KILROY WAS HERE

by

Brett Allen

A15 Publishing
5219 Monticello Avenue #5037
Williamsburg, VA 23188-9998
www.A15publishing.com

ISBN 978-1-970155-13-6

FIRST PRINTING

DEDICATION

This novel is dedicated to all the wonderful men and women I served with during my four years in the U.S. Army—and some of the not-so-wonderful ones, too. Also, I dedicate this novel to the members of Task Force Titan to whom I am forever bound by the bonds of war. And finally, to those who were lost, but will never be forgotten.

AUTHOR'S NOTE

This book is a work of fiction though much of it is based on actual events that occurred throughout my tour in Afghanistan. My experiences have been modified, twisted, and exaggerated for the sake of humor and story. Members of the real Task Force Titan may recognize roots of many scenes therein and I hope you recall those times with fond feelings.

It should be noted that, as a work of fiction, all characters in this book are also fictional. For those who were there, if you should suspect a piece of yourself in any of these characters, good or bad, you may be right. I carry pieces of you with me wherever I go in life. Figuratively, of course. I don't have physical pieces of any of you. Except, for the lock of hair I stole from Captain Michaud while he was sleeping. Anyway, I guess what I'm trying to say is don't get all whiny and aggrieved if you think a character is based on you and you don't like the way the character is portrayed. Suck it up, buttercup. A story has to have antagonists, right? It's not always about you. Stop being selfish.

Lastly, it is not this story's intent to downplay the sacrifice of veterans, but more to dispel the notion that merely wearing a uniform makes you a hero. Like the civilian world, the military is made up of all kinds: hard workers and sandbaggers, optimists and assholes, straight shooters and functional alcoholics. Most of us wore many of these hats at different times—sometimes all at once. We were never perfect, but we were always there.

Gallantly Forward!

Chapter 1: Bagram

December 25, 2008

I waited, itching for the sharp crack of antiaircraft guns and the spray of flak against the plane's steel skin. But there would be no enemy fire tonight. For most, there would be no grand trials-of-the-will in the coming months either. This was not the war of our fathers. There would be no whistle, begging brave men over the wall into No Man's Land. No storming beaches against fortified positions or jumping behind enemy lines under olive-drab canopies and cover of night. I thought about generations of dogfaced soldiers freezing in their foxholes. I thought about my father and his men, dropped into Vietnam's hot landing zones while violent death pinged casually off their shaking helicopters.

Instead, most of *my* travel companions were dozing off. Their biggest complaint from our glorious arrival to war would be stiffness from poor nap posture.

Thump, thump.

The Crew Chief pounded angrily on the intercom box above his jumpseat and it crackled back to life. The pilot was already mid-speech.

"...and out your left-side windows, you'll see Rukha, a tranquil mountain town along the Panjshir River. Their primary exports being lapis stones, radical militants, and exploding goats."

There was an obligatory chuckle from the passengers. The Crew Chief shook his head. I'm sure he'd heard the joke a million times and he didn't have much of a sense of humor anyway. Before we'd embarked, a smart-mouth Private had called him "stewardess" and he'd spent the rest of the flight sulking and mean-mugging us passengers.

"We are now beginning our descent into Bagram Airfield, where local time is 2100 hours. Local temperature is a balmy thirty-five degrees Fahrenheit. Please remain seated with seatbelts fastened and tray tables in their upright and locked position. We hope you've enjoyed flying with Air Force Air today and enjoy your stay in beautiful Afghanistan. God speed and Merry Christmas."

A collective groan went up behind me. I turned my head as far as I could, looking out over a sea of camo and Kevlar. One hundred and forty men and two women dressed exactly alike in digital camo pajamas. Everyone in full body armor and helmet. Everyone with a rifle leaning against his leg and everyone straddling bags stacked to his chin. One hundred and forty-two clones—off to war.

Two silver eyes watched me from the seat ahead. In thick black marker, a vandal's hand had sketched, around two rivets, a man's face peeking over a wall. Only half the face was visible and the figure's phallic nose and fingers hung with curiosity over a single line. *"KILROY WAS HERE"* was scrawled in ragged letters beneath the face. I ran my thumb over the graffiti.

"No respect," I mumbled.

Doc Jonston, our Squadron's senior medic, roused from his slumber. His thick eyebrows had nearly grown together and they twitched as he yawned and smacked his lips. He stretched his neck, wiping away a trail of saliva that tethered his chin to a dark, green spot at the top of his duffle bag. A seam in the bag had left a crease in his cheek.

"We there yet, LT?" he groaned. He poked his head above the Kevlar sea in search of windows that didn't exist.

"Just started our descent."

"Once more unto the breach," he quoted through another yawn.

I motioned to a black plastic case between our seats.

"What's in the case?"

A smile curled Doc's lips.

"Promise you won't rat me out, Sir?" he asked.

"Nope."

With considerable effort he rolled up the sleeve of his blouse, exposing a large black tattoo on his forearm. The surrounding flesh was crimson and swollen.

"It's the Batman symbol," he bragged.

"No, it's not."

"Well, that's what it's supposed to be," he said, running his thumb over the edge of the image. He winced as he touched it.

"It looks like a two-headed rhino."

"Whatever, it was my first try."

"You did that to *yourself*?" I asked.

"Yes, Sir," he said proudly. "Got the kit just before we left." He nudged the black case with his boot.

"Are you sure it's not infected?"

"Oh, it's infected," he said. "Medic, remember?" He pointed his thumb to his chest. "Before you ask, I'm not planning on giving out any tattoos. At least not until I've practiced some. Unless somebody asks, of course."

"I don't think they will," I said. "But if they do, about any of this, I didn't know about it."

"Hey, Sir, would *you* be interested in a tattoo?"

The plane's wheels bounced on the runway, as I explained I already had a tattoo—a souvenir from a Spring Break in high school. I confided it had nearly killed my mother. And my father, God rest his soul, had nearly killed me. Doc shook his head with secondhand remorse and didn't push the issue any further.

The C-17 ran continuous laps on the tarmac in an effort to best the world record for longest airplane taxi ever. Its mammoth body finally ground to a halt, which was followed by a symphony of thumps and hisses from various regions of its complex inner workings.

"It's a wonder this hunk-a-shit even flies," the stewardess groused and then turned to his audience. "Everybody remain seated until we've completed shutdown procedures and we've lowered the back ramp."

We all stood up simultaneously, or as much as our bags would allow, in an effort to stretch a collective leg cramp. Un-wedging our gear and ourselves turned out to be an exercise in team building. Soldiers in the aisle seats broke free first and turned around to help their neighbor and so on and so forth. The veteran non-commission Officers, or NCOs, filled the time with unsolicited advice for us first timers. I listened in on whatever I could, grateful for any information that would keep me from looking ignorant. Lieutenants have a bad enough rap in the Army.

Sergeant Hunter, our Sniper Squad Leader, offered a group of Privates dining tips for their temporary stay on Bagram.

"Now don't go bang'n away on a buncha Burger King and Pizza Hut just cause it might be the last time ya get it for awhile. I've seen some in shape, combat-killers go 'lardass' in just under a week here. I'm look'n at you, Smitty. Don't waste your money. The cafeterias are good here and half as bad for ya. Now, there's three main cafs, but two are garbage. Dragon Cafeteria's the way to go and it's down by the transient tents where we'll be stay'n. It's open twenty-four-seven, for all the off shift guys and they got chocolate chip cookies as big as your fuck'n head. Well, maybe not your head, Coucher. You got a bigass head."

Coucher *did* have a bigass head. Not freakish or anything like that, but definitely noticeable. I imagined that his birth had been a particular burden on his poor mother's nether region and this prenatal disappointment was just the first of many to come. Coucher had been a disappointment to me just months earlier. As a soldier in my old Platoon, he had been my most exhausting time eater. Not that he was mischievous or brash or confrontational. He was something far worse—he was lazy. In the Army, "laziness" is the original sin. And for his sins he was kicked out of paradise. When the Squadron Commander, or The SCO, demanded volunteers to fill his new Security Detachment Platoon, Coucher was the sacrificial lamb. Every Platoon in the Squadron had offered up their own "Couchers" for the good of the cause, leaving The SCO's platoon outfitted with the finest group of rag-tags and misfits you'd ever seen. By the time The SCO realized the grab-bag of grab-asses he'd inherited, it was too late.

The ramp of the C-17 dropped, letting a rush of winter air and jet fuel fumes flush the stank of tightly packed bodies from the cargo hold. Soldiers spilled out onto the tarmac, grateful to move. Behind the blinding runway lights, an inky curtain extended as far as I could see. A light snow was falling as I waddled down the ramp, hampered by all my gear. I felt an odd familiarity with this place. Like walking into a new town's grocery store.

Section Leaders circled the herd of straying soldiers like sheep dogs, barking orders at their chalks to form into ranks. We stumbled into our rank and file to be counted, recounted, and recounted again. I was in the front row, squinting into the lights. In the distance, beyond the hulking frames of airplanes and helicopters, I could see a large man running toward us, orange air traffic batons waving wildly over his head.

"Hey, Sergeant Hunter, I think this guy's try'n to get your attention," I said. Hunter turned to face the approaching man.

"What the got-damn hell is that?" Sergeant Hunter mumbled.

"Whatever it is, it's not coming fast," I said.

The man wore the olive suede boots and camo pants of an Air Force soldier, but was dressed from the waist up in a Santa Claus coat and cap. A white pom pom bounced back and forth over his head in time with his waving arms. After several minutes, he stumbled up to the formation, gasping for breath. He was an enormous man by military standards—which he clearly no longer abided by—but I admired him for his commitment to character. He had gone so far as to have his rank and a novelty name tape reading "Claus" sewn onto his costume. On his hands he wore thick black mittens with white fur trim at the wrists. He placed them on his knees as he doubled over his bowl full of jelly. I was sure he'd just run farther than he'd run in a long time.

"Welcome… to Bagram…Air Force… Base," he gulped, standing up and pacing in a small circle with his hands and batons resting on top of his head. There was a strong smell of eggnog as he passed. I saw storm clouds brewing in Sergeant Hunter's eyes.

"Take your time, Master Sergeant," said Hunter. I was glad he'd recognized his rank. Air Force rank patches looked foreign to me. MSgt Claus raised a mitten to buy himself a moment, then waved Sergeant Hunter away from the front of the formation.

"As I was saying, welcome to Bagram Air Force Base," MSgt Claus finally managed. "I don't normally have to make that run."

"No kidding," Sergeant Hunter grumbled, having joined me at the end of the first row.

"There's supposed to be a shuttle bus to pick y'all up and take ya down to the terminal for in-processing, but I couldn't find the driver. The terminal will send him down as soon as they can find him. Assuming he's not too deep in the eggnog," he chuckled. "While we wait, go ahead and dig out your reflective belts, cause you'll need'em. New regs, mandated by Bagram's own Command Sergeant Major Dragger, say you gotta wear those bad boys at all times. Some private got hit by a shuttle bus a few nights back, so we're taking preventative measures."

A groan came up from the clones and then the formation became alive with movement, as everyone began digging through bags to find their reflective belts, which are typically only used during exercise. I looped my belt over my right shoulder and let it dangle across my chest.

"Nothing like neon yellow over camouflage to make you feel like you're at war."

"We ain't at war, Sir," Sergeant Hunter said. "Might as well be at home."

MSgt Claus rambled on in front of the formation for several minutes, but he'd lost his audience. I caught bits and pieces of what he said over the excited chatter around me. It was mostly just cafeteria recommendations and tips on where to buy the best bootleg movie. I felt bad for him. Out of shape soldiers are quickly dismissed in the military.

"Alright," MSgt Claus called. "Everybody please quiet down." Everyone continued to talk. For good measure, a helicopter began to idle somewhere behind our C-17.

"Everybody shut your got-damn pie holes!" shouted Hunter.

The formation was silent.

"That's better," said MSgt Claus, as if he'd calmed the seas himself. His teeth chattered and the large sweat pools under his arms and neck were frosting over. He removed the radio attached to his hip and held it to his mouth."

"Terminal, this is Claus. Any sign of the bus driver?" He asked.

The radio crackled and festive Christmas music could be heard in the background.

"*Who?*" The radio asked.

"Oh for Pete's sake," grumbled MSgt Claus and lifted the radio to his lips again. "The bus driver. Airmen Rodgers. Have you seen him? We need the bus on the east end of the runway to pick up soldiers."

"*Haven't seen him, Big Sarge. You'll have to walk it in.*" The music was louder now. "*Merry Christmas!*"

There was despair and loathing in Santa's face as he stared west where the rows of lights came together. His radio arm hung limp at his side and he sighed.

"Too bad my sleigh isn't running tonight," he said forcing a chuckle through clicking teeth. "We'll have to hoof it, so load up your gear again." There was grumbling from the mob. "Don't worry, it's not far."

His crack about the sleigh was more believable.

Again we loaded up our gear over our body armor. I carried my rucksack on my back, and had managed to stack my assault backpack on it as well. I wore my olive drab duffle bag frontways across my chest, with three long cardboard tubes stacked horizontally across the shoulder straps and held in place by my chin. Each tube held rolled up maps, clearance level: Secret. In one hand I held a computer bag, containing my work computer and a clearance level: Secret computer. In my other hand, I held my rifle.

"Before we move out, I need everyone to put on their ballistic glasses," MSgt Claus yelled above the fray. Everyone stopped and stared. He now wore yellow shooting glasses under his festive red hat. "As mandated by Bagram's own Command Sergeant Major Dragger, regulations state that any personnel traversing the airfield should be wearing proper eye protection at all times."

This was the one "Bagram reg" we'd been briefed on before departure, so everyone had their glasses in easy reach. I leaned my rifle against my leg and fumbled my glasses out of my cargo pocket. Within a minute we were on the move, stretching into one long single file line. Beasts of burden crossing a flat, black desert in the bitter cold. And then we were stopped again.

I heard a sharp cry from ahead of me and I peered over my duffle bag and cardboard tubes to see what the holdup was. Four soldiers up, Private Coucher had gone ass-over-teakettle, feet kicking in the air and bulging rucksack burying his giant head in the tarmac. Blood sputtered from his mouth as he pleaded for help. Before I could drop my gear, the soldiers in front and behind him were helping him to his feet. His cheek looked raw and his lower lip was bulging. MSgt Claus trudged back to check out the commotion, stopping at the small puddle of blood on the oily tarmac. He bent down and scrunched something small into his palm. He stood to inspect it, revealing a bloodied tooth resting in his puffy mittened hand. Pinching it between his thumb and fingers, he raised it high above his head.

"The first casualty of war!" He shouted. I think he expected everyone to cheer.

He handed the tooth back to the bloodied soldier who was sitting dazed atop the pile of bags that had betrayed him. The soldier quietly put the tooth in his pocket and MSgt Claus disappeared back to the front of the line with all the impassive detachment with which he'd appeared.

The line of lights grew shorter as we approached the west end of the runway. My shoulders throbbed, being pulled in every direction by three different sets of shoulder straps. Sergeant Hunter kept the mood light by artistically stringing together swears as he recounted all the terrible things he'd do to Airman Rodgers if he ever came across him. The versatility of the "f-word" from the mouth of an NCO is one of the seven miracles of the modern military. Accompanied by enough appropriate—or inappropriate—hand gestures there is almost no need for any other nouns, verbs, adverbs, or adjectives.

Finally, it was over. Like drones, we filed back into formation in front of a small building whose sign read "Blackjack Terminal". MSgt Claus stood in the front of the formation again, waiting for the last of the caravan to fold in. I wiped beads of sweat from my face and was glad not to be cold anymore.

"Alright, everybody listen up," said MSgt Claus, clearly irritable from his unexpected workout. "In just a moment, you'll file through that set of doors into the terminal. Make sure you have your ID card in hand. You'll be scanned in and then you'll exit the terminal out the other side. If I understand correctly, y'all will be staying in the transient tents on the northeast side," he pointed back in the direction we came.

"This is bullshit. How are we supposed to get all the way back down there?" Doc asked from the back.

MSgt Claus shrugged.

"Not really my problem after you leave Blackjack Terminal."

Just then, a pair of headlights appeared from around the corner of the terminal, tires screeching behind them. A huge shuttle bus weaved to straighten out and sped straight toward the formation. I froze, but in a surprising show of "fat-agility" MSgt Claus leaped to place himself between the bus and the formation, waving his batons and shouting wildly. The bus veered off at the last second and I could swear the driver was dressed like a Christmas elf.

"You worthless son-of-a-bitch!" MSgt Claus shouted, shaking a balled-up mitten at the bus's tail lights as it headed down the runway to pick us up from where we used to be. He was pouring sweat again. He thumbed his reflective belt as he returned to the front of the formation.

"Y'all grumbled, but this thing prolly just saved your lives," he said. "Now everybody get inside before that lunatic comes back."

We were filing toward the doors when they swung open and a small female Airmen pushed her way out. In her hand she carried a single sheet of paper, which she delivered to MSG Claus with great urgency. He read it, shaking his head, while she darted back inside.

"If I could have your attention one last time," shouted an exhausted Claus. "As mandated by Bagram's own Command Sergeant Major Dragger, due to recent injuries sustained, mouth guards will now be required of all individuals walking on or around Bagram Air Force Base. Mouth guards can be purchased at the post commissary between the Burger King and the Pizza Hut." He crumpled up the paper and shoved it in his cargo pocket.

"Be careful out there and watch out for your buddies," he added, his face grim. "Welcome to the war."

Chapter 2: Shepherds

December 26, 2008

It started again. A beeping somewhere in the darkness, barely discernible above the howling heaters. Soon joined by another and another and another, until the vast tent was filled with a choir of electronic tree frogs, chirping away.

0600 hours.

"Shut those got-damn watches off!" Shouted someone in the dark. It sounded like Sergeant Hunter.

One by one, the alarms were silenced. Replaced with beams of light dancing over rows of cots and across the bare canvas walls and ceiling. Their owners searched bags for toiletries, fresh uniforms, and cigarettes.

This process had happened every fifteen minutes, for the last two hours.

On the cot next to me, a soldier rummaged through his rucksack, both his hands encompassed by a luminescent cone. He held a flashlight between his teeth, causing the cone to oscillate as he worked. Even with my eyes closed, I could sense the light swaying back and forth. I rolled over in my cot for the hundredth time and settled into another uncomfortable position.

I thought about my simple bed back home. Just a boxspring and mattress, flopped on the floor of my apartment bedroom. It sounded luxurious now and I worried about the living conditions on FOB Alternator. I wouldn't survive the year on a cot. I'd succumb to sleep deprivation, go mad, and be sent home within the month. A dull ache crept back into my shoulder, so I rolled over again. My neighbor's light had gone out. I closed my eyes again and started to drift.

"You sure do make a lot of ruckus when you sleep," came a voice from my neighbor's cot.

"Jesus!" I said. The voice seemed two inches from my ear.

"No, just me," he said. "I get that a lot though." I recognized the Texas twang of Captain Clark. At six feet, seven inches, there was no way he was comfortable on these cots either. 'Course, he was a beanpole, so maybe he just folded himself in half and slept that way.

"What time did you get in last night?" he whispered. He sounded right above me again. I squinted and slashed my arm though the space above my ear.

"Not 'til about twenty-three hundred," I said. "And I don't."

"You 'don't' what?"

"I don't make a lot of ruckus when I sleep," I said. "I haven't slept. I don't know how you could on these things." I flicked the tight fabric of the cot and it thumped like a conga drum.

"Eight hours in and you're already bitchin," he chided. "Unbelievable."

"I'm not bitching, Sir," I said. "I'm just hoping Alternator's got better living conditions."

"Why wouldn't it?" Clark asked. "It's only the most remote Forward Operating Base in the Logar Province. Five star, I'm sure."

I laid my head back down on the tightly rolled up pants I'd been using for a pillow.

"It's too early for sarcasm, Sir," I said. "I can't process it--"

"Stop calling me 'Sir'."

"I would, Sir, but you outrank me, Sir," I smiled, even though he couldn't see me.

Captain Clark sighed. I could hear his eyes rolling.

"Four more months?" He asked.

"Five," I said. "Mid May. And then I'll call you everything but 'Sir', Sir."

He was quiet for a moment.

"Captain Rye," he mumbled. "Sounds a lot better than 'Lieutenant Rye' anyhow."

In the distance, a wrist watch started beeping.

"Shut those got-damn watches off!"

It was most definitely Sergeant Hunter. I lay on my back, watching the ceiling as beams of light crisscrossed overhead.

"Where'd it get its name anyway?"

"Where'd what get it's name?" Clark asked.

"FOB Alternator," I said. "Was there some Sergeant Alternator who died gloriously on the field of battle, so they named some shit-stain in the middle of nowhere after him?"

"Nah," said Clark. "Hasn't been much fighting in Logar. Especially down south. What I heard was, there was a platoon of Scouts that were tasked to set up an outpost as far south as they could in Logar. You know, down in the Kherwar. But they only made it so far before they blew the alternator on one of their Humvees. They didn't have the parts to fix it, so they just set up shop right where they were. Boom. FOB Alternator."

"That's the lamest origin story I've ever heard," I said.

A flashlight clicked on behind our heads, the light darted between Captain Clark's face and my own. It was blinding.

"Will you two hens quit your got-damn clucking?" Sergeant Hunter said, lowering his light.

"Sorry, Sergeant," Captain Clark snickered, shielding his eyes.

"Should have known it'd be you two. Take your friggin pillow talk somewhere else. Some of us still got a little time to sleep," he said and faded back into the darkness. "Got-damn officers."

We kept our conversation minimal after that, both of us putting on our boots and tidying up our living area, which was nothing more than the two foot stretch between our cots. I carefully followed Captain Clark's winding trail to the exit, but tripped over three cots in spite of myself, receiving insensible scoldings from their occupants. We finally stepped through the tent flap and the temperature drop was astonishing. Morning light crept through an overcast sky, giving everything a gray, hazy hue. Our surrounding area was a series of green tents like our own, partitioned off by cement slab barriers lined up to make fences. These fences were meant to minimize and contain damage inflicted by mortar or rocket attacks, which happened about four times a year on Bagram. They reminded me of tombstones. Some had names or symbols scrawled on them in paint. One even had a phone number, available for any soldiers looking for a good time. I suspected it was fake or at the very least, poor Private Smitty's mother had no idea it was being advertised.

At the far corner of our concrete-encased courtyard, a small group of soldiers huddled shivering in the designated smoking area enjoying their breakfast cigarettes. I wasn't more than two feet out of the tent before one particularly chipper Staff Sergeant cast away his butt and rushed over to lecture me on the importance of wearing my reflective belt. The Sergeant hesitated when he realized we were officers, but then doubled down when he saw I was a Lieutenant. Sergeants love giving Lieutenants hell. The Sergeant assured me, through his tobacco teeth, he was close personal friends with

Command Sergeant Major Dragger and that his powerful friend would "have my ass on a platter" if he found out what a poor example I was setting for the lower enlisted. Captain Clark deflated my rebuttal with a shake of his head. Returning to the darkness of the tent, I could hear Clark making half-hearted apologies and guaranteeing the Sergeant that we'd be purchasing mouthguards shortly after breakfast.

Stumbling out of the tent with my reflective belt, I was pleased to see the Sergeant had returned to his sad smoking support group, no doubt bragging to anyone who'd listen that he'd just given the "what for" to a couple green officers.

"Why didn't you let me put him in his place?" I asked.

"He was in his place," Clark said, pulling a tin of chewing tobacco from his pocket as we walked. "Technically, you were in the wrong."

"You're taking *his* side? It's a stupid rule."

Captain Clark pulled an enormous pinch from the tin and packed it tightly between his bottom lip and gums. The chew looked like a muddy horseshoe around his teeth.

"But it *is* a rule and I'm not taking anyone's side," he said, spitting thick brown sledge into the gravel. "Once we get to Alternator, this 'Big Army' chicken-shit stops. It's just not worth the trouble."

"So just nod and smile for the next two weeks, huh?"

"Stay alert, stay alive," he sang.

We turned left on Disney Road, Bagram's main strip that runs parallel to the airfield. The road had been named after a Specialist who died in early 2002 when a piece of heavy machinery fell on him. The entire base had been required to wear helmets and body armor, day and night, for the next two months.

The surrounding mountains dominated the eastern skyline. Had it not been overcast, I imagined the sunrise would have been something to see. Coming up from behind us, I could hear a low rumble. It grew gradually, then faster and faster. It was coming from the runway, but I couldn't see beyond the wall of tents and plywood buildings that lined the south side of the road. The rumble graduated to a thunderous roar and, within seconds, the orange glow of a fighter jet's afterburners could be seen trailing away through the early morning haze. The shimmering dots headed east between two mountain peaks, like footballs through an upright.

"It's good." I said, raising both arms above my head.

"It's not good," Captain Clark said, pointing ahead of us.

On the sidewalk, a lone man stood with his back to us, watching the jet trail off. He was a sight to behold. On his feet he wore flip-flop sandals, I assume to draw attention away from the ultra-short running shorts and untucked, wrinkled undershirt that hung like a canopy over his paunchy frame. A brown bath towel was draped around his neck and his red hair was wild and deranged, giving him the air of an escaped mental patient. A group of crisply dressed soldiers heading toward us moved off the sidewalk, giving him the wide berth one would give a leper.

"Is that The GIF?" I whispered.

Captain Clark nodded.

"This should be interesting," I muttered as we approached the man. "Isn't he freezing?"

"Good morning, Sir," called Clark when we were nearly on top of him.

"Major Doyle, Sir," I said, rendering a salute.

Major Doyle spun around and slapped at my hand.

"Quit that, Rye!" He spat. The toothbrush dangling from his lips swung wildly as he checked his surroundings. "There could be snipers anywhere."

There couldn't have been. And when he seemed satisfied that there weren't, he sighed heavily.

"Sorry, Sir," I said. "It's my first day."

He reached up and placed a hand on my shoulder, giving it a firm squeeze.

"It's alright," his teeth chattered, "just pull your head out of your ass."

"Yes, Sir."

He turned his attention to Captain Clark.

"Mark! I'm glad you found me," he said, as though he'd been lost in the wilderness for days. "Can you tell me where the shower tent is?" He held out a wrinkled sheet of notebook paper. "Captain Garcia drew this map for me, but the idiot didn't mark which way was north."

Captain Clark glanced at the map.

"Yes, Sir, no problem," he said and pointed the direction we had just come. "Its two hundred meters down that way, on your right. There should be a sign."

"Great, thank you," Major Doyle said eagerly. "And Mark, you really shouldn't chew. It will kill you, if the Taliban doesn't. We'll speak with Doc Jonston about getting you some nicotine patches or at least getting you addicted to something less damaging."

"Yes, Sir. I know, Sir," Captain Clark said. "Bad habit."

Major Doyle had already pushed past us, heading for the showers.

"Have a good morning, Sir," I said, trying to be polite.

"Nobody likes a 'suck-up'," he called back. "Get to work, we have a war to win."

We watched him walk away, his sandals flip flopping along the way. His calf muscles were oddly well-defined. I imagined it was from tiptoeing around work his whole life.

"He's been here a week," Clark said, when he was out of earshot. "How is this his first trip to the shower?"

As the Squadron's Operations Planner, Major Doyle was legendary for his cunning and often audacious plans to shirk any and all responsibilities. A career officer, he had miraculously managed to avoid any combat deployments, despite the country's involvement in two wars for the previous eight years. Now charged with the responsibilities for which he had no personal experience, Major Doyle often concocted half-baked battle plans, which were usually in direct violation of the Geneva Convention. The spritely manner in which he'd flutter into a room, spew his mental refuse, and then flutter away, earned him the moniker, The Good Idea Fairy, or The GIF, among his subordinates, though none dared speak it to his freckled face.

We hurried through the breakfast line at the Dragon Cafeteria, which Sergeant Hunter had dramatically oversold. One runny omelet and a prepackaged muffin later we were back in the cold, heading to the Squadron's temporary Command Post. In my cargo pocket, two more muffins clunked together like rocks. Aunt Mary's Muffins were the official U.S. military's muffin of choice. The density and texture of the muffins were closer to that of a hockey puck, but I'd heard they were handy when bartering with local merchants or driving in reluctant tent spikes.

Large snowflakes danced lightly, swirling around us while we walked, before dashing themselves against the endless stretch of gravel and rusty mud. On either side of us stretched long lines of hastily erected plywood buildings that resembled chicken coops more than military constructs. Their only distinguishing characteristics were the small flags that flapped outside, announcing which unit headquarters currently held residence there. Ours was the only cavalry unit on the block, so the red and white guidon of our Squadron Command Post was easy to spot.

We entered quietly and found a briefing in progress. At the far end of the room, Captain Garcia, the Squadron Intelligence Officer, was speaking quickly and pointing to locations, marked with thin silver pins, on a map of the Logar Province. Captain Clark motioned for me to take a seat just inside the door.

"The old, blue truck has been spotted at these five locations, just after hostile incidents," we overheard Captain Garcia say.

The room was lined with similar maps, each showing different characteristics of Logar and the surrounding area. Some of these were the maps I'd carried with me on the plane the night before. The walls were lined with two rows of evenly spaced tables, which left a narrow aisle down the center of the chicken coop. At the table across the aisle from ours, behind a stack of green Vietnam-era radios, sat Private Coucher. He was leaned back in his chair with his large head propped against the wooden wall, wheezing slightly through his bulging lip as he slept. Both feet were resting on the table and he wore white running shoes instead of standard tan combat boots. Around the right ankle was a loosely wrapped bandage. No doubt another souvenir from his fall.

On either side of the aisle, directly in front of Captain Garcia, two men sat with their backs to us. On the left, sitting square and rigid, was Major Connick, the Squadron's Executive Officer. On the desk in front of him were two foam coffee cups, one of which still poured steam from its open lid. Next to the coffees was a hardcover notebook, in which he scribbled furiously, though he never seemed to take his eyes off Captain Garcia and his map. Major Connick's spirit animal was hummingbird and he often warned us, between long pulls of black coffee, of the dangers of getting too much sleep.

On the right was Lieutenant Colonel Fink, the Squadron Commander or The SCO. The SCO sat back in his chair with his shoulders slouched. The chair tugged down the collar of his uniform, allowing spider-like legs of hair to creep out of his undershirt. An unlit cigar bounced up and down from the side of his face. I don't know that I'd ever seen the man without a cigar, though I'd also never seen him smoke. He never moved his jaw when he spoke, for fear of loosening his grip. He would've made one hell of a ventriloquist if he had any sense of humor.

He reached up to scratch the small bald spot that had surfaced in his thin brown hair. It was his tell that he was about to destroy someone's self-confidence with biting criticism or simply just call them a dumbass and leave them wondering what they did wrong.

"You dumbass," the SCO interrupted through his locked jaw. Major Connick continued to write. "You're seriously going to waste this brief on some blue, beater truck and a cockamamie theory about a mystery militia? We already have vetted reports of fighters from the Afghan Taliban, the Pakistani Taliban, the Haqqani Network, Hizb I Islami, Al Qaeda, Chechen Rebels, Iraqi Rebels, Rebels without a cause," The SCO rubbed his eyes. "Now you're saying there's another force at play here?"

"Yes Sir," Garcia nodded. The SCO didn't let him elaborate.

"And even though there is only one road in and out of the Kherwar District, and it goes right past FOB Alternator, and we've never received any intel reports from their guards, it's your stance that they drive this piece-of-shit blue truck all over the Logar Province conducting their nefarious deeds."

"Yes, Sir," Captain Garcia hesitated. "Well, no, Sir."

"No?" The SCO bit down hard on his cigar.

"No, Sir," repeated Garcia. "Not nefarious, Sir."

"You're saying there's an organized group of Afghanis out there that *isn't* nefarious?" The SCO scoffed. "Well, stop the frick'n presses. And what is it you suppose these "Blue Truck Warriors" do down there, if not cause mayhem and sew fear into the local populous? Perhaps they're delivering Christmas presents to all the good little girls and boys."

"They don't celebrate Christmas here, Sir," said Captain Garcia. "And if they did, I'm not sure the girls would get presents."

The SCO's head dropped.

"Christ, Joe, I was making a joke."

"Yes, Sir," Garcia said. "It was very funny, Sir. And it's 'Jose', Sir."

"What?"

"It's 'Jose, Sir." Garcia repeated. "Not 'Joe', Sir."

The SCO removed the cigar from his mouth and sputtered bits of tobacco shrapnel across the desk in front of him. Major Connick had taken a break from note-taking to take a large pull from his coffee. I could see him smiling behind his cup.

"What's the frick'n difference?" The SCO glared.

"An 'S', Sir." Garcia said flatly. This was one of Captain Garcia's finest attributes. A perceived intellectual, it was assumed that he spent too much time with his nose in books to understand social norms. His brazen corrections of superior officers were simply accepted as characteristic of an introverted nerd. I knew better though. Captain Clark and I had seen him at more than a few bars back home. For a nerd, he was quite good with the ladies. Most smart-asses are in my experience.

The room was silent as The SCO gnawed the soggy end of his cigar.

"Ha!" he finally bellowed. "Well, I guess you're right, Joe."

I heard a sigh of relief from Captain Clark as The SCO went on.

"So, Joe, for argument's sake, let's say you're right and this blue truck shit is real. What do you propose these guys are up too?"

"Well, Sir, that isn't fully understood yet. Sightings of the truck are always made *after* so-called 'nefarious deeds'. In my experience, most insurgents do not hang about the scene of the crime after attacks. *My* theory is, perhaps the 'Blue Truck Warriors', as you called them, are simply trying to help. Maybe even fighting back against hostile outside influence."

"Let's hope we're not viewed as a 'hostile outside influence'," The SCO said.

Major Connick nodded in agreement as he wrote.

Suddenly, the door flung open, slapping violently against Private Coucher's table. A startled jump was all it took to remove the last two legs of his chair from the ground, sending the poor kid crashing. I like to think I would have helped him up, had the The GIF not flopped through the door and stood between us. A flurry of snowflakes blustered in behind him before he could shut the door. He was still dressed in the same attire from his shower excursion, only now his hair was wet and matted and his lips were blue against pale cheeks. He looked down at Coucher who was still in shock on the floor.

"Nice shoes," The GIF muttered.

"Bob!" The SCO barked. His face was murder red. "Where the hell have you been? You missed the whole goddamn brief."

Major Connick was taking another pull from his coffee, but his lips curled up from the edge of the cup. His shoulders bounced joyfully.

"It was his fault," The GIF stammered, pointing an accusing finger at Captain Garcia. "He drew me a shoddy map to the showers. I'd have froze to death if it wasn't for Captain Clark. He didn't even mark which way was north."

He held up the soggy sheet of notebook paper.

"Which way was North, Joe?" he yelled.

"The top of the page," Captain Garcia said calmly.

The GIF examined the page.

"Well that doesn't make a lick of sense."

"Bob. Get in my office," The SCO said through gritted teeth. His beady eyes were narrowed to slits as he pointed to an open door at the back of the room.

The GIF flip flopped down the aisle, his head hanging like a man being led to the noose. He gave one last deadly glare at Captain Garcia before disappearing through the door.

The terror alert on The SCO's face dropped to orange and he turned back toward us.

"Help that idiot up," he said pointing to Coucher who was still on his back rubbing his head. "And you," he said, pointing at me. "Go find a truck. You're my driver tomorrow."

I snapped out of my seat to the position of attention.

"Yes, Sir," I squawked nervously. His back was already to me and he disappeared into his office, slamming the door behind him.

I stood dumbfounded, while Captain Clark helped Coucher right himself.

"Where am I supposed to find a truck?" I asked. "I've been here twelve hours. I barely know where to find breakfast."

Major Connick had slammed his second cup of coffee and gathered his things. He wore a big grin as he walked toward us. The corners of his dashing smile pushed up the bags under his sleepless eyes. He could have been some celebrity's tired cousin.

"The top of the page is north," he chuckled as he slapped a piece of notebook paper into my chest. I looked down at the page, finding another crude map of Bagram.

"Good luck," Connick called back as he opened the door. More snow swirled into the room. "You might not want to stick around here. Walls are paper thin. Major Doyle might want some privacy for his ass-chewing."

****

The Outer Loop. The inside perimeter of Bagram's outside fences made a nice eight mile running loop, if you're into that sort of thing. Captain Clark and I sloshed swiftly across the rutted muddy road. We'd spent the majority of the afternoon acquiring a truck from a surly government contractor, who felt it was his sworn, sacred duty to be defender of the civilian motor pool. We'd finally convinced him that our need was legitimate, but I suspected he gave us a lemon anyway. Captain Clark then suggested we take a break, which, according to him, we were doing by running in the snowy cold.

I stared off through the chain link fence, huffing and puffing as I bitterly analyzed the years of poor life choices I must have made that led me to be here on this miserable run. Beyond the fence was a dingy brown moonscape of rocks and rubble as far as the eye could see. There was absolutely no vegetation. Occasionally we would pass the distant ruins of some mud structures that could have been as ancient as Alexander the Great or as recent as the Soviet occupation.

Up ahead, a herd of rawboned goats caught my attention. They tripped along over the rubble just outside the fence. Behind them, in the hollow of another clay ruin, an old man and a young boy hopped lightly from rock to rock following the direction of their herd. The man's gray beard did little to hide the scowl on his sun-weathered face and he used his walking stick to take vicious swipes at the boy when he got too far ahead. They paid no attention to us as we approached and even less attention to their goats. They could not have been more than twenty feet from the fence.

"What's to keep one of them from lobbing a grenade over the fence?" I asked as we ran.

"Arthritis and a lack of arm strength," said Clark pointing to the old man and then the boy.

"No, seriously. Why do they allow them to get so close?"

"See those guard towers?" Captain Clark pointed to one of the wooden box structures that lined the fence. There had been one every hundred meters along the way. "'Cause each one of those contains no less than two maladjusted, GED carrying, disgruntled Privates with a 240-Bravo machine gun, just looking for an excuse to shoot something."

I was suddenly more worried about the towers than the shepherds. The old man and the boy were now behind us and I checked over my shoulder to make sure neither was throwing anything.

"Look at it this way," Clark continued. "What would *them* attacking *us* gain? They'd be dead in seconds. Best case scenario for them, they killed two useless planning officers."

I was mad that I was a useless planning officer and that I was dead in anyone's "best case scenario".

"I should be out there," I said, looking off through the fence again.

"Herding goats?" Captain Clark asked.

"You know what I mean. I should have a platoon. Be running missions. Helping the locals. Making a difference."

"Herding goats," Captain Clark affirmed. "You'll have The SCO's ear tomorrow. You should tell him how you feel. He loves to hear about feelings."

"Maybe I will," I said. I turned my head for one last look at the shepherds and was just in time to see the old man's cane connect crisply with the poor boy's skull, sending him reeling into the rubble among the goats.

"Just be careful what you wish for, man," huffed Clark. A truck rounded the corner ahead and we both jammed our mouthguards back in.

"You might not realize how good you have it," he garbled.

Chapter 3: Wink

December 27, 2008

I stomped the gas pedal, but it was too late. The truck's engine coughed through the turn onto Disney Drive, its insides rattled like a bag of spent brass. There was shotgun blast and the engine died. A group of soldiers nearby leapt for the safety of the cement tombstones; I assume mistaking the backfire for a mortar attack.

"Sorry," I mouthed through the window. "Sorry, Sir," I said toward The SCO. I fumbled to restart the engine as we rolled to a stop. There were daggers from the passenger seat.

"If we could get there sometime today, that would be outstanding, Lieutenant," The SCO said. "We'll be scraping the bottom of the barrel as it is. If I get a couple duds because you picked a P.O.S. truck, so-help-me-God."

He spat flakes of tobacco from his lip onto the floor mat and reinserted his cigar. It was nothing but a nub now.

"Sorry, Sir," I said, still unsure of the purpose of our trip. "This was all they had."

"Then what the hell are you sorry for?" He grumbled as the engine struggled back to life.

The wide grin of Command Sergeant Major Storms filled the rear view mirror. His teeth were brilliant white against his skin, which was as ashy-black as the stock of his rifle. He leaned back and rested his head against the back window, his flat-top running perfectly parallel to the top edge of the glass. The man had a haircut you could set your watch to. As the Squadron's senior NCO, CSM Storms had learned to embrace The SCO's surly demeanor.

Heading west, the transient tents disappeared, replaced with permanent structures that made up the oldest section of Bagram. I imagined that someday, these too would be piles of rubble for the goat herders to navigate, but right now they were a hive of activity. Groups of soldiers, sailors, and airmen, of every uniform traversed the thin sidewalk, on their way to and from whatever duties they were dodging, all united by their common reflector belts. Occasionally, I'd see a group of foreign uniforms and wondered where they were from. None of *them* were required to wear reflective belts, so it's hard to say if any of them survived the war.

We pulled into the Task Force Headquarters parking area just as the engine stalled again. Luckily, we had enough momentum to coast into a spot, sparing me the humility of a restart. I'd been looking for an opening to ask The SCO about getting another Platoon, but in the ten minutes of painful silence that preceded, I hadn't found an opportunity to interrupt. The SCO reached for his handle and I went into "now or never" mode. I vomited words.

"Sir, Platoon. Will I get one? Again?" Instant self-loathing.

The SCO dropped his head and closed his eyes. For a moment I thought he was pretending to be asleep.

I glanced in the mirror. CSM Storms was grimacing the way you do when you witness a car crash or when someone says the "f-word" around your mother. It was too late though, so I tried again.

"Sir, I'm just wondering if I'll ever have the opportunity to lead a Platoon again? My knee is back to a hundred percent and I could use the field experience."

"No," The SCO said flatly and went for the handle again.

"Can I ask, why not, Sir?"

There was a groan from the back seat.

"No, Jacob. You can't," The SCO growled. "But since you already did, I'll explain it to you. All of my Platoons are staffed. And even if they weren't, I still wouldn't make you a Platoon Leader again. You'll be a Captain soon and Captains don't lead platoons. Now if you don't mind--"

"Captain Applegate is still a platoon leader," I stated.

"Captain Applegate's a nimrod," The SCO asserted. "He doesn't lead anything. His Platoon Sergeant does his job. He's there because that's where he's least dangerous and I haven't found a way to get rid of him."

"So, I'm too valuable to be wasted on a Platoon, Sir?" I smiled, hoping to ease some tension.

"Tell yourself whatever you want, Jacob."

"It's Jared, Sir."

"Who cares?"

The SCO opened his door, then stopped.

"You can showcase your value by watching the truck," he said climbing out.

"Aye, Sir," called CSM Storms from the backseat. He put a large hand on my shoulder and addressed The SCO. "Might be a good professional development opportunity for the L.T. here to come in with us, Sir."

Senior officers like The SCO were always looking for opportunities to "professionally develop" junior officers. It looked good on their evaluations. The SCO bent down and spat more tobacco flakes.

"I don't give a damn what he does, as long as the two of you hurry the hell up," he grumbled and slammed his door.

"Don't take anything' he says personal," Storms winked. "He's just a grouch. But if he thinks your name's 'Jacob', well, you might wanna just be 'Jacob' for a bit."

"Roger, Sergeant Major."

"Bingo. Even if he think's your name's 'Roger'. Try not to say anything dumb inside, Sir," he gave me another wink on his way out his door. "Actually, try not to say *anything* at all."

****

The walls surrounding the building were high enough that I couldn't see over. A single strand of concertina wire spiraled along the perimeter giving it the feel of a prison. We entered the compound through a gated space in the wall at the other end of the parking lot. A pair of sedated Specialists, guarding the gate, rendered salutes to The SCO as we entered, which he ignored entirely. I was trailing a few steps behind, but was not extended the same courtesy.

Stepping through the gate and into the courtyard was like stepping out of Bagram completely. It was a pleasant place. The first one I'd seen since arriving. A cobblestone sidewalk ran through its center, ending at a circular patio with wooden benches around its edge. At its center sat a weathered cement fountain, which had been shut off for the winter months or just didn't work at all. On top of the fountain was a regal statue of a man in Afghani garb.

On either side of the sidewalk was honest-to-God, green grass, which was also the first I'd seen. As far as I know, it was the only patch of grass on the base, maybe in the whole province. Scattered along the interior of the perimeter walls were small wood-chipped beds where flowers must have grown in the summer. These were also turned off for the winter. Amongst all of this, milled small groups of command teams, consisting of high-ranking officers and NCOs. The groups bounced off one another like billiard balls, exchanging salty smiles, awkward salutes, and insincere handshakes before bouncing away on a new trajectory, only to collide with the next group a few feet later. I was by far the lowest ranking officer in sight.

"One goddamn mortar could take out half the command of Eastern Afghanistan," the SCO said. "Let's get this over with and get the hell out of here. This place is a prime target."

The SCO turned his attention toward the building, while CSM Storms waved to familiar faces and I searched the air for the incoming projectiles I hadn't been worried about before.

"Sweet Jesus, there's only five left," The SCO pointed his nub cigar at the building. "Thanks to your P.O.S. truck."

Along the building wall where he looked, a wooden platform had been erected on which five Afghan men stood in a row facing out into the courtyard. Four of them were dressed in typical Afghan "man-jams", loose fitting linens which hung on their wiry frames like laundry on a clothesline. They looked like they hadn't eaten a meal in days. The fifth man looked like he hadn't missed a meal his whole life. On his feet he wore a pair of new tennis shoes instead of sandals, which were probably needed to support such a rotund build. Like the others, he wore "man-jams", but they seemed stressed in certain areas and their bright white color was outshone only by the idiot smile he wore on his face.

"What is this?" I whispered to CSM Storms as we followed The SCO toward the stage.

"What do you mean, 'what is this'?" he whispered back. "He didn't even tell ya where we were goin'?"

I shook my head.

"This is Terp selection, L.T.," he said. "Incoming commanders get to select two interpreters that they'll work with over deployment. You don't wanna get a bad terp."

Before we could climb the platform, a voice boomed across the courtyard.

"Daniel!"

The SCO cringed. The meandering groups of command nebulas parted, leaving a path across the courtyard back to the fountain. Down that path strided Colonel John J. Gunn, our Brigade's Commander, The SCO's direct boss and least favorite person. He looked like a giant passing through the other commanders and was rumored to have an ego to match. I'd never met him, but I'd heard the war stories and rumors. Allegedly, as a young Major in Iraq, he'd cleared an entire building by himself, after his convoy of Rangers was pinned down by enemy fire. They say he killed ten men along the way. More extreme versions say he killed the last three insurgents with a plastic spoon he'd saved from his field rations. The *most* extreme version said he kept the spoon and used it for dinner that same night.

"Daniel!" He called again, raising a hand high above his head to make sure we noticed. He was impossible to miss. He wore mirrored aviator sunglasses and a smile that threatened to escape the strict confines of his chiseled jaw. Behind him, trailed his own small nebula of followers, consisting only of two female soldiers. There were rumors about them too.

The woman to his right was Second Lieutenant Sarah Barrett. A medical officer by trade, she could have just as easily been a bikini model. She'd been chosen as the Colonel's personal assistant for the duration of the deployment after what I'm sure had been the world's shortest interview process. I'd seen her at a few officer parties back home, but found her looks intimidating. I assumed women like that preferred the strong silent type anyway, so I always practiced the latter and kept my mouth shut.

To the Colonel's left, was the equally beautiful Staff Sergeant Lisa Loredo. She was exceptionally young for her rank and as a motor pool sergeant she had a reputation for having a hot Latin temper. Her smoldering brown eyes could level you faster than the twelve inch crescent wrench she was usually carrying. She'd also been mysteriously assigned to the Colonel's staff just before deployment. Probably because she got his engine running.

The SCO turned crisply to face all three, forcing a smile. He rendered a salute when the Colonel closed in, but this time it was his turn to be ignored.

"Daniel, it's good to see you," Colonel Gunn said. "How come you haven't come to see me yet? You've been here a few days already, have you not?"

"I have, Sir," The SCO mumbled. "Been very busy. Lots of intel to comb through."

"Take that god-awful cigar out of your mouth, Daniel," Gunn said. "It makes you sound like a mush-mouth."

"Sorry, Sir," The SCO said, removing the cigar. There was loathing in his eyes. He could mask his expressions, but he couldn't mask the color he was turning.

"I hope you're not talking to other superior officers like that," Colonel Gunn continued. "I can understand you being disrespectful to me, we have history."

He then turned his attention to me.

"And who's this strapping young warrior? The Commander's apprentice?"

I straightened up and gave a salute which was also ignored.

"Lieutenant Rye, Sir," I said. "I'm the Commander's driver for the day."

I heard a throaty groan from CSM Storms and the Colonel's two harpies snickered behind him. The Colonel's eyebrows raised above his mirrored lenses.

"A First Lieutenant. As a driver?" He asked. "Are you being punished for something?"

"I-I don't believe so, Sir," I stammered.

"Daniel," he said, turning back to The SCO who was now shooting daggers at me again. "Daniel, why do you have a First Lieutenant as a driver? Are you that overstaffed with junior officers? Perhaps we should disperse some to other units."

"No, Sir," The SCO responded quickly. "Jacob here will be one of our Battle Captains. He may need to work closely with the Terps, so I wanted him involved in the selection."

This was all news to me. And not good news. "Battle Captain" translated to "command post babysitter". It would be my job to run and find an adult if anything bad happened in our area of operations.

Colonel Gunn considered this.

"Either way, Daniel, I need you to come by Brigade Headquarters. There've been some major developments in your future area of operations. Specifically in the Kherwar District. Messy business. I'll have our Intel Officer fill you in on the details," he then turned to me. "Have your 'driver' drop you and Sergeant Major off when you're finished here."

"Yes, Sir," said The SCO. Colonel Gunn and his entourage had already started on a new trajectory. Lieutenant Barrett winked at me on her way by. It was probably insincere.

"You just couldn't keep your mouth shut, could you?" The SCO growled, placing the cigar back in its rightful place. He was still shaking his head as he climbed the stairs to the platform.

CSM Storms chuckled, slapping me on the back.

"You got the worst luck, Sir," he also winked at me on his way by. I wished people would stop winking at me.

I followed them up the stairs and we began making our way along the row of terps. The SCO had a series of questions for each one.

"What's your name? Where are you from? Why do you want to be my terp? Are you secretly a terrorist?" These were the typical questions.

"Ahmed. I am from Kabul. To earn money to go to America. No." These were the typical responses.

The SCO would then check the terp's muscle tone and teeth before moving on. It was demeaning, but there's not much use for a sickly Terp, especially in combat. The SCO looked unexcited about his choices and continued to grumble about the quality of truck I'd acquired.

The fourth man in line was the heavyset terp in white. A pencil mustache traced the dopey smile he still wore on his chubby face.

"What's your name?" The SCO asked.

"Frank," he said. He had no trace of an accent.

"Frank?" The SCO said excitedly. "That's a goddamn American name. I love it. Where are you from, Frank?"

"San Diego, California, Sir."

"San Diego? That's a goddamn American city," The SCO exclaimed. "Well, I'll be damned, Frank. You're not pulling my leg are you? What brought you over to this shit hole?"

"I'm from here," Frank explained. His smile faded. "My family immigrated to America when the Russians invaded. I've seen the suffering going on here and I wanted to give back to my people."

"Shoot. Sorry. That's very noble. It's a lovely country you have here," The SCO lied. I'd never heard him apologize before and I don't think I ever did again.

"Just kidding," Frank's smile roared back. "I heard this job paid a shit-ton and it's get'n me away from the wife and kids for a while."

I braced myself.

The SCO roared with laughter so loud even CSM Storms jumped a little.

"I love this guy!" yelled The SCO. "Come on, Frank! You're coming with me. Wait, let me see those teeth first."

Frank opened wide to display his pearly whites.

"Goddamn American teeth." The SCO said proudly. "Come on, Frank."

The four of us moved on to the final interpreter. The poor guy didn't have a chance of living up to Frank.

"What's your name?"

"Ahmad Fazil Ahmadzai."

"That's a damn mouthful, isn't it?" The SCO grunted. "Where are you from?"

"Kabul, Sir."

"Why do you want to be my terp?"

"I want to do something to better my country, Sir. It saddens me to see what has become of--"

"Yeah, yeah, yeah," The SCO motioned for him to stop. "I've heard it." He stepped back and motioned the rest of us to step back so he could see the remaining interpreters he had just interviewed.

"Okay, Akmed, er, Armed, er uh, Terp 2, you win by default. Come with us."

Terp 2 smiled and joined us as we continued off the platform. The platform ended near the concrete fountain and I could now see the pockmarked statue was dressed in the similar fashion of our new Terps. On his head he wore a traditional pakol hat and along his side he carried an AK-47. I looked around the fountain's base, but didn't see any placard or inscriptions.

"It's Ahmad Shah Massoud," Terp 2 whispered behind me.

"I thought it was Ahmad Fazil-something," I said.

"Not me. The man on the fountain" he said with reverence. "Ahmad Shah Massoud. 'The Lion of Panjshir'. A great warrior against the Russians and the Taliban."

"Ah, yes, I know 'The Lion'," I lied. "I just didn't recognize him in that hat."

Terp 2 smiled. I was ready to deck him if he winked at me.

"I'm not riding anywhere in that deathtrap of a truck you got," The SCO called back as we navigated through the command nebulas toward the gate. "The Sergeant Major and I will walk to Brigade Headquarters. You get these Terps back to our H.Q. for inprocessing, then find me a truck that's not a heap-a-shit."

"Worse case, just have one of our mechanics look at it," CSM Storms chimed in. "If those boys can fix a broken Humvee, ain't no reason they couldn't tune up a pick-up."

We exited through the courtyard gates between the two guards who were now busy flipping through tabloid magazines. I headed down the parking lot with Frank and Terp 2 in tow. Frank was chattering away about missing the warm San Diego weather and how everything was so dusty here. I didn't hear a lot, mostly because I didn't like him already, but also because my attention was on a group of soldiers who'd congregated around the hood of my truck.

"Can I help you, gentlemen?" I asked impatiently.

They all turned to face me and I recognized a number of them from our maintenance group. They were all Specialists, which seemed odd. One soldier, who'd been sitting on the hood, jumped down and puffed his chest.

"We need a ride, yo," he announced.

I looked down to make sure my rank was visible. For those unfamiliar with military customs and courtesies, "yo" is not an acceptable substitute for "Sir". Before, I could respond, the group split and a fat little Specialist sauntered through. He barely came up to the chests of his compatriots and he was as wide as he was tall. His black mustache was lustrous and matted down with wax and he scratched at the stubble along his jaw. It was ten in the morning and he had a five o'clock shadow. His other hand rested limp on the top of his stomach beneath a mangrove of chest hair bursting from the top of his undershirt. When he stood directly before me, he squared up and gave a crisp salute.

"You'll have to excuse my ill-mannered friends," he mumbled, shooting a sideways glance at the group who now stared down at their boots. "They lack discipline and respect. But my associate was correct. We request that you provide us transportation to the bazaar near the front gates."

"Who *are* you?" I asked. The odd soldier's name-tape was missing from his uniform.

"My name is inconsequential," he replied. "Who I am is a man who is tired of walking. It's 'new release day' at the bootleg movie stand and if we don't arrive soon, the selection will be picked over. I would consider this a great favor to me. A great favor which I would repay."

"Um. Okay," This was shaping up to be the oddest interaction of my military career. "I guess that wouldn't be a problem, except the truck barely runs. I'm not sure I'll even make it back to headquarters."

"My associates have already taken care of it," he smiled and directed my attention to the grease covered hands of some of his friends. "She purrs like a kitten."

His friends were climbing into the bed of the truck. He gave me a wink and headed for the passenger door.

Chapter 4: Handboy

January 6, 2009

Thump, thump.

I exhaled and let fog creep back over the window glass. The Blackhawk cruising next to us blurred to a dark mass and then returned to clarity. I'd be lying to say I wasn't nervous. The helicopter bobbed with the changing air temps. I didn't particularly care for that, but drumming rotors soothed me some. It was early and the sun was still low in the east, casting long shadows over the rocks and ruins below. The brilliant sunshine and the crisp air gave my spirit buoyancy, even when the helicopter didn't.

Across from me, Captain Clark watched out his window, grimacing through heavy gulps of the tobacco juice he wasn't allowed to spit on the chopper floor. Behind him, a young looking door-gunner with a dirty mustache stood behind his machine gun and scanned the ground for targets. Every now and then he'd point to the ground, yell something back at us, and wait for our confounded nods of fake approval. Whatever he was yelling was lost between the rotors and my ear plugs. Whatever he was seeing was beyond my field of vision.

Terp 2 sat next to me on the canvas bench seat, nervously wringing his hands every time the helicopter dipped. He'd pulled his head so tight to his shoulders, the baby fat of his cheeks was pushed up by the stiff collar of his flack-jacket. He looked like a turtle that couldn't quite fit in its shell.

"How much farther?" He yelled.

I shrugged, Clark apparently didn't hear him.

He'd been assigned to us by default after The SCO unofficially chose Frank as his own personal assistant. Frank and The SCO had become thick as thieves in just a few short days and were rarely seen apart. It was disgusting. Poor Terp 2 had been given the cold shoulder and had taken to loitering outside the Squadron Command Post, hoping to be of use to anyone needing his services. Even more demeaning, the Squadron Supply Sergeant, had ordered both interpreters cloth name-tapes for their uniforms and, not knowing Terp 2's real name, had his unwanted nickname stitched on instead.

Across the cabin sat a large olive case packed full of Vietnam-era communications equipment, which we'd been tasked to deliver to the Afghan National Police (ANP) platoon currently stationed in the Kherwar District. To be fair, I really hadn't been tasked with anything, but Captain Clark had and I'd begged obnoxiously until The GIF caved and let me come along. A hundred meters away, the second Blackhawk carried Sergeant Hunter and his sniper squad, who'd had been tasked to keep two worthless staff officers and their terp out of trouble.

According to our briefing, communication with the Kherwar Outpost had always been terrible due to the mountains that enclosed the district. Even so, the outpost would get a message through every couple days with nothing new to report or a request for better food in their supply drops. A few weeks back even the spotty communications had stopped. Several conflicting intel reports had come in, ranging from "everything's fine" to "they're out of food and starving" to "they're all dead as doornails". None of the reports were from reliable sources. Reliable sources are hard to come by in Afghanistan, let alone in some podunk district.

There was only one road into the Kherwar and it was supposedly a white-knuckler to drive. We were told it was usually socked in with snow during the winter anyway, so sending in a convoy out of FOB Alternator was out of the question. I'm sure the boys stationed there weren't at all disappointed to hear that and since we were the incoming unit, it was decided this was the perfect opportunity to make introductions. The GIF had wanted to do a couple flyovers, airdropping in care packages and the commo gear, but since we couldn't confirm the outpost wasn't now occupied by violent Taliban extremist, The SCO quickly put the kibosh on his plan and demanded boots on the ground.

"Two minutes," called the door gunner. I read his lips more than heard his voice. He raised two fingers and pointed out the window. We had dropped into a valley, checkered with patches of snow across its barren floor. At the center, rising from the landscape, on the crest of a slight rise, stood a rectangular concrete structure. The lone two-story skeleton had been a government funded schoolhouse in the early 1960's. It looked out of place to say the least and had clearly been stripped of any amenities over the decades. Even the windows and doors were gone, leaving gaping holes like empty sockets in a skull. Decaying bones of a more prosperous Afghanistan.

We saw no sign of people. I wasn't surprised. With no doors or windows they were probably huddled inside, trying to stay warm. The helicopter wheels touched down lightly on the open field south of the schoolhouse. We slid the doors open and stepped into ankle deep snow as the second Blackhawk touched down behind us. The mountain walls circling the valley looked like the grandstands of an ancient gladiator arena.

"Those who are about to die, salute you," I said to myself.

"What?" Yelled Clark over the thumping rotors.

"I said, where is everyone?"

Clark shrugged and pointed back to the helicopter where the door-gunner was beckoning us back.

"How long you gonna be?" the door-gunner yelled.

"Not long," Clark yelled back. "Twenty to thirty minutes. Less, if there's nobody home."

The door gunner nodded approval and relayed the message over his radio to the pilots. The snipers unloaded the commo gear from our chopper and took up a defensive position just outside the reach of the rotor blades. The door-gunner was still listening to the pilots and nodding. He finally waved us back in.

"We're going to run up to FOB Shank for fuel. Shouldn't be more than forty five minutes," the door gunner explained.

"You're leaving us here?" I asked. This was a very "un-gladiator" thing to ask.

The door gunner grinned at my discomfort.

"Well, we sure aren't gonna sit here and be target practice," he yelled. "If the ANP try to murder you, just pop red smoke and those boys will turn this place into the wild west." He thumbed toward the sky where our two Apache Gunship escorts were circling like angry hornets.

I took comfort knowing the Apaches were staying on station. Armed with Hellfire missiles and thirty millimeter chain-guns, Apaches were the scourge of the skies. Clark tuned his radio to drop onto their frequency. We joined the sniper team in their semicircle and the Blackhawks lifted off, kicking up a blizzard of snow and dirt. As soon as they were clear we picked up and moved toward the building. Over Clark's radio I could hear the Apache pilots chattering away. Their conversation was mostly a string of dick jokes, so Clark turned the volume way down.

We approached a small guard shack, which stood along the only road in the province. A toll arm reached halfway into the road, but had been snapped off at the middle. From the guard shack, the road stretched west, ending at a cluster of red clay qalats about a mile away. These earthy compounds made up the village of Kherwar, which was much smaller than I'd imagined. To the east, the road stretched on for miles before disappearing into a pass between the mountains.

The shack was filthy, its floor littered with food wrappers, cigarette butts and crumpled porno mags. The smell was enough to gag a maggot. A ramshackle desk sat against the front wall. Its surface was oddly trash free. In the center of the desk was a notebook, sitting perfectly centered and square. Being careful not to disturb the rubbish, I tiptoed over and tossed the notebook back to Terp 2 who fumbled it, picked it up, and nearly fumbled it again.

"What is it?" I asked.

"I am sorry, Sir," he replied. "I am nervous."

"No," I said. "I mean the notebook. What does it say?"

Terp 2 began flipping through pages.

"It is traffic journal," Terp 2 said. "In it is written, all vehicles that pass here."

Clark was looking over Terp 2's shoulder.

"Any other notes?" He asked.

"No," Terp 2 said. "Very strange."

"What is strange?"

"There are many pages, but only records one vehicle," he continued to flip pages. "Oh my!" He shouted and dropped the notebook again, looking away in disgust.

"What?" I asked, picking up the notebook by its spiral binding in case there was something gross inside.

"In the back," Terp 2 said. His head was turned away, but he watched from the corner of his eyes.

I flipped the notebook open to the last pages. Where the log ended, the guards had found a new use for their time. Filling the final three pages was a compilation of erotic drawings. Mostly naked women in various stages of sexual ecstasy. Portions of the female anatomy had been exaggerated, but other than that, the drawings were rather impressive. The shading was impeccable.

I turned the notebook to show Clark the artistry. Terp 2's face flushed. I thought he might snap his neck if he turned his head any farther.

"Must'a been pretty lonely out here," I said. "Isn't this one your sister?" I pointed to a particularly curvaceous young woman toward the bottom. Terp 2 looked at Clark with horror.

"Good one," Clark said. "Let's take the notebook. Captain Garcia will want to see it."

"Yeah, he will," I said.

"Shut up," said Clark. "Let's keep moving. Maybe there's somebody inside the schoolhouse who can explain where everyone went."

As we walked, Terp 2 apologized profusely to Clark for "gazing upon his sister's naked form", while Clark tried to explain that I'd been joking. My concentration was fixed on the village of Kherwar, which seemed as dead as the schoolhouse. There was no movement at all. Not even a feral dog emerged to bare testament to some inhabitants. Perhaps they all went south for the winter. I imagined Afghan "snow-birds" playing shuffleboard and drinking Mai Tai's on some Pakistani beach.

"Aye, Sir," called Sergeant Hunter. He'd taken point on the walk to the schoolhouse and now had his rifle raised toward the door. "We got somethin' here."

From the snow emerged cement stairs that led to the side door of the schoolhouse. The morning sun had melted the snow from the steps, revealing a crimson trail of splatter marks that ascended the stairs and disappeared down the hallway inside. Anxiety rushed through me, but Captain Clark seemed unfazed. He shook his head.

"Nothing in this damn country can ever be easy," he grumbled.

"Blood's dried on, Sir," said Sergeant Hunter. "Probably been a while."

"Let's take it slow and clear rooms as we go," I said, regaining my calm. "Can't be too careful."

Sergeant Hunter nodded to be polite. He'd already made that assessment. The snipers joined him at the top of the stairs. They formed a single file line and entered the building, clearing one room at a time, ping-ponging from one side of the hall to the other. Clark, Terp 2 and I entered behind them keeping watch on the far end of the hall. Each room was the same, completely stripped of any furniture, but like the guard shack each appeared to have been ground zero for a vicious dumpster explosion.

The hallway, like the rest of the building, was gray cement blocks and lacked any adornments. There were no light fixtures, because there was no electricity, but the bare doors and windows allowed sufficient light into the dingy corridor, making it easy to follow the blood trail. The sniper team cleared the last room before the hallway spilled into a large open vestibule with the main entrance off to our right. Directly opposite the entrance was the staircase leading to the second floor, which wrapped back toward us from a landing halfway up.

"Got-damn," said Hunter, pointing his finger toward the door. "You don't see that every day."

The blood trail wrapped around the vestibule wall and ended in a dried puddle beneath a desk in the corner. On top of the desk, was the source. A human head sitting front and center. The face was waxen. Its jaw hung low, its mouth frozen in a desperate moan. Above the mouth was a thick black mustache, whose size was dwarfed only by the long nose above it. The birds had already gone a round on it and, had the eyes remained, they'd have sunk into the sockets. Some of the stringy bits of its neck cascaded over the side of the desk, ending in dark red blood-sicles.

Anyone who says my generation is desensitized to violence is full of shit. I'd have thrown up right there had Terp 2 not beat me to it.

"Get it together, man," I told him, suppressing my own gag.

Some of the snipers had moved on ahead, for a closer look. They were split fifty-fifty on whether it was really gross or really cool and dared each other to touch it. One finally did, trying to close the mouth, but rigor mortis had set in and the whole head tipped backwards making crackling noises as frozen flesh separated from the desk.

"Leave the damn thing alone," I said. "It's disrespectful."

There were eye rolls, but they stopped.

"The L.T.'s right," said Sergeant Hunter. "Quit dick'n around and go clear the rest of those rooms." He pointed down the hallway opposite the one we'd entered from.

Captain Clark put in another dip. He didn't say a word about the severed head. In fact he didn't look surprised in the least.

"Were you expecting this?" I asked.

"I wasn't *not* expecting it," he replied. I got the feeling his last deployment left him jaded. "Not really sure what anyone expected. Leaving a platoon of poorly armed police out here, cut off from everyone, with nothing to do but jerk off and smoke hash."

"Where do you think the rest of them are?" I asked.

"They're all in the wind by now," said Clark.

"Or in a shallow grave out back," added Sergeant Hunter, as he watched his men zig-zag down the far hallway. Terp 2 had taken a seat against the cement wall. His face still a shade of green.

"What do we do now?" I asked.

"We wait until the birds come back and we go home, I suspect," said Clark taking a seat on the staircase.

"I'll have the boys clear the rooms upstairs next, just to be sure," said Hunter.

Clark nodded.

"So we're just going to leave?" I asked. "We just found a frick'n head. Shouldn't we do some investigating? Maybe go down to the village and ask what people have seen?"

"Grand idea, Sir," Sergeant Hunter said. "Let's take our eight, minimally armed guys, down to an unfamiliar village, when there's clearly hostiles in the area, with no back-up. What could go wrong? Maybe they'll stack our heads next to your buddy's over there."

I was getting no support from Captain Clark, who was now spitting into a brown chew puddle between his feet.

"We have back-up," I said pointing up.

"The Apaches won't be much cover if we have to go into the village," Clark said. "And I don't think anyone down there is gonna come out to greet us. Sergeant Hunter's right. We're under-manned. And it's not our mission anyway. We came here to deliver radios and make introductions."

He looked at the head on the table.

"I feel we've been properly introduced," he added.

Suddenly, we all went quiet and listened. There was noise from the second floor.

"Probably just a couple rats fighting over more body parts," I said.

There was more rustling and then the unmistakable sound of broom handle slapping concrete. That was enough to drive Clark from his seat. The sniper team was still on the far end of the second hall and I was tired of standing around. I started up the stairs.

"Where do you think you're going?" Clark asked, grabbing my arm.

"To shoot some rats," I smiled and tugged my arm away. I continued up the stairs with my rifle trained on the landing at the top.

"Get back here," hissed Clark, following me up.

"Got-damn officers," grumbled Sergeant Hunter as he too followed us up.

As soon as my head crested the top of the stairs, I zeroed in on the source of the noise. Across the hall was a door, slightly ajar. It was the only door I'd seen in the whole building. From the small opening, a broom handle extended out across the dusty floor. There was no light from inside, but I could hear the sound of paper shuffling. I motioned to Clark that I was going over. He and Sergeant Hunter moved up the stairs so they could watch down both ends of the hall. I stepped lightly across the hall and reached out past my rifle to swing the door open. Just as my finger touched the handle, the door burst open.

"Shit!" I shrieked.

The edge of the door connected with my nose and my heal connected with the broom handle. I sprawled backward onto the floor, as pain flashed through my face. The sound of thunder cracked inside my kevlar helmet as it struck the concrete. The impact interrupted my view of a child's frame as it leapt over me. It dodged a swinging grab by Sergeant Hunter and hurtled down the stairs.

"Stop him!" Clark shouted to anyone downstairs. Blood streamed from my nose. I felt like a turtle as I rocked on the armor plate in the back of my tactical vest.

"I got him," called Terp 2 from downstairs. "I got him!"

Captain Clark and Sergeant Hunter helped me to my feet and we ran down the stairs. Turning on the landing, we found Terp 2 grasping the upper arms of a boy no more than thirteen. My eyes were drawn to his right arm. His wrist and hand were gnarled and disfigured and a cluster of metal rods surrounded it, as if to keep it in place. Around the rods, a series of thick wires were woven to form a cage around the lower arm. The boy took one look at my blood-soaked chin and panicked. With one swift motion, he planted his heel firmly into Terp 2's testicles and was off again. He sprinted down the long hall we'd entered from, outrunning the sniper team who'd heard the commotion and given chase. Unfortunately, a soldier in fifty pounds of body armor and weapons doesn't stand a chance against a hundred and ten pound teenager running for his life.

"Titan Three Alpha, this is Cobra One, we have a runner from the main building," crackled one of the Apache pilots over the radio. "It looks like he's stealing a birdcage. Would you like us to engage?"

"This is Titan Three Alpha," replied Clark. "It's just a kid, over."

There was moment of silence before the pilot came through again.

"So, that's a negative on engaging the kid, correct?"

"Jesus," Clark said before squeezing the handset again. "Roger, Cobra One, do *not* engage the kid. Keep an eye on where he goes, over."

"Will do. Kids heading for the village. Not really anywhere else to go out here," he replied. "Cobra One, out."

We were standing around Terp 2 when the snipers finally came back. Terp 2 was still laying on his side on the floor grasping his manhood and glubbing air like a fish out of water. He'd gotten more than he bargained for today. I sat down on the stairs and tilted my head back to stop the bleeding. My hands were covered in blood. Captain Clark and Sergeant Hunter went upstairs to look for more clues, returning a few minutes later with a stack of old yellowed papers.

"I think we found our erotica artist," Clark said, showing me a collection of nude drawings. "They were in the closet where the kid was hiding."

"Kid's a little pervert," Sergeant Hunter chuckled, folding up a few of the drawings and putting them into his breast pocket.

"They're not half bad though," I said, taking a few from Clarks hand. "Especially from a kid with a wonky hand."

"Somebody prolly found him drawing this smut and put the hurt on him," said Hunter. "These religious extremists don't mess around out here. Prolly why he bolted so fast. Didn't wanna get caught again and lose the only dick-beater he's got left."

"Your nose broke?" Clark asked, changing the subject.

I shook my head. The thick taste of iron was running down the back of my throat.

"Just got a good bashing," I said.

"Your nuts broke?" Clark asked Terp 2, he pointed to his crotch.

Terp 2 looked confused for a moment, but then nodded with a half smile. Clark reached down and helped him to his feet.

"Thanks for try'n to help," he said. "That's more than most terps would've done."

Terp 2 nodded, wincing painfully as he straightened his back.

"Alright, let's get moving. Birds will be back soon," Clark said. He removed a small digital camera from a pouch on his body armor and tossed it to one of the snipers. "Get some pictures of the building, inside and out, and get a bunch of pictures of the head. Maybe we can get an ID on the guy when we get back."

"What do we do with the head?" I asked. "Seem's wrong to leave it out on the desk."

Captain Clark thought a moment, while the snipers snapped their pictures of the gory scene. Once they'd finished, he walked over to the desk and opened the large filing drawer on the side. He grabbed the head by one of the ears and drug it over the edge of the desk, letting it fall into the drawer with a metallic thud. He shut the drawer hard with his foot. Even Sergeant Hunter was stunned.

"What?" he asked. "The ground's frozen and I don't see any shovels around here, do you?"

"Ruthless," I said.

"He's not gonna mind," Clark said. "I promise."

He wiped his hands distastefully across his thighs and pulled the tin of dip from his pocket once again.

Chapter 5: Insurgent Cookies

January 10, 2009

It'd been four days since The SCO tore into Captain Clark and me for a variety of perceived missteps in our handling of the Kherwar schoolhouse situation. He was furious that we hadn't approached the village to speak with any town elders. I wanted to tell him that I'd proposed it, but I couldn't break from my unified front of failure with Clark. Useless staff officers need to stick together. Besides, The SCO had moved quickly to a new topic, chastising me for allowing a teenager to get the drop on me and for staining up a perfectly good uniform with all my disgusting nose blood. He'd brightened momentarily at the prospect that "Handboy", as he'd been dubbed, could be a valuable public relations victory if we could find the depraved, young artist and provide him proper medical attention. The SCO seemed least upset about Clark's solution to the severed head, though he submitted we should have just punted the thing into a nearby ditch and left if for the feral dogs. The only saving grace of the mission had been the traffic log, which confirmed Captain Garcia's blue truck theory. Garcia seemed equally excited about the nude drawings, which mysteriously disappeared soon after.

The GIF had then taken another verbal beating from The SCO, simply because Clark and I were his subordinates. Shit rolls uphill in the Army. Since then, I'd been doing anything and everything to stay busy and away from the Command Post until things cooled down. I tried keeping a low profile, but the incident at lunch today was going to draw some negative attention. That's probably why The GIF was summoning me to the CP now anyway. The man loved to add insult to injury.

I tripped through the gravel, following my flashlight along the corridor of command posts. It was late and nearing the end of dinner hours at the Dragon Cafeteria, so my path was clear, save for a few straggling soldiers hurrying to chow. I kept my fingers crossed that I'd find the Command Post the same way. I stopped at the foot of the stairs, shining my light on the door. A sheet of paper wriggled to free itself from under a tack. I felt my face flush. On the paper was a picture of two large chocolate chip cookies, with the words: WANTED across the top in large, bold font. Below the picture read:

"BOLO: Taliban Cookies. Wanted for the attempted assassination of 1LT Jared Rye. Should be considered extremely delicious. Kill or Capture. Do not eat. For more details, inquire within."

I tore it down, stuffing the crumpled sheet into my cargo pocket. I'm sure Clark and CSM Storms had giggled like schoolgirls making the sign. I slammed the door open expecting to find a room full of hecklers. The door struck hard against the first row of tables, startling Captain Applegate who'd been sleeping with his head down on a table a few rows in. He whipped his head around, wiping saliva from the corner of his mouth.

"What the hell, Lieutenant?" he screamed.

"Sorry, Sir," I said. "Door got away from me."

I poked my head around the door. Private Coucher sat behind the radio desk, where he'd been most of the last few days. He still had tennis shoes on and this time his left arm was in a sling. He wiggled his fingers in a half wave with his bad arm and went back to flipping through his magazine.

"It's about time you got here," Captain Applegate said, shaking off his nap. "I'm starving."

"Oh no, Sir. I'm not here to relieve you," I said. "I was told Major Doyle wanted to speak with me."

"The GIF isn't here," Captain Applegate said and smiled. "Yeah, that's right. I heard what you guys have been calling him behind his back. Seems pretty disrespectful if you ask me, Lieutenant."

"I don't use that name, Sir," I lied and sat on the edge of a table.

"Bull," scoffed Applegate. "And how about you stand at attention when you're talking to a superior officer."

"I'd use the term 'superior' loosely," I jabbed, with a grin.

Captain Applegate jumped to his feet.

"What did you just say to me?" He snapped back. I hopped down from the desk and stood at attention.

"I'm sorry, Sir. I was just joking," I said. "I didn't mean any offense."

Applegate got up in my face and stared me down. Years of acne had scarred his cheeks with pits and ridges, not unlike the landscape outside the Bagram fences. His forehead was dotted with fresh ruins and flakes of dandruff drifted past from his coarse black hair, like some kind of grotesque snow globe. I wondered how anyone could have such a dry scalp with such an oily face.

"I don't care if you only have a couple months left, you'll show me respect until the day you're promoted," he said through clenched teeth. "Understand me?"

"Yes, Sir."

"Here's what's going to happen, L.T.," he went on. "The first convoy leaves for FOB Alternator tonight and Major Connick was very explicit about there being an officer on duty in the CP during the movement. So you're going to sit here while I go grab some grub and if you're lucky, I might even come back when I'm done. And if you're *real* lucky, I won't tell The GIF about your little nickname for him next time I see him."

"But you *haven't* seen him, Sir?" I asked.

"The GIF? No. And you won't either. He's on the convoy to Alternator. So is The SCO. Probably why Major Connick wants an experienced officer like me in here," He boasted. "In case they call up or run into any trouble. Whoever told you The GIF was going to be here was full of crap."

The door banged open again and The GIF fluttered in. He was dressed in full battle-rattle and wore fresh panic on his face. He barely looked at Applegate or me, frantically scanning the room. I cleared the aisle as he pushed Applegate out of the way and charged through.

"Where the hell is it?" he grumbled.

The radio crackled and The SCO's voice boomed through the air like the voice of God.

"Titan TOC, this is Titan Six, do you copy?"

The GIF froze. Private Coucher fiddled with the knobs to lower the volume and slowly lifted the handset to his face.

"This is Titan TOC?" he stuttered.

"Good God, man, are you sure?" The SCO said through the static. "Is that son-of-a-bitch Doyle there?"

"Yes, Sir," Coucher replied before realizing The GIF was vigorously shaking his head and making sweeping hand motions across his throat.

"You tell that son-of-a-bitch to hurry the hell up. He's holding up the whole damn convoy. Titan Six, out."

Coucher looked at The GIF nervously.

"Sir, The SCO says to hurry the hell up."

"I heard what he said," The GIF grumbled. "Now if you idiots could help me look for my rifle, I could get out of here. You're holding up the whole damn convoy."

"I'd be happy to help you," Applegate smarmed. "Where'd you last see it?"

"Shut the hell up, Applegate," The GIF said. "If I knew where I last saw it, I wouldn't need your damn help."

We looked under and around tables, but there weren't many places for a rifle to hide. Beside one table, some degenerate had graffitied the plywood with another crudely drawn man peeking over a wall, his nose and fingers hanging over the edge. Below it was the same message: *Kilroy Was Here*. The same graffiti I'd seen on the plane. I couldn't think of any "Kilroy" in our Squadron. Must have been someone from the previous unit.

"Sir," Private Coucher called and all three of us looked over. "Major Doyle, Sir. Have you checked the rifle rack yet?" Coucher pointed to the metal rifle rack opposite the door from him. A lone rifle leaned against it. I felt like an idiot.

"What a dumb place to put a rifle," the GIF grumbled. "Anybody could have reached in the door and stole it."

He slung his rifle across his back and turned to me.

"You wanted to see me, Sir?" I asked.

"Yes. I wanted you to come down here and find my rifle. But since you took your sweet-ass time, I had to come find it myself."

I was both annoyed and relieved. Maybe he hadn't heard about the lunch incident.

"And Rye," he said. "If you've recovered from your near death experience today, make sure this rifle rack is moved to the front of the office."

With that, he was gone, the door slapping shut behind him. Applegate smiled.

"Well, looks like you have some work to do while I'm gone," he gloated.

"You *are* coming back though, right Sir?" I asked. "I have things I need to get done tonight."

He just shrugged as he walked out the door.

"What a jerk," Coucher mumbled from behind the radios.

"You're not kidding," I said. "What'd you do to your shoulder?"

"Doc thinks I pulled my rotary band," he said, rolling the affected shoulder.

"I mean, how did you hurt it?"

"Sword fighting," he said, as if it wasn't a strange response.

"Never mind, I don't want to know," I said. "Are you sure Doc said 'rotary band'?

"I don't know, something like that, Sir," he said. "Say, you want me to move that rifle rack for ya?"

"Nah," I said. "The GIF's not coming back and if your shoulder's messed up, you shouldn't be moving heavy objects anyway."

Coucher stood and pulled the sling from around his neck with smile.

"It really is feeling better, Sir," he said. "I'll have it moved for you in a jiffy." He went to work moving the rack, which, from the look on his face, was substantially heavier than he'd anticipated. He pulled one side first, scratching it loudly against the plywood floor, then the other side with the same effect.

RRRRRRRRRRRT... RRRRRRRRRRRT

I was about to protest further when the door swung open again and the Squadron Chaplain stepped in.

"Hey, Sir," I said, getting to my feet again. Chappy was new to the Squadron and I didn't know him well enough to be lax on courtesies. He was an odd man and kind of a hardass. In a former life, he'd been an infantryman and a Drill Sergeant, and had seen his fair share of action in Iraq before deciding to attend Officer's Candidate School. Somehow, during his stint in OCS, a hiccup in the Army's personnel records earmarked him for the Chaplain Corps instead of his beloved Infantry. Human Resources, of course, vehemently denied it was a mistake. Not being a Godly man at the time, Chappy fought the assignment tooth and nail, but eventually conceded to the notion of possible divine intervention. Even now he described his relationship with God as a tenuous and begrudging respect that he was sure was mutual.

"Don't get up on my account," he said, waving a hand. "And call me Chaplain or Chappy, please."

He paused a few feet inside and looked around the TOC, as if taking it in for the first time. He wanted to say something, but didn't know how to start.

"What brings you by tonight?" I asked after a few moments of awkward silence.

RRRRRRRRRRRT

"Funny you ask," said Chappy. "I ran into The GIF a few blocks down the road. He had his panties all in a bunch about something and ordered me down here to talk to you."

"Did he say what it was about?" I asked. I was surprised how many people were aware of Major Doyle's nickname.

"He said you attempted suicide today." Chappy said matter-of-factly.

"Jesus Christ," I said, then remembered my company. "Sorry, Chappy."

"Don't apologize to me. It ain't *my* name you're taking in vain. Now you start sling'n around 'Billy Mast' like that, well, then I'll fight you," he grinned. "So why'd you try to kill yourself? Deployment blues? Sexual confusion? Some hoe back home got you down?"

"Good God," I said. "What kind of Chaplain are you?"

RRRRRRRRRRRT

Chappy eyed Coucher as he moved the rifle rack.

"It's not like that at all," I continued. "I had a choking episode in the cafeteria."

"Well, why'd The GIF say 'attempted suicide'?"

"Well," I hesitated. "It may have been a self-inflicted choking episode."

This brought Chappy's attention back from Coucher. His eyes got wide and he leaned in close.

"Autoerotic asphyxiation?" he whispered.

"What? No." I exclaimed. "Listen, it was a bet. CSM Storms was giving me crap at lunch for having a big mouth around The SCO. One thing led to another and he bet me I couldn't fit four of them huge cookies in my huge mouth."

"Those are some damn good cookies," Chappy nodded.

RRRRRRRRRRRT

Chappy's eye twitched.

"Anyway, long story short, it took some doing, but I got all four in there. The problem was they got a little too far in there and Major Connick had to give me the Heimlich in front of the whole cafeteria."

"Wait. Major Connick was there too?" Chappy interrupted. "You're telling me the Squadron Command Sergeant Major *and* the Squadron Executive Officer were both witness to this?"

"Witness?" I said. "They instigated it. Major Connick brought me the cookies."

Chappy leaned back against a table.

"Ooo-eee," he said. "That's pretty frick'n funny. But what's the big deal? If the higher-ups already know about it, who cares?"

"There may or may not have been a table of 'full-bird' Colonels two tables down from us," I explained.

"Oh," said Chappy.

"Who were having lunch with a two-star General," I went on.

"Oooooh," sang Chappy.

"Who then presented me with a challenge coin for, and I quote, 'surviving my own idiocy'."

"Ouch."

RRRRRRRRRRT

Chappy lost it.

"Goddammit, Private. Can't you see we're having a fucking conversation here. If you move that fucking rack one more inch, I'll rip your miserable guts out."

Private Coucher darted back to his corner with his tail between his legs, throwing the sling back over his injured shoulder as he went. Chappy's hands were white and shaking. He took a deep breath before turning back to me, his face placid again.

"Well, it sounds like the worst is over. I'm sure you'll get a fair amount of harassment from the fellas, but it's nothing to kill yourself over," Chappy said as he headed for the door. "Though, no one would blame you if you did *now*."

"Where are you going?" I asked. "That's all you got for me?"

"You say it wasn't suicide. I believe you," he shrugged. "Plus, you got me all hot and bothered for one of those cookies."

"Well, thanks a lot," I said. "I may have just destroyed my Army career."

“Maybe,” said Chappy. “Were Storms and Connick laughing?”

“Yes, Sir,” I admitted.

“Well, then you may have helped your career. That General forgot you two seconds after he walked away.”

Chappy stopped at the door and turned to Private Coucher.

“Sorry for the outburst, Private,” he said. “I shouldn’t have done that. I just get very frustrated when I see excessive amounts of stupidity. Feel free to come talk to me about your feelings anytime. You have a blessed night.”

And with that he stepped out into the night. Coucher and I sat staring at the door, until finally the radio crackled to life, killing the silence.

“Titan TOC, this is Titan Six,” The SCO’s voice crackled over the radio. I could hear the cigar in his mouth.

“This is Titan TOC,” Coucher responded.

“Glad to see you’re sure this time,” The SCO said. “For better or worse, we finally have all personnel and equipment. We’re leaving Bagram. Titan Squadron is heading for FOB Alternator. Over.”

Chapter 6: St. Valentine's Day Shura

February 14, 2009

The courtyard reeked of goat dung and body odor. The whole town of Pul-i-Alam did. We'd come to the capital of the Logar Province to hold a meeting, or shura, with the elders of the surrounding district, Baraki Barak. The SCO was adamant that we needed to win the hearts and minds of the people in Baraki Barak first. They were the linchpin in his plan to move south.

"We need to control Baraki Barak before we can take Charkh," he'd said. "And we need to control Charkh before we can take the Kherwar."

The SCO made it clear that he and Frank were the only ones to speak with the elders. Clark and I were to keep our mouths shut and our pencils to paper. We were there only to take the minutes of the meeting. He'd even gone out of his way designate Clark the primary note-taker and me the secondary. An unnecessary distinction made simply to demean. Further showing his favoritism, The SCO put Clark in charge of the Squadron's "contingency fund", which was nothing more than a backpack full of cash used to pay for accidental damages incurred during acts of war or acts of negligence.

We sat on a large rug facing into a circle of weathered, elderly faces. The old men sat cross-legged on decorative rugs, fidgeting like a classroom of first graders. Some twisted their beards while studying the patterns beneath them. Others sat proudly with straight backs and cold eyes. The SCO sat at the head of the rug with Frank to his left. Years of marching and training had left The SCO unable to sit cross-legged like the elders before him. Years of fast food and physical neglect had left Frank unable to do the same. Instead, the two sat with their legs stretched in front, toes pointed skyward. It was the first time I'd seen The SCO without a cigar and he habitually ran his tongue over the yellow-stained corner of his mouth. He'd forced his temporary tobacco ban on Clark as well, forbidding him from chewing during the meeting.

"Does The SCO know they aren't listening to him?" I whispered.

"Shhhhh," hissed Clark.

"Most of 'em don't even look awake," I said. It was true. A few elders appeared to be nodding off. "I can hear someone snoring."

"Shhhhh," Clark hissed again.

"Stop shushing me so loud. Are you trying to get us in trouble?" I asked.

Clark shook his head, refusing to look at me.

The SCO had started the meeting by giving the elders a lengthy narrative of his experiences, achievements, likes and dislikes and a few uncomfortable personal facts, offered up in the spirit of good faith, I'm sure. Frank, looking uncomfortable in his sitting position, echoed The SCO's dictation in local dialect, adding grand gestures to spice up the stories. Frank's efforts proved fruitless though and The SCO's impressive resume was lost on the old men who'd never been outside a ten mile radius of their respective villages and had no idea where West Point was. After The SCO's long winded introduction, he asked those who were still conscious to give their names, village of origin, and any other personal notes of interest. The SCO motioned to Clark and I to be writing this down, but Frank offered no reverse translation, so anything after the gentleman's name was lost on us.

While the elders were daydreaming, dozing, or chatting, not so discreetly amongst themselves, The SCO took the opportunity to gloss over details of his plan he felt would normally ruffle the old men's feathers. Most notably, his plan to establish an outpost in Baraki Barak, the creatively named capital town of the Baraki Barak District. He then quickly guided the meeting along by giving the elders an opportunity to voice their ideas for district improvement projects that could be undertaken by U.S. forces to improve the lives of the citizens. This perked interest among the oldtimers and they went around the circle nudging each other awake and shouting suggestions, which Frank struggled to translate.

"I would like the old, Russian minefield, behind my home, removed," one weathered old man stated. "It exploded five sheep last year alone."

The SCO looked back at Clark and I to ensure we were taking notes. Clark was writing furiously in his green notebook. I dropped my eyes and began to write as well.

"Exploding Russian Sheep"

The suggestions continued to roll in, getting more advanced as they went. Improved school houses and supplies, elaborate irrigations systems, paved roads, a water purification plant, a hydroelectric dam on the Logar River.

"Good God," The SCO grumbled. "I'm surprised they haven't asked for a casino and titty bar yet."

He quickly elbowed Frank, who'd begun to translate.

With all of the activity inside the shura, I hadn't noticed the steady roar building from beyond the courtyard walls. Soon I could hear sporadic shouts in both English and Pashto from outside. The SCO's radio operator shuffled over and knelt beside me, tapping the earpiece that was connected to a radio handset on his shoulder.

"Sir, there's a mob forming outside," he said. "They're getting restless."

The SCO looked back. Apparently our sidebar conversation was more insulting than all the sidebar conversations between the elders.

"What?" he growled.

"Sir, there's a mob forming outside," the radioman said again. "They're getting restless."

The SCO raised his hand to take the cigar from his mouth before realizing it wasn't there.

"I don't care if they're flipping cars and burning couches. You tell Captain Applegate to get his shit together and get that situation under control," The SCO said.

The soldier looked nervous, tilting his head to the handset.

"Raven One, this is Raven Three," he radioed. "Titan Six says he ain't done here yet and to 'get your shit together and get the situation under control'."

I thought I could hear Captain Applegate's shrill voice screaming into the radio from beyond the wall. He'd recently been assigned as Platoon Leader for The SCO's security detachment of misfit soldiers. The SCO called it a promotion. He was providing Applegate the opportunity to see 'command decisions made up close'. But we all knew The SCO just wanted to keep a thumb on him. I think he secretly liked his opportunities to abuse Applegate, even more than he liked abusing me.

"What's a boxer without a punching bag," I'd accidentally overheard him tell The GIF.

The noise from outside calmed briefly and The SCO changed the direction of the shura once again.

"As I've explained, we're the Coalition representatives for the entire province of Logar. As I gathered from your introductions, all of you fine gentlemen live here in Baraki Barak. It is our hope to offer help to other districts as well and I was hoping one of you might be able to offer advice of who to speak with in the Charkh District. Or possibly to make an introduction, if that is not too bold."

Clearly The SCO was uncomfortable asking for favors. Even more clear was the discomfort of the elders at the mention of the Charkh District, a sparsely populated region of Logar separating the lowlands of Baraki Barak from the mountains of Kherwar.

The elders exchanged glances and kept their heads low. The man with the exploding sheep began to stand, but his neighbors grabbed his wrist, pulling him back to the rug. Not to be deterred, he leaned forward, rubbing the roots of his dusty beard as he spoke.

"The land of Charkh is dangerous ground," he whispered. "It will not be welcoming for you and your men. Bad men there."

"Who are these bad men?" The SCO asked. "Taliban? Local militia?"

The old man would not say more. The radio operator tapped me on the shoulder.

"Sir, Captain Applegate is reporting that the crowd is now throwing rocks at them," he whispered to me. I looked to Captain Clark who simply shrugged.

"Sir," I called to The SCO. "The mob outside is getting out of control. They've started throwing rocks."

The SCO dropped his head.

"How big are the rocks?" He asked.

"Sir?"

"I said, how big are the rocks?" He barked.

The radio operator relayed the question and waited for the response.

"Sir, Captain Applegate reports that they have worked their way up to medium size and growing," the radio operator reported. "He says they sting a bit."

The SCO knew his shura was coming to an end. He quickly crammed in one last question for the elders.

"We've heard of several incidences around Logar involving a little blue truck," he said.

I expected looks of confusion from the elders, but Frank's interpretation of this was all it took to stretch grins across their leathery faces. Apparently, the world of Logar is rather small.

"So you know who owns the truck?" The SCO asked.

"Nasir," called out the exploding-sheep-man. "He is a fine boy. I knew his uncle very well. Nasir, helps the people very much."

I wrote down the name.

"How does he help the people?" The SCO leaned in.

"He protects those that can't protect themselves," the man said. "From those that would wish to control us."

The SCO nodded his head and licked his lips.

"And where would I find this 'Nasir'?"

A shot rang out from beyond the courtyard walls. The shura was over. The old men suddenly became much more agile than they'd let on, popping up from their rugs and moving quickly to the exit or the safety of the attached buildings. Clark and I rushed around, frantically encouraging everyone to calm down and remain seated. Frank nervously followed The SCO's lead and stayed seated on the rug. The SCO was a stone, his eyes closed and his fists tugging at the tassels of his rug.

"That was one of our guns," he said. His voice was the eye of a hurricane. "What the hell happened out there?"

The radioman shuffled timidly over to The SCO.

"Sir, Captain Applegate is reporting a negligent discharge," he squeaked.

"Christ," said The SCO, getting to his feet. "The most important meeting of the deployment, ruined by an N.D. You tell Applegate that I want to know who's responsible immediately."

The SCO removed a plastic sandwich bag from his breast pocket. The inside was smeared with the soggy end of his cigar.

"It was Captain Applegate's weapon, Sir," the radioman reported. "Applegate was responsible for the discharge."

"Christ," said The SCO. "Stop saying 'discharge'."

"At least no one was hurt," I said.

"Someone was hurt," the radio man relayed before The SCO could bite my head off.

"Christ!" yelled The SCO, biting his cigar instead.

We exited the courtyard through a door in the red clay walls. The scene we entered was dramatically different from the empty streets we'd arrived on. Our MRAP vehicles had been moved to form a semicircle barricade around the front entrance of the courtyard. Between each hulking machine, soldiers from Raven Platoon filled the gaps and beyond them was a sea of Afghani men milling angrily up and down the crossroad. In the middle of it all, a small group of soldiers and civilians had gathered, their attention on the ground before them where a number of high pitched shrieks were now emerging.

I followed The SCO as he pushed his way through the circle. Lying at the bottom of the crowd, an Afghani man writhed in pain. Doc Jonston was already working on him, cleaning and dressing a large wound at the end of his foot. Beside them sat Captain Applegate. His face was the color of spoiled milk and he stroked the Afghani man's arm, mumbling apologies with the repentant tone of a religious litany. Terp 2 sat on his knees behind the man, propping his head up and offering him drinks from his canteen, all while relaying Captain Applegate's ramblings the best he could.

"What the hell happened?" The SCO barked.

Captain Applegate's eyes were filled with horror.

"I'm so sorry, Sir," he blubbered. "They hit my hand with a rock. My finger shouldn't have been on the trigger."

"Save your apologies for the court-martial," The SCO said. "Doc, what's the damage?"

"He'll probably lose his big toe, Sir," Doc replied without looking up from his work.

"Only the one?" The SCO asked.

"That'd be my guess, Sir," Doc said.

"Captain Clark," The SCO called. "How much is a toe worth?"

"Sir?"

"There's an index card in there," The SCO said, pointing to Clark's contingency fund backpack. "How much is a toe worth?"

Clark pulled a small laminated card from the top of the backpack and ran his finger down a printed list.

"Says here, two thousand dollars, Sir."

"For *one* big toe?" The SCO choked.

Clark consulted the card again.

"Oh. Sorry, Sir. *Big* toes are five thousand each."

The SCO spat flakes of tobacco from his lips in Applegate's direction.

"Pay the man," he grumbled. He turned and pushed back through the crowd. "Let's get the hell out of here before we all get stoned to death."

"Good idea, Sir," Frank said, hot on his heels. "These fools will be cutting off all kinds of appendages once they realize we're paying for them."

Captain Clark removed five large bundles of cash from the backpack and handed them to the wounded Afghani man. The cash served as an incredible anesthetic and the man flipped through his new crisp bills in pure ecstasy. Seeing that the man was no longer concerned with his foot, Doc wrapped one last bandage and gathered his gear.

"Drink lots of water and change your socks regularly," I heard him tell the wounded man. Terp 2 translated and then stood, letting the man sink on to his back in the dirt while he waved his new fortune in the air for his friends to see. I saw the disgust on Terp 2's face, but I wasn't sure if it was for us or the man on the ground.

The whole ride back to FOB Alternator, I kept thinking about the wounded man's bloody foot and the index card of body parts. I waited until we were back in the Operations Office before voicing my disgust to Captain Clark.

"I'm just saying, it's obvious these things happen too frequently if we've got laminated cards prepped and ready," I said hoisting my feet onto my desk.

"I don't disagree," he said, spitting brown chew-juice into an empty water bottle. "But what other option is there? You can't cart the guy off to give him proper medical. It'd look like an abduction."

He stood and walked toward the door.

"Bottomline," he said, "war is messy. Admittedly, messier around folks like Applegate, but the fact is civilians get hurt sometimes. Think of all the wars past and the millions of civilian casualties. I'd say we're making pretty good progress. Something to consider anyway. You coming to chow?"

I begrudgingly agreed with his assessment, but decided to skip dinner anyway. Clark hadn't been gone two minutes before The GIF kicked open the door and I wished I'd gone with him. I dropped my feet to the floor and started to stand, but he motioned for me to stay seated.

"Save it," he said. "And keep your feet off the desk. This isn't your damn dorm room, Rye."

"Yes, Sir."

Major Connick entered behind him, checking his watch. The bags beneath his eyes told me he was operating on another level. Time of day was no longer relevant to him. His watch was just a reminder that his subordinates were mere mortals and still operated under the archaic constructs of a structured day. He leaned back against a desk, waiting for The GIF to do his thing.

"The SCO has a job for you," The GIF said.

My heart started pounding. I'd assumed Applegate would be fired. And I'd feared I'd be his replacement. I wanted to be a platoon leader again, but not like that.

"The SCO wants you to develop some reconnaissance missions over Baraki Barak and Charkh," The GIF continued. "The enemy knows we're coming and he wants eyes on major routes to prevent placement of roadside bombs."

"*Over* Baraki Barak and Charkh, Sir," I asked.

"Yes, Rye. *Over*," he said, flapping his hands like a bird. "Like, with helicopters."

"Sir, I've never created missions for helicopters before," I said. "I don't even know where to begin."

He pointed to the phone on my desk.

"Call up the piloty guys at Brigade Headquarters," he said turning back toward the door. "Also, ask them about Bambi Buckets."

"Bambi Buckets, Sir?"

"The riot in Puli-e-Alam has gotten bigger since you all left," The GIF explained. "We need a deterrent to prevent gatherings in the streets."

"I'm confused, Sir. What is a Bambi Bucket?"

"Rye, don't ask so many questions, it makes you look dumb. You've never heard of Bambi Buckets? And you call yourself an air support expert?"

"No, Sir. I don't."

"Good, 'cause you're terrible," he said, shaking his head. "They're buckets that dangle from helicopters. They use them to drop water on forest fires, but I thought they might be good to disperse an angry crowd."

The GIF was quite pleased with his idea.

"Sir, you're not serious?" I asked. I looked to Major Connick for help, but his eyes were closed and his chin had slipped to his chest.

"Why wouldn't I be serious?" The GIF asked.

"Well, I mean--," I started, trying to think of a way to phrase it gently. "Dropping that large a volume of water from that high up--. Couldn't that kill someone?"

The GIF laughed, relieved that civilian deaths was the only downside to his brilliant idea.

"Rye, it's water," he spoke to me like he was explaining quantum physics to a first grader. "Water is soft. It's not like we're dropping buckets of bricks. I swear, sometimes I don't know where your head is at. Worst case scenario, these people actually get a bath for once and we rinse all the goat shit off the streets."

He flicked Major Connick on the shoulder as he moved toward the door. Connick startled awake.

"I'm going to chow before they close," he said.

"I'm right behind you," Connick yawned.

"Are you alright, Sir?" I asked once The GIF had gone.

Major Connick smiled.

"I haven't slept in seventy-two hours," he said. "I'll be honest, I'm at capacity. I think I may have to check out for a while."

"Sir, I don't think that's healthy," I said with concern. I'd seen him weaving down the hall of the Command Post earlier. I didn't know him well and he'd kept us at work for many late nights in preparation for deployment, but he'd always been a fair and rational human being, which was more than I could say for a lot of Majors. Not to mention he'd saved my life from the Taliban cookies back in Bagram.

"If sleep deprivation is my biggest threat while I'm here, I'm doing okay," Major Connick replied. "The real question is, how are *you*?"

"Fine, Sir," I said, not wanting to complain to a man working himself to an early grave.

He eyed me suspiciously.

"Good to hear," he said. "If you're ever *not fine*, my door is always open. And Rye, don't worry about this helicopter mission stuff. You'll figure it out."

He tore a sheet of paper from his notebook and handed it to me.

"There's the number for the Brigade's aviation unit. Call them and ask to speak with their Ops planner. His name is Major Oran. He's good people. Ask him for examples of previous missions. After that, it should be 'plug and chug'."

"Thank you, Sir," I said, taking the paper.

"And Jared," Connick went on. "If you own this, we might be able to make Air Planning a full time gig for you and get you out of that Battle Captain junk."

"That'd would be great, Sir," I said. "But what about Major Doyle's Bambi Buckets. Do I ask Brigade about it?"

"Good God, no," he said. "Just forget you ever heard it. I'm sure he's already forgotten he told you."

Major Connick leaned over and picked up the Battle Captain guide book that was laying on my desk. "I'm going to give this to Captain Applegate. I've got a feeling he won't be leading any more platoon missions for The SCO."

Chapter 7: Jingle Air

March 5, 2009

I never liked Ivan until they peeled him off the rocks in the Tangi Valley and by then it was too late. Ivan didn't like me because Ivan didn't like anyone and because I never had vodka. He was always drunk when he landed his helicopter on my airfield, but he was always wrecked because it helped him land without wrecking. Ivan had been a pilot for the Russian military in the mid-80's, flying combat missions in the very same region. His promising military career was shot from the sky by the Mujahideen and a Stinger Missile, stamped "Made In The U.S.A.". He'd crash landed his bird and evaded his would-be captures, but hadn't been able to land sober since. Or at least that's the story he told me every damn time I saw him.

"Ver do you vant the load?" Ivan shouted over the rotor wash of his Mi-8 helicopter.

"The same damn place you dropped the loads last time," I yelled. A shortage of Army Aviation in our area had forced us to rely on contracted pilots like Ivan, known simply as "Jingle Air", for "milk-run" resupply missions.

"Red smoke?" Ivan slurred.

"Yes, red smoke. Just like before."

"Vodka?" Ivan pulled a silver flask from inside of his jacket.

"No, Ivan. I don't want any."

Ivan shook his head.

"No. Do you 'ave?" He pointed to the flask, holding it upside down.

I checked my watch. It was 1000 hours.

"Let's get these loads in the air," I shouted, tapping my watch.

Ivan shrugged and shuffled back to his idling aircraft. It was hard to gauge his level of drunkenness from his awful English, but the weave in his step provided some insight. I'm sure that flask had been full before breakfast.

Ten foot tall cement barriers walled in my airfield. My airfield. I'd taken Major Connick's advice and took ownership of the air missions. I'd worked myself out of the Battle Captain job, becoming the permanent Squadron Air Officer. It wasn't a glamorous position. Some argued it wasn't a real position at all. But it got me out of the Command Post more and out from under the watchful, beady eyes of The SCO and fanciful, schemes of The GIF.

I walked back toward the gap in barriers that served as the airfield's entrance. The Squadron Sniper Team was waiting there and I gave the signal that Ivan was ready to go. The Taliban are apparently fair-weather fighters and with most of the jihadists in hibernation, there'd been terribly little to snipe. They'd spent the last week target practicing, but with all the FOB's feral dogs now dead, Sergeant Hunter had signed them up to assist me with airfield operations. With helmets, goggles, and gloves, they jogged off to the cargo nets that were staged at the opposite end.

Each cargo net, called a sling-load, carried food, water, ammunition or fuel destined for delivery to OP Spur, an outpost the Squadron had established on a high mountain ridge, overwatching the district of Baraki Barak. OP Spur had been deemed necessary after three roadside bombs were discovered the hard way along routes in the district. Armed with a platoon of scouts and a TOW-missile, OP Spur would serve as a healthy deterrent against what The SCO felt was a growing insurgency caused by Applegate's chronic incompetence.

Sergeant Hunter was directing his men to the first load when I jogged up in my helmet and goggles.

"What the got-damn hell are you doing, Sir?" He asked.

"Never ask somebody to do something you aren't willing to do yourself," I said.

Hunter shook his head.

I climbed six feet to the top of the load, using the webbing of the cargo net. One of Hunter's soldiers was already there holding the metal eyelet I'd need to hook the load to the bottom of the chopper. He gave me a peculiar look.

"What the hell are you doing, Sir?"

"Never ask somebody to--" I stopped and pointed to the eyelet. "Gimme that. I'm bored as all hell, man. I'm hooking this first one."

The soldier was suspiciously eager to surrender his duty. Throwing the eyelet to me, he rolled off the load in one fluid motion.

"Watch your noggin, Sir," He shouted with a smile. "Be ready to roll if he dips. He dips a lot."

I looked down to find myself perched atop a pallet of MREs. I imagined myself squashed between the belly of the chopper and the pallet; guts and gore intermingling with globs of pristinely preserved imitation pork rib, veggie omelets, and shrimp jambalaya.

"Pay attention, Sir," shouted Sergeant Hunter, waving his arms.

Thump, thump.

Ivan had lifted off and began creeping forward. The round, chopper bounced like the pale carcass of a dead whale on dirty waves. Ivan's abrupt changes in elevation were unsettling. He smiled at me through the windshield, before turning his attention to swatting an unseen bug flying through his cockpit.

I lost Ivan as the helicopter crept overhead. The rotor wash ripped savagely at my sleeves and pant legs. Bits of gravel assaulted my face, forcing my head down. When I looked again, the helicopter was hovering three feet from my helmet. Through a slot in the center of the floor, a pair of tired eyes stared back at me. The Eyes must have belonged to Ivan's copilot, whom I'd never met before.

I reached up to set the eyelet, but the hook was too far to reach. I shook my head. The Eyes rolled and disappeared. Seconds later the chopper dropped an inch. Reach. Still too far. The Eyes rolled again and again disappeared. The chopper dropped three inches. This time it was enough and the eyelet of the cargo net slipped over the hook. I looked back to The Eyes and gave the thumbs up. The Eyes squinted menacingly and disappeared. The chopper dropped fast. I rolled desperately off the load and crashed hard into the gravel below. I scrambled away, as the helicopter hovered just inches over the load before taking off.

"What the hell was that?" I shouted. "He did that on purpose."

The snipers were roaring.

"He could've killed me."

I gave Ivan's bird, "the bird". Sergeant Hunter wiped tears from his eyes.

"Sir. You gotta jump for those," he said, catching his breath.

"What?"

"When the chopper gets that close, you gotta jump to hook it. Lower'n a chopper a few inches ain't easy. That was your warning not to be so picky."

"That's one hell of a warning. Why the hell didn't you guys tell me to jump?"

"Cause we're bored as hell out here too, Sir," Hunter grinned, slapping me on the back. "You're alright, Sir. We got the rest. You've had enough for one day."

"Screw you 'I've had enough', I got the next one."

At the base of a large mountain we'd all dubbed "Mount Krumpit", FOB Alternator sat higher in elevation than almost anywhere in the province. From the top of the cement barrier wall, we could watch Ivan's entire trek to OP Spur. We could even see the red smoke used to signal him in. I watched him go and come back and we repeated the process all over again.

The day slid away slowly and the sun moved high into the sky. Finally there was one sling-load remaining. I squinted from my perch to see Ivan returning from the Spur. Just then, a trail of black smoke curled up like a viper from the ground in Baraki Barak. The snake streaked past Ivan's helicopter, just missing his blades. Ivan took evasive action, forcing the bird into a steep climb. I jumped down and grabbed the airfields radio.

"Titan TOC, this is Titan Three Air, my Jingle Air just took rocket fire over Baraki Barak. Copy?"

"This is Titan TOC. Good copy. Just got the same report from OP Spur. We're sending Titan Two to the airfield to debrief the pilot. Don't let Jingle Air leave."

Just as Ivan's chopper was landed, an out of breath Captain Garcia jogged onto the airfield. His face was flushed and he doubled over, hands on his knees.

"I hope he's sober enough for questioning," I said, while Garcia caught his breath.

"I don't need much," Garcia said pulling a map from his breast pocket. "OP Spur gave me a general location. I just need Ivan to pinpoint where he saw it. If he saw it."

"Might be harder than you think."

I joined the snipers sitting along the barrier wall. They watched Garcia eagerly. The long rotors still swung quickly around Ivan's aircraft, muting the drama. The fusion of grand hand gestures and gravel kicking, was a beautifully choreographed dance, pitting alcoholism against exasperation. Garcia pointed frequently and emphatically to the map that struggled to escape in the swirling wind.

Ivan only shrugged his round shoulders and waved his flask in Garcia's face. Garcia swatted viciously at the flask. In retaliation, Ivan slapped the map from Garcia's hands, pointing and laughing as the, once proper, Captain chased after it as it danced in the rotor wash. Victorious, Ivan took one last, long pull from a paper-bagged bottle he'd pulled from his cockpit.

"Well, that should do it," I sighed.

Within seconds, Ivan was unconscious, stretched across the seats of his cockpit. Garcia made his way back to where we sat, his face gnarled in rage.

"How the hell is he flying that thing?"

"Doesn't look like he's flying anything anymore, thanks to you."

"What do you mean, 'thanks to me'? He was drunk off his ass before I even got here."

"No, Sir. He was drunk *on* his ass when you got here. You riled him. *Now* he's drunk off his ass. A drunk Ivan can fly. An unconscious Ivan can't. Now I've got a six ton paperweight taking up my entire airfield."

Captain Garcia was in no mood.

"I'm real sorry he's clogging your bustling airfield," Captain Garcia snarled, motioning to all the helicopters that weren't there. "But I'm about to have The SCO's boot ankle deep in my ass. He's sending Cherokee Troop out to find the shooter, with or without a solid grid coordinate. I, for one, would like them to be a little prepared, so they don't get caught with their pants around their ankles."

Garcia knew how to get under my skin. I had familial ties with Cherokee Troop. I'd been a Platoon Leader there before a knee injury sidelined me to Squadron Headquarters.

"Did you ask 'The Eyes?'" I asked.

"The what?" Garcia demanded.

"Ivan's co-pilot," I explained. "The guy who gives him height adjustments while we're hooking sling-loads."

Garcia's face got even redder.

"There's nobody else on that damn bird," he spat, pushing his glasses up by the bridge.

I contemplated the implications of this—Ivan dashing back and forth between his controls and the slot in the floor, while his six ton helicopter hovered inches over my head. I decided never to hook a sling-load for Ivan again.

"Give me the map," I said. "You buy some time with The SCO. I'll work on Ivan."

Working on Ivan proved more difficult than I'd imagined. We started out small, attempting to shake him awake, holding coffee under his nose, and then vodka, but nothing roused him. Sergeant Hunter and the snipers grew impatient and the efforts escalated to face slaps, nipple twists and the dreaded ball-tap. Still no response.

"This ain't doin' shit, Sir," Hunter complained. "I'm gonna bring out the big guns."

Before I could ask, he whistled at his men.

"Make yourselves useful," he said with a grin. "Get the man another drink."

The sniper seemed to understand without explanation. Each man grabbed an arm, a leg, or belt loop and hoisted Ivan to their shoulders. Like pallbearers in a funeral procession, they began a slow trek down to the shower tent.

****

The map was wet, but readable. I rushed across the loose gravel toward the Command Post, cursing every time my ankles rolled. It'd taken Sergeant Hunter and his men longer than expected to wake Ivan and most of them had ended up just as wet. I hadn't been overly confident that Ivan would be in any condition to read a map, but the vodka-soaked aviator had proven surprisingly cognizant after a shower. He'd put his soggy finger to the map with confidence. The information was crucial, so I was rushing the map back to Captain Garcia and his team of intel nerds.

"Rye!"

I cringed.

The GIF stood outside the exit of the cafeteria adjusting the brim of his wrinkled patrol cap. He started toward me and I snapped to attention, rendering a salute out of habit.

"Sir, I--"

"Jesus Christ," yelped The GIF. He ducked down as if someone had swung at his head. "Are you mad? There could be snipers anywhere."

The only vantage point a sniper could have was from Mount Krumpit and would require a miraculous four mile shot. I dropped my salute.

"Sorry, Sir," I mumbled, trying to make a getaway.

"Not so fast," The GIF said, stepping in front of me. "Was that Jingle Air I saw flying in here earlier?"

"Yes, Sir."

"What were they doing here? Were they lost?"

"No, Sir. We were sending resupplies up to OP Spur," I said. "As directed, Sir."

The GIF's eyes narrowed.

"Directed by who?" He asked.

"By you, Sir."

"I gave you no such order," The GIF huffed. "Why are you not using Army birds?"

I chose my words carefully.

"Sir, per our conversation two days ago, I was under the impression that Army helicopters had more important things to do than run resupply missions to small outposts."

"'Per our conversation'?" He repeated. "What, are you reciting an email to me?"

"No, Sir."

"You know why people don't like you, Rye?"

"People don't like me, Sir?"

"I sure-as-shit don't right now. And you know why?"

"Because I'm a terrible scapegoat, Sir?"

"Because you blame everyone else for your shortcomings." The GIF sighed.

He took a step back and looked to the sky pensively.

"I hope you all are paying attention," he went on. This was how he began all his lectures. There was no one else around. "There's a lesson in this. Just because I tell you to do something, doesn't mean I've told you the correct way to do it. I expect you to be able to sort out what I mean, over what I say. You're all adults. Start acting like it."

"Sir, Ivan's helicopter took surface-to-air fire," I blurted. "Almost took him out. He was able to pinpoint on the map where it came from."

I held the map up and The GIF eyed it opportunistically.

"That so? And where are you going with that?

"To Captain Garcia, Sir," I said. "He needs it to brief Cherokee Troop before they head out to make trouble."

The GIF's demeanor changed. He reached up and placed a freckled hand on my shoulder, smoothing down a wing of red hair protruding from his patrol cap with the other. His tone became fatherly.

"Jared, I understand what you're trying to do and I can respect it."

I was concerned. The GIF went on.

"I know your job here is insignificant and you want to feel like you're making a difference. Like you're useful."

There it is, I thought.

"But you need to stop and think, because this is a good lesson if you become a Commander some day. Would you really trust the lives of your soldiers to the incoherent words of a drunken Russkie?"

"But, Sir," I pleaded.

He waved me off.

"I tell you what we'll do," he said, slowly plucking the map from my grasp. "I'll throw this in the trash for you. And while I do that, you take your happy-ass back, sop up your Russian puddle, pour him back in his chopper and get him the hell off my post."

"Sir, he's in no condition to be flying. He can barely stand."

"My point exactly," said The GIF. "And yet you trust him to point out accurately on a map where he *thought* he saw enemy fire come from while flying hundreds of feet overhead?"

I felt my face flush.

"Now if you'll excuse me," said The GIF, "the dust out here is giving me a migraine. I'm going to my quarters. Get back to work."

Before he could make his getaway, he too was stopped.

"Doyle," came another voice from the cafeteria exit. This time it was The SCO, with Frank trailing close behind. It was shaping up to be an awful afternoon.

"Doyle, why the hell is Jingle Air doing our resupplies to OP Spur?" The SCO barked as he approached. "That Russian is a liability."

The GIF puffed his chest.

"That's exactly what I told Lieutenant Rye here, Sir," he said, pointing to me. "He's been given strict instruction to never use them again. I've just finished reprimanding him on the same topic."

"Good," The SCO slimed his cigar to the other corner of his mouth and took notice of the map in The GIF's hand. "What's the wet map about?"

"Oh, yes Sir," The GIF held it out proudly for The SCO to see. "I was just on my way to get this to Captain Garcia. The Jingle Air pilot was able to pinpoint exactly where the surface-to-air fire came from. This information could be a great asset to Cherokee Troop before they head out."

The SCO studied the map. I studied the pale tissue of The GIF's neck, imagining my hands wrapped tightly around it.

"I can't believe I'm saying this," said The SCO, "but excellent work, Doyle."

"Thank you, Sir," The GIF said, more surprised than proud.

"And you," The SCO said turning to me. "I imagine that communist sympathizer is still on my FOB? I want him and his aircraft out of here A.S.A.P."

"I was just telling him that too, Sir," The GIF butted in.

"Shut up, Doyle," The SCO waved him off.

"Sir, Ivan is in no shape to fly," I said. "He's coherent but still very drunk."

"He's drunk?" The SCO shouted. "Even more reason to get him the hell out of here. The last thing I need is Colonel Gunn on my ass because some civilian succumbed to alcohol poisoning on *my* base. You'll be doing the paperwork if he dies."

Frank laughed like a hyena behind him.

The sound of rotor blades filled the air and within seconds the whale carcass, piloted by Ivan, buzzed low over the tent village, directly over our heads. I held my breath, unsure that Ivan would pull up in time to clear the FOB walls. The SCO stood on his toes to verify the exact second the chopper crossed the boundary of FOB Alternator.

"There. No longer my problem," he stated matter-of-factly, turning back to me. "Nice work, Jeremy. You didn't even screw up this time."

"It's Jared," I muttered, then checked to make sure no one heard me.

The SCO, The GIF and Frank left for the Command Post, leaving me standing alone and empty handed. Kicking rocks, I headed to the cafeteria, fully intending on overdosing on Aunt Mary's Muffins. Before reaching the entrance, I spotted Private Coucher walking toward the Staff Building, south of the Command Post. His tennis shoes and arm sling were gone, but he wore a thick white brace around his neck.

"Coucher," I shouted. "What happened now?"

He turned his whole torso to see who was speaking, exposing a new rank on his chest and patrol cap. He was no longer "Private Coucher", but "Specialist Coucher". He gave me a startled look and darted into the building, faster and more reckless than a neck injury should allow.

There was no way in hell I was getting snubbed by a Specialist, after just getting crushed by two field grade officers. I ran to the building and climbed the six steps in two bounds. I swung the door open ready to make Coucher earn his neck brace, but the hall was empty.

The Staff Building, as its name implied, housed offices for the non-combat members of the Squadron Staff. These included the Squadron Supply Team, the Squadron Adjutant (which is a fancy way of saying Human Resources), and the Squadron Public Affairs office. Even Chappy had an office and impromptu confessional, which was usually occupied by Captain Applegate. Directly across the hall was the Squadron conference room, where all major operations were briefed. Like the Command Post, the building had been constructed entirely from plywood and sound traveled freely. I stepped lightly down the hall, listening for signs of life. From the conference room, there were low voices and footsteps. There were no operations being briefed today.

I pressed my ear against the door, hoping to recognize a voice from inside. I tried the handle but found it locked. I raised my hand to knock, but my wrist was grabbed from behind. I swung around to find Chappy, shushing me with one finger over his lips.

Chappy slapped his hand over my mouth, dragging me into his office. He shoved me toward a chair in the corner and shut the door carefully behind him.

"What the hell, Chappy," I whispered, though I didn't know why.

"Keep it down," he demanded. He pressed his face against the door, peering through a peephole he must have drilled himself.

"What the hell are you doing?"

Chappy held up his hand for me to wait. When he was satisfied we hadn't been heard, he turned back to me.

"Sorry, Rye," he said. "But some weird shit is going on over there."

"Some weird shit is going on in *here*."

"Rye, please try not to cuss in my chapel," he said. "Just about every Specialist in the Squadron is in that conference room over there right now. Every. Single. One."

Wrinkles formed on Chappy's bald head as he delved deep into thought. He removed his uniform top, exposing an extraordinary canvas of interwoven tattoos running up both arms and disappearing under the sleeves of his undershirt.

"So, what do you think they're doing?" I asked.

"I don't know, but it's not the first time they've met," he said. He'd pulled a large buck-knife from his pocket and began picking grime from under his fingernails. "Those sons-a-bitches have been meeting in there at least once a week since we got here."

"So what's the big deal? They're probably just helping each other get ready for the promotion board."

Chappy rolled his eyes.

"I have faith in God, Rye," he said. "But not much in people. They're up to no good. And I'm gonna find out what."

"What'll you do then? If you rat them out, soldiers will never confide in you again."

Chappy's eyes widened.

"Jesus. I hadn't thought of that," he said.

"I'm sorry, are you talking to me or God?" I asked, heading for the door.

"Sorry. You," he said, and then he looked as though he'd had a small epiphany. "*You.* You'll expose them, *won't* you?"

"What?"

"If I figure out what sinister, perverse deeds these little bastards are up to, you'll turn them in for me, won't you?" Chappy was too excited to stay seated.

"I mean, I guess."

I assumed it was an agreement I'd never have to fulfill. "But only if the deeds are *both* sinister and perverse.

"Outstanding," Chappy yelled smacking me on the back with a massive hand. "The investigation is officially open."

Chapter 8: Beer Bitch 11

March 6, 2009 (Very Early Morning)

The cafeteria was out of energy drinks. Those of us who couldn't stomach coffee, survived the long days and nights consuming abhorrent amounts of Sergeant Drill's Freedom Juice, a dangerously caffeinated concoction, created solely for the military by one of America's largest soda conglomerates. Normally, the squat, half-cans of cancer inducing, battery acid were plentiful in Alternator's cafeteria beverage cooler and were restocked as fast as bleary-eyed soldiers could pack them into their greedy cargo pockets, but a hiccup in the Army supply chain caused a two-day delay in delivery. Around 1930 hours the evening prior, reports began to trickle in of soldiers being found asleep in bathroom stalls, concrete bunkers, and behind machine guns in watch towers. An especially dedicated few, truly jonesing for their fix, formed a mob outside the cafeteria doors, but proved too sleepy to become unruly.

Squinting through a yawn, I checked my watch; 0245 hours. From the activity in the Command Center, you'd think it was noon. Officers and NCOs filtered in and out, hoping to bear witness to the Squadron's first major combat action of the deployment. A direct result of Ivan's shower map. With precise coordinates in hand, Cherokee Troop had discovered a hive of enemy fighters.

At the front of the room were two large flat-screen televisions. The first received a live, infra-red video feed from the Apache helicopters, whose support I had coordinated earlier in the evening. Their eye-in-the-sky cameras followed enemy "squirters" that scurried like bugs from a lifted log every time the choppers made a pass. Only to be stomped out of existence by devastating bursts from the Apache's thirty-millimeter chain-gun, leaving a glowing spatter on a normally dark background. The second monitor was split between a live feed map, with moving icons representing U.S. forces, and a chat message box where ground forces could communicate directly with the Squadron and Brigade Headquarters, the pilots, and anyone else with their hand in the combat cookie jar. The whole setup looked like an old school, real-time strategy video game.

I sat along the back wall, listening to the voices crackle back and forth over the radio. Voices of men whose faces were streaked with sweat and dirt. Voices of men whose vision was hindered by the grainy green glow of night vision goggles. Voices of men who were bringing the fight to the enemy and actually making a difference. I gagged a little as I sipped the cold remains of coffee at the bottom of my cup.

Clark sat on the tabletop in front of me, swinging his long legs and making calls like he was watching a football game unfold.

"Oh, come on. He's right in front of you. You've gotta hit that," he slapped down hard on the table as patches of hot dust kicked up around the image of a fleeing insurgent. He made it another ten feet before a second volley expanded his heat signature across the ground.

The GIF stood at the front of the room, as close as he could get to the video feed.

"Yeah, baby," he said, pumping his freckled fist.

Major Connick stood in front of the tactical screen, coaching Captain Applegate through each new scenario. Poor Applegate had only been the nighttime Battle Captain for less than a month after being fired as The SCO's Security Platoon Leader. It had been a quiet month, but now he was in a full-on tailspin. Whenever Major Connick wasn't calming him down, Applegate stalked the front desk, belittling anyone he outranked.

"Find out how that damn Romanian is doing," he snapped at the radio operator.

An hour earlier, FOB Alternator's resident Special Forces Team had arrived to the battle with a team of Romanian Special Forces under their tutelage. Their first order of business was to clear a qalat where eight insurgents had taken refuge. As they breached a side door, a Romanian soldier stopped a bullet with his chest and the assault went to hell. Fortunately for the Romanian, one of the Apache gunners had a set of brass balls and, after landing in the middle of the fray, gave up his seat so that the Romanian could be evacuated. Now the gunner wandered the battlefield with only a pistol, thin breastplate, and previously mentioned brass balls for protection. I wondered if I would have been so brave.

"I'm gonna get some more coffee," I told Clark. "You want any?"

"Nah," he said, oozing chew juice into a Styrofoam cup. "I've got enough chemicals flowing through me. If I drink coffee now, I won't sleep."

I looked around.

"Is anyone sleeping anytime soon?"

Before I could step foot into the aisle, the Command Center door flung open, nearly knocking me over. The SCO stepped right into my face.

"Major Doyle put you in charge of air support, did he not?"

"Yes, Sir," I stammered.

"Then why the hell don't I have any drones on station yet?"

"Sir, I--," I began, not recalling any conversation about drones.

"Save it," he grumbled. "I've already made the call for Task Force level assets."

"I tried to tell him, Sir," The GIF butted in.

"Shut up, Doyle," he said brushing him off. "Major Connick, give me a rundown of where we stand."

Major Connick began to respond but The SCO raised his hand to silence him.

"On second thought," The SCO said, grinding his cigar, "I'd like to hear the report from our new Battle Captain."

The craters on Applegate's cheeks pooled red.

"Uh, yes, Sir," he stuttered. "Third Platoon, Cherokee Troop is reporting that they don't have contact anymore. They think all the runners have been, er, neutralized. The Apache pilots are saying the same thing. Third Platoon is heading back to ground-zero to reinforce the security team around the qalat. Captain Keegan's Special Forces Team is reporting between eight and ten armed men inside the qalat, but they haven't tried to breach again."

"What do you mean they haven't tried again?" The SCO asked. "We've already lost the element of surprise, now they're just giving these clowns time to dig in."

"Captain Keegan says it's too risky, Sir," Applegate said.

"Of course it's risky, it's goddamn war," The SCO said. "You tell that son-of-a-bitch to take that qalat."

"Yes, Sir," Applegate said, nodding to the radio operator to relay the message.

"Major Connick, what is the situation away from the qalat?" The SCO asked.

"Sir, Third Platoon swept south of these two qalats here," he said motioning to the map. "They pushed squirters out into the open for the Apaches to finish. I'd say we've got six or seven that way, but most of the fighters have holed up in the qalat that Captain Keegan's trying to take."

I watched The SCO pace back and forth between the two monitors. He didn't acknowledge Major Connick. He just shifted his cigar anxiously from one side of his mouth to another.

"No sign of any little blue trucks?" He finally asked.

"Nothing reported yet, Sir," Applegate piped up.

"We did issue the BOLO to Cherokee Troop, right?" The SCO asked, looking at Major Doyle. "They are aware to keep their eyes peeled for that truck?"

The GIF's face went blank.

"When you gave the Operations Brief to the Commander and Platoon Leaders," The SCO lead him, "you told them to be on the lookout for a blue truck, right?"

The GIF looked desperately to Captain Clark.

"Yes, Sir," Clark said. "They were made aware."

"Christ, Doyle, try to be present for your own order briefs," The SCO lectured. "You're lucky you did such a fine job getting that map from the Jingle Air fool. It nearly makes up for your gross incompetence. Nearly."

I clenched my fists. The GIF beamed over the backhanded compliment.

"Sir, Captain Keegan is saying it's a 'no-go' for another breach attempt," the radio operator reported to every "Sir" in the room. "He's requesting a JDAM to eliminate the target completely."

The SCO roared.

"He wants me to drop a five hundred pound bomb next to the first village we're trying to bring into the fold? He's out of his goddamn mind. You tell him he'll get no such authorization from me," The SCO barked. The radio operator looked like he wanted to crawl under his desk.

The SCO turned to me and pointed his finger. All chatter in the Command Center stopped and everyone stared at me. My mind raced to figure out what I'd done now. I removed my notepad from by breast pocket, just in case I was being tasked with something.

"You. Go get me a beer from the cafeteria," The SCO growled. "And while you're at it, get one for the rest of the boys in here. It's going to be a long night."

I kept my head down, so no one could see how red my face was. I wrote "Beer Bitch" in my notepad just to give my shaking hands something to do. I quickly counted eleven heads in the Command Center and wrote that down as well. The cafeteria only provided "near beer", which was a non-alcoholic substitute tasting like pure concentrated disappointment. I was sure no one else would want one, but it wasn't up to them anymore.

"And don't take all night, goddamnit," was the last I heard before the door swung shut behind me.

****

I was livid. I cursed continuously as I followed my flashlight to the cafeteria. I'd been reduced to an errand boy in front of half of my peers. I was The SCO's cabana boy, on the world's least luxurious resort. This wasn't what I'd joined the Army for.

The bodies of sleeping soldiers littered the ground outside the cafeteria's rear doors. I stepped over and around, careful not to disturb the junkies waiting for their beloved Sergeant Drill's. There'd be a violent stampede once it arrived.

The blackout doors creaked as I pushed them open. A hand grabbed my ankle.

"You got the juice?" A voice came from a mass next to the door.

"No. Get off me, you bum," I grumbled, kicking at the gloved hand with my other boot.

The first set of blackout doors swung shut behind me and I pushed through the next. The transition from blackout conditions outside to bright lights inside left me momentarily blind.

"Well, holy shit!" Boomed a voice. "Were your ears burning?"

"What?" I yelled, rubbing my eyes and squinted into the light. On the far side of the long mess hall, Chappy sat twisted in a metal folding chair. The lights on the far side of the cafeteria were dim compared to the retinal burning atrocities hanging over the exit. "What are you doing in here? It's three in the morning."

"This is a sign from God," said Chappy. He looked up, searching for God in the tan canvas overhead. "We were just talking about you. I was telling Coucher here, that you were on our side as well."

By now, I was halfway across the room and I could finally see Coucher sitting opposite of Chappy's enormous frame. He was still wearing his ridiculous neck brace.

"On your side of what?"

"You said he knew," Coucher whined. His eyes darted around the room and he started to stand. "I shouldn't be talking to either one of you."

"Sit your ass back down," Chappy pounded his fist on the table. Even I jumped a little.

Coucher dropped back to his seat.

"He does know," Chappy said more gently. "He just doesn't know about *you* yet."

"Christ, Chappy, I'm standing right here," I said. "And I'm aware of Coucher, in all his battered and bruised glory."

"Right," said Chappy, getting excited. "But you don't know he's working for *us* now."

"Us? What 'us'?"

"Our investigation," said Chappy.

"*Our* investigation? No, no, no, this is your deal. I said I'd back you up if you found anything. I don't want to be part of any cockamamie investigation."

Chappy looked hurt at my reticence to join his crusade.

"Coucher has agreed to be my weasel," Chappy said.

"Mole," corrected Coucher.

"Right, mole," said Chappy. "Whatever you wanna call it. He's gonna be a snitch and get us dirt on what the Specialists are doing at their secret little meetings."

"I'm no snitch," groaned Coucher.

"Of course you are," said Chappy, "and you're going to be great at it."

Coucher gave a weary smile.

"Has he given you any valuable information?" I asked.

"No," Chappy conceded. "He's been goddamn useless so far, if I'm being honest, but he just got promoted so he doesn't think they're telling him everything yet."

"What is he getting out of all this?"

"I had to promise him eternal salvation," Chappy whispered, as though Coucher couldn't hear him.

Coucher smiled proudly.

"How'd you get that neck brace?" I asked Coucher.

"Doc Jonston gave it to me," replied Coucher.

"Well, obviously," I said. "I mean how'd you get hurt?"

"I fell asleep in the guard tower," he said sheepishly. "My Section Sergeant startled me awake. Doc thinks it might be whiplash."

With anyone else, I'd have been surprised, but Coucher's head was big enough to make the diagnosis believable.

"And what happened there?" I asked. Coucher's uniform sleeve had bunched up on the table, revealing a large white bandage taped over his forearm.

"That's nothing," he said, quickly pulling his sleeve back down.

"You got a tattoo from Doc, didn't you?" I asked.

Coucher slowly nodded.

"It's the Batman symbol, isn't it?"

Coucher nodded slowly.

"But it doesn't look much like a bat, does it?

Coucher shook his head.

"Nothing better than deployment tattoos," Chappy piped up. "I got four or five on my first tour in Iraq. Got'em from a buddy in my platoon named Lazlo. They all got infected really quick. I nearly died. They were going to get Lazlo for involuntary manslaughter if I croaked. Boy was he worried."

He roared laughing. Coucher looked a titch nervous.

"I'd love to stay and hear more about this, but I've been tasked by The SCO," I said. I turned my back to them and headed for the beverage cooler.

"They're still out of Sergeant Drill's," Chappy informed as I opened the cooler doors.

"I know," I called back. "I'm on a beer run."

I began loading my cargo pockets with cans of beer.

"That nasty non-alcoholic crap? Chappy asked.

"Unless you know where I can get the real stuff," I said.

"Write that down. That's another task for you," I heard Chappy tell Coucher.

BOOM!!!

The tent floor shook. The glass of the beverage cooler door was still rattling as I pulled my head out. Coucher was under the table with his hands over his head like a grade schooler in a tornado drill. Chappy sat square and upright in his chair listening for more.

"Mortar?" I asked Chappy, trying not to sound alarmed.

"Nah," he said. "Too far away and too big."

It dawned on me what the explosion was. I could still hear Chappy calling after me as the mess hall's double doors smacked shut behind me.

****

The SCO was sitting by himself on the far side of the TOC when I burst in. I'd ran the whole way and my knees and thighs were tenderized by the continuous pounding of the beer cans in my cargo pockets. A glance at the overhead surveillance feed confirmed my suspicion. The screen showed a smoking crater where the qalat had stood. Debris stretched out in chaotic arches of twisted metal, mud, and wood. The men who'd been holed up inside were undoubtedly painted into the Pollock. Over the radio, voices still crackled back and forth as leaders on the ground reported ammunition levels and confirmed body counts.

Major Connick sat at the front of the room writing notes and rubbing his eyes. The other officers and spectators had either left voluntarily or been kicked out. Only a skeleton crew of the Command Center staff remained. Connick stood and gathered his papers. Suppressing a yawn, he shuffled down the aisle toward me. Pausing briefly at my side, he lifted a tired hand to my shoulder.

"Boom," he said, forcing a half smile. I couldn't tell if he was winking or if half his face had fallen asleep. I had so many questions. But it wasn't the time.

He exited the Command Post and I intended to follow suite. I turned to the nearest table and started unloading beers from my pockets into a neat row. From my peripheral, I could see The SCO was watching me. He stood and slowly walked along the front row. With the last beer on the table, I turned toward the exit, trying not to look too hurried.

I can make it, I thought, reaching for the door's handle.

"You missed it," The SCO growled from behind me.

"Sir?" I asked turning toward him. I don't know why I thought playing dumb was the best option.

The SCO moved his cigar skillfully across his mouth and adjusted his belt. He looked like he'd lost weight. It didn't seem like the appropriate time for a compliment.

"You missed it," he repeated. "It's a shame. You could have learned something valuable about command here tonight."

"Yes, Sir," I said, gritting my teeth. "I was in the mess hall getting beers. Like I was asked, Sir."

"Hardly the time to be drinking, if you ask me, Jeremy."

"Jared, Sir."

"You seem to miss a lot, Jeremy. You're going to have a rough time later in your career if you don't start picking up some of these combat lessons. You might want to speak with the Chaplain about your drinking problem."

The SCO continued down the aisle until he stood in front of the beers. He picked one up, analyzing the can.

"Personally, I don't know how you drink this non-alcoholic garbage. Tastes like piss."

He set the can back down and I stepped aside so he could reach the door, but he stopped in front of me.

"Get some sleep," he said. "If you're sober enough, you're coming with me tomorrow."

"Yes, Sir," I said, fighting to keep my shoulders from sinking. "Where are we going, Sir?"

I followed The SCO's bloodshot eyes toward the television screen, still playing the feed of the smoking crater.

"I'll show you first hand the brutality of war. Maybe then you'll take this seriously."

I kept watching the smoking crater as The SCO exited.

"Sir?" the radio operator called.

"What?" I said with a little too much bite.

"Sir, are you going to drink *all* of those beers?" he asked.

I felt bad for him. I'm sure his night had been worse than mine. I began passing the beers out to the remaining workers in the Command Center, bypassing Captain Applegate who was sleeping with his head hidden behind a computer monitor. I kept one beer for myself and sipped it slowly as I trudged through the gravel back to my room. The SCO was right about one thing, it did taste like piss. But it was the closest I'd had to a beer in four months.

Chapter 9: Collateral Damage

March 6, 2009 (Midday)

Thin strands of smoke curled from beneath charred, splintered boards and twisted metal, like snakes dancing to a charmer. I was amazed to see patches of glowing coals twelve hours after impact. We'd have been there sooner, but our departure was riddled with delays. The brass in Bagram had made it clear the Afghan National Army, or ANA, was now to "spearhead" all major operations in an attempt to legitimize the government and its military in the eyes of the people. A last-minute effort before the summer's Presidential election. Captain Keegan and his team were tasked with training and babysitting three platoons of Afghani soldiers on their compound attached to the southwest corner of Alternator. Getting the Afghani soldiers ready for movement had been like herding cats and had left The SCO on the verge of an atomic meltdown.

I was standing on the edge of the bomb crater watching the forensic teams work when Terp 2 came up beside me.

"Who are all these people?" Terp 2 asked.

The Brigade Commander, Colonel Gunn, had arrived before us, bringing teams of soldiers for every investigative task imaginable. Groups of soldiers in clean, pressed uniforms milled around the bombsite, poking and prodding. There was a team taking pictures of every inch of smoldering rubble, a team measuring the crater, its radius, depth, and blast pattern, a team collecting body parts from under charred rock and wood, and a team reassembling bodies into Frankenstein-like amalgamations to assure an accurate body count. Lieutenant Barrett was there, but was busy babysitting a gaggle of journalists. They'd undoubtedly come to get a juicy story about 'excessive use of force' and did their best to stray from Barrett's watchful eyes. Sergeant Loredo was there as well and escorted a team from the bomb's manufacturing company. They wore collared shirts and ties under their kevlar body armor and boasted loudly about the size of their bombs. There was also a team managing angry locals who'd gathered to hurl insults, and a few stones, at the "American murders" and complain about long damaged property they could now blame on last night's explosion. That team was followed closely by another team shelling out handfuls of cash from a big, black duffle bag.

"I don't know who all these idiots are," I lied.

The SCO had asked Colonel Gunn the same thing when we arrived. Colonel Gunn's reply had been just as curt.

"They're here to gather evidence against you," Gunn had said. "In case you made a mistake and we have to Court Martial you."

The SCO had gone white.

"I'm sure everything is on the 'up and up' though. Standard procedure," Colonel Gunn added with a smile. He then invited The SCO to walk with him and discuss "alternative courses of action" he might have taken rather than leveling the equivalent of a city block. I was clearly not invited on this lesson in warfare humility and was left standing around with no real purpose. I wasn't surprised though. The SCO had forgotten he'd invited me anyway and asked me three times that morning "what the hell I was doing there." I would've liked to have heard their conversation though. I'd been racking my brain over what had changed The SCO's mind about dropping the bomb.

"Do you think he did the right thing?" Terp 2 asked.

"You mean dropping the bomb?" I asked. "Yes. I do."

Terp 2 was silent a moment, staring into the crater in front of us.

"What if there were women or children inside?"

"There weren't," I said.

"No one could have known for sure."

"He knew for sure that a friendly had already taken a bullet to the chest," I said, kicking a rock into the crater. "There's not always a clear answer. Sometimes you've gotta make a decision with the information you have and risk being wrong."

One of the soldiers from the photography team shot me a dirty look and rushed over to snap pictures of the rock in its new resting place.

"Even if being wrong is to mean killing innocent people?" Terp 2 asked. His face more curious than accusing.

"See that guy over there?" I pointed to one of Captain Keegan's men who'd been on the ground the night before. He was scratching his bushy beard and giving instructions to two Afghani soldiers guarding the perimeter. "That guy's probably alive right now because he wasn't forced to fight his way inside that qalat."

"He is a soldier though," Terp 2 replied. "His *job* is to fight his way inside."

"Easy to say from the sideline," I said and started to walk away. "You're a Terp. Your job is to interpret, not to question tactics."

I stopped. I was being harsh. I looked around at all the ANA soldiers guarding the perimeter.

"Why didn't you join the military?" I asked. "You're young. You seem fit. Well educated. Why choose 'terping'?"

"Money is better as a interpreter."

"With your education, you could've been an officer though, right?" I asked. "That's gotta pay better."

"It does, but only the sons of wealthy families are officers. My family has no such connections."

"I've seen some of the officers walking around," I said. "They seem arrogant and disconnected. And god-awful lazy."

"Wealth does not mean competence," Terp 2 lamented.

I smiled and stepped back to the edge of the crater. The snakes of smoke were thinner and fewer.

"Once you make your fortune 'terping', what will you do?" I asked him.

"I will move my family far away from here," he said without hesitation. "I will move them away from the violence of this country."

"Great countries are forged in fire," I said, before realizing he probably didn't understand the analogy. "They're built with great effort and self-sacrifice. Imagine where we'd be if everyone just picked up and ran whenever things got hard."

"This is easy to say from the sidelines."

I smiled at him.

"Fair point. I'm not saying I don't get it, I'm just saying, sometimes you have to stand and fight if you want things to change."

I puffed my chest, inspired by my own speech.

"You mean like those men did?" Terp 2 asked, pointing to the half assembled corpses, which the photography team was now cataloging.

"Well, yes," I said, shaking my head. "Just don't choose the wrong side."

There was a commotion from beyond the far side of the crater and Afghani soldiers scurried everywhere in complete disarray. Captain Keegan's head popped out from behind a tall mound of debris and pointed to us.

"You!" He yelled. "Get over here, quick!"

Disregarding the shouts of the photographers, I dashed through the twisted wreckage around the crater. Terp 2 tripped his way behind me.

"What is it, Sir?" I puffed, finally reaching Captain Keegan. "How can I help?"

"Not you, kid," he said. "The Terp."

Kid?

I'd have given him a piece of my mind, if I wasn't terrified of all the ways he knew how to kill me. Keegan had a reputation of being condescending, but he always did it with a smile and a "half-joking-not-sure-if-you're-being-a-douche" tone. He was a fraternity brother on steroids.

"We've got a vehicle approaching about a half mile out," Keegan said. No smile now. He spoke quickly and pointed to a dust trail that was rising from a white van in the distance. "This is the only road into town. That van's going to come right through our set-up here. We'll need to stop and search it before it can move through. Good opportunity for these ANA guys to learn how to do a proper stop-and-search checkpoint."

Captain Keegan started shouting orders at confused ANA soldiers while they scuttled about like spooked turkeys. Terp 2 translated his commands as quickly as he could.

"Use your big-boy voice," Keegan shouted at Terp 2.

Terp 2 started shouting. It was awkward and choppy at first, but he grew confident. The ANA soldier began moving in logical, deliberate directions, quickly setting up the hasty checkpoint of Keegan's design. The soldiers grabbed rolls of razor wire that had been bundled and hooked to the sides of their vehicles. With thick leather gloves, they stretched the wire across alternating sides of the road, creating a serpentine path that would force the van to slow to a stop before reaching the perimeter.

The van kept coming and was now about two hundred meters away. I guess that wasn't surprising since the driver's only alternative was to turn around.

Terp 2 relayed Keegan's direction to move two soldiers to each side of the checkpoint while another was tasked to collect identification and paperwork from the driver.

At a hundred meters out, the van was not slowing. I could see perspiration on Keegan's forehead and his voice was more agitated.

"I guess we're doing some Escalation of Force training," Keegan shouted.

He walked forward, waving his rifle and his freehand over his head.

"Stop!" he shouted. "Stop the van."

The van kept coming. Kneeling behind a mound of dirt, I positioned myself to have a clear shot and took my rifle's safety off. The ANA soldiers looked cautiously from Keegan to the van. Terp 2 had stopped translating and moved back toward me on the side of the road.

The van hit the farthest coil of razor wire without touching its brakes.

"Warning shot," Captain Keegan announced. He fired a single shot, aiming just over top of the van. There was no reaction from the driver. There was, however, a reaction from the ANA soldiers. With no one translating Keegan's announcement, the soldiers believed Keegan was engaging the van. What followed was ten seconds of the most violent volley of gunfire I'd ever been witness too. You can fire a lot of rounds in ten seconds.

"Cease fire, cease fire," Keegan waved his arms up and down, screaming at the ANA soldiers over the barking guns and the jingling of spent brass. "Goddammit, cease fire!"

The van's hood was swiss cheese and the driver's silhouette was no longer visible through the spiderwebbed windshield. The van had plowed through the second row of razor wire during the melee, but before reaching the final row, it veered sharply and slammed into the ditch on the far side of the road, nearly rolling in the process.

Then there was silence. Anyone with a brain between their ears was hunkered behind anything thick enough to stop the shrapnel of an exploding van. I went flat, but an explosion never came. I peered over the mound of rubble, imagining one of the van doors winging by and severing my head clean off.

I looked around, waiting for someone to make a move. Keegan was farther down the ditch, waving in more reliable help from the remainder of his Special Forces team.

"What the hell is going on here?" Came a voice from behind me. I rolled over in my protected position to find The SCO standing tall behind me. He had removed the cigar from his mouth and pointed the wet nub at me. "Why the hell are *you* down *there*?"

"The van tried to blow through the checkpoint, Sir," I said.

"Well, no shit," The SCO said, spitting flakes of tobacco from his lip.

"ANA shot it up pretty good," I continued.

"I'm amazed they even know where the trigger is," said The SCO.

"Captain Keegan and his team are going to clear the van," I said. "I think."

"There's nothing in the damn van," The SCO said.

"Sir?"

"Those knuckleheads just sprayed three hundred rounds into that van. If that hooptie had explosives on it, they'd have blown it sky high already."

I got to my feet, straightening the strap that connected the butt of my rifle to the chest of my armored vest. The SCO shook his head. By now, Captain Keegan and three of his men were approaching the van. They'd let their dog go first. A German shepherd by the name of Bigsby. They'd bestowed upon Bigsby, the explosives sniffing K-9, the rank of Sergeant. It was Sergeant Bigsby's crucial duty to let his two-legged team members know when he smelled a bomb, but now he danced happily back and forth along the side of the van, even hopping up along the windows to get a look inside.

Keegan approached the passenger door with one of his men, while two others swept around back to the rear doors. They signaled a countdown of three and swung the doors open simultaneously.

"What the hell is going on here?" Colonel Gunn demanded, coming up beside The SCO and me. The SCO looked at me to respond.

"The van tried to blow through the checkpoint, Sir," I said. "The ANA shot it up pretty good."

"What an astute summary," Colonel Gunn said, shaking his head. "Perhaps you'd like to point out something besides the glaringly obvious?"

"They're clearing the van now, Sir."

I honestly hadn't intended to sound like a smart-mouth, but I managed to draw a half-smile from The SCO. He loved anything that irked Colonel Gunn.

There was shouting from the van and Keegan backed away with his rifle raised at something inside.

"Oh, God. What now?" Colonel Gunn groaned.

As Keegan back-pedaled, a man miraculously descended from inside of the van. The ANA's hail of bullets should have made him ribbons, but the man didn't have a scratch on him. He didn't crawl from the van or slump down in a bloody heap, he simply hopped from the seat and stood there, scratching his head and surveying the damage.

"How's that even possible?" I asked.

"Goddamn ANA. Can't hit the broadside of a barn," The SCO grumbled.

"Lucky for you they can't," Colonel Gunn stated. "That improper escalation of force would have been an unfortunate addition to the investigation against you."

"What investigation?" The SCO demanded. "Captain Keegan isn't even under my command."

"I apologize, I meant 'potential' investigation," Colonel Gunn laughed. "And don't be so sure about Keegan. He may not be your soldier, but this is your *crime* scene."

He chuckled again and shook his head.

"Of course, I mean battlespace, not crime scene," he smiled. "And since you didn't manage to kill anymore unidentified combatants or civilians, I think I'll head home."

With that, Colonel Gunn was gone.

Captain Keegan's men had the driver on the ground, his hands zip-tied behind his back. The ANA soldiers had helped the man to the ground in an assertive nature resulting in a bloodied nose. Small inky puddles formed under his face on the road's clay surface.

"He's gonna want money for that van," I observed.

The SCO's cheeks flushed. Capillaries were bursting in his bloodshot eyes. I stayed as still as possible, hoping he'd forget about me and move on.

"Let's go find out what this ass-hat wants," he growled.

I looked around. Apparently he was talking to me, so I followed on his heels. I waved to Terp 2 to joining us, since The SCO's beloved Frank was probably still hiding in a ditch somewhere or mooching food off the locals.

“Why the hell didn’t you stop?” Keegan shouted. He had his knee pressed firmly into the back of the man’s gray tunic. Terp 2 translated.

“I didn’t see you,’ the man lied.

“What do you mean, you didn’t see us?” Keegan shouted. “Are you fucking blind?” He bounced on the man’s spine.

“I was reading a text message,” the man said. Terp 2 had some difficulty relaying the term “text message,” but we eventually got it.

“You’re not supposed to text and drive, you dumbass,” I said.

Keegan bounced again, sending all the air from the man’s lungs.

“What’d the text say?” Keegan demanded. “What was so damn important?”

The man gasped for air.

“The text was not for me,” he groaned.

“Then who was it for,” I said, trying to get involved while The SCO was there to take notice.

“The message is for Squadron Commander Fink,” the man wheezed.

The SCO held up a hand and motioned for Keegan to stand the man up. Keegan yanked the man painfully to his feet by his wrists. Red dust covered half his bloodied face.

“I am Squadron Commander Fink” The SCO said. “What message do you have?”

The man stared down at his dust covered ‘man-jams’.

“The honorable Mohammad Nasir, requests an audience with Squadron Commander Fink. In one week at FOB Alternator,” the man said. He’d sounded like he’d practiced his line a hundred times.

The SCO didn’t say a word. He just smiled behind his cigar and headed back to his truck. Perhaps that had been his play all along. A boring old firefight wouldn’t have done the trick, but dropping the bomb was certainly a bold enough action to draw out this Nasir fellow. And now he could find out what this Robin Hood of Kherwar was truly about.

Chapter 10: Nasir

March 13, 2009

Clark pulled a volleyball from the care-package resting on his lap.

"Why don't they play beach volleyball over here," I wondered aloud. "They've got the sand for it."

"Cause they're too busy banging goats," Clark mumbled. He rifled through the box pulling out celebrity gossip magazines and logs of chewing tobacco.

A platoon from our maintenance troop had done a supply run to the Brigade FOB to restock our coolers with Sergeant Drill's and had stumbled across a shipping container with a month's worth of mail for our Squadron. It had been mis-labelled and was two days away from being shipped back to Bagram.

"Seriously," I said, turning to Garcia. "Volleyball aside, why aren't sports more popular here? Seems like this country could use a little teamsmanship."

"My mom always buys the wrong kinda chew," Clark scowled.

"Probably a lot of reasons," said Garcia. "Lack of equipment for one."

"I don't buy that," I said. "American kids used to play baseball in the streets with a broomsticks and rag-balls. People make do with what they have."

"Lack of exposure," Garcia suggested. "Maybe they just don't know how to play most sports."

"I don't know how to play most sports, but that doesn't stop me from trying."

"Stuffing cookies in your face isn't a sport," Clark said, ducking to dodge the pen I threw at him.

"Fine. Lack of joy?" Garcia suggested. "Maybe they're focusing all their energy on 'not dying'. Just maybe they don't feel like hittin' the volleyball court when it's littered with old Russian toe-poppers."

"I could buy that," Clark said, thumbing through a tabloid newspaper.

"But isn't that what this country needs?" I asked. "Something unifying? Right now, it's just a patchwork group of tribes that hate each other over centuries old familial disputes."

"That's probably why they don't do sports. The teams would end up killing each other," Garcia offered. "They do have Buzkashi, though."

"Buz-what-shi?"

"Buzkashi. It's Afghanistan's national game," Garcia explained. "It's where a group of riders on horseback try to throw a goat carcass into a goal."

"You're not serious," I said. "How could you hate your neighbor while you're doing something as lighthearted as dead goat tossing."

"People making do with what they have," Clark chimed in again.

"Well, I'm going to make do with what I have right here," I said, pulling a box of my own off my desk. I ran my pocket knife lightly across the top and flipped open the cardboard flaps.

"You gotta be kidding me," I said.

"What'd you get?" Clark asked, poking his head above his newspaper.

I flipped the box, raining packages of cellophane wrapped, neon marshmallows onto my desk.

"Who sends somebody a box full of Peeps?" Garcia asked.

"Apparently my mom does," I said, picking up a note that was half buried in the sugar-coated blobs.

> *Dear Jared,*
>
> *I hope you're staying safe over there. Carol Walters from church said she saw something on the news about a suicide bomber, but she couldn't remember where. Did you hear about that? That wasn't close to you was it? You remember Carol, right? Tim Busko's mom's cousin? She said she'd say a pray for you. Who knows if she'll remember though, she's always been a bit of a spacecadet. Nice woman though. Things have been pretty*

uneventful here. The house is still very quiet with your dad gone, but I'm keeping busy. I had to give Mr. Furbottom two baths yesterday because he rolled in deer poop outside. I hope you know he would have been proud of you and what you're doing. Your dad that is. Not Mr. Furbottom. Although I'm sure he is too. I am too. Proud of you. I just wish you could do it from home. Anyway, Walmart had their Easter displays out already and I know how much you love Easter candy. Don't forget to share some with your friends. Brush your teeth. Please stay safe.
Love,
Mom

"What'd it say?" Clark asked. "Why all the Peeps?"

"They were on sale," I said, stacking the packages into a neat pyramid behind my laptop. "She buys them every year. I don't have the heart to tell her I hate them."

The door swung open and The GIF sauntered in. A yawn pushed his freckles into brown blobs at the top of his cheeks. Frank followed on his heels.

"Rye," he said. "Just the person I'm looking for."

Every conversation ending with me doing something miserable started that same way.

"This Nasir fella will be visiting the FOB today," he said, as if we hadn't been briefed a dozen times already. "The SCO would like you and Frank," he pointed to Frank, like I didn't know who Frank was, "to greet him at the gate and escort him in. I don't think I need to tell you how important this is. Any questions?"

"Just one, Sir," I said, smiling. "Who's Frank?"

"Nobody likes a smart-ass," The GIF said, rolling his eyes.

"The SCO requested me personally?" I asked.

"Sure," he shrugged. "Just make him feel at home. The SCO wants this guy as an ally to keep the Kherwar district in check. At least until we can set up down there."

"How do I make a warlord feel at home?" I asked. "Frank could give him a backrub. Or a front rub."

"I'll rub *you*!" Frank threatened.

Frank's relationship with The SCO had made him comfortable to the point of cocky. His perceived position of power prompted him to make tasteless jokes at anyone's expense, which he considered good-natured ribbing. None of us felt bad about returning the favor.

"No one's rubbing anyone," The GIF said, rubbing his forehead. "And I'd suggest starting by not calling him 'warlord'. Gaining his trust could really lighten the resistance going into Kherwar."

Garcia swiveled back around in his chair, pinching the bridge of his nose.

"Sir, we don't know a lot about this guy," he said. "We don't even know how the Kherwar villagers truly view him. I don't think we should be crawling into bed with him just yet."

"Whoa, whoa, whoa," I said to the GIF. "You said 'make him feel at home' not get him into bed."

The GIF pretended not to hear me.

"You can voice your concerns to The SCO," he said to Garcia, jerking his thumb toward the door. "He wants to see you in his office to go over intel reports one more time."

The GIF headed for his desk, but stopped short.

"Has someone been sweeping in here?" He asked, his nose twitching. "It seems dusty."

"No, Sir," said Clark. "I don't think it's any dustier than usual."

"No. It is," The GIF winced. "My migraine is coming back. Dust allergy. I'm gonna go lay down."

He rubbed his forehead for good show.

"Rye, don't forget to go have sex with Nasir," he added on his way out, grimacing a smile through the terrible pain of his phantom headache. "And take Frank with you."

****

FOB Alternator's front gate was an elaborate serpentine of Hesco barriers and razor wire, designed to stop speeding vehicles and would-be suicide bombers. On either side stood guard towers, each manned by sleepy ANA soldiers behind dusty machine guns. The

FOB's entrance was two hundred meters off a not-so-busy road, so the instances of cars approaching the gate were few and far between.

The snow was gone, but there was still a spring chill in the air. I sat on the ground, with the collar of my uniform pulled up and my back against the metal mesh of a Hesco barrier wall. I watched vacantly as a group of Specialists lugged large boxes marked with red crosses from the guard hut to a group of locals who'd come to receive aid. They could have been handing out boxes of hand grenades and I likely wouldn't have noticed. I was busy fantasizing about how rich I'd be, if I'd been smart enough to invent the Hesco barrier. It was the simplest invention. An open-top box made from chain link fence, lined with a thick burlap sack and then filled with dirt. Put enough in a row and you have an immovable wall. The military was using them by the thousands, building outposts and FOBs like ours all over Afghanistan and Iraq.

The sound of crinkling cellophane hijacked my daydream.

"When is this guy gonna show up?" Frank grumbled, unwrapping another package of Peeps he'd stolen from my desk. He'd sat closer to me than I would have liked. He massaged one of the yellow marshmallows between his dirty fingers.

"How the hell am I supposed to know? You were the one who talked to The SCO," I snapped. "I thought you said he was on his way?"

"He is, he is. Calm down," Frank laughed through a mouthful of yellow goo. "The SCO said he'd be here before dinner."

I looked at my watch and slammed my head against the wall behind me.

"It's only 1400," I said, rubbing the back of my head. "You're telling me we could be waiting all afternoon?"

Frank apparently decided this was a rhetorical question and filled his mouth with another Peep.

"You're a paradox, Frank. A marshmallow eating a marshmallow."

Frank rolled his eyes and continued chewing. He made sucking noises trying to keep the sugary yellow saliva from escaping down his chin.

"Mind if I sit," came a voice from above.

I looked up to find Terp 2 standing just down the wall from us.

"The SCO sent me to take over for Frank," he explained, pointing to Frank as though I might not know who he was. "He said he has an important task for Frank before the guest arrives."

Frank slapped my leg and smiled. A stream of yellow spit trickled to the ground while he rolled over his gut and struggled to his feet. His cheeks still bulging, he waved tersely over his shoulder, as Terp 2 took his place along the wall. We sat quietly for a long while. It was the first time I'd seen Terp 2, since our conversation at the crater. He was probably still sore with me for insinuating that he was quitting on his country. I thought maybe I'd apologize.

"It's Tuesday," I said. "There should be new bootleg movies at the shop."

The SCO had begrudgingly allowed five local merchants to set up shops on FOB Alternator at the behest of CSM Storms, who insisted it would improve the morale among the soldiers. Three of the five shops sold exclusively bootlegged movies, many of which had not been released in American theaters yet. They were making a killing.

"Three years ago my father attended a funeral for an anti-Taliban Imam in Kabul," Terp 2 said. He didn't want to talk about bootleg movies. "As he was leaving the mosque, a man dressed in a police uniform detonated a bomb in the entrance. He and eighteen others lost their lives."

I studied my boots.

"My family has experienced many," he paused to find the right word, "*hardships* since then. It is not easy for a widow in Afghanistan. And my little sisters are not old enough to be much help."

"I'm sorry, I didn't know," I said.

"How could you have? You did not ask," he said. "This is why I want to leave Afghanistan. Not for me, but for my mother and sisters."

I was about to apologize again, when a whistle came from a Private on guard duty by the gate.

"I think your friend's here, Sir," the Private called, pointing down the way to where an old blue truck crept off the main road toward the serpentine barriers and wires.

Terp 2 and I watched the truck advance through several security checkpoints, each one manned by a pair of nervous soldiers who'd hadn't had the opportunity to put their training into practice enough times be confident. At the first station two Privates ran mirrors attached to long poles along the underside of the vehicle to check for explosives. At station two, another interpreter questioned the men inside the cab, while two more Privates opened both doors to inspect the interior for weapons. Finally, at station three, an exuberant Sergeant Bigsby, on loan from the Special Forces team for the day, padded lightly around the truck wagging his tail and proclaiming once and for all that the truck was threat free.

"Why don't they put the dog at the first checkpoint?" Terp 2 asked.

"Those dogs are way too expensive to train. They wouldn't risk losing one," I said. "Plus I think he's the highest ranking soldier on this guard duty anyway."

The truck rolled slowly through the gate and stopped. The glare from the overhead sun made it impossible to see more than a silhouette through the passenger window. Before we could reach the truck, the window slid down.

"Good afternoon, my friends!" Sang a voice from inside the cab. The window revealed a face no older than mine. Coils of black shiny hair spilled from the edges of an unformed black beret. Pinned to the front of his beret was a United States Army Combat Infantry Badge; pinned on his face was a sparse adolescent mustache draping the biggest smile I'd seen in three months.

"Good afternoon," I fumbled. "Which one of you is Nasir?"

I figured Nasir must surely be the driver who was a statue in dark sunglasses. He never bothered to look our direction. The young passenger's smile defied logic and widened further. His white teeth seemed to glisten against the dull entirety of his home country.

"Guilty as charged," he sang with a laugh. The black coils of hair bounced across his forehead.

For a second, he restored my hope in Afghanistan. Maybe this country wasn't beyond salvage. I returned his smile, but quickly stopped with the realization that mine couldn't compare to his. Then I may have blushed a little. Terp 2 tapped me on the lower back and suddenly I realized I'd let too much time go by without saying anything.

"Wonderful to meet you, Sir!" I spasmed.

"Sir?" Terp 2 murmur behind me.

I ignored him.

"I'm Lieutenant Rye," I said, extending my hand, which he grasped like a vice. "I'll be escorting you in to meet with the Commander. If you'd like to have your companion park the truck along the wall, we can get started. The walk isn't far."

Terp 2 started to interpret, but Nasir held up his hand.

"The pleasure of meeting you is mine," he said. His English was quite good. "But if you do not mind, I would ask that you allow the truck to take me as far as it can. I have an old knee injury and I do not enjoy walking on the stones you Americans use on your bases."

"I don't blame you, this stuff is treacherous," I said grinding a hole in the gravel beneath my boot. "Just drive slow, Sir. We'll walk out front to show you where to go."

I turned to walk and caught an odd look from Terp 2.

"By the way," I said. "This is Terp 2." I jerked my thumb over my shoulder in his general direction.

"Nice to meet you," Terp 2 said, without reaching for a handshake. "Sir."

Nasir's smile retreated some.

"Again," he said. "The pleasure is mine."

The tense moment was interrupted by a shout from down the road.

"I said make him feel at home, not chat him up."

The GIF was struggling up the hill from the Command Center as fast as his stubby legs could carry him. By the time he reached the truck, beads of sweat were forming under the bill of his patrol cap, where tufts of orange mane matted to his forehead. He approached the driver side window and put his hands on his knees. The window lowered slowly.

"My apologies," he panted after he'd regained himself. "I'm Major Doyle. I'm in charge of Operations. I'm sorry you had to deal with my underlings here. I was attending to some important business."

He'd apparently come from shaving. Two small, blood-dotted squares of toilet paper still clung to the underside of his chin. I'm sure either The SCO or CSM Storms had directed him to clean up before the meeting. He'd probably been directed to greet Nasir personally from the beginning, but had subcontracted the duty to me so he wouldn't have to sit at the front gate all day.

Nasir's driver glared at him through his sunglasses, while Nasir waved politely from the passenger seat.

"I am Nasir," he called. "It is nice to meet you."

The GIF looked annoyed at the inconvenience of walking around the truck, but he mustered a smile.

"We'll show you down to the building where the meeting will be held," he said. He stared down the road from which he'd just come.

"Rye," he shouted.

"Sir?"

"You and Terp 2 guide them in," he said. "I'm going to bum a ride, if our guest is okay with this."

Nasir nodded with equal parts politeness and curiosity.

The GIF shooed us along as he dropped the tailgate and hopped on board.

****

The conference room looked completely different. Walls, normally plastered in secret and classified maps, were now naked plywood. The whiteboards at the far end of the table were spotless and the smell of cleaning agents still hung in the air. The conference table yawned an assortment of treats and beverages, surrendered by the cafeteria staff. At the center of the magnificent spread were two large silver bowls, one heaped high with a medley of Aunt Mary's Muffins, the other containing iced down cans of everyone's favorite poison, Sergeant Drill's Freedom Juice. Nasir sat at the far end of the table, silhouetted by the white boards. On his left arm, his driver stood. His stoic demeanor had subsided and he propped his sunglass on top of his head, eyeing the bounty in front of him. The rest of the chairs, minus one reserved for The SCO, had been removed from the table and lined along the outer walls. We sat against the wall opposite Nasir, trying not to stare.

The SCO had not yet arrived. I assumed that keeping his guest waiting was some sort of power play.

The sound of heavy footsteps could be heard coming down the hall. The door swung open and we all began to stand, until Frank entered carrying another bowl of apples, oranges, and overripe bananas.

I leaned over to Terp 2 who sat rigid in the chair next to me.

"Man, they really rolled out the red carpet for this guy, huh?"

He looked at me with confusion. Usually, interpreters were not allowed in the conference room, or any headquarters building, because of operationally sensitive information. This was the first time he had been allowed in. I leaned toward Captain Clark who sat on my other side.

"Man, they really rolled out the red carpet for this guy, huh?" I repeated.

"Shush," Mark reprimanded, but then added. "His smile is something else, isn't it?"

"See! That's what I said!" I swatted Terp 2 on the leg. "Isn't that what I said?"

Terp 2 rolled his eyes.

"I think you might kiss him if you get the chance," he whispered.

"All of you shut up," hissed The GIF from the other side of Clark. He was sour about not getting to sit at the table and went back to rolling between his fingers the little squares of toilet paper he'd discovered under his chin.

Nasir checked his watch and leaned back casually in his chair, clasping his hands behind his head. He began to rock his chair slowly. At the same time his driver reached for a muffin. Nasir halted him and shook his head.

In the hallway, the door leading outside could be heard swinging shut through the thin plywood walls. The room fell silent, except for the rhythmic creaking of Nasir's chair, as he bobbed back and forth. Low voices could be heard approaching down the hall. The door swung open, still catching me off guard.

"*Atten--tion!*" Major Connick called entering the room. He quickly stood to the side at the position of attention. The four of us along the wall jumped to our feet, while Nasir continued to rock lazily in his seat.

The SCO was a bull entering the room. His uniform appeared brand new and was adorned with all the badges he'd earned over the years. His suede tan boots had been brushed spotless and the little remaining hair he had was combed off to the side. Even his cigar was brand new.

Without a glance at us, The SCO paced swiftly across the room with all the pomp and pageantry of a commanding general. Nasir rose to his feet, walking around the table to greet him.

"Mr. Nasir, it is my absolute pleasure," The SCO extended his hand to shake, but Nasir went in for a hug. My heart soared. The SCO was completely caught off guard by the embrace. His arms were pinned by the young Aghani's bear hug and his hands flapped like a giant baby duck.

"This is the best thing I've ever seen," I whispered.

"Shush," scolded Clark. The GIF shot daggers.

Nasir held tight for an awkward moment. The SCO's face was red, but not his usual shade. Captain Garcia's face was more the rage-red I was expecting. He'd entered the room behind The SCO and wasn't pleased to be there.

The SCO coughed as Nasir released him.

"Well, that was, um, unexpected." the SCO stumbled. "Thank you. For that. Mr. Nasir."

"No. Thank you, Mr. Lieutenant Colonel Fink, for meeting with me today, and please, it is just 'Nasir'."

"And you can just call me, Daniel," said The SCO before realizing we were all still standing at attention.

"At ease," he growled, as though our presence was an inconvenience to him. "Take your seats."

The SCO took his seat at the table adjacent to Nasir.

"I hope you and your man will enjoy some of the refreshments we've set out," he waved his hand over the grand feast he'd provided.

Nasir's driver salivated.

"With respect, Mr. Daniel, I did not come here today for American treats, generous as it is," Nasir responded. "I came here to discuss your intentions for my home. You see, Logar is my home. It always has been. And I have worked very hard to promote peace here."

The SCO removed the cigar from his lips and wiped the corner of his mouth with his thumb. He cleared his throat before launching into his discourse.

"Nasir, I agreed to meet with you today because I understand that you are a man of considerable distinction and influence in this region. It is also my understanding that, though young, you have a rich personal history when it comes to fighting the Taliban and keeping your province free of outside influence."

Nasir nodded as The SCO continued.

"It is the concern of my commanding officers, that the success of U.S. and coalition forces in other regions of the country will force Taliban forces to seek out new areas of refuge in order to continue conducting their operations. Because of the unique geological conditions of the Kherwar District and its truly austere location, it may become the focus of Taliban efforts to regain a foothold in the region. Therefore, it is my proposal to you, Nasir, that we form a sort of 'unofficial alliance' between our forces to ensure that never happens."

It was The SCO's turn to lean back in his chair. He inserted his cigar and waited. For the first time, the broad smile melted from Nasir's face and he aged ten years before my eyes.

"Mr. Daniel, first of all, let me tell you how I appreciate you taking this meeting. There are many other commanders in your army who would have dismissed my request. I see this as a sign of mutual respect. We are both men of action and I assure you that I have taken *much* action to maintain the security of my beloved Kherwar. I will be dead before I allow Taliban dogs to enter my boarders."

He swept a curl of hair behind his ear as he leaned in on his chair.

"It is my understanding that you have already established an outpost to the north of here near Baraki Barak. Do you intend to establish more throughout Logar?"

The SCO had not expected Nasir to be so well spoken. He nibbled the end of his cigar before removing it again.

"Well, Nasir, as you probably know, it's hard to influence an area without physical presence. And influence is the name of the game. We'd like to help the people of the Logar by supporting infrastructure projects that can better their lives. In order to do these projects, though, we need security and in order to have security, we need to have a temporary presence in those areas. At least until we can hand the job off to the Aghani Army or national police."

A smile returned to Nasir's face, but not the same one.

"You are right, Mr. Daniel. Influence *is* the name of the game. But I think we both know, that it will be a long time before the ANA or the national police are able to successfully influence *anything*."

The SCO obliged him by flashing a half smile.

"That may be," said The SCO, "but right now they are the only representation we have of a legitimate Afghanistan government."

"Legitimate?" Nasir scoffed.

"I'm sorry?" The SCO asked.

Nasir restrained.

"I am too, Mr. Daniel," Nasir said, "here you've extended the olive branch to me and I've responded with mistrust. Of course, I will help maintain the peace and control of the Logar Province in whatever way I can. I only ask that you allow me to continue to maintain the security of the Kherwar district by myself, without outside influence."

The SCO grimaced.

"That's not up to me, Nasir. I have to follow orders, but I can run it up my chain of command and see what I can do."

"Then it is settled!" He said, slapping the table. "Let today be the beginning of a lasting alliance."

He leaned forward taking three cans of Sergeant Drills from the bowl of ice. He cracked one and placed it in front of The SCO, the second he handed to his driver, and the third he kept for himself.

"Perhaps, you will honor me with your presence in my home district of Kherwar before long? Then I can show you first-hand how secure we are."

The SCO took a reluctant swig of the neon soda.

"I will be sure to send one of my Troop commanders to visit you very soon," he said.

"You will not visit yourself?" Nasir asked. He sniffed the contents of the can then set it back on the table. "Have I done something to offend you?"

Nasir's driver slammed his empty can down on the table and grabbed another from the bowl. A sheen of sweat covered his forehead.

"No! No. You haven't offended me," The SCO begged. "It's just not common practice for a man of my stature to make many visits to the battlefield."

Nasir furrowed his brow.

"Battlefield? Mr. Daniel, I assure you that the Kherwar is not a 'battlefield'. It is the most secure district in Eastern Afghanistan."

I wondered if The SCO would bring up the severed head we'd found there only months earlier and I was surprised he hadn't addressed the mystery of the missing ANP platoon. But who was I to question high level tactics?

"What I meant to say is that my duties here do not often allow me to leave for long," The SCO hesitated. "But I will make an exception in the name of our new friendship. I would be happy to visit your district personally."

Nasir tossed his hands in the air.

"You have honored me," he exclaimed. "Let us say, one month?" He suggested, looking down at his watch as though it had a calendar.

"One month," The SCO said, mimicking his enthusiasm. "I look forward to it."

There was a moment of awkward silence and the rapid tapping of the driver's toes filled the room.

"Well, I'm sorry to cut our meeting short," Nasir said, looking back to his watch and then up at his driver, "but it would appear that my driver has consumed too much Freedom Juice."

Nasir rose from his seat, followed by The SCO who looked put off by not being the one to conclude the meeting. The SCO opened his arms for the goodbye hug, but was greeted only by a handshake. Behind Nasir, his driver slipped another Sergeant Drills and an Aunt Mary's Muffin into his tunic pocket. I hoped the caffeine and sugar wouldn't kill him.

The GIF and Frank took it upon themselves to escort Nasir and his driver back to the front gate, but not before filling their pockets with snacks as well.

As soon as Nasir had left the building, Captain Garcia spoke up.

"Sir, I still don't think this is--," he was cut off when The SCO raised his hand.

"Enough, Joe," The SCO said without looking up from the blank pages of the notebook he'd just set in front of himself. "Everyone out."

Major Connick motioned for the rest of us to exit and we were more than happy to oblige.

"Except you, Jacob. Hold tight a minute," The SCO said. The other guys looked around curiously.

"I'm Jacob," I muttered.

The rest needed no further explanation and headed for the door.

"Good luck," Major Connick whispered on his way by.

The door creaked shut and there was silence. For a few long minutes The SCO sat with his head resting in his hands, staring down at his notebook. He seemed distressed and I feared he was about to unload some all too personal confession or some other uncomfortable heartfelt display of emotion. Perhaps he was sick from the swallow of Sergeant Drill's. I stood at the foot of the table, waiting for some type of instruction.

Finally, The SCO lifted his head and looked across the table. Without looking directly at me, he beckoned me to come closer. As I shuffled nervously across the floor, I had an unlikely thought. Perhaps he'd had a change of heart. Perhaps he'd taken notice of my success running the Squadron's airfield. Perhaps he was going to give me the important, combat oriented, assignment I'd been hoping for.

"Jacob," The SCO said.

"Jared, Sir," I said instinctively.

Stupid.

"What?" The SCO looked up.

"Nothing, Sir."

The SCO rose from his chair and looked around the room.

"Clean all this shit up," he said, with a sweeping gesture over the table. He shifted the cigar from one side of his mouth to the other and sputter bits of tobacco leaf onto the table in front of him. He picked up his notebook and exited the room.

Chapter 11: Mission Brief

April 11, 2009

"Alright, everyone, let's get back on task," Major Connick said, clicking to the next slide. The conference room was packed with officers and NCO's being briefed on the upcoming mission to Kherwar. Major Connick was a hummingbird. He zig-zagged around the room between maps and whiteboards of auxiliary information in order to facilitate the presentation being delivered to The SCO. I guarantee, if you checked his office, you'd find a stack of empty Sergeant Drill's cans.

"Lieutenant Rye is up next with 'Air Support'."

Startled by the sound of my name, I sprang to my feet, banging my thigh against the conference table on my way up. This was my first time speaking in a major operations brief and I'd been rehearsing my notes all day.

"Wait, wait, wait," Captain Jaxon interjected before I could begin. "I'd like to talk this through. You're telling me this Nasir guy knows when we're coming?"

He leaned forward in his seat, massaging the white-walled sides of his 'high and tight' haircut. As the Cherokee Troop Commander, Captain Jaxon would be leading the mission into the Kherwar.

"Doesn't this seem like a bad idea to anyone else?" His gray eyes searched the room for supporters. Captain Jaxon was the only person in Afghanistan that The SCO seemed to like and because of this, he was the only one with a free pass to speak his mind. And he did speak, often and loudly.

The room was silent. All eyes were fixed on the SCO who sat at the head of the table, gnawing his cigar and making notes in his notebook. I wasn't even sure if he'd heard Jaxon's complaint from the other end of the table.

Captain Garcia broke the silence reluctantly.

"We have no evidence that Nasir has negative intentions toward us," he said with all the steadfast conviction of a man with a gun to his head.

I took my seat again between Clark and The GIF. The GIF was doodling in his notebook and had drawn a surprisingly accurate rendition of a Chinook helicopter on one side of the page. He was now putting the finishing touches on a rocket-propelled grenade arching its way toward the ill-fated helicopter from a stick-figure in the opposite margin.

"What do you mean, 'no evidence'?" Jaxon exclaimed. "Didn't Clark and Rye find a frick'n dead body there three months ago?"

"Just the head," I said. "No body."

Clark jabbed me with his pencil under the table.

"There's nothing tying the murder of the Police Chief to Nasir," Garcia said. "Or anyone else for that matter. With the whole police platoon missing, all evidence points to mutiny anyway."

"Mutiny?" Jaxon scoffed. "Forty five men. Correction. Forty five *Afghani* men, were able to make that collective decision."

"Exactly," said Garcia. "Kill the boss and everyone scatters. That simple."

"And what about this *evidence*?" Jaxon complained. "Screw the evidence. Why hasn't anyone just asked Nasir straight-up about it? God knows it's not for lack of opportunity. The slick bastard's here every other day."

The SCO stopped writing. Everyone seemed to notice except Captain Jaxon. It was true, Nasir had been a frequent visitor to the base over the last month. So much so that he knew most of the front gate guards by name. He even started bringing Sergeant Bigsby treats. He and The SCO always met in private. One on one.

"Alright, back to the brief," Major Connick eased in, his eyes on The SCO. "Let's get this done and save comments for the end. Rye, you're up."

I stood up again.

"Garcia, have you ever been in a Chinook that's being shot down?" Captain Jaxon interrupted again.

I sat down again.

"No," Captain Garcia said flatly. "Have you?"

"No. And I'd like to keep it that way."

The GIF was adding flames to the back of his Chinook doodle.

"It's a sign of respect." The SCO said, finally looking up. His face looked thinner. "We weighed our options, Jaxon. We were invited by a man who clearly holds sway over the district. His reach may go even further. We go in there on our own, when we aren't expected, we're going to stir a pot that doesn't need stirring. Now you're right, we don't know a lot about Nasir," he shot a cold glance at Captain Garcia, "but we do know he's not Taliban. He's actually quite opposed to the Taliban. So what do they say? 'The enemy of my enemy is my friend', or some shit? Our job here is stability and right now the Kherwar has it. Let's not rock the boat if it doesn't need fixing."

I watched from the corner of my eye as The GIF fiercely jotted The SCO's broken axiom under the flaming Chinook.

"Ultimately, the brass at Bagram is going to want an outpost," The SCO continued. "So I guess the question is, would you like to build an outpost with the *help* of the locals or being *shot at* by the locals?"

"Sir, I know we want to go down there and dole out hugs and pink-powdery, warm fuzzies, but I gotta be honest, I ain't comfortable flying into an unfamiliar district, into an unfamiliar Landing Zone, in a hostile country, when the locals know we're coming. Maybe Nasir ain't bad, but you know damn well that everyone down there knows we're coming by now. This is Afghanistan, news like that goes viral here."

"We'll just go in on a different Landing Zone," The GIF said, finally peeling himself away from his artwork. "They won't be expecting us to do that. Then you'll have your element of surprise."

"Jesus! You told him where our LZ is going to be?" Jaxon was mortified. "Did you give him Stinger Missiles while you were at it?"

The SCO slammed his fist on the table and the room jumped. At least I did. The SCO pulled his cigar from the corner of his mouth, where yellow matter had formed. He tongued away flecks from his lips while he murdered Jaxon with his eyes.

"You're going. And that's final," he said, calmly concealing his rage.

Captain Jaxon settled back into his chair and placed his hands behind his head, satisfied with his disturbance.

Major Connick nodded to me. I stood up.

"Of course, Sir! Cherokee Troop can handle it," Jaxon burst, a smirk smeared his square jaw.

I sat back down.

"We'll win some hearts and minds," he laughed. "And if we have to, we'll give them two to the heart and one to the mind." He fired an imaginary rifle at me and I pretended to duck.

Major Connick had his head in his hand. I often got the feeling he felt like the only sane person in the room. The SCO stared at Jaxon for an uncomfortable minute and the tension slowly eased from his face. Finally a smile erupted and he roared with laughter.

"That-a-boy! That's the spirit!" He shouted, placing the cigar back in his mouth. "The rest of you sad-sacks could learn a thing or two from Captain Jaxon here. Not afraid to speak his mind. Not like you goddamn 'yes men'."

Everyone at the table nodded.

"You all disgust me," The SCO reiterated.

This wasn't the statement I'd hoped to follow for my portion of the presentation. Fortunately for me, Jaxon wasn't finished. I like to think that he was trying to help me out. He'd been *my* Troop commander for three months before my knee surgery sidelined me to the Squadron staff. We'd developed an affinity for each other based on mutual respect.

"Before Lieutenant Dingle-nuts starts blabbing," he said pointing at me. "I'd like to apologize to the group. It's not my place to question the plans. As long as you're comfortable going in these conditions, Sir. I am too."

The SCO cleared his throat.

"I will not be going," he said, scribbling some notes in his book.

"Sir?" Captain Jaxon seemed genuinely alarmed for the first time.

"I said, 'I will not be going'," The SCO went on. "I have other missions to prep, long term strategies to consider, equipment to sign for and on and on. I don't have time to lollygag around Kherwar if this mission turns into a goddamn turkey-shoot. Captain Clark will go in my stead. He's been there before, he'll be a valuable asset."

"Sir?" This was news to Captain Clark.

"Goddammit, Bob," The SCO shouted at The GIF. "Didn't you brief Clark that he's going?"

The GIF frantically searched back through pages of doodles.

"Captain Clark, I'm sorry you weren't informed, but you're going in my place," The SCO said.

I heard Clark swallow hard, no doubt gutting a mouth full of chew juice in the process.

"Yes, Sir," he said.

"It'll be fine," The SCO said reassuringly. "Jaxon and Cherokee Troop will escort you and Frank down to the village, you'll meet with Nasir and other village elders, then you'll come home. In and out. No sweat."

"You said it was about respect, Sir," Captain Jaxon piped up again. "Won't Nasir be disrespected if you don't show?"

"He'll get over it," The SCO grumbled and turned back to Clark. "You've met him once already. Just inform him that I was called away and regret not being able to make the trip. He'll pout about it for a few minutes and he'll be fine. Make sure you put a bug in the elder's ears about us using the schoolhouse for a voting station in the summer elections."

Clark nodded and I saw an opportunity.

"Sir, I've also been there before and have met Nasir," I squawked. "Maybe I should go too."

"Shut up, Dingle-nuts," The SCO said looking down at his notebook again.

Captain Jaxon winked at me.

"You're the Air Planner," The SCO went on. "This is an *air* mission. You need to be here to run the *air*-field. Clear?"

I nodded.

"Sir, what about Hand-Boy?" I asked, filled with instant regret. "I could link up with his family and see if we could help him."

The SCO's eyes narrowed.

"I don't give a rat's ass about Hand-Boy," he growled. "I thought I told you never to bring that name up again."

"Sorry, Sir." I said, averting my eyes.

"For all we know that little handicapped pervert was the mastermind behind the police mutiny and the severed head," The SCO raged. "I'll be damned if I go out of my way to help that little heathen."

"Yes, Sir," I mumbled, keeping my chin glued to my chest. I wanted to sink through my chair.

"Now let's get this atrocious briefing over with," The SCO barked. "Who's up next?"

I got to my feet.

****

The rest of the brief had gone quickly enough. My portion was awkward and clunky, just like I'd practiced. I'm sure I'd messed up a few places, but by that point everyone was so anxious to get the hell out of there that they didn't bother correcting me. Even The SCO was mum and he's usually the first to crucify for "briefing sins". In retrospect, nobody was listening at all, which was fine by me. I was just happy to get out of there.

I skipped the last two steps on my way out of the Staff building and landed hard in the loose gravel, almost falling on my ass. Rounding the staircase, I headed for my room. I was free for a few minutes while The SCO laid waste to The GIF for failing to brief Captain Clark. I'd barely taken a step before a hand emerged from underneath the staircase and grabbed my arm.

"Sir," exclaimed Specialist Coucher. He was crouched below the stairs, his face a sickly yellow. "Sir, I need to talk to you."

"Good, God,' I said. "What's the matter with you?"

His neck brace was gone, replaced with a vile rash he'd developed while wearing it. The crimson lesion wrapped around his entire neck, ending under his chin. The rash had apparently prevented him from shaving and his face was covered in a sparse beard. The beard was blonde and probably all but invisible from over ten feet away, which is probably the only reason no senior NCOs had stomped him yet. All of this did little to distract from the purple bruising that puffed his right eye shut.

"They're onto us," he hissed.

"There is no 'us'," I hissed back.

Coucher's left eye darted around, looking for sinister figures who might be watching. He looked like an iguana about to snatch a dragonfly.

"You have to let Chappy know, Sir," he squeaked. "I'm getting too close. I think they know I'm snooping."

"Did they do that to you?" I asked, pointing at his eye.

"This?" Coucher dabbed his eye, as though he'd forgotten about it. "No, this was my fault. I fell off the treadmill in the workout tent. That's not what I need to talk about. I'm in danger. The other Specialists are up to something. Something big. Bigger than FOB Alternator and that's all I know. And that's all I *will* know, if they have their way."

"I think you're being paranoid," I said. I tried to turn away, but he grabbed both sides of my uniform collar.

"Sir, please," he groveled. He looked truly terrified.

"Fine," I sighed, brushing his hands from my chest. "I haven't seen Chappy today, but when I do, I will let him know. In the meantime, lay low. Don't be out alone or the big, bad 'E-4 Mafia' will get you."

"Thanks, Sir,' Coucher stammered. "I'll try to."

"Rye," called a voice from above.

I took a step back and looked up to find Major Connick standing on the landing above. He had his elbows on the railing and a tired grin on his face.

"Excellent job on your portion of the brief," he said.

"Really, Sir?"

"God, no," he said smiling. "But it wasn't bad for a first attempt."

"Thank you, Sir," I said. "I guess."

"Rye," he said. "Anything could happen with this Kherwar mission. Keep your bags packed."

He winked, convinced I understood. I didn't, but I was sure as hell going to make sure my assault pack was ready to go. Major Connick went back through the door and I was left staring up with a gaping mouth. I was expecting Specialist Coucher to be gone when I looked down, but he wasn't. The guy was a constant disappointment.

"Is there something else you needed?" I asked.

Coucher shook his head. His color had returned and he was less skittish.

"I could use some dinner," he said. "Would you go with me?"

"Hell no," I exclaimed. "You just told me some shadow organization has your number and wants you whacked. I can't be seen with you."

I'd meant it as a joke. Coucher's face drained and without another word he bolted around the corner of the building, on his way to God-knows-where.

Chapter 12: Last Minute Change

April 12, 2009

In the center of the airfield, two Chinooks dozed in the twilight. Their rotors bowed like palm branches and their tailgates yawned, patiently waiting to devour soldiers. It had been a long time since I'd seen a Chinook at rest, but the pilots had arrived early to make last minute arrangements before taking Cherokee Troop into the Kherwar. I was always amazed at how such a beast could take to the sky.

The airfield was serene in contrast to the chaos outside its concrete walls. The road running along the northern boundary was a swarm of heavily armored and heavily armed bodies. The entire eighty-six man Cherokee Troop had set up their staging area and now milled about within smaller groups chewing, smoking, laughing, and calling each other "fuckers". I weaved in and out among them, pretending I knew what I was supposed to be doing. Most were younger than me but already had a combat tour, either here or in Iraq, under their belts. Section leaders checked the equipment of the nervous newbies and imparted nuggets of air assault wisdom. I eavesdropped and pretended to check items off my clipboard, which held nothing but an obsolete flight manifest and a rough sketch of the airfield.

"Hey Sir," came voice from behind. "Don't look so lost."

I turned to find CSM Storms smiling at me through the fading light.

"That obvious?" I asked.

"Nah," he waved his huge hand. "But I know a 'Lost Lieutenant' when I see one."

I rolled my eyes. NCOs loved to hassle Lieutenants for "looking lost".

"The SCO gave me a huge Field Manual to read on airfield operations, but none of it applies to an airfield this small," I said. "I'm sure I should be doing something, but I'll be damned if I know what."

Storms put his hand on my shoulder.

"You're doin' just fine, Sir," he said in his most fatherly tone. "The SCO's got big ideas, that's all."

We started walking again and he steered me through the crowd.

"These used to be your boys, right?"

"Yes, Sergeant Major. I was Third Platoon Leader for Cherokee Troop."

"You miss it?" he asked.

I nodded, but something was puzzling me.

"With all due respect, Sergeant Major, I haven't seen you out lately. What are you doing up here?"

Storms pretended to be insulted.

"I'm the senior NCO on this base," he said matter-of-factly. "I'm making sure our troopers are squared away."

"You miss it too, don't you?" I said.

"All this?" he asked, looking around us. "Miss the grind? The mountains of gear? The backaches? The knee aches? The tiredness? The dirt?"

"Yes," I said.

"Every goddamn day," he whispered.

He slapped me on the back and nearly knocked me over.

"But there are other ways to serve," he said. "Or so I've been told. You don't have to pull a trigger to make an impact."

Static came over the radio fixed to his shoulder and Sergeant Hunter's voice crackled into our conversation.

"Anyone out there seen Lieutenant Rye? Over."

Hunter was manning the Command and Control Humvee on the other end of the airfield. CSM Storms cocked his head and spoke into his hand mic.

"I got him right here. Whaddya need?"

"I need him back at the command truck," said Hunter. "The SCO would like a word with him. Several words actually. Mostly of the 'four-letter' variety."

"He's on his way," Storms replied over the radio.

I swallowed hard and Storms flashed his big white teeth.

"Dead man walking," he called as I walked away.

****

I spotted The SCO before he spotted me. Even in the diminished light, I could tell he was heated, as he pointed to different areas of the airfield while Frank nodded aggressively at his side. Frank wore his helmet and his body armor, both of which appeared to be two sizes too small.

The hard life of a 'yes man', I thought.

An idea hit me.

"Sir, you were looking for me?" I said as I approached.

"Goddammit, Jacob," The SCO said. "What kind of operation are you running up here?"

"An air operation, Sir?" I replied. The blood thumping in The SCO's ears must have drowned out my sarcasm.

"This is the shittiest excuse for an air assault I've ever seen," he growled. "Your airfield set-up is atrocious. What do you have to say for yourself?"

"I'm sorry, Sir. You're absolutely right, Sir. Do you have any suggestions on how I can improve, Sir?"

A dash of disingenuousness made the self-loathing more palatable. The terror level in The SCO's face dropped from red to orange.

"I do actually, but I don't have time for that now," he said chomping his cigar nub. A tiny, yellow bubble of spittle oozed from its tip. "I have another manual you can go over later. Much thicker than the first one."

He scanned the area around the entrance.

"Where's your kit and helmet?"

"My kit and helmet, Sir?" Now I really *was* confused. Surely he didn't expect me to run the airfield in "full battle-rattle". "My helmet is in the truck, Sir, but I never bring my armor up here."

"How do you expect to go on this mission, if you don't have your damn gear?" he asked. The Chinooks were starting to churn up their engines. The daylight was gone, but I thought I might be glowing.

"Go along on the mission, Sir?" I asked with excitement.

The terror level rose a shade.

"What are you, a damn parrot?" He snapped. "Stop repeating everything I say as a question."

"Repeating, Sir? Sorry, Sir. I wasn't informed I'd be going along on the mission," I said, assuming The GIF had forgotten to tell me. "Will I be running air operations in Kherwar for the return flight?"

The SCO removed his cigar.

"You can barely run air operations here. Why would I want you running them there?" He asked. "Major Doyle has come down with another case of his bullshit migraines and Doc Jonston put him on bed rest. I need Clark to stay here, since he's the only one who knows what the hell is going on in that damn Operations Office."

He sputtered a few flakes of tobacco from his lips and I felt one land on my chin before he continued.

"Major Connick seems to have some unwarranted faith in your abilities and has recommended I send you instead."

I resisted the urge to wipe my chin, fearful it'd jinx the moment.

"Yes, Sir," I exclaimed. "So you want me to lead the shura with Nasir and the elders?"

"Good God, no," The SCO said. "That's too important. Captain Jaxon will handle that now. Your job is to find Handboy."

I felt like I was being tricked.

"Sir, I thought you weren't concerned with Handboy?" I asked.

"Of course I'm concerned with Handboy," he boasted. "What type of heartless clod wouldn't be?"

I swallowed hard. I didn't want to blow my one shot at going on this mission.

"I don't know, Sir. I just thought that--," I started, but was cut off.

"Handboy's our best chance to win some brownie points with these Kherwar elders and proper medical attention is one thing Nasir can't provide. We'd have to be idiots to pass up this opportunity for good press. I want you to convince his family to let us fly him to Bagram to fix his wonky hand."

I nodded.

"If *you* didn't know you were going, then Doc probably doesn't know he's going either," The SCO said, pulling his chin. "Go to the Aid Station and tell him to get his ass up here. Then go get your own gear, if you can still find it."

I thanked God that I'd heeded Major Connick's advise and kept a bag packed.

"Is Frank going?" I asked. Frank was struggling to breath in his tight vest.

"What? No," The SCO said. "Frank's been getting a number of death threats from the local shopkeepers and our cafeteria staff. I'm making him wear his gear for his own good. He's far too important to be risked on a mission of this nature."

He smiled at Frank, who grimaced back.

"Find your own terp," he said, flicking his wrist. "Now go. We'll hold the birds until you get back."

****

Terp 2 was easy to find, as he'd been loitering outside the Command Post again, waiting to be needed. He was oddly excited for the mission and ran off to find his gear before I'd even finished giving him the details. I think he was happy just to have something to break up the boredom. I was too, but I had to find Doc if I wanted to avoid The SCO's wrath.

I was out of breath coming through the Aid Station door. The lights were blinding compared to the darkness outside and simulated exceptionally well, the sterile luminescence of a real hospital. The sick bay was quiet. Six beds sat empty along the opposing wall, their white linens neatly tucked and cornered. I was surprised The GIF wasn't occupying one. A droning buzz came from behind a set of double doors in the back.

"Can I help you?" A voice asked from beside me, making me jump.

Beside the doorway, wedged back into the narrowing tent wall, a clerk's desk sat, piled high with cases of latex gloves, fake prescription notepads, and boxes of nicotine patches. Behind the desk, a bleary-eyed Specialist sat with his heels propped on the table, his chair tilted, and his nose buried in a vintage looking copy of a *The Flash* comic book.

"I'm looking for Doc Jonston," I said, clearing my throat after my near heart-attack. The clerk dropped his feet to the floor and righted his chair when he realized he was addressing an officer, but remained seated when it registered that I was only a Lieutenant.

"Sorry, Sir," he yawned. He pointed to the double doors at the far side of the tent. "Doc's busy in back."

"I'm sure he won't mind if I interrupt."

I started walking back, when I heard the Specialist scramble to his feet.

"You better let me get him, Sir," he said, stumbling around the desk and knocking over a stack of ibuprofen bottles. "He doesn't like to be bothered while he's, um, working."

"Fine," I said, conceding to let the clerk go. "But I know what he's doing back there."

The clerk hobbled past me, his left pant leg rolled up to just below his knee. On his calf, the skin was crimson and shiny with some type of ointment.

The buzzing stopped as the clerk entered the back room and seconds later Doc Jonston burst from behind the doors, like a nerdy gunslinger entering a ghost town salon. His uniform top was missing and he wore dental magnifying glasses, attached to his government issued ballistic shooting glasses. On his hands he wore latex gloves, their fingertips stained black.

"How can I help you, Sir?" he asked with a smile.

"One, you could try not to be so obvious," I said, pointing at his gloves. On his forearm, the Batman tattoo was substantially larger than before, but also much more accurate. "Two, and most importantly, I need you to pack your gear. Right now. The SCO wants you on the mission to Kherwar tonight."

Doc looked back cautiously at the double doors.

"Right now isn't a great time for me," he said. "I'm kinda in the middle of something."

"I don't want to know," I said and then added. "But The SCO will. Now, I won't rat you out, but you can be sure The SCO will be down here snooping around if you don't get up to the airfield."

"This isn't going to go over well," Jonston sighed, looking back again.

"Who do you have back there anyway?" I asked.

"I thought you didn't want to know, Sir?" he said, with a grin. "I can't tell you anyway. Hippocratic Oath and all."

"The Hippocratic Oath doesn't apply to Army Medics or tattoo artists," I said. "Did I see *The Flash*'s logo tattooed on your poor clerk's calf?"

I looked around, but the clerk had not returned from the back.

"He's satisfied with the final product," Doc boasted.

"Is the final product 'hepatitis'?" I asked. "He doesn't exactly seem like 'The Flash' material."

"The antibiotics make him sleepy, Sir."

"Well, if you'd like to continue to operate with impunity, I'd suggest meeting me at the airfield in about twenty minutes with all your gear."

Doc shook his head and held out his tattooed forearm, but I'd already started for the door.

"I'm getting better, Sir," he said with a smile.

"Sure, sure," I called back as I pushed through the exit "Twenty minutes!"

I stepped into the gravel and waited for my eyes to adjust. I had to make one last stop at my room to gather my gear before heading back to the airfield, but I'd forgotten my flashlight and the moonless night was nearly impenetrable. The blackness was the best case scenario for a nighttime air assault. It was the worst case scenario for trying not to walk face first into the side of a building or trip over rogue tent lines.

With no ambient light, it was possible to see thousands of stars. Off on the horizon, two small circles of red-orange light hovered in the air. The afterburners of two jets streaking away.

That's odd, I thought.

I squinted into the dark. The dots bounced erratically. These were no afterburners. And they weren't off in the distance. They were the cherry tips of two lit cigarettes and about the time of this revelation, two gorilla hands had grasped my arms and a third slapped painfully over my mouth.

I thrust and kicked and tried to shout, while the two shadowy figures dragged me down a small embankment to the concrete mortar shelters that ran parallel to the Air Station. The hand covering my mouth smelled of oily workshop rags and cigarette smoke. I gagged at the thought of all the places the hand had likely been that day.

Inside the mortar bunker, one of the lit cigarettes leaned in so close I thought it'd burn my eye.

"You'll keep yer mouth shut, if ya know what's good for ya," grunted a huge shadow behind the glowing embers. The hand lifted from my mouth.

"What the--," I started to yell before the hand slapped down again. This time it was followed by a solid fist to the gut. Pain flashed white in my eyes and I sucked air through the closed fingers of the oil rag hand.

"Boss wants-ah talk to ya, so shut yer friggin mouth," one of the cigarettes garbled, threatening to sear my eye again.

A bright light flooded the bunker from the far side. I squinted and tried to turn my head away, but the gorillas to either side of me kept my head held straight. The light bounced closer, followed by a raspy, labored breathing.

“Lieutenant Rye,” welcomed the man behind the light. “I hope my men didn’t startle you much.”

I knew the voice. The fat Specialist who’d haggled a ride from me in Bagram.

“If we uncover your mouth, can I trust you not to shout?” He asked.

The oil rag hand nodded my head for me.

“Splendid,” said the voice and the hand lifted from my mouth.

“You gotta be out of your goddamn mind,” I hissed. “Why did I get jumped by these goons?” I swung my head wildly from side to side. I recognized the gorillas from the Squadron motorpool. Both Specialists.

The flashlight lowered revealing the round face and greasy mustache I’d expected. The shadows cast by his light made his face appear to sag, as though melting. On his chest, he wore a name-tape this time. Specialist Thedon.

He waved his hand and his goons released my arms.

“Old habits, I guess,” he said smiling softly.

“I guess so,” I said, rubbing my sore biceps and wondering what the hell he was talking about.

“I guess you’re probably wondering why my men snatched you and why I wanted to speak with you tonight.” From his pocket he removed a folded handkerchief and dabbed it lightly across his forehead.

“No guessing. I literally just asked you that five seconds ago.”

He ignored me.

“I told you,” Thedon said, “that I’d call on you. It's time to repay the favor.”

“You never told me that at all,” I said. “In fact, it’s you that should owe me a favor.”

Specialist Thedon was unfazed.

“You remember,” he insisted. “You remember when your girl was seeing that other man back at Fort Drum. And you came to me. *You* came to *me* for help. And we took care of them both for you. Did we not?”

“Jesus, you have the wrong person,” I groaned. “I haven’t had a girlfriend in years.”

The gorillas sniggered.

"You haven't?" Thedon asked. He tilted his head like a dog trying to understand music.

I shook my head.

"This is inconsequential," he said, waving me off as he turned to face the back of the bunker.

"This seems very consequential," I stammered. "You should be talking to someone else."

Thedon turned back toward me. His chin tucked into his chest while he sauntered up and stood toe to toe. He was a full head shorter than me, but he raised himself on his tiptoes and pointed his chin at mine.

"You're a good boy," he said, "but you talk too much." He gave my cheek a firm slap.

"Okay," I said. "I'm going to go ahead and leave now. This was a fun little game, but I need to be to the airfield in five minutes. You're lucky I'm in a hurry or I'd report your asses right now."

I turned to leave, but the goons were blocking the only exit.

"That is precisely why I wanted to speak with you. You see, I have this Soldier who has been a constant disappointment to me and this organization."

"What organization?"

"Hush now," Specialist Thedon scolded. "For that reason, he is being given one last opportunity to prove himself useful. I would like him to accompany you as part of your personal security detachment for this mission."

I was equal parts frustrated and fascinated by the audacity of this low ranking, obese soldier.

"First of all," I said. "I can't just add new people to the flight roster. Second, my rank doesn't warrant a personal security detachment. And third, I wouldn't take him even if I could. This little organization of yours clearly isn't sanctioned by the Army."

Specialist Thedon chuckled and mopped his brow again.

"*Little* organization?" He said, raising his eyebrows. "My dear boy, you have no idea. There are Specialists in every facet of military life. You can not imagine our influence. We can make this war a very dangerous place for you."

He stuffed the handkerchief into his pocket, replacing it with the gold handle of a folded pocket knife. He flicked the blade open and began picking at his fingernails.

"Are you threatening me?"

"Not threatening, Mr. Rye. Informing."

"*Lieutenant* Rye," I corrected.

"Inconsequential," he said.

"Stop saying that."

"I'm merely educating you on the extent of my organization's influence. Our mutual friend has already been added to the flight manifest and to Cherokee Troop's permanent roster. If you don't take him, you will have a soldier that is unaccounted for, which I doubt will go over well with The SCO. From what I've heard, he already finds your airfield operations--," he paused, "unsatisfactory."

Thump, thump.

In the distance, I could hear the second chaulk of helicopters lifting off. If I didn't get there soon, I'd delay the whole mission, put everyone at risk, and likely get murdered by The SCO.

"Fine," I said. "But when I get back, you're gonna tell me everything there is about this organization of yours. You got that?"

Specialist Thedon grinned, pulling down on the edges of his mustache. Light from his flashlight glinted off his blade as held them together in one hand.

"Best you hurry, my boy," he said. "You've got a war to win."

With that, the goons grabbed my arms and hurled me out of the bunker. I landed on my chest, face down in the gravel. I turned to protest, but the light was gone.

"Hi, Sir," came a sad voice. A new, much dimmer light clicked on in front of me. Its shaking beam barely lit a slipshod pair of uncuffed pant legs spilling carelessly over dirty tennis shoes. Behind the light, I could make out the outline of a neck brace supporting an oversized helmet.

"Son-of-a-bitch," I mumbled. "I should've known."

Chapter 13: Return Of Handboy

April 13, 2009

Captain Jaxon loved indulging in the grittiest aspects of warfare. His bravado, fueled by his men's keening, caused him to regularly subject them to easily avoidable hardships and trials of physical discomfort. He was of the mindset that suffering for suffering's sake builds character and his Troop, by God, would be the greatest in the Squadron. His men griped often and loudly, but loved him in spite of it, or possibly because of it. And because he'd earned them the reputation of being the toughest sons-of-bitches in the whole Brigade. I could usually get behind his mentality, but I certainly wasn't going to pour sand in my drawers just to feel the grind.

It was for this reason that I wasn't surprised to find myself trudging through sloppy clay on the road to Kherwar Village, while the sun barely peeked over the mountains on our shoulders. We'd been at the schoolhouse for only an hour after the Chinooks left, when Captain Jaxon decided we should stroll into town. Storm clouds were looming over the western mountains and he wanted to get the shura completed before they hit. Sleep was a luxury anyway.

"You should roll around in the dirt."

I jumped. People were always startling me from behind.

"You should roll around in the dirt," Captain Jaxon repeated, walking up beside me. "Might help you fit in better."

I looked around at the dusty, worn uniforms of his soldiers, then down at my own bright fresh gear.

"I fit in just fine, Sir," I muttered. "Half these men used to be mine anyway."

Second and Third Platoon were taking the walk into the village with us and they walked in two long, staggered lines on either side of the road. First Platoon stayed in reserve at the schoolhouse, in case there was trouble and reinforcements were needed.

"We're all just relieved to finally have an operations slideshow expert along on a mission. Could really help out in a jam," Captain Jaxon looked pleased with his wit and nudged my shoulder with the butt of his rifle.

"Don't you have more important things to do, Sir," I asked.

“I don’t,” Jaxon said. “But I would like you to explain to me, once more, how it came to pass that Specialist Shit-For-Brains got assigned back to my Troop.”

Specialist Coucher walked ahead of us on the side of the road. He looked back dejectedly. His neck appeared fine, even after Captain Jaxon had ferociously ripped away his brace and ordered him to put on a pair of regular boots.

“The SCO wants the recently promoted Specialists rotated back to line Troops, to get some real experience,” I lied. I’d been practicing on the flight down.

Captain Jaxon eyed me suspiciously.

“Just like you say The SCO flip-flopped and wants you to find Handboy now, huh? Offer him some good ol’ American health care?”

“Yes,” I replied. It had occurred to me late last night that The SCO had explicitly told every officer involved in the planning and execution of this mission of his hardline opposition to assisting Handboy in any way. I was the only person, aside from Frank, aware of his extreme policy reversal.

“Changed his mind last minute,” I continued. “He thinks that lending Handboy a hand will win the hearts and minds of the village.

Jaxon scoffed.

“I know how to win ‘hearts and minds’,” he sneered, raising his rifle and pretending to aim at an imaginary target. “Two to the heart and one to the mind. Pow. Pow. Pow.”

“Yes, Sir,” I said. “You’ve said that before.”

“Don’t get lippy with me,” he scolded. “You’re lucky I didn’t make you stay back at the schoolhouse and clean up that head you and Clark left in the desk. Good God, that thing stunk.”

“Yeah, sorry about that. I wasn’t expecting to see *him* again.”

Captain Jaxon shrugged.

“I bet *he* wasn’t expecting to be back here either,” he motioned to Terp 2 who hadn’t strayed far from my shoulder since we’d arrived. Doc Jonston followed close behind him, but appeared to be asleep on his feet. “I wish you’d have told me you were bringing your whole damn entourage. I wasn’t expecting four more mouths to feed.”

My stomach rumbled at the mention of food. A preservative packed, hermetically sealed, vegetable omelet bounced in my cargo pocket. I was hungry, but not that hungry.

"Kudos to you for adapting to a mission change so quick though. There's hope for you yet," he said, jabbing my shoulder even harder with his riflebutt.

He suddenly got serious and nodded toward the village.

"When we get there," he said, "I expect you'll handle your little side-mission-bullshit on your own. I'm meeting this Nasir-mofo and the town elders to let them know 'whaz-up'. Cherokee Troop is comin' down to stay and there'd better not be any trouble. You can ask some of the elders about Handboy if you want. It's a small village. Somebody will know where to find him."

"Like one of *them*," I said, pointing toward the village. "Looks like we have a welcome party."

Captain Jaxon squinted. A small group of villagers loitered on the road, just outside the village.

"Anything to be concerned about?" I asked.

"Two hundred years ago it would have been, but unfortunately, armies don't line up and march toward each other anymore."

I raised my rifle to look at the group through my magnified scope.

"Doesn't look like much of an army," I said. "I don't see any weapons. Most of them look old anyway."

"Never underestimate the tactical value of baggy clothing," Captain Jaxon said. "I learned that in Iraq."

Captain Jaxon radioed his platoon at the schoolhouse to update them on our situation. The group outside the village continued to grow, but the closer we got the more obvious it became that the group posed little threat. The majority of the men who milled about could barely maneuver their canes, let alone a rifle.

I walked with Captain Jaxon to the front of the formation as we neared the welcome party. As we approached, the group of old men parted, making way for four, much younger, men. Leading the smaller party was Nasir, a wide grin fixed, as always, under his shining curls and black beret. He was no longer dressed in typical Afghan garb, but wore military style cargo pants and weathered, black boots. His men were similar in dress and I recognized one behind his sunglasses as his driver from a month prior. The two new men carried AK-47s across their backs.

"Are they allowed to have those?" I whispered to Jaxon.

"Not really, but if I lived here, I'd sure as hell have one," he said.

Nasir threw his hands out wide.

"My friends!" He shouted, but then frowned. "Where is Daniel? He agreed to visit my home in person."

He stood on his toes to look down the long line of soldiers still spaced out in columns down the road.

"He sends his sincere apology," I said. "He was called up to Bagram by his superi---"

I was cut off by Captain Jaxon clearing his throat.

"If you don't mind, *Lieutenant*," he said, shooing me with the hand that rested on his rifle handle. "This ain't your show."

He turned to Nasir and extending his hand.

"You get me instead," he grinned. "Captain Marvin Jaxon. Pleased to meet you."

Nasir hesitated, barely hiding his contempt, before shaking Jaxon's hand. He forced a smile under his thin mustache.

"Should we head in and get this shura started?" Jaxon asked, nodding to the closest alleyway into the village.

Nasir looked at the alley as though it were miles away. He sighed and then, as though a weight had been lifted, he stood straight and held his head high.

"I think it would be wise for us to conduct our meeting here today," he informed.

"Out here on the road?" Jaxon asked. "Doesn't seem real official."

Nasir nodded.

"It will be very 'unofficial'," Nasir confirmed. "I had promised these men that they would be meeting with the commander of these new American forces. I mean no offense to you, but they will be displeased, as am I, that Daniel sent one of his, how you say, 'underlings' and did not deem this important enough to attend himself. I fear that unless we hold the meeting here and quickly, many of these men will simply wander home."

Captain Jaxon ground his teeth at the term "underling".

"I assure you, I hold great influence with my commander," Captain Jaxon said. "I myself am the commander of all the soldiers you see behind me. I am perhaps a better person to speak with anyway, since I will be the one establishing our base here."

Nasir's caterpillar mustache curl downward.

"I was unaware that you would be establishing a base here," Nasir said. "I assure you that an American occupation of my district is unnecessary. We are quite capable of protecting ourselves from the Taliban."

I looked at Nasir's three stone-faced bodyguards. They hadn't moved a muscle since he started talking.

"It's not always the Taliban that's the threat," Jaxon said, eyeing the bodyguards as well. "And it wouldn't be an occupation. We're here to assist. And to help make sure no one else loses their head. Though I have no doubt you know how to handle yourselves."

Nasir shook his head.

"A terrible tragedy," Nasir said. "I was fond of Captain Ahmed. They say his men were not so fond and turned against him."

"Yeah, curious bit about his men," Jaxon said, raising a brow. "Any idea where they all disappeared to?"

"Home, I would imagine," Nasir said with a smile. This wasn't a completely impossible explanation. The Afghan National Police were notoriously disorganized and dissatisfied members had the habit of simply abandoning their posts.

Captain Jaxon wasn't done sizing Nasir up. He motioned toward the pin on his beret.

"I notice you're wearing an American Combat Infantryman's Badge," Jaxon said. "May I ask how you came by one of those?"

Nasir lifted his eyes, as if he could see the beret on his own head. The wide smile returned to his face.

"It was a gift," he said proudly. "Given to me many years ago for assisting one of your Special Forces units on a mission."

"I'd like to hear that story," Jaxon replied.

"Perhaps another time," Nasir smiled and looked around. "I think we should begin our gathering before these poor men begin to die—of old age that is."

He turned and began walking toward a flat clearing to the south of the road, with Captain Jaxon walking beside him.

"Hey, wait a minute," I shouted. "What about *my* mission?"

Jaxon turned back and rolled his eyes. Nasir looked at me with puzzlement.

"Yes," Captain Jaxon sighed. "There's a small boy we believe lives in your village. He has a gnarled-up hand and Lieutenant Rye here has been sent down to find him. I don't suppose you know who I'm talking about?"

"I do, actually," Nasir seemed surprised. "You refer to my younger brother, Amir. What could you want from Amir?"

"We don't want anything from him," I said. "We'd like to offer some assistance. Our Squadron Doctor would like to take a look and see if there is anything we can do to help."

Doc Jonston gave Nasir a dopey wave. Nasir considered this a moment and then beckoned one of his rifle-carrying guards to his side. He whispered something and the man strolled off into the alleyway.

Nasir turned back to me and smiled.

"I have sent my friend to find my brother," he said. "I have instructed him to bring Amir to the village square."

He pointed into the village.

"Amir will not come out here. He is very afraid of you Americans," he said in response to our confused looks. "You see, the wound on his hand was his gift from the same Special Forces men. The fewer Americans, the better chance you'll have of speaking with him."

Captain Jaxon looked eager to change the subject.

"Take Third Platoon and find the square. Spread'em out so you don't spook the boy," he muttered. Nasir gave us both a smile and headed off to herd the wandering elders to the clearing. Captain Jaxon pulled me in close.

"Just keep your radio on. And don't stray too far," he told me. "This is uncharted territory. If shit hits the fan, I don't want my Dingle-nuts," he poked my chest, "hanging in the breeze. Always expect worst-case-scenario. I learned that in Iraq. Stay alert, stay alive."

Terp 2 gave me a worried look.

"Well, what happens if they attack *you* during the shura. You're one platoon short?" I asked.

"I don't expect that'll happen," Captain Jaxon said. "They're not gonna shoot us up when all their granddads are sit'n around chatting."

He slapped me on the back and gave me a grin.

"Don't take all day," he said. "Be back in an hour whether you find him or not."

I nodded and he headed off to where Nasir and the elders had started to form a circle in the clearing.

The Third Platoon Leader, Lieutenant Creed, and his Platoon Sergeant, Sergeant First Class Hopkins, were not at all thrilled about venturing into the village on some wild-goose-chase, but, like me, they didn't really have a say in the matter. Using overhead imagery they'd picked up from Captain Garcia before leaving Alternator, we were able to identify a route to the village square. We entered the village down a walled roadway, barely large enough for single vehicle traffic. The stone and clay walls rose high on each side and the tightness of the corridor brought on a tightness in my chest. I watched the top of the walls, expecting to glimpse the business-end of an AK-47 or the smoke trail of a rocket propelled grenade right before my demise.

I knew the rest of the soldiers could feel it, too. It was early but the village was alive. Villagers eyed us suspiciously, gathering at corners and intersections to watch us pass. I scanned each person for outlines of weapons or unnatural bulges beneath their billowy linens. Every time a young man would slip out of sight, I'd assume his intentions were nefarious, retrieving a weapon or evading an impending explosion. One of the villagers smiled at me as I passed and nearly broke me mentally. Finally, our skittish parade culminated as we stumbled into an empty village square.

The Third Platoon soldiers fanned out and made hasty security positions at each entry point into the square. Oddly enough, the square was the one place we'd seen this morning that was completely deserted.

"Shit. The SCO's going to have my nuts on a platter if we don't find this kid," I said.

Terp 2 looked confused. He and Doc had walked with me the whole way in.

"Nuts is another word for testicles," Doc clarified, but Terp 2 clearly didn't know that word either.

"My balls," I said, pointing to my crotch. "The SCO's going to cut'em off."

Terp 2's face went pale.

"It's a figure of speech," I said. More confusion. "Geez. He's not really gonna do it. It's an American saying. It's supposed to be funny."

"I knew a boy once, who had his 'balls' cut off for looking upon a man's daughter," Terp 2 said, shaking his head sadly.

"Well, it's not real funny anymore," I said and tried to change the subject. "Doc, what exactly are you gonna be able to do for this kid? If we even find him."

Doc sat down on the crumbling remnants of a clay wall and took out his med kit.

"Well, if the wound is infected, I can put some ointment on it. If it hurts, I can give him some ibuprofen. I got lots of that."

"I think he's been living with this condition for quite a while," I said. "I imagine he's got a way of managing that stuff already."

"If he's addicted to cigarettes, I've got nicotine patches."

Doc looked longingly into his med kit for answers.

"You think he'd want a tattoo?" he asked.

"Good God, Doc," I said. "That's all you brought?"

"Nobody, told me what the hell we were doing," Doc said defensively. "And you do realize I'm not actually a doctor, right? I got a few weeks of training on how to stop somebody's bleeding long enough to get them to an *actual* doctor. If somebody shoots Handboy, *then* I can really shine."

"Well, I think it would've been safe to assume we weren't going to be giving the locals tattoos. Can you at least assess the damage to his hand?" I asked. "You know, figure out if an *actual* doctor would be able to do anything?"

"Sure," Doc said. "If his hand is all jacked up, I can confirm that it's all jacked up."

"Wonderful," I said, sitting down next to him.

We waited. Ten minutes and nobody came. Twenty minutes and nobody came. Lieutenant Creed paced by, tapping the face of his watch and commenting on how exposed we all were. Thirty minutes and still nobody. Lieutenant Creed started pointing to the surrounding walls and then making gunfire hand gestures and pantomiming explosions. I flipped him off.

Even Terp 2 started to check his watch.

"You have somewhere else to be?" I asked him.

"It is odd that the village square would be so empty for so long," Terp 2 said.

"What do you mean?"

"The square should be the heart of the village. No one has even attempted to come in since we arrived."

"They probably don't want to be caught in the middle of the ambush we're about to experience," I said.

Doc rolled his eyes as he finished rearranging the contents of his med bag.

I checked my own watch.

"Well, it looks like we've been stood up. We'll have to pack it up and head back."

Terp 2 looked concerned.

"But, Sir, The SCO is going to have your 'nuts on a platter'."

"You're right," I said. "The SCO will have my nuts. But I'd rather lose my nuts than my life, so let's get the hell outta here."

The radio on my shoulder crackled.

"This is Cherokee Six to Dinglenuts, over," came Captain Jaxon's voice. "Come in, Dinglenuts."

"I'm not responding to 'Dinglenuts'," I said into the hand mic.

"Seems like you just did," Jaxon said. "Where are you guys? Did you locate Captain Hook? Over."

"Negative," I said. "We're still in the square. Haven't seen a damn soul. Just about to head your--"

"Stop! Stop right there!" Came a shout from behind us. I nearly fell off the half-wall were we sat. On the backside of the square, two soldiers were shouting down a narrow alley. Beyond, I could see a young man walking slowly toward them. Handboy.

I was on the ground and closing the distance to the soldiers.

"Shit, Sir! He ain't stop'n!" one soldier called back over his shoulder. "I'm gonna have to blast him."

The soldier's helmet was enormous.

"You're not blasting anyone, Coucher," I yelled. "Hold your damn fire."

The boy finally stopped advancing. His eyes darted from soldier to soldier, a sheen of sweat on his brow. A dusty tunic draped his body and concealed his arms within. The flowing clothes made the shape of his figure indiscernible and gave the appearance he was swaying in the breeze. There was a low rumble of thunder in the distance.

"Tell him to show his hands," I instructed Terp 2, who'd been on my heels the whole way over. Lieutenant Creed had been on the opposite end of the courtyard and was still running toward us.

Terp 2 translated. Handboy worked to free his hands from the loose fabric.

"Tell him we're here to fix his hand," I said.

Terp 2 translated. I heard him use the name "Handboy" in English. I smacked him on the shoulder.

"He has no idea he's 'Handboy'," I snapped. "Call him Amir."

Terp 2 re-translated. The boy, who still had not shown us his hands, struggled to free himself from his snag. His choice of attire was suspicious, but his failure to show his hands was making everyone nervous.

"Tell him to take the whole damn tunic off," I said.

Terp 2 translated.

The young man slowly lifted the tunic over his head. As it lifted above his waist, he exposed a bulky canvas vest strapped across his torso.

I squinted at the vest.

"Suicide vest!" Coucher shouted.

The shout sparked a chain reaction. Handboy, with the tunic now draped over his head and obstructing his vision, blindly stumbled forward. My heart leapt to my throat and I heard Captain Jaxon's warning in my mind.

Always assume worst-case-scenario.

Training took over and I went to the next phase in the "Escalation Of Force". The warning shot. Everything became a blur. I raised my rifle and aimed at the wall above and to the left of Handboy. I heard Creed yell something from behind me right before I pulled the trigger. It sounded a lot like "stop", but I assumed he was yelling at the boy. Lightning cracked from the storm clouds overhead. The recoil surprised my shoulder and a puff of dust kicked from the clay alley wall in front of where I'd aimed. The zing of the ricochet was masked by thunder. A red-pink mist spouted out from behind the tunic and Handboy shrieked from inside his shroud. His body swung violently and dropped to the ground.

"Oh shit," I mumbled.

Terp 2 translated.

Chapter 14: A Glint

June 5, 2009

I'd shot Handboy. By the way everyone overreacted you'd think I tagged the poor kid between the eyes. In actuality, the ricocheting bullet winged him in his good hand, passing right through the palm. Needless to say, Handboy was near hysterics and if Terp 2 hadn't been there, it would've been much worse. Terp 2 was able to talk him down enough to let Doc bandage him up. Handboy even seemed to *like* them both by the end of it. Just not me, no matter how profusely I apologized. It *was* a bit ironic that the flak vest Handboy wore for protection against Americans was ultimately what got him shot.

Captain Jaxon, was surprisingly cool about the incident at first. In fact, he even started referring to Handboy in the plural, "Handsboy", but once The SCO got word, all joking went out the window. The SCO lit into me over the radio back at the schoolhouse. The trouble with getting chewed out over the radio by a superior, is you can't hang up on them. You gotta sit there and take it, while everyone watches and laughs.

The odd thing was, the person who seemed least upset was Nasir. He seemed downright indifferent. At one point, seeing how distraught I was, he slapped me on the back and said something to the effect of, "shit happens". In retrospect, he was probably just familiar with the Contingency Fund process, which would explain his greedy smile when Captain Jaxon finally whipped out the backpack.

Captain Jaxon's shura hadn't panned out either, but at least it hadn't result in the maiming of an adolescent cripple. The elders, like Nasir, didn't care for the idea of an American outpost and even less-so after Captain Jaxon eloquently explained he "didn't give two shits" what they thought. My blundered warning shot had been the cherry on top.

Long story short, I'd spent the majority of the last two months avoiding everyone, which was impossible given we lived on a postage stamp in the middle of nowhere. It was awful. Everyone who outranked me had some snarky comment to make or glaringly obvious advice to give.

Aim higher.

Stick to slide-shows.

Shooting kids is bad.

Fortunately for me, the Army's "time-in-service" promotion schedule made me a Captain in early May and the number of people on base who could freely give me shit had gone down. This hadn't stopped Major Connick from cracking Handboy jokes all the way through the small promotion ceremony though. Harassment aside, being a Captain felt good, even though I hadn't had much time to enjoy it. The mission to refurbish the Kherwar schoolhouse as an outpost had started in late April and my airfield had been a hot-zone of supply runs ever since. The Taliban's Spring Offensive had overlapped with our construction, pulling a lot of Apache helicopters into combat missions. The Chinooks we used for supply runs weren't allowed into the Kherwar without Apache escorts, so I found myself spending many a night stretched across my Humvee's windshield counting shooting stars.

Terp 2 had taken to joining me for the late night supply runs. Not because we needed an interpreter, but because he was bored and it was way to break up routine. I didn't mind either. I was glad to have him around most nights. It was nice to have someone to talk to, since the sniper team usually kept to themselves. That night they were all lined up, sitting against the concrete barriers. The moon had waned itself into oblivion and all that could be seen were the glowing tips of their cigars bobbing in a single file line.

"Why do they always have to smoke up here?" Terp 2 asked.

I jumped a little, cracking my elbow against the windshield glass. He'd been silent in the darkness for so long, I'd forgotten he was there.

"Just their way of passing the time, I guess."

"I do not know how they can stand it. The smell is terrible," Terp 2 complained.

"I love the smell," I said, putting my hands behind my head.

"How could anyone love that smell?"

"Reminds me of my dad," I said. "He smoked a lot of cigars. On Sundays, after church, he'd smoke right outside the backdoor, but my mom would always make him go to the far edge of the lawn so he wouldn't stink up the house."

Another shooting star streaked overhead. Number five.

"Sometimes I'd stand out there with him," I said. "He'd tell me stories from his youth or talk about the morning's sermon.

Sometimes, if his mood was right, he'd tell me about his time in Vietnam. Not often, but sometimes. He always seemed more distant during those stories. Weird thing is, I can remember wanting that. Wanting to have interesting stories of my own. It's an odd thing, being jealous of scars."

Terp 2 was quiet.

"How did he die?" He finally asked.

"Cancer. Probably from the damn cigars."

"I am sorry," Terp 2 said.

"Thanks. It's not like my mom didn't warn him a million times," I said. "What about your dad? Did he have any quirks like that?"

"Quirks?" Terp 2 asked.

"Special traits or characteristics? Something that's always in your memory of him?"

More silence in the dark. I feared I'd broached a topic he wasn't ready to discuss, so I changed the subject.

"I wish they'd just call off this damn mission. We've only got forty five minutes until sun-up," I said. "They wouldn't have time to take a single load out at this point."

"My father used to walk to work," Terp 2 said in a far-away voice. "His walk would take him through a very poor neighborhood. Before he would leave each morning, he would fill his pockets with any food we could spare. He would give these foods to those on the street. I think his saddest mornings were when he had no food to give."

We sat silent for a moment, listening to the snipers snicker at some unheard joke, the cherry ends of their cigars burning brightly between alternating puffs.

"He sounds like he was a great man," I finally said. I wanted to say more, but the radio crackled to life inside the truck.

"Titan Three Air. This is Titan TOC, over."

I rolled off the Humvee hood, wincing from the stiffness of lying on its unforgiving surface. I grabbed the hand mic and acknowledged the Command Post.

"Titan Three Air, we just got word the birds are down for the night. We're calling off the supply run."

It was Captain Applegate and I could tell he was smiling. Hard telling how long he'd known the mission was off.

The snipers must've overheard the transmission. Their cherry embers bobbed by in single file out of the airfield.

"Titan Three Air?" Applegate crackled again.

"Yeah, send it," I said.

"SCO's pretty pissed you didn't get the supplies out. I'd steer clear of the Command Post. Fair warning."

I should've been numb to it by now, but I threw the hand mic anyway. The SCO had been on the warpath. At first I figured it was because of Handboy, but recently he'd been targeting all his other staff officers too. Two weeks ago, he'd ripped the Chaplain apart in front of God and everyone for using the New International Version in his Sunday service. The SCO preferred King James.

I climbed out of the Humvee, ready to vent to Terp 2, but he must've had enough of our heart-to-heart and followed the snipers out. By the time I'd policed up the airfield equipment and got to my bunk, the sun was almost up. Sleep trumped hygiene, so I left my toothbrush on the table, kicked off my boots, and climbed the ladder into bed. I checked my watch. 0703 hours. I pulled the blanket over my ears.

One of life's new normals was occasionally being woken by outgoing artillery fire from FOB Alternator's resident 155 millimeter cannons. Being in close proximity to their barrage was something akin to being slapped in both ears simultaneously and repeatedly. The concussion was such that the ceiling, two feet above my bed, had cracked, sending concrete dust and bits of rubble showering onto my face with every forceful blow.

I checked my watch. 0735 hours. The next ten minutes were spent praying for silence with my pillow hotdog-bunned over my ears. The ten minutes after were spent praying for the ceiling to give way, ending my misery entirely. Neither prayer was granted. I made a mental note to file a complaint with Chappy. Finally giving up my fruitless quest for sleep, I slid down the ladder and back into my boots. If I couldn't sleep, I might as well see what all the fuss was about.

****

I stumbled to the Command Post and found CSM Storms standing atop the entrance landing with binoculars to his eyes. Stopping at the foot of the stairs, I followed his gaze to the top of Mount Crumpit, where the rounds were impacting.

"What're they shooting at?"

"There's a glint," Storms said, squinting into the lenses.

"A glint?" I asked.

"A glint," he reiterated. "Something metallic. The SCO thinks it might be the enemy conducting reconnaissance. Or even worse, a sniper."

"That would be one hell of a sniper shot. Can you see anything?"

Storms sighed.

"No. Whoever or whatever it was, must be long gone."

"What do you think it was?" I asked.

"A glint," Storms responded matter-of-factly.

Another round thundered out. Seconds later a dirt-cloud burst from the rocky mountain wall, sending debris in all directs and a time delayed rumble through the valley below.

"If they don't have a confirmed target, why are they still firing?" I asked.

"They have to neutralize the threat," He responded. The binoculars never left his eyes.

"The threat of the glint?" I asked. "Aren't those rounds super expensive?"

"Exactly," Storms said in response to both questions.

I watched another round strike the mountain wall before climbing the stairs. I don't think CSM Storms even noticed as I slipped behind him and into the Command Post.

****

The Operations Office was empty. The firefight that'd preoccupied my Apache escorts and left me in a lurch on the airfield had kept the operations staff up all night as well. But unlike me, they weren't going to let a little cannonade deprive them of their respite. I'd known Captain Clark wouldn't be there. He was on his two weeks of stateside "R & R". Within hours of his departure, the wheels had fallen off in the Operations Office. The GIF, unfettered by Clark's common sense, was back to concocting half-baked missions, most of which were direct violations of The Geneva Convention. He was currently passionate about placing fake security cameras on posts spread out from the FOB's perimeter. His theory being that if anyone tried to mess with the cameras, they were clearly terrorists and the

Sniper Team would be justified in shooting them dead. Sergeant Hunter had been appalled.

"That's called 'baiting'," he told The GIF. "You can't even do that to deer back home. You ain't using my guys for that shit."

For the last several days, Captain Garcia and I had secretly been paying a number of Specialists to sweep the office at regular intervals, in an effort to induce The GIF's now infamous dust migraines and drive him from the office.

With the room to myself, I slumped into my chair and hiked both boots into the air, bringing them down softly on the corner of my desk. Slouching down, I leaned my head back. The cannons were firing at slower intervals now, but not slow enough to sleep through. With my right index finger, I picked at the plywood countertop next to me. A chip of the wood cracked away and fell to the floor. Its impact on the floor matched perfectly the explosion of another round against the mountain wall. The activity had exhausted me and I yawned triumphantly.

"What in the name of holy hell do you think you're doing?" Came a voice from the doorway.

"Holy sh--," I caught myself. The SCO stood before me and I nearly went ass-over-tea-kettle, swinging my legs down from the table. I sprung to the position of attention.

"Sorry, Sir. Good morning, Sir."

The SCO studied me with bloodshot eyes. I apparently wasn't the only one who'd gone without sleep. His yellow tongue shifted his cigar nub from one side of his mouth to the other.

"Sorry for what?" He growled. "Being a lazy shit? Or destruction of government property?" His eyes dropped to the wood chip on the floor.

"Sir, it'd been loose for a while--."

"So has your mother!" The SCO shouted.

A triumphant smile spread across The SCO's face. I furrowed my brow. It seemed like a trap.

"You got me, Sir," I finally said.

"Shut up, David," he growled. "Where the hell is the Chaplain?"

"It's Jared, Sir."

His eyes narrowed menacingly.

"Where. Is. The. Chaplain?"

I looked around the empty room to convey he wasn't there. The Chaplain's office was in the next building over.

"I couldn't say, Sir," I said. "I'd guess he's in the staff building. In *his* office."

"You're borderline useless," The SCO said. "We've got an angry mob forming at the front gate. The family of that worker who died is here looking for compensation."

Two days earlier, a local construction worker was jackassing around on the front of a crane and was accidentally catapulted face first into a concrete barrier. It was his own dumb fault, but the family wanted money all the same.

"I don't think the Chaplain has the contingency funds, Sir," I said.

"No shit, Sherlock," The SCO growled. "Clark's on leave and Major Doyle lost the damn backpack, so we're shit-out-of-luck for money. I need the Chaplain to smooth things over with them. Maybe say a few prayers or something."

"I'm not sure--" I started to protest, but then stopped. "Would you like me to go find him, Sir?"

"Implied task, genius," he said, shifting his cigar again. He was standing uncomfortably close. His lips were chapped and cracked. "Tell him to get his big, bald head down to the front gate."

"Yes, Sir," I said.

"Where is your gear?" The SCO asked, searching the room.

"Sir?"

He rubbed his eyes. I thought I better expound before he bit my head clean off.

"Sir, my gear is in my room."

"Well, I hope you're packed. The birds should be here in two hours."

Now I was really confused.

"Sir, I don't follow. What do I need to be packed for?"

"Goddamn Doyle," he muttered. "You need to be *packed* because you're coming with me to Kherwar to un-fuck the situation you created with Handboy. I'm not sure how you don't know this. I'm holding a shura to address the summer elections and you'll be making a public apology."

If Captain Clark were here, I'd have known.

"Sir, the boy charged--," I stopped myself, as The SCO clenched down on his cigar.

"You'll make a public apology for shooting the child," he said, through gritted teeth.

"Sir, he was hardly a child."

"You'll do it," the SCO growled.

"Yes, Sir," I said, as he walked back to the door, "he was at least a teenager."

The SCO ignored me, but paused in the doorway.

"Tell the Chaplain to pack his shit too. He needs to get outside the wire."

He spit cigar debris onto the floor and was gone.

Chapter 15: The Kher-Shur

June 6, 2009

"I think I'm being used," said Chappy.

He sat on the edge of a crumbling, clay wall in the Kherwar village square. The same wall I'd sat on almost two months ago. He ground the tip of his boot in the red clay.

"You're definitely being used," I said, sitting next to him.

"You think so?" Chappy burst, thrilled to have someone to confirm his suspicion.

"For sure," I said. "One hundred percent."

A moment passed with only dead air and dust between us. I stared off across the square toward the alley where I'd shot Handboy. I could feel Chappy boring a hole in my skull, but the SCO was pacing nervously a few meters away and I wasn't sure he was out of earshot. Every now and again he'd shoot a glance at Chappy, but Chappy was oblivious.

"Well, Jesus, don't just sit there," Chappy whispered, "tell me why you think I'm being used?"

"You use the Lord's name in vain a lot."

He ignored me.

"I'm sure it's the same reason you feel like you're being used," I said, eyeing The SCO.

Chappy pivoted toward me, lowering his head with his voice.

"No, I want *your* opinion," he whisper. "Why do you feel like I'm being used?"

"You're a chaplain in a war zone," I sighed. "I think everybody here thinks about the afterlife a smidge more than normal and anybody who's on-the-outs with God is gonna try to use you for a shortcut 'in'."

"What do you mean, 'shortcut 'in'''"?

"You know, a deathbed repentance," I suggested. "Afghanistan being our deathbed."

We sat silently watching The SCO, who muttered sound bites of his shura speech as he marched back and forth. The town elders began to arrive, entering through a crude security checkpoint on the main road into the square. The checkpoint was manned by none other than our beloved SPC Coucher.

"I can't believe they brought that guy, let alone have him running a checkpoint," I said, nodding at Coucher. "His screaming is half the reason I shot Handboy."

"You gotta stop beating yourself up about that," Chappy said.

"Easy for you to say, you've never shot a kid before."

"That you know of," he said. "I was a whole different person before the Army issued me God."

"Yeah, but you never shot a kid before," I reiterated. "Right?"

"No," he said. "No, that *is* pretty fucked up."

He put a hand on my shoulder and the ink from his sleeve tattoo poked out from under his cuff.

"What I mean is, it's easy to second guess yourself, but the fact is, you made a hard call in a hard situation, that potentially could have saved some soldier's lives. Hell, if nothing else, by taking the shot, you undoubtedly stopped Coucher's dumb-ass from shooting ol' Handboy right in the brain. So there you go, you saved Handboy from certain death and Coucher from a lifetime of pocket-holding in Leavenworth."

"You really think he would've shot him?" I asked.

"Hell yes. I wouldn't put *anything* past that little shit-bird," Chappy grumbled. "And now that he's off Alternator, my investigation's gone to shit. So there's another thing he's messed up."

"Sorry, Chappy. I know how much you wanted to bring their little mafia down," I said.

Chappy hung his head and went back to digging in the dust with his boot.

"There's one more thing." I whispered. "About you being used."

Chappy perked back up.

"One more thing?" He asked.

"I'm pretty sure The SCO hopes that by having you around, he won't get hurt. Like some sort of 'God-forcefield'. I'm positive that's why he had you come."

Chappy's jaw dropped.

"Get out." He said. "That's awful. But it makes perfect sense. That's why he had me sit next to him in the chopper and that's why he made me walk the outpost's perimeter a few steps ahead of him last night. Come to think of it, that's probably why he made me eat the first bite of his breakfast this morning."

Chappy nodded in agreeance with his own assessments.

"Kinda cool, actually," he said. "The SCO thinks I'm invincible."

"Or expendable. He knows how much you curse, so he probably thinks God's more likely to take you first," I said.

"God doesn't work like that," he said in a way that sounded more like a question.

"I'm not privy to how God smites."

"But you do think it's more of a 'sacrificial lamb' scenario than a 'God-shield' scenario?" He asked. "I feel closer to Jesus already."

"It certainly fits The SCO's disposition better."

"Between you and me," Chappy whispered. "I hear the SCO's made quite a few enemies in Logar. I've heard about some shady behind-the-scenes shit."

"Yeah, right," I rolled my eyes. "Who'd you hear that from?"

"I'm a Chaplain, people tell me lots of things. I can't tell you who though."

"Chaplains shouldn't gossip," I said.

"Okay, fine, I'll tell you. It was Lieutenant Carrier, The SCO's new Security Platoon Leader. He said the SCO met with a couple of elders in the Chark District two weeks ago. The meeting ended in a shouting match. He said, Frank said, the men were making death threats and mentioning Nasir a lot. Carrier thought something else was up though. He said the guys didn't look old enough to be elders. That shit is pretty crazy, huh?"

I rolled my eyes.

"I'm sorry, I'm pretty amped. I had a Sergeant Drill's before we left the outpost."

"Well, I wouldn't put too much stock into what Lieutenant Carrier tells you. The guy's been here less than a month. He's got no idea what he's seeing."

"Chaplain!"

I jumped. Chappy didn't. The SCO was staring at us from the end of the worn path he'd carved in the dust. He looked sickly and the bags under his bloodshot eyes were ready to burst. Behind him the elders had taken their seats on an array of ornate rugs laid out by Captain Jaxon's men.

"Chaplain, get up here. I'm about to start this shura. You're going to do the opening prayer."

"The opening prayer, Sir?" Chappy asked.

"Did I stutter?" The SCO scowelled. "You open all my meetings with prayer. This one's no different."

I'd never been to a single meeting that Chappy had opened with prayer.

"Yes, Sir, but--," Chappy stammered, surveying the elders.

"Spit it out, Chappy."

"Sir, these men pray to a different God. Won't we offend them by forcing them to sit through our prayer?"

The SCO gnawed his soggy cigar and glared at Chappy. It was hard to tell if he was weighing Chappy's words or plotting ways to kill him.

"Do a silent prayer then," he finally said. "Tell them they can pray to whatever God they want. You pray to *our* God though, you understand?"

"Yes, Sir. Of course, Sir," Chappy gritted at me, once the SCO turned away.

The silent prayer was awkward, as expected. Frank put forth his usual lackluster effort in explaining to the elders what was about to happen. In the end they just watched in confusion while Chappy stood silently, his head bowed, eyes closed, and lips moving along to his inner monologue.

"Amen," Chappy said aloud, letting us know he'd concluded. He looked to Frank who shrugged.

Chappy nodded to his bewildered audience and turned back toward me, but The SCO grabbed him by the shoulder before he could take a single step.

"Whoa," eased The SCO. "Don't run off just yet. We may need some religious guidance throughout the meeting, so why don't you stay put."

The SCO's hands were on both Chappy's shoulders now. He guided him backward to face the old men, who still had no idea what in someone-else's-God's-name was happening. The SCO leaned forward and whispered something into Chappy's ear. At the same time the two men sat down cross-legged right where they'd been standing, with Chappy to the front left of The SCO. The SCO then motioned to Frank, who sat next to Chappy with his legs splayed out like a child.

"What is going on?" Asked Terp 2, who'd taken Chappy's spot on the wall.

"The SCO's adding some extra body armor," I said.

The shura kicked off and The SCO launched right into his rhetoric, detailing the intricacies of the upcoming presidential election. It was all stuff I'd heard before; dates, times, who the candidates were and which candidates were favored to do best. Frank's translations droned on in the background like a white-noise machine. It was obvious he was barely comprehending the words his mouth was regurgitating. Occasionally, an elder would stand up with a question, which Frank would translate with great annoyance. The SCO largely ignored these inconvenient interruptions and went on with his own agenda. I kept stealing glances at Terp 2, who's face had reddened and hands shook.

"This is much bullshit," he finally whispered. It was the first time I'd heard him curse. "This election is the most important in Afghanistan's history, but that fat bastard has barely gotten a single translation right."

"And finally," the SCO announced, "it's been decided that, for security reasons, the voting will be held at the old schoolhouse. As you all know, my men have set up a security post there, so your voting station will be provided the highest level of security."

"And what if we don't want you Americans interfering with our election?" Came a voice from the back of the square.

I looked over to see Nasir, swaggering across the courtyard, his black beret cocked forward over his black curls. There was no shining smile on his face this time. SPC Coucher was still at his post chewing slowly on regret, his chin digging a hole in the chestplate of his body armor. The SCO's face was a new shade of yellow. He scooted a few inches forward to be more directly behind the Chaplain.

"Nasir! So good to see you," The SCO forced his best fake smile, nearly dropping his cigar. "Forgive me for not inviting you, I didn't realize you were considered a village elder."

"I am not," Nasir replied flatly, "but I have many friends and trusted advisors here. I have come to lookout for the interest of my countrymen."

Nasir continued at a swift pace through the crowd of seated old men, until he stood between Frank and Chappy.

"And you don't believe that having your election site in the most secure location in Kherwar is in the best interest of your countrymen?" The SCO asked, leaning back to look up at him.

Nasir squatted low to meet The SCO, eye to eye.

"Colonel Fink," he said calmly, "the most secure location in Kherwar is wherever I happen to be standing."

He stood up and spoke louder for all the elders to hear.

"I fear that holding this election within an American facility will taint the results amongst my comrades. I fear the rumors of American interference will be abundant. And if that happens, the people will not recognize or respect the Afghani government."

Nasir looked to Frank who looked to The SCO.

"Frank," Nasir called sweeping an arm over the gathered elders. "Frank. Ask these men if they approve of an Afghani election in an American facility?"

The SCO nodded and Frank garbled through his translation. Old heads dropped. Frightened eyes stared at the ground in front of them, like someone had just shot their prize goat. Some shook their heads slowly.

The SCO's face was no longer pale, but a deep rage-purple. Chappy still sat cross-legged in front of The SCO. He was the only one still smiling, his right hand wrapped tightly around the handle of the Kabar sheathed to his belt. I half expected him to jump up and gut Nasir. It seemed The SCO need only give the order.

"There. You see?" Nasir said, but was interrupted before he could continue.

An old man stood in the back of the crowd. His beard, dyed a vivid red in homage to the Prophet Muhammad, stood out against the wrinkled leather of his face. When he spoke, his voice was deep and smooth. Even in his aged state, I could tell he'd been a fighter in his youth.

"Why would we not take the opportunity for security?" Frank translated. "This opportunity to vote would have never come to pass without the Americans. What sense does it make to turn down this opportunity to vote, free from the threat of the Taliban—and other criminals."

Red Beard said this last part looking directly at Nasir.

Nasir seethed a response in Pashtun. But this time it was Terp 2 who translated for the benefit of The SCO.

"Sit down old man. You're tired."

"There, this gentlemen gets it," The SCO said, pointing to Red Beard. "There's only benefit to our involvement in the election security."

"This was not part of our agreement," Nasir snapped at The SCO. "This is a violation of our terms and you have greatly overstretched your boundaries. Your presence is not welcome here."

I wasn't sure what I was hearing or what agreement the SCO had made with this sorted man. The SCO's face drained. His eyes became shifty and he scratched nervously at the back of his neck.

"You translate any of this and I kill you," he said to Frank.

He removed his cigar before continuing.

"Nasir, my boy, I think it best we all calm down. As for our—agreement, I made it very clear from the beginning that its terms were subject to alterations, given changes in orders from my superiors. You must understand, I am under direct orders from my Commander to ensure the voting for this election is held where U.S. forces can most effectively protect the people of Kherwar. My hands are tied in this matter. And besides, the people's safety is paramount here. There are no ulterior motives. I assure you."

"Safety? Protection?" Nasir was nearly yelling now, his thin mustache buckled at its center. He translated his own words to ensure the elders could hear him undermining this representative of oppression. "Where was your protection when my poor brother was mutilated by an American for the second time. By one of your own men."

Nasir pointed a ragged finger directly at me. My stomach turned at the word, "mutilated". The elders were looking at me now too, but their collective disapproval was no match for the pure hatred pouring from Nasir. Nasir beckoned to the checkpoint. My heart sank as Handboy stumbled slowly into the square. SPC Coucher had given up, putting up no resistance to yet another person breaching security. The SCO turned to me.

"Apologize, Jacob," he growled.

I swallowed hard. This was why I'd come, but I'd only anticipated apologizing to the elders, not Handboy himself. I wasn't expecting to see Handboy ever again.

"I—er—Handboy," I stammered.

Frank opened his fat mouth to translate, but Terp 2 beat him to it.

"Amir," Terp 2 corrected.

I felt a bit more confident with him beside me.

"Yes. Amir. Excuse me," I said. "I understand the pain I've caused you and I know I cannot take that back, but I would like to give you my heartfelt apology not only for the physical pain I've caused, but also for the unfair bias I displayed in assuming you had negative intentions, based off from how you looked, behaved, and the general fact that your vest looks exactly like a suicide-vest. And that you're also apparently hard of hearing and can't follow directions."

The SCO cleared his throat in warning.

"I hope that you could find it in your heart to forgive me," I finished.

Terp 2 stumbled in a few places as he translated, but all-in-all he sounded smooth. After he'd finished, he looked at me nervously. We waited for anybody to say something to break the awkward silence.

A wide grin spread across Handboy's face. Not at me, but at Terp 2. He nodded his head to Nasir, who nodded back, his face still set in stone.

Nasir turned back to address the elders.

"These Americans disrespect us. They do not believe in our ability to provide for our own future. They do not want to give us that chance. They want only to conquer, so they come here in sheep's clothing to manipulate and undermine, all while slowly dripping their poison upon us. Let us take no more part of this deceit. Come. This meeting is over."

Nasir took a few steps toward the gate, but then stopped. The elders sat motionless, their eyes to the ground.

"You see, Nasir," The SCO said, still sitting in solidarity, or laziness, with the elders. "*This* is democracy. The people have spoken and they have chosen a safe environment for their elections."

Nasir, studied the bowed heads of the Kherwar village elders and then walked back to stand between Chappy and Frank again. Putting his hands on his knees, he squatted down before The SCO. Chappy calmly began sliding his Kabar from its sheath.

"I have people everywhere, Fink," Nasir hissed. "*Everywhere.*"

The SCO gulped.

"Just apparently not here," I said, my hand poised on my rifle handle. I don't know why I said it. I was thinking it, then my mouth opened and there it was.

Nasir turned his head. He smiled a malevolent smile as he stood.

"Yes, Jacob," he said, as he walked back toward Handboy. "Apparently not here."

With his hand on his brother's neck, Nasir guided them both back past a nervous Coucher.

"It's Jared," I called, as they exited the checkpoint.

Chapter 16: AWOL

June 7, 2009

Moonlight spilled across the floor of our room in the schoolhouse, illuminating mounds of rubbish left by the police before their sudden departure. Hands folded behind my head, I studied the cracks of the ceiling in our second-floor room. They were new and interesting cracks, with much more to offer than the tired, boring cracks above my bed at Alternator. Chappy snored aggressively a few feet behind my head and Terp 2 spooned his backpack against the opposite wall.

I couldn't sleep. My bladder was about to burst, but the pain didn't yet outweigh my desire to avoid the trek downstairs and outside to the latrines. The noise from the helicopters coming in and out of the outpost didn't help either. They were running a resupply mission from Alternator. A mission I'd planned long before learning I'd be coming to The SCO's shura. So I guess, if I were back at Alternator, I wouldn't be sleeping there either.

I laid awake thinking of the shura drama. The revelation The SCO could be making illicit behind-the-scenes deals with local militants was bad, but he never said another word about it. Maybe I just don't understand the high level politics of war. Either way, Nasir's interruption had ended The SCO's shura in a hurry and he'd been unbearable ever since. I can't say I blamed him though. He'd been thoroughly humiliated by Nasir in front of all the village elders. He redirected this humiliation by channeling his post shura-rage on Coucher for allowing Nasir and Amir through the checkpoint uncontested. As far as The SCO was concerned, the shura had been a complete failure. And it was one hundred percent Coucher's fault. He was brutal in his badgering and beratement, even going so far as to follow Coucher's every move for the rest of the day. I almost felt bad for Coucher. At one point, I witnessed The SCO hurling insults through the latrine door, while Coucher used the toilet inside.

I checked my watch. 0432 hours.

"You awake, Sir?" Terp 2 asked.

"Yup. Have been for a while."

"Me too," he said. "I have been thinking a lot about yesterday."

"About the shura?"

"About Nasir-- and what he said. I think maybe he's right," Terp 2 said.

I sat up on my elbow.

"Right about what? That the voting shouldn't be here?" I asked.

"That Americans shouldn't interfere," he said.

"We're not going to *interfere*," I said defensively. "We're making sure you all don't run it into the ground. It's a complicated process."

"What *is* the process?" Terp 2 asked.

"How the hell should I know. Like I said, it's complicated. I think."

Terp 2 was silent.

"Listen, you wouldn't teach a kid to drive a car by just handing him keys and telling him 'good luck'," I said.

"I've never driven a car," said Terp 2.

"Okay, so you wouldn't teach a kid how to herd goats by giving him the flock and sending him on his way, right? You gotta show him what 'right' looks like."

Terp 2 scowled.

"You think we're all a bunch of goat herders here, don't you?"

"More or less," I grinned.

"Go eat some McDonalds you fat American shit," Terp 2 grumbled.

"Don't talk about McDonalds," Chappy moaned. "I'd murder everyone on this outpost for an Egg McMuffin."

"Very Chaplain like," I said.

"I'll murder both of *you* if you don't quit gabbing," he grumbled. "What the hell time is it anyway?"

"Time to take a piss," I said, kicking back the flap of my musty sleeping bag.

The dim red glow from my flashlight gave the hallways a ghostly aura. A few soldiers who couldn't sleep sat against the walls, drifting into my cone of light like silent apparitions and then drifting out again just as fast. I got the impression the whole outpost was awake, but refused to admit it.

I clicked my light off, as I stepped out onto the southern stoop. From there, I could navigate by moonlight. Passing a ramshackle guard tower, I could barely make out the silhouette of a soldier hunched over his weapon. I wondered if he was awake.

The latrine was essentially a repurposed semi-trailer set halfway to the southern outpost wall. Two sets of blackout curtains served as doors to block the intense white light inside. I squinted down the long aisle of partitioned stalls and foot-pump sinks. There on the wall, next to the first soap dispenser was a familiar face. Set boldly in sweeping black strokes, Kilroy peered from over his imaginary wall.

"Kilroy Was Here," I read aloud.

The vandal's tool still balanced precariously on the edge of the plastic sink, its cap had gone rogue and was resting against the drain stop below. The sweet smell of permanent marker hung in the air, fighting for survival over the rancid funk of stagnant MRE shits. I bent down to see beneath the curtains that served as doors for each toilet stall. At the farthest end of the latrine a pair of boots were visible behind the last curtain.

"You think it's funny to deface government property?" I called down to the boots. There was no movement in the stall.

"At least have the balls to come out and own your artwork," I called again.

Still no movement.

I walked swiftly down the aisle, the toilet curtains billowing in my wake. I was a man on a mission. I was going to find out who this joker was once and for all. I squared up before the final curtain and threw it open.

"Ah-hah!"

****

I shook Captain Jaxon frantically.

"Sir, we're missing someone."

Captain Jaxon groaned in rhythm with the squeaking joints of his cot.

"Immagonnakillya," he mumbled.

"Sir, did you hear me?" I asked, still shaking.

"What do you mean 'we're missing one'?" he slurred without opening his eyes.

"No, Sir," I said. "We're missing *someone*."

The emphasis of "someone" cut through the haze of sleep like Chappy's Kabar. Captain Jaxon's eyes snapped open. His hand shot up, gripped my collar and pulled me in so close our noses nearly touched.

"What do you mean, 'we're missing *someone*'." he hissed.

"It's Coucher, Sir," I explained. "He's gone. I checked with Third Platoon. He's not in his rack."

Captain Jaxon relaxed his grip.

"Stop calling me 'Sir', we're the same rank now," he said. "Third Platoon's on guard duty tonight. Coucher's probably on the wall somewhere."

"Not unless he's on the wall naked, Sir."

Captain Jaxon ran his hands over his face.

"Explain," he said.

"I found his uniform folded up in a latrine stall. His boots, rifle, body armor, NVG's-- everything was there with it. His helmet is still stuck in the toilet bowl."

Jaxon closed his eyes and drew a deep breath.

"Rye?"

"Sir?"

"Next time, you should lead with that information. That's pretty fucking critical information," he said. "Understood?"

I nodded.

Within five minutes, the whole outpost was on high alert. Red beams crisis-crossed every which way, as teams of soldiers scoured every inch of the base for signs of Coucher. I'd headed back upstairs to tell Chappy and Terp 2, neither of which were surprised Coucher was on the lam. Part of me wasn't surprised either. Not after all the hell he'd taken the day before.

Undoubtedly The SCO had already been informed of Coucher's exodus and was now on a tirade in the command post downstairs. I kept listening for the sound of him yelling as the three of us rushed back down the stairs, but the only obscenities were clearly coming from Captain Jaxon.

"Did you know he was leaving?" Jaxon snarled, pointing an accusing finger at me before I was even in the room.

"What?" I stammered. "Why the hell would Coucher tell me he was leaving?"

"Not Coucher," Jaxon yelled. "The SCO."

"What about The SCO?"

"The SCO is gone," Jaxon threw his hands up.

"You think he ran off with Coucher?" I asked.

"Yes, they're having a secret love affair and now they've run off to join the Taliban," Jaxon rolled his eyes. "No, Dingle-Nuts, The SCO is back on Alternator. Him and that fat-ass terp of his must've hopped on one of the resupply birds last night. Apparently everybody just assumes they can come and go off my outpost whenever they feel like it."

He kicked a metal folding chair for effect and it clanged across the bare concrete. I looked back at Chappy, who was already bored by the situation and was stuffing chunks of an MRE pound cake in his mouth. Terp 2 stared with wide eyes.

"I can't believe he didn't tell us he was leaving," I said.

"Tell me about it," lamented Jaxon.

"How the hell are we supposed to get back to Alternator now?"

"Don't know. And don't care," Jaxon said switching gears. "I've got a soldier who has run off into hostile territory. I've gotta find this asshole before he gets his head lopped off."

"So you're sure he ran off?" I asked. "Couldn't have been kidnapped or something? Coucher's dumb, but running off is downright suicidal."

My Officer's Basic Course instructors had made us watch some rather gruesome videos of Taliban beheadings. They said it was to make us understand the consequences of soldiers getting separated and captured. I always assumed it was just to scare the shit out of us. Either way it worked. I didn't even like walking close to the perimeter wall by myself. I'd vowed a long time ago that I'd suck-start the muzzle of my rifle before I ever let myself get captured.

"Well, most kidnappers don't change their victim's clothes at the scene of the crime before making their getaway, dumbass," Jaxon continued, handing me a piece of notebook paper. "Plus we found this folded into Coucher's uniform."

I read the paper with Chappy and Terp 2 hanging over my shoulder.

To Who It Concerns:

Dew to iraqoncilable diffrences, I, Joseph Coucher, hear buy give my resignation as Specalist in the army. I no longer feal like I serve under component leedership and that the mishons I am being asked to do are not in the best intrest of the United State or the Afgans. There four, I've decided to take it upon myself to seak out the Taliban, peal to their cents of reason and make a piece deel, so this nation can begin to heel.

Please do not try to find me. When the time is rite, you will no wear I am.

Love,
Joseph A. Coucher
Formerly of the army

I could hear Chappy scratching the stubble of his bald head.

"I can't believe he spelled 'resignation' right." I said.

"Why'd he sign it "love" at the bottom?" Chappy asked.

Captain Jaxon snatched the note back, folded it up and put it safely in his breast pocket.

"Gonna need that evidence for Court Martialing his ass," he said patting his pocket lightly. "Assuming he isn't dead already."

A wave swept over me. In any other scenario, I'd have been filled with rage toward Coucher, but I couldn't muster it today. In fact, as crazy as it may sound, I was jealous. Not jealous of his situation because his situation was about as bad as situations get. I was jealous of his simple mindset. His blind, albeit misguided, confidence in his own abilities and beliefs drove him to walk out into enemy territory unarmed. I was jealous that his need to make a difference was so great he was willing to ditch every ounce of familiarity to strike out on his own with the soul intent of leaving a positive mark on this world. Jealous that he was shaping his own destiny. Jealous he'd probably never have to deal with The SCO again.

"Kids fucked six ways from Sunday," Jaxon growled. "We'll find him though. Gotta find him. They say you got twenty four hours to find'em before the leads start to go dead. I guess if we don't see him on YouTube, he's probably still doing okay.

"Sir?" Called Jaxon's RTO from the radio at the control desk. He had an open laptop in front of him. "Sir, I think you need to come see this right away."

The four of us lined up behind the RTO's computer. And there it was, in all its shaky, hand-cam glory. SPC Coucher, dressed in a pair of muddied man-jams, being ushered into a dog cage by four masked men. His captors, armed with AK-47s and brandishing hefty arched knives, taunted Coucher as he crawled. To his credit, Coucher was remarkably calm at first. When his captors grilled him for information, he responded only by reciting his name and social security number, just as he was trained. It was only after being denied the phone call he felt entitled to and the opportunity to use "the little boy's room" did Coucher begin to panic.

"Son-of-a-bitch. He couldn't even last six hours outside the wire on his own," Jaxon shook his head. "Now he's gonna be famous."

"Infamous, more like," I said. "What can we do to help?"

"The media's gonna make this kid into some sorta goddamn hero. If they let him keep his head, he'll probably get a book deal out of this," Jaxon scowled. "And *we* aren't going to do anything. *I'm* gonna stay right here for damage control. *You three* are gonna get on the first thing flying and get the hell off my outpost. I don't have the supplies to feed another three damn mouths."

****

We sat on our packs on the edge of the outpost's small airfield. The sun was already scorching the valley and the shade from the Hesco barriers was shrinking every minute. I scootched my boots closer to my ass whenever I felt the heat rising on my toes. Terp 2 dozed next to me, his head leaning so far back I thought his neck would snap. On the other side, Chappy was flipping pages in his camouflage covered Bible and shaking his head.

"I don't think you're allowed to disagree with anything in there," I said.

Chappy rubbed his eyes under his sunglasses.

"I was thinking about something else," he said.

"Coucher?" I asked.

"I know he was picked on a lot and, I get it, he got tons of shit from the SCO yesterday, but common. Now we gotta dedicate all our assets to finding the stupid kid, instead of doing what we came here to do," Chappy slapped the Bible shut. "It was a dick move. He's putting a lot of people in unnecessary danger."

"I'm not sure I've seen a whole lot of 'necessary danger' since I've been here," I said, pulling my feet in closer as my toes smoldered.

Terp 2 stirred a little.

"You know what I mean," grumbled Chappy. "I talked with Coucher a bunch over the last months. He was a nervous little shit, but I never thought he'd bug-out like that. Never thought he was even close. He must have been pretty scared The SCO was going to pull him back to Alternator after his screw up yesterday."

"You never really know what somebody's thinking," I said. "Maybe it *was* delusions of grandeur. He thinks he's going to single handedly win the war. Anybody here says they've never fantasized about playing the war hero is a liar. Going 'Rambo' or 'John Wayne' on the enemy. Hell, the military thrives on men with those fantasies."

Chappy continued venting, but I drifted into a daydream. I was now single-handedly fighting off hordes of Taliban, who fiercely stormed the outpost walls. Bullets cracked against the schoolhouse walls and Hesco barriers, conjuring tiny puffs of dust that vanished in a blink. Those bullets that didn't find a home screamed recklessly past my head before vanishing into the ether. I crawled from cover to cover firing rounds at the advancing radicals, each round finding its mark, as gray curls of smoke arching in every direction from the tails of enemy rockets. Just when the situation was most dire, and I could hold the hostiles off no longer, the familiar thump-thump of rotary wings cut through the air. Reinforcements were on their way.

Chappy rapped my chestplate with the palm of his hand. My heroic fantasy crumbled, but the "thump-thump" remained. Choppers inbound.

The birds weren't coming for us. We weren't special enough. But one group was. Coucher's disappearance had spurred an "all hands on deck" initiative across all of Eastern Afghanistan and Captain Keegan's Special Forces Team, along with teams from other nearby bases, had been spun up and sent to Kherwar to help bolster the search.

The Chinooks touched down in a churning brown cloud of their own creation. Captain Keegan and his men came sauntering down the ramp. Their rugged beards swept the air, catching a fine coat of dust, but they all smiled as they adjusted their "cool guy gear" which seemed to have been individually tailored to their hulking triangular frames. Half of them had their sleeves rolled up. I wished I could roll my sleeves up. They moved in dramatic slow motion through the rotator wash, toward where the three of us had been spilt against the wall with our disheveled gear forming a half circle, hopefully shielding our embarrassment.

What a bunch of asshats, I thought, trying not to stare. I stood and saluted Captain Keegan as he passed.

"Good luck, Sir!" I shouted, hoping that the rotor wash covered the crack in my voice.

"We'll take it from here!" Keegan shouted. He returned my salute with a genuine smile of perfect, gleaming teeth and a charming wink.

Prick.

"What did he think he was taking over from you?" Chappy asked after the team had passed. "Did he think you were somebody important?"

"I am important. Or at least that's what my mom tells me."

"You do know you're the same rank as him, right?" Chappy continue. "You don't have to salute or call him 'sir' anymore."

"I was being respectful."

"I bet if you asked him, he'd let you clean his boots," Chappy smiled. "Maybe polish his rifle."

I led Chappy and Terp 2 across the airfield toward the ramp of the Chinook, but as we approached, the ramp started to rise. I ran forward wildly waving my arms to catch the attention of the tail gunner, who seemed to purposefully avoid looking in our direction. I was finally too close to ignore and he begrudgingly dropped the ramp and met me halfway up. He leaned forward, putting his head right alongside mine.

"What can I do for you, Sir?" He shouted into my ear. I could still barely hear him inside the rotor wash.

"We're supposed to hitch a ride back to Alternator." I shouted, motioning to my two companions behind me.

The tail gunner shook his head.

"Screw yourself, Sir." He shouted.

"What?" I yelled back.

"I said, not on this bird, Sir," he shouted back.

"That's not what you just said," I shouted back, but he continued like he didn't hear me.

"We've been tasked to find your missing douchebag. *All* aircraft have been."

I never understood why tailgunners were such jerks. Probably because they had to deal with so many hitchhikers.

"He's not *my* douchebag," I yelled back. "I'm just the Squadron Air planner."

"Looks like you're really good at your job," he shouted.

"What?" I yelled.

"I said, there's a civilian aircraft coming in behind us to pick you guys up," he pointed off to the east.

"That's not what you said," I shouted again, but he was already walking back up the ramp. The three of us retreated back to the airfield wall, as the Chinook's engines wined. Two escort Apache gunships circled overhead like angry hornets looking for something to sting.

"That tail gunner was a dick," said Chappy. "If he'd have talked to me like that, I'd have punched him in the neck."

"You heard that too?" I yelled as the Chinook left the ground. "I thought I was just hearing things."

We sat there silently baking in the hot sun again, wondering if there was actually a civilian helicopter coming to get us. After a moment, Terp 2 broke the silence.

"Sir, what did you mean earlier when you said you hadn't seen a lot of 'necessary danger' over here?"

I'm sure my face was red.

"I don't know," I said. "I guess I thought it'd be more obvious we were helping. I thought we'd be stacking more bodies than bricks."

We all sat in silence again and I could tell Terp 2 wanted to speak. I was about to head to the command post and radio for another helicopter, when he tugged at my uniform sleeve. His eyes were earnest.

"Sir, it's not always the grand actions that make the most difference," he said.

"What are you, a fortune cookie now?" I joked.

Terp 2 looked confused.

"Nevermind," I said. "I get what you're saying and I'll keep it in mind."

Terp 2 smiled. I made a mental note to learn how to pronounce his real name. It'd been bothering me for a while, still calling him what The SCO called him.

Thump-thump.

Rotors cut through the air again.

"Well hot damn," I said, "looks like they sent another bird after all."

My joy was short lived. The small white body of a helicopter bobbed merrily along through the eastern pass. It weaved like a drunk taking a sobriety test. Ivan was at the wheel. Chappy looked as sick as I felt watching the shaky little helicopter land hard on the red clay. By the time the rotors slowed and we reached the cockpit, Ivan was passed out at the wheel. It was another five hours before he was sober enough to fly us back to Alternator.

Chapter 17: Independence Day

July 4, 2009

Coucher's big head must've been a good luck charm for the Squadron because once he was gone, the wheels fell off. More likely, it was the end of The SCO's shaky alliance with Nasir that did it, but either way, hostilities in the province were on the rise. I felt worst for Lieutenant Harper. As the Squadron's Route Clearance Platoon leader, his unpleasant job was to seek out roadside bombs along key roads and disarm them. His soldiers had been busy.

"Some of them are quite ingenious," Harper had said, while his shaky hand tried to light a cigarette. His right eyelid twitched as he took a long first drag. "What those bastards'll do is put a tire in the middle of a paved road and light it on fire. The heat from the fire softens the asphalt. They scoop out the asphalt, put in their bomb and then smooth it back over. The good ones'll make it look just like new."

"Damn," I said. "How do you find those?"

He took another long drag and rubbed an oily spot on his filthy uniform.

"Most effective way we've found is to run over'em with a truck and get blown the hell up. Then ya know right where they were."

Four days ago, one of the civilian "jingle trucks" delivering food to our cafeteria, struck a bomb and blew our Fourth of July dinner sky high. I didn't see the aftermath personally, but I'd heard it was hard to look at. The thirty foot cargo trailer had been split down the middle. Steaks and lobster tails littered the clay banks along the road. Freedom isn't free, I guess.

This was all insignificant compared to two days ago. Jaxon's boys in Kherwar had finally been able to get their vehicles through the Nazzi Pass, the only known road in and out of the district. The pass had been too treacherous during the wet spring season, but drier weather now made it worth the risk. With their new found mobility, Jaxon had tasked Second Platoon with a mission to the outer reaches of the district in an effort to identify new mountain passes in and out of Kherwar. Routes where the enemy could have smuggled Coucher. Where vehicles go, the bombs followed. The blast rattled the schoolhouse and a billowing black cloud rose from the far side of the village. At Alternator we huddled tensely around the Command Post radio waiting for updates from Captain Jaxon, while Captain Applegate chastised everyone for being in his way. Jaxon could be a jerk, but he was a stone under pressure, even after learning one of his men had died. And here I was, pouting about some squandered surf and turf.

From the reports, it was miraculous only one soldier was killed. The buried bomb had slashed through the engine block, but left the interior of the truck untouched. The only crew member with exposure was the gunner. He'd been standing with his torso through the hatch, scanning the village for threats as they approached. The truck's hood spun off like a boomerang and the gunner's gory lower half had slumped into the hatch's swing seat before anybody even knew what happened. His name was Specialist Boyd. He'd just turned twenty and had a fiancée back home. Seems like they always have a fiancée back home. Or a newborn they hadn't met yet. Or something equally tragic.

It was the Squadron's first KIA and a dark gray cloud settled over FOB Alternator. Obviously, the soldiers in his Platoon were hit the hardest and they were brought back from Kherwar for a few days of rest and relaxation. Whatever that means in rural Afghanistan. We'd even had a memorial service for Boyd, the afternoon before his platoon was to return to Kherwar. To Chappy's credit, the service was tastefully done and he managed through it without cursing once.

After the service, CSM Storms pulled me aside and handed me a folded paper, with instructions to deliver it to The SCO. I tried to refuse it, with no luck. The SCO had been under the weather and no one had seen him for days. When I asked what the note was, Storms smiled his huge smile.

"It's a surprise," he said. "And it's for The SCO's eyes only."

Twilight was fading as I crunched across the gravel toward The SCO's quarters. He had his own private building on the far side of the Squadron Motorpool and, until this point, I'd made it a point to stay away at all cost. I dreaded the conversation to come and prayed he'd be too sick to open the door. My mind strayed as I walked and I imagined myself discovering his near lifeless body on the floor of his room. A discovery that would of course save his life. He'd remember my name then.

Around the building, the ground was littered with shovels and half-filled sandbags. Along the walls, filled sandbags had been stacked chest high in a neat row. Two complete rows lined the roof from end to end and a third had been started. Alternator had never been mortared since we'd been here, but clearly The SCO wasn't confident that luck would hold.

I stepped over a fallen shovel and knocked firmly on The SCO's wood door.

Be assertive and confident, I coached myself.

"Who's there?" Came an angry shout.

"Captain Rye, Sir," my voice cracked.

Dammit.

"Go away, Roy. I'm contagious," The SCO said.

I shook my head.

"I have a note from CSM Storms, Sir. I was asked to deliver it."

There was a moment of silence and then the knob squeaked. I expected light to pour from inside, but the door only opened an inch with darkness behind it. I stood at attention, but my eyes were downcast.

Be confident, dammit.

I set my shoulders back and raised my eyes until they met the barrel of the 9mm pistol The SCO had leveled to my head.

"What the hell?" I stammered, stumbling backward.

"What the hell, *Sir*!" The SCO corrected.

"Sorry. What the hell, Sir?" I repeated, shielding my face with my hand, as if it would stop a bullet.

"Were you followed?" The SCO snarled. He opened the door further now. Maybe six inches. He looked like hell.

"What?"

"Were you followed?" He demanded.

"I-I don't think so," I stammered. "Sir, everyone already knows where you live."

The SCO considered this and lowered his pistol. His eyes were wild and he poked his disheveled head out the door, checking along the sides of the building for any would-be assassins. Satisfied I hadn't been sent to kill him, he opened the door further and smoothed down the wrinkles of his stained undershirt.

"You can't be too careful these days."

His cigar was new and he wrestled it with his tongue to keep it in place as he reached out to collect the note. His hand was nearly transparent. His fingernails long and brittle yellow, except for one he'd been chewing on. I placed the folded note in his hands, avoiding contact, then backed away. My legs were still quaking from having a pistol pointed at my face.

He unfolded the note and I studied him as he read. Even in the limited light, I could tell he was not well. His feet were bare and close in color to the cold concrete underneath them. His toenails rivaled his fingernails in length. I cringed as he raked a big toenail across the concrete while he read. His uniform pants were wrinkled to match his undershirt and his bare arms showcased a skin irritation of crimson sores and sunburn-like flaking. He'd lost weight. His face was pale and gaunt. Darkness hid in the recesses of his cheeks. His eyes carried heavy bags and his hair was reduced to wisps.

"Take a picture while you're at it?" He growled.

"Sorry, Sir." I muttered and studied the ground instead. "Are you feeling any better?"

The SCO stared at me a moment, his jaw set hard on the cigar which was now splitting open in his tight lips. He lifted the note to eye level and glanced at it again, then at me.

"Absolutely not," he growled. "Are you all out of your goddamn minds?"

He crumpled the note and bounced it off the bridge of my nose. Turning on his heels, he slammed the door behind him, leaving me alone in the darkness with the shovels and sandbags.

****

I poked my head into CSM Storms's office. He was leaning back in his pleather office chair, his heels resting next to his keyboard, both hands strapped behind his perfect flat-top. On the corner of his desk sat Major Connick. They were whispering, but I caught the words "batshit crazy" as I entered the room.

"Sorry, to interrupt, Sir and Sergeant Major, the SCO gave the 'go ahead'."

The two men glanced sideways at one another. I could tell they didn't believe me. Major Connick nodded.

"Ok, well, we'll get it underway," said CSM Storms.

I still didn't know what "it" was, but I was afraid to ask what I'd just committed everyone too. I nodded and turned to the door.

“How’d The SCO look?” Major Connick asked. His face was grim. I got the feeling he already knew the answer.

“He looked pretty rough, Sir.”

Connick nodded.

“Thanks for doing that, Jacob,” he said, smiling.

“You’re a jackass, Sir,” I said.

****

The funk that had dogged the Squadron all week had followed Second Platoon to the airfield. There they waited in the dark for their ride back to Kherwar. It was time to bury their feelings. It was time to get back to work. I sat on my Humvee hood and watched their silhouettes drift silently by. Most of the Soldiers sat quietly, leaning against the concrete barriers. No doubt thinking of their lost friend or contemplating the fragility of their own morality or wishing they’d used the bathroom before coming to the airfield. They shifted their asses in the loose pea gravel until they’d dug themselves into makeshift reclining chairs. The American serviceman is, by necessity, a master of ergonomics. Central to their survival is their ability to find comfort where there appears none.

“Rye!”

“Jesus!” I shouted. I was still jumpy from staring down the barrel of a 9mm earlier.

“Hell, Rye, you’re high strung,” Captain Jaxon rested his elbows on the Humvee hood. He’d flown back to Alternator earlier in the day for the memorial.

“Give a guy a warning cough or something next time,” I sighed. “It’s been a weird day.”

“I’d be thankful for a weird day if I still lived here,” he said. “I’ve been back six hours and I’m already contemplating suicide. I don’t know how you stand it.”

“I live vicariously through others, Sir,” I said.

“Stop calling me ‘sir’, Dingle-Nuts. We’re the same rank now.”

“So can I make up a fun nickname for you, too?” I asked. “How about Baldy McShithead? Or just ‘McShit’ for short?”

He smiled.

“If you want me to force feed you your own teeth,” he said.

“Are we winning in Kherwar?” I asked him.

"Winning?" He chuckled. "I don't know, I guess. How do ya gauge winning in a war like this?"

"Body count?" I suggested, trying to pander to Jaxon's typical, hard-charging, "kill'em all and let God sort'em out" machismo.

"That's not really the war we're fighting anymore," he said. "We've started a lot of infrastructure projects; building a schoolhouse closer to the village, building dams, expanding their electrical network, we've even got their radio station repeater up and running. So yeah, I think we're winning. Or at least not losing."

"What a delightfully political answer," I said.

Captain Jaxon stood straight, his bald head reflecting moonlight as he looked from side to side.

"What about The SCO?" He asked.

"What *about* the SCO?" I shifted uncomfortably.

"I've heard he's become—difficult to work with," Jaxon paused. "That he's not *handling* the deployment well."

"He's just been sick lately," I said.

"No bullshit," Jaxon leaned in.

"He's your direct supervisor," I said. "Shouldn't you have a better bead on him than me?"

"I haven't heard a lick from him in two weeks," Jaxon said. "The only people I hear from are Major Connick and The GIF. And fifty percent of those individuals are useless."

"As long as we have Connick, I think we'll be alright," I said.

Captain Jaxon nodded.

"No bullshit," I said. "I don't know what's going on with The SCO, but that altercation with Nasir got him rattled."

Jaxon stayed quiet.

"Do you know what kind of deals he made with Nasir?" I asked.

Jaxon sighed.

"Do I know *exactly* the deal? No," he said. "I do know that he'd assured Nasir he could retain control of Kherwar with a certain, um, autonomy. I think he made the deal before realizing what kind of person he was dealing with."

It was I who leaned in now. My stiff lower back screamed as I pulled up from the Humvee windshield.

"And what kind of person *is* he dealing with?" I ask.

Jaxon backed up a step.

"Easy there, Gabby Gossip," he said. "We've gathered from the locals that he's a pretty bad dude. Even though most of'em are too scared to talk to us. Looks like Garcia was right about this guy afterall. He's a lot worse than The SCO wanted to believe."

"You think he's secretly Taliban?"

"Nah, not Taliban. Sounds like he's got a deep seeded hate for the fanatics. The people that have talked say if he finds out you're Taliban, he whacks you right there on the spot. So, silver lining, the Kherwar hasn't been bothered by the Taliban in a long time."

"If there aren't any Taliban in Kherwar, who's planting bombs?" I asked.

Jaxon ran his hand over his bald head.

"When are those birds supposed to get here?" He asked, searching the sky.

"Come on, dude," I said. "Throw me a bone here. Nobody tells me shit."

"I said you don't have to call me 'sir'. That doesn't mean you get to call me 'dude'," Jaxon chastised. "And this stays between us."

I nodded.

"It may be Nasir and it may not be. He's not exactly popular in his home district. Could be somebody trying to stir up trouble," Jaxon said. "But there's definitely truth to the stories we've been hearing."

Jaxon looked around again and lowered his voice.

"How much did they tell you about the bomb that killed Boyd?"

"That there was a bomb and it killed Boyd," I said.

"After interrogating the bombsite," he whispered, "it's clear Second Platoon missed some obvious warning signs. You know, telltale signs of roadside bomb."

"Why'd they miss'em?" I asked.

"Something was drawing their attention elsewhere," Jaxon said ominously.

"For the love of—," I whispered. "Just spit it out, goddammit."

Jaxon chuckled. Only he could turn a serious topic into a cat and mouse game.

"You remember the old dude with the red dyed beard? The one that spoke up at the Shura?" Jaxon lead.

"I remember him," I said. "Nasir didn't like what he had to say. What about him?"

"Second Platoon found his head on a pike."

"No bullshit?"

"No bullshit," he said. "Posted just a ways outside the village. They hit the bomb right before they got to it."

"Damn, I kinda liked that guy," I said, shaking my head. "I guess that explains The SCO's sudden 'illness'."

"Seemed like a pretty clear message to me," Jaxon said. He checked his watch. "So, really, when are these birds going to be here?"

"BOOM!"

I nearly fell off the Humvee. Even Jaxon took a knee.

A smaller blast rumbled through, as the shell impacted the side of Mount Crumpit. The exploding shell spewed an inferno across the rock face, leaving a glowing patch, burning high on the mountain. One hundred and fifty-five millimeters of white phosphorous.

CSM Storms's voice came over loudspeakers.

"Good evening, Titan Squadron," he called. "In honor of America's birthday and as a final send off for our fallen brother, we have a special treat for you tonight. Keep your eyes on Mount Crumpit. Thank you for all you do to serve our great country. God bless America and God bless Boyd. Now let's burn that mother to the ground."

There was some static in the speaker and then Led Zeppelin's "Stairway To Heaven" began to play. I fumbled my ear plugs in as a barrage of fire unleashed from the Squadron cannons. It was a spectacle to behold. The shells were all white phosphorus and the whole mountain appeared on fire within minutes. Not a single Soldier remained sitting. Every last one was standing, shouting, whooping and hollering. When the song ended and the last round had fired, the soldiers clapped and cheer.

I watched the mountain burn, as Jaxon went to regain control of his men. The mystery of the message in The SCO's note was solved. I was happy to have played my part, even though I hadn't known it would be such a lofty bill for the taxpayers back home. The boys of Cherokee Troop deserved the pick-me-up, but I swallowed hard. CSM Storms had plausible deniability. I'd lied. I was going to be murdered by the SCO after all.

Chapter 18: Election Jitters

August 13, 2009 (Morning)

A bloody, crimson cast washed the gray from the eastern rock walls and flooded the Kherwar valley. The sky was terrifically dyed, as if the clouds themselves were bleeding out. It was fiercely beautiful from the school's window, but I knew the locals would not feel the same. A bad omen. And on the day of Afghanistan's elections.

I looked around the room. My wards were still asleep. The SCO had been giving me garbage chores since the Fourth Of July incident, the latest was to escort a two-man team of Afghan election officials from Alternator to the outpost in Kherwar, where they'd be setting up their polling station. The two officials had arrived to Alternator, by way of Kabul, yesterday evening and we'd made the final leg to Kherwar shortly after midnight. Officially, I was tasked as a personal liaison of sorts, to ensure their trip was smooth. Unofficially, I was there to make sure neither of the corrupt little tallywackers tried to stuff the ballot boxes. Government officials there, as everywhere, were notorious for being easily bought. I was not to let them out of my sight.

I'd been looking forward to getting out from under The SCO's thumb, until The GIF announced he'd be joining the journey. He'd been aching to get some "safe" field-time and had been volunteering to go on recent convoy missions now that the possibility of a small firefight or roadside bomb was on the rise. His hope was for a mortar or rocket to land in his general vicinity or a bomb to blow up a nearby truck, allowing him to write up a few awards for himself and get his Combat Infantryman's Badge.

"The locals will find the voting more 'official' if there's a field grade officer present," he'd said.

The civilian population, especially in Kherwar, had no idea what the U.S. Army rank structure looked like and really didn't give two shits one way or another. I spent that night avoiding conversations with The GIF, which wasn't easy considering he'd taken to giving me baseless tips for going into combat. Fortunately for me, Terp 2 was coming along as well. At least I'd have someone sane to talk too. Though he occasionally had other missions, Terp 2 had become, for all intents and purposes, my own personal translator. My trust in him had single handedly restored my faith in his country.

The two of us sat on the floor of our room with our backs against an old iron heat register that had probably never worked. The election officials slept a few feet away on dirty bedrolls provided by Captain Jaxon's men. Their locked ballot box was placed in the center of the room, reflecting the bloody sky off its dingy aluminum exterior. Terp 2 said he didn't believe in bad omens.

"Now, where will you go to university when you get to the States?" I quizzed.

"Michigan State University?" Terp 2 answered.

"Damn right," I said. "And why will you go there?"

Terp 2 rubbed his eyes and thought for a moment.

"Sir, it is too early for all these questions," he grumbled. "Can I not get more sleep while our guests are also resting?"

We'd arrived shortly after midnight, but Captain Jaxon had only provided a supplemental guard for two hours. The GIF had, of course, commandeered half of Captain Jaxon's sleeping quarters moments after arrival and we hadn't seen him since.

I sipped instant coffee from my canteen cup.

"This is serious. Why Michigan State?" I grilled.

"Because their women are the most beautiful?" Terp 2 answered.

"There ya go," I said, giving him a thumbs up. "He can be taught."

Terp 2 smiled proudly.

"This is if I can ever make enough money to go to America," he said, his smile fading.

"Getting to America isn't the issue," I said. "It's paying for college once you're there that's the real challenge."

Terp 2 looked even more down.

"Don't worry," I continued. "You'll find a way. Maybe write a letter to a university and explain your situation. Most schools are run by bleeding-heart, liberal douchebags anyway. They'd probably eat that shit up and give you a scholarship on the spot."

He smiled again and took a small notebook from his breast pocket.

"How do you spell, 'douchebags'?" he asked.

"Don't they have any universities here?" I asked.

"None are any good," Terp 2 said shaking his head. "There is university in Kabul, but there are few good teachers there."

I tried to picture what a university in downtown Kabul would look like.

"What would you study?"

"I have not decided," said Terp 2. "Politics? Maybe business?"

"Well you better decide that first, before you go writing to the schools. They're going to want to see you have a plan. That you have a passion."

"I want to learn something that will help me make a positive difference when I come back here," he said looking around the room.

I knew he was talking about Afghanistan, but the way he said it made me feel like he meant this dirty side room in the Khewar schoolhouse.

"I didn't think you planned to come back," I said.

"Plans often change," Terp 2 said.

He rested his head against the grooves of the cold heater.

I shut my eyes and daydreamed about an attack on the outpost. This attack was more intense than my last daydream. This time I was wounded rather badly but forced myself to fight on through the blood and gore. For some reason I had a beard like Chuck Norris. Somewhere along the way my daydream became a real dream and then Terp 2 was shaking me awake.

"Sir, are you okay?" he asked. "You were crying in your sleep."

Confusion gave way to embarrassment.

"I wasn't crying," I said. "I was reacting to enemy fire."

Terp 2 tilted his head.

"I don't understand, Sir,"

"I was having a—," I started. "Shut up. I'm fine. Quit looking at me like that."

Terp 2 leaned back against the heater, but watched me from the corner of his eye.

"I said, I'm fine,".

"I know, Sir. I've just never heard a man cry like that," Terp 2 smiled.

"Tell anyone and I'll kill you," I said, jabbing him softly with my elbow.

Thump-thump.

We both looked up, as the distant sound of rotors grew louder. I checked my watch.

Who would be coming to the Kherwar now?

Walking to the eastern window, I searched the red horizon. A familiar white dot bobbed and weaved in the distance. Jingle Air was heading our way.

I snagged a Specialist from the Command Post to watch over the sleeping election officials and headed to the airfield with Terp 2 in tow. Captain Jaxon already stood on the cement stoop outside.

"You expecting company?" He asked.

"I'm not, Marv." It irked Jaxon when I used his first name, so I tried to do it as often and unnecessarily as possible. "The SCO's not coming down until later today, if he comes at all."

The helicopter's bloated white carcass made its approach.

"Ivan's flying straighter than normal," Jaxon observed.

I nodded. He *was* flying straighter. Which meant Ivan was either sobering up or just starting to drink. The helicopter hovered over the airfield and then touched down on the first attempt. I'd never seen Ivan touchdown on the first attempt. As the rotors wound down, Ivan hopped down from the cockpit and ran, not staggered, around the side of the aircraft to open the door for his passengers. His hair was combed and parted, not moving an inch, even in the stiff rotor wash.

"This isn't good," said Jaxon. "Whoever's on there is gonna be an asshole."

"Probably just The SCO coming in early," I grumbled.

"I stand by my statement," said Jaxon. "Listen, I ain't got time to be bogged down by his bullshit all morning. I gotta make sure the election station is setup right for when the villagers start coming in. I can't believe we're letting every asshole and their brother on my base. Mark my words, this is a dumbass idea. If the SCO asks where I am, just tell him I'm 'around' getting stuff squared away."

Jaxon ducked back inside the building and I cringed at the thought of escorting The SCO around all morning. I briefly entertained the idea of hiding in the latrine trailer. The only thought that kept me there, was knowing there'd be hell to pay if no one was there to greet The SCO on the airfield.

"You don't have to stick around for this if you don't want to," I told Terp 2.

"I don't think it is The SCO," he said.

"Why's that?"

"He is worried that the Indian cafeteria workers are trying to poison him," he grinned. "Anyone that paranoid is not going to fly with Ivan."

I couldn't argue, so we waited and hoped that Terp 2 was right.

Ivan had folded out a small step ladder that reached halfway to the ground. He held his hand up to help the first passenger. A portly figure emerged from the cabin and stepped onto the first rung. It flexed under his weight.

"You can't be serious," I mumbled.

I knew who it was before I even saw the mustache. I shouldn't have been surprised. It'd been two months since Coucher had walked off the outpost. An outpost Specialist Thedon had banished him to. I had some suspicions, but Thedon had all but vanished after the incident. I suppose this was his triumphant return. He took a small jump from the bottom rung with all the grace of an individual not accustomed to leaving the ground. Ivan gave him a small bow.

Thedon looked in our direction and doffed his helmet, as his two goons descended the ladder behind him. Together, they hurried toward the north end of the airfield where a small receiving party of Specialists had magically materialized.

"So damn weird," I mumbled.

The show wasn't over though. Ivan went back to the ladder. Even in full body armor, helmet, and eye protection, I could tell the next two passengers were female soldiers. Being on deployment with a unit composed almost exclusively of men for eight straight months really gives a guy a sixth sense for that sort of thing. Behind these androgynously dressed, yet somehow sexy, female soldiers stepped a large male figure. In full kit, his chest filled the entrance of the helicopter. His mirrored aviators barely moved as he bypassed the ladder and hopped effortlessly out of the bird. He was a futuristic gunslinger, with his pistol holstered to his thigh. Colonel Gunn had arrived.

They spotted us immediately and began walking in our direction. Lieutenant Barrett and Sergeant Loredo were already shedding their cumbersome body armor. Barrett removed her helmet and shook out her long locks like she was in a damn shampoo commercial. Or at least that's how I remember it. It was all in slow motion.

"This is going to be bad," grumbled Terp 2.

"Might not be *all* bad," I said, still watching the Colonel's assistants.

I stood at attention and rendered a salute as the Colonel approached.

"Captain—,' Colonel Gunn called, returning my salute.

His eyes dropped to my name tape.

"Captain Rye," he said, flashing his broad smile. "Good to meet you. I've heard a lot of good things about you."

I looked around to see if there was another, more deserving Captain Rye standing behind me. Seeing as there wasn't, I gave a half wave and suddenly couldn't remember if I'd already saluted or not. I snapped to attention again and rendered another salute. The whole series of movements was seizure-like in nature. Barrett and Loredo giggled behind the colonel.

The Colonel returned my bobbled salute with a crisp, clean one and only a hint of annoyance. With both hands on his hips, he took a moment to take in his surroundings. He looked like he should be wearing a cape.

"So this is the Kherwar Outpost," he marveled with a chuckle. "Rustic!"

"Yes, Sir," I said. I'd fully intended to elaborate on that impressive response, but the words died in my mouth before they could circumvent my teeth.

Silence is golden, thought half my brain.

You're a moron, thought the other half.

Loredo laughed. I was counting that as a win. The Colonel was unfazed by the level of awkward I'd achieved.

"Where's The SCO?" he asked. "I'd have thought he'd come out to greet me."

"Um, well, Sir," I stuttered. "He's not here yet. I believe he's coming down later this morning or early afternoon."

The Colonel looked disappointed, but dismissed it just as quickly.

"I could go get Captain Jaxon for you, Sir," I suggested. "He's in command here."

"Nonsense," said the Colonel. "He needs to focus on the tasks at hand. I'm not staying long. Just making my rounds to the voting stations."

I was impressed he was flying with Ivan, unarmed, in broad daylight, with no armed aerial escorts.

"Well, Rye," he continued, checking my name tape again, "since you're the only one here that had the balls to receive us, you get to show us around."

With that, the Colonel turned and walked swiftly along the side of the schoolhouse. His posse followed suite, while Terp 2 and I jogged to catch up.

"You can begin tour guiding anytime now," Colonel Gunn called over his shoulder.

I looked at Terp 2 for support. He only shrugged. I could tell he was looking for any justifiable excuse to cut and run.

"Sir, I'm probably not the best person for that. I don't—"

"I'm not looking for a book report, Rye," he interrupted. "Just tell me what you know."

"Yes, Sir," I said. "Well, as you already know, this building used to be a schoolhouse back before the Soviet's occupation. Most recently, it was home to a platoon of Afghan National Police, but every last one of them disappeared. Well, everyone but their captain, whose head we found inside."

The Colonel was silent a moment. I wasn't sure if he was listening at all.

"You're right," he finally said. "I did already know all that."

He tossed a pity-grin over his shoulder. Again, I looked behind myself to confirm it was I he was addressing. As I looked back, I saw Captain Jaxon dart from the schoolhouse to the latrine trailer. With a cocky smile, he flipped me the bird before ducking inside.

"Do we know why the police platoon packed up so quickly?" the Colonel asked.

"My guess is the decapitation of their commander was a motivating factor," I said. I honestly wasn't trying to sound like a smartass. Barrett and Loredo raised their eyebrows and I held my breath through an eternity of silence.

The Colonel's laugh rolled like thunder.

"I guess I should have clarified," he chuckled. "Do we know for sure who's lopping heads off down here?"

"Captain Jaxon would be better suited to answer that, Sir," I said.

"Well Captain Jaxon isn't here."

"I believe they have a list of suspects, Sir," I said. "But nobody has definitive proof."

"And what do *they* think about this Nasir fella I've been hearing so much about?" The Colonel raised a curious brow.

"I believe he made the list, Sir. But nobody has definitive proof," I repeated.

"Have you met the man?" He asked.

"I have, Sir. Multiple times."

"The SCO seemed to have trusted him, but I know he was opposed to the outpost. Do you trust his intentions?" The Colonel asked as we reached the northern end of the building.

"I trust him as far as I can throw him, Sir," I touted. I checked to see if Barrett and Loredo were impressed with my bravado. They were hiding it well.

"I don't trust the intentions of *anyone* from this country." I added and immediately wished I hadn't. I could taste the boot in my mouth. I hoped Terp 2 had made his escape and hadn't heard me, but when I looked back he was shaking his head, his eyes fixed on the dirt.

We rounded the corner of the schoolhouse to find The GIF pumping vigorously on the foot pedal of a portable water station. He apparently wasn't concerned about the outpost's limited water supply, as he diligently bathed himself in the meager flow of water. We were directly behind him before he realized he had an audience. He turned to meet us, his face dripping and his orange hair matted to his scalp. He rubbed the water from his eyes and then realized who stood before him. He snapped to attention. Water trickled from his chin and pinballed through the sparse hair of his bare chest, disappearing under the fold of his man-boobs. His salute was even more awkward than mine had been. Barrett looked nauseous.

"Good morning, Sir," The GIF sputtered. "I wasn't expecting to see you here."

His toes curled anxiously across the top of his flip-flops.

"Why would you be expecting me, soldier? I hadn't told anyone I was coming," the Colonel said, returning his salute.

My heart was overcome with joy as it registered with The GIF that Colonel Gunn didn't recognize him. His frustration was delightful and I tried hard not to do one of those embarrassing snort-laughs.

"Now, son," Colonel Gunn said, putting his arm around The GIF's bare shoulders. The Colonel was a mountain by comparison, though The GIF bested him in circumference. "I know we're a long way outside of regular Army life, but it's important for us to uphold our standards. Do you understand?"

The Colonel motioned to The GIF's physical state, from head to toe.

"Without our standards, we're no different from the enemy. Isn't that right?" He asked.

The GIF's pale complexion shifted to neon red so quickly he reminded me of heating wires inside a toaster. For a brief second I longed for the breakfast I'd missed.

"Yes, Sir." The GIF squeaked. "I'm sorry, Sir."

"Don't be sorry, son. Just be all you can be. You'll make a great soldier someday."

I hoped, with all my being, the Colonel would call him "slugger" and give him a rap on the chin or a pat on the ass.

"And as far as *this* goes," Colonel Gunn said, giving The GIF a playful pat on his protruding stomach. "Maybe lay off the MRE pound cakes a while."

Gunn gave him a wink and The GIF, with a nod, put his chin on his chest in defeat.

I snorted.

Shit.

I finished the rogue giggle into an elaborate sneeze as cover. It must've been too elaborate. Barrett and Loredo backed away in disgust.

"Good God, Captain. Are you dying?" The Colonel chuckled.

I pretended to wipe my nose, but I knew I hadn't fooled The GIF. I was going to pay for that later.

"Alright son, go get your uniform on and get to work" The Colonel said, turning back to The GIF. "We've got a war to win."

The GIF rendered the saddest salute and trotted off toward the schoolhouse, his tail between his legs. The Colonel watched him until he disappeared through the building's doorless entrance. He folded his hands behind his back and raised himself on the balls of his feet.

"Find out who that man's squad leader is," he said, "and make sure he's on shit burning duty for a week."

"I don't think they burn their shit here, Sir," I said, "they've got a latrine trailer."

"Well, have the latrine removed. Or have that guy's squad leader burn the latrine itself. I don't care, but somebody in that boy's life needs to be burning shit. I want that guy's leader to make his life a living hell until he knows how to act like a soldier. Undisciplined assholes like that will get people killed."

"Yes, Sir," I wished I could tell him "that guy's leader" was actually the SCO. I imagined The SCO on shit burning detail and made a mental bookmark to come back to that fantasy later.

We proceeded with our tour toward a large green tent north of the schoolhouse. Late last month, Captain Keegan's Special Forces Team had rotated back home to America and a new National Guard Special Forces team had taken their place at Alternator. Last night, the new team had flown into Kherwar with a platoon of forty-four Afghan National Army soldiers, with the intent to put an "Afghani face" on the election by having them provide the outpost's security for election day. The new SF team's job was to provide guidance, keep the undisciplined soldiers from abandoning their post, and keep them from accidentally, or intentionally shooting each other. A job commonly referred to as "herding cats". The green tent, meant to accommodate the entire newly arrived force, had already become too hot for the Afghan soldiers to bear and the ground outside the entrance was littered with sleeping bodies, as if the tent itself had spewed them out.

The Colonel stopped and surveyed the mess.

"When did you say The SCO will be arriving?" He asked. "I would hope he'd instill some discipline on this post once he arrives."

"I believe he's coming down later this morning, Sir," I said.

"And what was his reason for not being here already?" The Colonel probed.

I didn't want to cover for The SCO, but I didn't want to throw him under the bus and ultimately screw myself either.

"I believe he's trying to arrange to have medical supplies brought down for Handboy," I lied.

"Ah, yes, Handboy. And what all can you tell me about this 'Handboy'?"

"That he's an excellent artist and a bit of a perv," I said.

The Colonel's eyebrows raised over his aviators.

"We know that he and Nasir are brothers," I offered up. "The SCO has had—mixed feelings—about helping him."

"I should hope so," Colonel Gunn scoffed. "That could end up a media disaster. We don't even know how the little bastard mangled his hand in the first place. Maybe he was trying to blow up some Americans and it backfired on him. Maybe the boy should stay a cripple. It's harder to plant bombs with a wonky hand."

"Nasir claims Americans did it."

"See!" The Colonel shouted. "Our soldiers don't go around shooting adolescents for nothing. They must have had a good reason. Do we know when it happened?"

"Early 2002," came a voice from the tent entrance. "A Special Forces' breach team accidentally blasted his hand with their shotgun. Kid grabbed the inside door handle at the wrong time."

From the dark interior of the tent stepped a man more akin to a train-hopping drifter than an U.S. soldier. Behind me, I heard Loredo whisper something about how tragic the "homeless veteran epidemic" had become.

"Captain Russell, Sir," the drifter said, holding out his hand to the Colonel, who looked at it curiously. Captain Russell looked around at the surrounding hillsides. "Forgive me for not saluting, Sir, but the walls of this outpost aren't very tall and we don't exactly have the high-ground."

The Colonel looked at him like he was a leper. Easily in his forties, Captain Russell's hair was long and unkempt, his beard wild and dusty. His uniform top had been discarded somewhere and his undershirt was painted over an oval belly that drooped far below the bottom of his rigger belt. His pants were cuffed at the bottom, exposing flip-flop thongs over his tanned feet. I'd met him only once before on Alternator, where he'd addressed me as "dude", "man", and "brother" within the span of thirty seconds.

"Aren't you a sight to behold," The Colonel said, reluctantly shaking his hand.

"Assimilation, Sir," Captain Russell smiled cheerfully behind his big beard. Crows feet gathered at the corners of his eyes.

"Setting quite the example for your elite squad here." The Colonel motioned to the regurgitated soldiers on the ground. "Perhaps the assimilation should've gone in the other direction."

The smile never faded from Captain Russell's face.

"How did you come by your information?" The Colonel asked. "Our intel guys haven't reported that to me yet."

"I have a—unique—history with this region," said Captain Russell. "Plus, our team has access to some--unconventional intel avenues."

"Have you told The SCO that yet?" I asked. I felt like a child interrupting an adult conversation.

"Have you told The SCO yet?" The Colonel asked.

"I did, Sir. He was rather distraught about the whole thing."

"If I were Handboy, I'd be pretty angry," The Colonel said. "Nasir too. Especially after that boob of a Lieutenant accidently shot him earlier this summer."

More giggling from Barrett and Loredo.

Suddenly, there was shouting from inside the tent. The altercation was in Pashtun and I had no idea what was being said. For the first time, Captain Russell's smile sank.

"What the hell is it now?" He grumbled turning toward the door.

A shot rang out, as a bullet ripped through the tent wall.

Chapter 19: Election Elation

August 13, 2009 (Afternoon)

I was glad I wasn't the only one dick-down in the dirt. By the second shot, even Colonel Gunn was soiling his fresh-pressed uniform. The only one left standing was Captain Russell and when the second bullet was ripping out of the tent, he was running in. He was agile for a man of his age and waistline. Effective too. In seconds, the "all clear" came from within. There was shouting and the sound of a struggle, followed by the distinct sound of flesh impacting flesh, and then silence. Captain Russell emerged, flanked by two more Special Forces hippy-drifters. Behind him, he dragged a mildly conscious ANA soldier, whom he thrust into the dirt next to us. The soldier's hands were already zip-tied behind his back.

Colonel Gunn was first back to his feet. His pistol drawn, he brushed the dust from his puffed-up chest with his free hand. He looked back at the rest of us disparagingly. Frankly, I was impressed with my reaction. I'd never been shot at before, even if it was indirect. I was more relieved I hadn't stood around like a slack-jawed clod than I was relieved to be alive. Barrett and Loredo were next up and dusted each other's chests and thighs. In retrospect, they were probably dusting themselves, but I prefer to remember it this way. Lieutenant Barrett caught me staring and gave me a dirty look. Not the good kind. She nudged Loredo, who already looked pretty cross about the whole ordeal and discreetly flipped me the bird.

Captain Russell had his hands on his knees. The sudden physical exertion had caught up with him. The Afghan soldier spit the dirt from his mouth, as his left eye inflated. He began shouting frantically.

"He's says he's innocent," Terp 2 said, still down on a knee. "He says it was self-defense."

"Of course he does," wheezed Captain Russell. "That's what you say after you shoot somebody dead."

"Who'd he shoot?" The Colonel demanded. He craned his neck for a peek inside the tent.

"His platoon leader," Captain Russell shook his head. "Nothing like dealing with an inter-platoon homicide before my morning bowel movements."

"Plural?" I asked.

"What was the altercation about?" The Colonel asked.

"Altercation, Sir?" Captain Russell scoffed. "ANA officers are typically rich-kid-asshats that only look after themselves. They don't usually last long. Although, normally their soldiers have the common sense to wait until they're out on a mission before they frag'em."

The ANA soldier was still rambling in Pashtun through gulping sobs. Captain Russell was fluent and followed the whole thing. The Colonel pretended to understand, taking cues from Russell's body language, nodding in most of the right places on a two second delay.

"What is he talking about?" I whispered.

"He claims the platoon leader tried to recruit him to help disrupt the election. When he refused," Terp motioned to the soldier, "the platoon leader threatened him with his pistol. He says he wrestled the gun from him and shot him."

The Colonel looked relieved to finally know what was going on.

"Ask him why his platoon leader wanted to disrupt the election," he directed Captain Russell. The soldier began spattering again out the side of his mouth, with his face half in the dirt. His left eye was swollen shut, so I'm sure all he could see was our boots.

"He says he doesn't know why," Captain Russell rolled his eyes. "He thinks maybe the guy's family had connections to a candidate. Makes sense. These young Afghani officers will often get their position through political connections."

Two more Afghani soldiers emerged from the tent carrying the corpse on the canvas cot he'd died on. A thick green blanket covered from head to shin and two grunge, bare feet pointed out in either direction.

"If you can't trust your officers, who can you trust?" The Colonel grumbled.

"I couldn't agree more," I thought.

The soldiers bobbed the cot along the schoolhouse toward the airfield.

"Sir, can 'the stiff' hitch a ride back with you guys?" Captain Russell asked. "It's a beast getting air support and custom dictates they bury the dead within twenty-four hours of expiration.

The Colonel turned up his nose.

"Ivan won't be happy," he said. He looked at Barrett and Loredo whose mouths were turned down in grotesque displeasure. "But he'll make do. Desperate times."

The man on the ground now sat cross-legged in the dirt, his hands still zip-tied behind him. The right side of his face was caked with dust and dirt. He resembled a sad Phantom of The Opera.

"And what about this one?" The Colonel asked, pointing with his pistol at the man's head.

"We'll keep him here while I do more *investigating*," Captain Russell said, digging the toe of his sandal in below the man's ribs. "I believe Jaxon has a makeshift detention center we can throw him in for now."

"I'll take him," I quickly volunteered. Anything to get out of this tour.

The Colonel used his pistol to point at me now.

"You're my tour guide. You're not going anywhere," he said.

I wished people would stop pointing guns at me.

"Speaking of Captain Jaxon, I haven't seen that bastard yet," Gunn continued. "Where do you suppose he's hiding?"

He wasn't looking for an answer. Without so much as a 'goodbye' or 'good luck' to Captain Russell, the Colonel continued on his walk.

We made a full lap of the perimeter before arriving back at the schoolhouse entrance where we'd began. Ivan's chopper sat lifeless, an unnatural, brilliant white against the red clay backdrop. Ivan's legs protruded from the cockpit door. The dirty feet of the deceased ANA officer stuck out from the passenger door on the other side.

The Colonel checked his watched and surveyed the area. He tapped his foot impatiently.

"0828," he said. "Two minutes and we'll be out of your hair."

"Should I go wake up Ivan, Sir?" I asked.

"You can really see the whole outpost from right here," he said, shaking his head. "Kind of makes our whole little tour seem a bit asinine, don't you think?"

"I guess, Sir."

"Well, why'd you let me do it then?" He seemed annoyed all of a sudden. "Were you trying to waste my time?"

I could hear his two harpies sniggering behind me. Terp 2 faded back a step. I swallowed hard and stood straight.

"Far be it from me to question your directives, Sir. Besides, it's important that the men see the leaders they admire out among them."

The Colonel smiled.

"Ryan, you're right. That was a fine decision on my part; getting out in the dirt with the fighting men. Suffering and enduring with them. I feel renewed. And I bet they feel the same."

"Did you want to tour inside the schoolhouse, Sir?" I asked.

"Oh, God no. That place looks like a disease-infested, shit-hole."

From the north end, two uniformed gorillas entered the airfield with Specialist Thedon in the lead. Thedon was visibly upset at the sight of the dead ANA officer. One of his goons picked up a barefoot and let it drop, his head bouncing in rhythm with the foot. The second goon made his way around the bird and shook vigorously on Ivan's legs. Through the windshield, Ivan's torso shot into view and he sat rigid in his seat. The chopper's blades slowly began turning as he geared up the engines.

"We'd best be off, so we don't get left behind," the Colonel said. "He's on a tight schedule."

"What, Sir? I asked, as the rotors thumping grew louder and faster.

"I said, I'm on a tight schedule," the Colonel said. "Tell Captain Jaxon it's bad form not to greet a senior officer when they visit his outpost."

"Yes, Sir."

"Also tell him to smoke the shit out of that chunky, orange haired Private we saw taking a bath at the handwashing station."

"Yes, Sir."

I couldn't wait to tell *everyone.*

"And Captain" he shouted, "mixed feelings or not, if America's responsible, the SCO needs to help that Handboy. If you see Handboy today, you tell him help is on the way."

I was impressed by Colonel Gunn's concern.

"The press will eat that shit up," he added. "We'll look like goddamn heroes."

Obligation lifted my hand to salute, but the Colonel had already turned his back.

"And don't salute," the Colonel yelled without looking back. "If I get shot in the face, I'm going to be very upset with you."

The Colonel's vipers hissed at me and followed their charmer. Terp 2 and I watched them walk away with considerable interest. Within minutes the *thump-thump* was fading off into the skyline and the outpost returned to its dust-muffled silence. Tension eased from my shoulders.

"So, what'd *he* want?"

"Jesus!" I nearly jumped out of my skin.

"Nope, just me," grinned Captain Jaxon.

"That's Chappy's joke. It's a sin to steal a Chaplain's joke."

Jaxon rolled his eyes.

"What'd he want?"

"To see the polling station," I said.

"But he didn't come into the polling station," he argued.

"He also wants you to vet Handboy. Find out if it's true that U.S. soldiers caused his mangled hand. And if it was our fault, get him help. Regardless of what The SCO wants."

Jaxon rolled his eyes again.

"Did you tell the Colonel *you're* responsible for one mangled hand?" He asked.

"I didn't see how that would've been beneficial to our conversation. But he wants to make Handboy a priority."

"I'll send him a 'Get Well Soon' card," Jaxon said. "The SCO radioed while you were out for a stroll with your new friends. He's not coming. He doesn't want the election to look like an American-led ordeal. He said it would put more of an Afghani face on it without him here. He's also really pissed at you."

"Pretty standard," I sighed. "What'd I do this time?"

"He's pissed about the Colonel coming down."

"How the hell is that my fault?" I asked.

"He said, and I quote, 'Rye's the goddamn Air Officer, he controls the airfields, he shouldn't have let the helicopter land'," Jaxon laughed. "Anyway, he forbids you from talking to the Colonel unsupervised in the future."

I could feel the pulse in my palms and my knuckles ached from clenching. I decided, then and there, to submit my paperwork to leave the Army at the end of my contract.

"Don't kill the messenger," Jaxon said, raising his arms as he walked back into the schoolhouse.

****

The polls opened promptly at 0900 hours. Villagers trickled in shortly thereafter and by 1100 hours we actually had a line forming at the front gate. The gates were manned and regulated by ANA soldiers, who were manned and regulated by Captain Russell and his band of Jerry Garcia look-alikes. Everyone had a job today. Everyone except me. So I sat with Terp 2, who'd been tasked to provide verbal instructions to everyone arriving to cast their vote. The instructions were simple:

Put your thumb in the ink. Press your thumb under the name of the candidate you'd like to win.

The voting station consisted of one table, the large steal ballot box, two stacks of ballots, and two purple ink pads. All day long, villagers quietly filed in and out, leaving their smudged, purple print on history. I wondered how many had any concept of how momentous this day was for them. It certainly wasn't lost on Terp 2.

It was the most excited I'd ever seen Terp 2. I was happy for him, but he was still bitter toward me for the disparaging comments I made to Colonel Gunn. He wasn't talking, so I was bored out of my skull. You can only watch people pressing purple appendages for so long. To curb my boredom, I made myself 'Hall Monitor Supreme' for the day. A few Purple Thumbs had become disoriented on their way out, so I took it upon myself to keep everyone out of the south end of the school house, where the ANA soldier was being detained.

The makeshift prison cell was guarded by two more ANA soldiers who'd been handpicked by Captain Russell himself. They were the best he had. The cream of the crop. They lay on the floor on either side of the door, with their caps pulled low over their eyes. Every hour, I'd walk down and kick their boots to make sure they were still conscious. Most of the time, they weren't.

This was on top of my original responsibility of making sure the, so-called election officials didn't shit the proverbial bed. An hour into voting, one official was asleep on the floor. The other rested his chin on the rickety-ass, voting station table, flicking his pencil and watching it roll back to him over and over.

"Better not be stuffing each other's boxes in here," Captain Jaxon shouted as he entered the room. He took the chair vacated by the sleeping voting official. "How goes it? Good turnout?"

"Good as can be expected, I guess," I said. "They all look suspicious. Like we're gonna detain'em and ship'em off to Guantanamo."

Most of the voters were wild-eyed entering the room and Terp 2's fast talking excitement wasn't helping. They had the air of beasts being lured onto the slaughterhouse floor.

"Half of them probably deserve it," Jaxon sneered. "They'd just as soon kill ya, as look at ya."

Terp 2 cleared his throat.

"Common, don't piss on his parade," I said to Jaxon.

"Course, it won't be too long and we'll be outta here," Jaxon continued. "And they can go back to kill'n each other over goats."

Terp 2 cleared his throat louder.

"Get a goddamn drink if you're parched," Captain Jaxon yelled at him.

"Leave him alone, Marv," I said. "Guys like him are the only chance this country has, so quit dumping on the one thing that's making him optimistic."

Jaxon shook his head.

"Sorry, if I offended your girlfriend. I just don't think a forced democracy is much of a democracy," Jaxon explained, standing back up again. He checked his watch. "Break time's over, ladies. Back to being a badass. Two more hours of this clown-show and we're closing the front gate."

Pop.

We all heard it. We all froze.

Pop. Pop. Pop.

Jaxon bolted out the door and rushed down the hall in the direction of the gunfire.

"Don't take your eyes off the ballet box," he called as he ran.

There were shouts from outside and then the guard tower machine guns began returning fire. The shots were coming from the front gate and I wanted desperately to check out the action.

I looked back into the room to find the remaining voters sitting calmly on the floor, huddled in a windowless corner. They looked like they'd done this before. Finally, something familiar for them.

It figures I'd be stuck on the bottom floor of a cement building during the only firefight I'd ever been close too. I briefly considered leaving Terp 2 in charge and going out to join the fray. The voters were placid enough, but the two election officials were awake and alert now. They watched me with interest and I could tell the crooked bastards were waiting for me to abandon post, so they could do all sorts of sordid things to lady liberty.

My angst was short-lived and the firefight was over as quickly as it had started. By the time the Apaches began buzzing overhead, the outpost was back to its normal activities. The exchange of gunfire had served its purpose though. As soon as it was safe, the locals began to leave, many without casting their vote. Terp 2 was furious.

Before long, Captain Jaxon reentered the room. He still wore his armor and dust clung to the sweat on his forehead and jaw.

"Everything alright in here?" He asked, still puffing.

"Haven't seen anybody new since you left," I said.

"I doubt you will," said Jaxon. "Harassing fire from the south hills. Lots of caves up there, so the Apaches didn't get a bead on anything. Too far off to be accurate, but either way, the message to the voters was clear. The whole outpost is clearing out."

Suddenly, Jaxon looked puzzled. He leaned back and poked his head into the hallway.

"Where are the guards?"

"The guards?"

"The guards. The ANA turds that were guarding the other ANA turd that killed the ANA officer turd."

"They're not there?" I asked.

Jaxon closed his eyes in tired frustration.

"How the hell am I supposed to know?" I grumbled. "You told me to stay here."

Jaxon hurried from the room, muttering under his breath. I followed close behind with Terp 2 on my heels. If the guy was gone, it was gonna be my ass on the platter. Not because I was responsible for him, but because I'd been the officer geographically closest to him.

Jaxon jogged down the hall, reaching the door a few steps ahead of me. He flung it open, quickly turning and walking back toward me.

"He's still there," his face was gray. "He's still there. Shit. Shit. Shit."

I kept on past him until I too stood in the doorway. Terp 2 crowded in behind me, only for a second before he turned and heaved his lunch back into the hallway. The prisoner was still there alright. He lay on his back in an inky pool. His face was expressionless, but the smile carved in his neck was ear to ear.

Chapter 20: Night Of The Purple Thumbs

August 14, 2009 (Barely)

"Are you still awake?" I asked. I could barely see Terp 2's outline across the room. An ocean of black poured through the window and flooded the space between us. No moon tonight.

"Of course I am," he whispered. "Because you keep asking me if I am awake."

"Sorry," I said. "I can't stop seeing it."

The ANA soldier and his gashed neck, hovered over me like a bloody specter. The face was pale between smeared patches of crimson warpaint, its tongue lolling from the corner of sagging lips.

Not even the severed head of the former ANP Captain had affected me so much. Only two other events in my life had seared an image into my brain so permanently. The first was the dripping carcass of a whitetail deer. My father had shot, skinned, and hung it from its neck in our garage when I was five years old. I'd refused to eat meat for a month. The second was the centerfold of a July 1986 Playboy my friend David Fitz had lifted from behind his dad's workbench. I was twelve at the time and my relationship with meat improved dramatically.

"Seeing the ANA soldier's slashed neck has really got me thinking," I said. "I know I keep complaining about being a combat officer that's never been in combat, but between you and I, I'm not sure I could handle seeing that carnage all the time. I don't know. Maybe you get desensitized after a while. Maybe everyone starts out this way. Maybe it's like television violence and rap music; you just have to shock your way into indifference. You know what I mean?"

The blackness absorbed my words and I squinted into the void.

"Terp 2, did you hear me?"

I was answered by a light snore.

Lucky bastard.

The silence was almost as unbearable as the paranoia that came with it. After all, there was a murderous, throat-slicer somewhere in the area. I pictured my own throat cut ear to ear in the same ghastly smile. I tried to shake the image from my mind.

Sitting up on my elbows, I strained to see the two lumpy silhouettes of the election officials. I almost felt bad for them. Almost.

They'd taken a vicious verbal assault from Captain Jaxon at the end of the day, but they'd earned it. Seconds after we'd discovered the dead ANA soldier, we realized the voting room had been left unsupervised. Jaxon looked more nauseated by this realization than he had about the body. We both started running and entered the room to the sound of folding chairs scratching across concrete. Both officials sat where we'd left them, fervently studying the far corners of the room and refusing eye contact. Both their thumbs were dyed deep purple. The stack of ballots was gone and the metal voting box overflowed from the slot in its lid. It was about this time The GIF made his second appearance of the day, giddy with excitement about the firefight he hadn't participated in and the possibility that he could now get his Combat Infantryman's Badge. To Captain Jaxon's credit, he calmly excused himself from the room before succumbing to a meltdown.

After some investigation, it was determined the election officials' voting fraud had been a target of opportunity and unrelated to the dead ANA soldier outside of its convenience as a distraction. Captain Russell was brought in to account for his two missing guards and after a chaotic roll-call, it was discovered that one was missing. The missing guard's uniform was found later in a broom closet two doors down from the voting station. He'd likely changed into civilian clothes, cast a vote, and then slipped out with the other purple thumbs. The second guard had excused himself to the latrine. Upon his return, he saw the commotion and, deciding we had the situation under control, excused himself again to take a nap. Or at least that was his story. He was tasked with mopping up the dead soldier's blood.

Somewhere in my recollections of the day, I finally drifted off to sleep. In a dream, I watched from above as three dark figures hovered over my sleeping body, quietly arguing over who'd get the pleasure of slitting my throat.

"Wake up, Dingle-nuts."

I yelped and grabbed for my rifle.

"Relax," coaxed another voice. I could faintly see the outline of Captain Russell's unruly beard.

"What time is it?" I grumbled.

"Does it matter?" This time it was The GIF. I quickly flipped from confusion to annoyance.

"It matters, Sir, because people are getting their throats cut and you three are creep'n in the dark," I said with a little too much sass.

A red-lens flashlight clicked on, illuminating the three men's faces in an eerie red glow.

"We're in Afghanistan, smartass. There are murderers on the loose all day, every day," said The GIF.

"What is going on?" Terp 2 mumbled from across the room.

"What's going on, is we've got a situation at the front gate," said Captain Jaxon.

Jaxon paused just to piss me off. I took the bait.

"For God's sake, just spit it out," I barked. "How's a situation at the front gate involve me *at all*?"

"There's a visitor and he won't speak to anyone else."

"Really?" I asked, suddenly feeling important. "They asked for me?"

"Not you. Him," said The GIF. His stumpy finger pointing at Terp 2.

****

The front gate of the outpost was miniature replica of the gate on FOB Alternator. The Hescos were shorter, the serpentines tighter, and the guards, fewer. The location of the gate had been dictated by the location of the old ANP guard shack, which was now being used for its original purpose. The sole window in the shack had been boarded up and white light escaped through the cracks in its warped, plank door.

Terp 2, Captain Jaxon, Captain Russell, The GIF, and I entered the small building. The GIF, being the last to enter, left the door hanging wide open. He frequently and unsolicitedly explained this bad habit as an attempt to improve ventilation and prevent the onset of his ridiculous dust-migraines.

The guard shack was larger than I remembered. The mounds of trash that had made the floor unwalkable, were gone and the only remaining feature from our first visit was the rough desk where we'd found the traffic log so many months ago. At that same desk, Handboy sat, where he'd probably sat months earlier sketching his busty fantasies. In front of him sat a small notebook and he tried clumsily to sketch a picture with his bandaged hand. With a rogue wire off his caged hand, he scratched frustrated grooves in the table's surface and gritted his teeth with every misplaced pencil stroke. He was so intent on his drawing, he barely acknowledged us entering. A weathered black backpack was slung over the shoulder of his chair, half hidden in the shadow of the single light bulb that swayed overhead. It was the classic "interrogation room" setup.

When he finally noticed our arrival, or to be more accurate, Terp 2's arrival, a broad smile washed the frustration from his face. He was less excited to see me. He slid his bandaged hand beneath the table and out of view. He was trying to make me feel bad and it worked. Captain Jaxon had discouraged me from coming, fearing my presence would frighten the boy into silence and blow an opportunity for good intel. I reminded Jaxon that Colonel Gunn had tasked me in the Handboy matter and he begrudgingly allowed me along.

Before I could ask, Terp 2 was laying on another round of apologies for me. He and Handboy chatted excitedly while The GIF lamented loudly about the brightness of the single lightbulb and the excessive noise from the generator humming away outside.

"Terp 2, just find out what he wants," The GIF instructed impatiently. "And tell the son-of-a-bitch, if he lies to us, we'll know. And we'll have Rye here shoot him in the hand again."

"Jesus, don't tell him that," Captain Russell said, shaking his head. "The poor kid is probably scared shitless already."

The GIF crossed his arms and scoffed.

"He doesn't look too scared to me."

Terp 2 and Handboy continued talking at a ferocious tempo. They both used large hand gestures, which was surprising considering the state of Handboy. We waited intently for a break in the conversation, so Terp 2 could provide a recap.

Captain Jaxon cleared his throat.

"He says his brother is a bad man," reported Terp 2.

"Well no shit, Sherlock," grumbled Jaxon. "All that flailing about and that's all you got? Did he tell you anything we *don't* already know?"

"If you'd let me finish, I'd tell you," Terp 2 bit back. Maybe it was the lack of sleep or maybe he was still sour from Jaxon's badgering during the election, but that was the first time I'd seen Terp 2 stand his ground.

Jaxon gnawed his cheek.

"Fine, go on," he finally said.

"First, you must understand that this is very difficult for Amir, to come here and speak with us," Terp 2 continued. "He says his brother has always been very good to him, but he has been very bad to many people."

"Wait," interrupted The GIF, "who the hell is Amir? And what's his brother have to do with anything?"

Captain Russell slapped his forehead.

"Handboy is Amir, Sir," I said. "And Nasir is his brother."

"Well why the hell didn't he just say, 'Handboy'?" The GIF asked

Captain Russell's face was red and his clenched hands were shaking.

"Amir—I mean, Handboy, says that Nasir has been supporting anyone who will resist the U.S. occupation of the Logar Province."

"It's not an occupation," grumbled The GIF.

"He says, Nasir punishes anyone opposing him. He says Nasir spent today intimidating people coming to vote."

"Well, they must not have been too scared," Jaxon boasted. "We had higher than expected turnout today."

Terp 2's face was grim.

"About that, Sir," he said, nodding to Handboy. "There's something you need to see."

Handboy unhooked the backpack from his chair and held it out as best he could with his caged hand. With his bandaged hand and a great deal of difficulty, he unzipped the bag and beckoned for us to look. I was hesitant, but assumed the gate guards had done their due diligence and cleared him of anything deadly. Captain Russell produced a small flashlight from his pocket and we all exchanged glances as we leaned in to inspect the contents of the bag.

The smell forced my head back and my dinner up. I plugged my nose and went back in. At the bottom of the bag, about six inches deep, were dozens upon dozens of purple stained thumbs.

"Good God," murmured Captain Russell.

My stomach turned.

"I don't buy it," announced The GIF.

"You what?" Asked Captain Russell angrily.

"I don't buy it," repeated The GIF. "Those aren't even fresh thumbs. Some of'em look like they could be a week old or more. "

His head was nearly inside the bag, inspecting the thumbs up close.

"Yes, I'm sure of it. He didn't get all of these today," The GIF declared, scowling at Handboy. He slapped the bag from his weak hands. "What kinda shit are you trying to pull here?"

Handboy looked to Terp 2 with confusion, but Captain Russell held up his hand to stop him from translating. Captain Russell was on the verge of a meltdown. I was excited by the prospect of these two overweight, middle aged officers turning to fisticuffs in a small, dirty guard shack in rural Afghanistan.

"Sir, are you really questioning the authenticity of a bag full of severed thumbs?"

"Well, Captain," The GIF said in his most condescending tone, "this boy, who has every right and reason to hold a vendetta against us by the way, claims these thumbs were all taken from people voting today, but clearly these are not fresh thumbs. Look at that one there. It looks like a shriveled old prune. Without the thumbnail, you'd never even know."

"It's a bag full of goddamn human thumbs," Russell exploded. "Who the hell cares when he got'em?"

"I'm just saying, he could've cut them off folks that were already dead," The GIF said cooly.

While The GIF and Captain Russell argued over the source of the purple appendages, Captain Jaxon pulled Handboy and Terp 2 aside for questioning. Handboy kept checking a cheap plastic watch that he wore under his wire cage and glancing warely at the open door that creaked back and forth in the breeze.

I bent down and picked up the backpack. In a small section across the front, the remnants of an olive drab thread still frayed out in a rectangular outline, where a patch had recently been torn off. Morbid curiosity took over and I opened the bag. Holding my breath, I examined the grisly contents. To The GIF's credit, some of the thumbs *did* look pretty old, but one thumb in particular caught my attention. I flicked a thumb out of the way to get a better look. This particular thumb *was* fresh and a shade lighter than the rest. I reached in and pinched the thumb between two fingers like a grab-claw in a Vending Machine of Horrors. With my prize in hand, I dropped the rest of the bag on the table.

"Everyone, shut the hell up a minute," Captain Jaxon yelled.

The GIF and Captain Russell fell silent. I suddenly felt awkward standing at the edge of the room with a human thumb in my hand.

"Tell them what you just told me," Jaxon told Terp 2, slapping him casually in the chest with the back of his hand.

Terp 2 straightened up.

"Amir has informed us that Nasir has recently been in contact with some men from Pakistan. He believes they are Taliban."

"Bullshit," Captain Russell spouted. "Nasir hates the Taliban."

Terp 2 held up his hand.

"If I may finish?" he asked. "Amir believes he is arranging deal with these men. One that would buy this district time, free from Taliban interference. Interference he claims began after the creation of this outpost. Amir says he overheard a conversation about 'turning over the American' as part of the deal."

Captain Russell's jaw dropped. The GIF's would have too, if he hadn't been mid-yawn. Captain Jaxon wore a confident smile and nodded as if he himself had supplied the news.

"You gentlemen know of any dip-shit Americans in need of rescue?" Jaxon asked. "'Cause I think I know of one."

The GIF groaned.

"So the kid brings us a bag of bloody thumbs and we're supposed to take his word on some conversation he thinks he overheard that may or may not be about Coucher?" The GIF asked, continuing his stubborn streak.

"I think I found proof of life here, gentlemen," I said, holding up the white thumb, like I'd found the Golden Ticket.

Everyone crowded around to get a better look.

"Terp 2, ask Handboy where this particular thumb came from," I instructed.

Terp 2 turned around. Handboy was gone. The black backpack was gone. For a moment, the only sounds were the creaking of the door that still hung wide open and the hum of the generator. Then came the whistle of an incoming mortar.

Chapter 21: REFRAD

September 7, 2009

There were two guards posted outside The SCO's office doors. They were dressed in full battle-rattle, standing rigid with their backs pressed against the sandbag-reinforced wall The SCO had demanded be built in the hallway outside his office. Between the sandbags and their body armor, the guards clogged the corridor almost completely. I recognized them as the two nimrod Specialists who'd been Thedon's muscle a few weeks earlier. Both now wore Sergeant's stripes.

I clomped down the hall and stood in front of them, facing The SCO's door. Neither bothered to break concentration on the opposing wall.

"Got kicked out of your little club?" I asked, pointing to the new rank patches in the middle of their chests. The soldier on the right, who I'd always deemed the brainier of the two, only grunted.

"Why don't you get a couple chairs?" I asked. "The Taliban's not breaching the FOB walls anytime soon."

"Can't, Sir," grumbled the second guard. "SCO says chairs'd clog up the hall. Might trip'em up if he had to evacu-ate."

I stepped in to knock on the door, but the left guard held up his hand to my chest.

"Gotta frisk ya first, Sir," he said with a big grin.

"Seriously? I have a rifle slung across my back," I said, tugging at the strap across my chest. "Everyone does."

"SCO's orders," he said and went into patting me down from armpits to ankles. When he'd finished he nodded approval to his friend.

I shook my head and rapped on the door.

"Enter," came a growl from inside, followed by a shout. "Wait!"

I froze with my hand on the knob.

"Who's there?"

"Captain Rye, Sir."

Silence.

"Who?"

"Captain Rye, Sir. You requested to speak with me?"

"Who told you that?"

"Sir, you radioed me a few minutes go," I said. "I walked down here just now, from the airfield."

The right guard giggled.

"Sir, could we speak *inside* your office."

"I am inside my office," The SCO replied. "You're not. Fix it."

I opened the door and nearly sprawled to the floor. My toe had caught a sandbag. The whole floor was covered in a single layer of full sandbags. I looked around in awe. On either side of the office, the walls were stacked to the ceiling with sandbags. Throughout the center of the room, sandbags were suspended from the ceiling at varying levels with paracord. I would later learn these were intended to stop shrapnel in the event of an explosion.

The door swung shut behind me. Remembering my military bearing, I reported in proper procedure. Stopping two steps in front of The SCO's desk, I stood at attention and rendered a crisp salute.

"Captain Rye, reporting as ordered, Sir," I snapped. I always felt a little proud when I didn't jack up the reporting process. Like a gymnast sticking the landing.

The air in the office was stale. Wafts of tobacco and piss pummeled my nostrils in alternating waves. A water bottle, with its bottom cut off, had been tacked upside-down on the far wall as a makeshift urinal. A tube connected to the neck spiraled down between a gap in the sandbags and into a hole in the floor. I didn't let my eyes wander long. The SCO still stared at me and I was still saluting. Custom stated he had to acknowledge me before I could stop.

"We're at war, we haven't got time for that 'customs and courtesies' shit," he said. "Take a seat."

There were no other chairs in the room, so I simply took a few steps back. The floor groaned, already stressed by the weight of the sandbags. The plywood floor bowed noticeably in the center of the room. The SCO bowed from stress as well. His uniform hung like a tent off his shriveled shoulders. The only place he hadn't lost weight was in the bags under his bloodshot eyes. His skin was translucent yellow and he ran a paper hand through what remained of his hair.

"Where are we at on today's air assault?" He asked. With the revelation that Coucher was still within grasp, The SCO had demanded multiple search and rescue missions per week.

"Captain Russell's team is still out, Sir," I said. "They've reported back they've acquired one detainee."

The SCO smiled. It was terrifying. His teeth were stained a deep brown underneath receding gums.

"It isn't Nasir, Sir," I said.

The SCO scowled. Every mission he planned had a "kill on sight" clause dedicated to his arch-nemesis and every time the teams came back empty handed another piece of his sanity slithered down the coiled piss tube.

"There was no sign of Coucher either, Sir."

"Who?" he asked. "Oh. Right. Too bad."

He stood up and hobbled across the room to the water-bottle urinal. Turning his back to me he continued to speak.

"Captain Garcia has come across some new intel. I have a few missions in mind, but I can't seem to find Major Doyle anywhere."

After a fair amount of gosselling, the tube spiraling between his legs turned an alarming amber.

"I haven't seen him, Sir," I said. "But I'll go look for him, for you."

In actuality, no one had seen much of The GIF since the mortar attack in Kherwar. After returning to Alternator, he'd spent the next several days hunched over his keyboard, drafting numerous award recommendations for himself for alleged acts of valor that no one had witnessed during the chaos. After that, he'd spent the next several weeks in and out of the Aid Station trying to get diagnosed with low level Post Traumatic Stress Disorder. I only know this, because Doc Jonston kept complaining in the chow hall about The GIF driving customers away from his black market tattoo parlor.

"No," The SCO said, the tube was clear and the gosselling began again. "We have other matters to discuss."

He returned to his desk and lowered himself into his chair. Leaning forward on his elbows, he removed the cigar nub from his lips and looked at me with something akin to kindness.

"Do you know what 'morale' is?" He asked.

I nodded.

"How would you define it?" He asked.

I thought for only a moment.

"A soldier's will to fight, Sir," I said.

The SCO smiled and sat up straight in his chair. I thought he might slide through the neckhole of his uniform.

"Bravo," he said. "I couldn't have phrased it better. And how would you say the morale is among the soldiers in this Squadron?"

"Good, Sir."

"And how would you say your personal morale is?" He asked.

"Good, Sir," I lied again.

The SCO fell silent and his smile fell as well. He narrowed his eyes suspiciously.

"So what's *this* shit about then?" He growled, holding up a manila folder.

I swallowed hard. Days earlier, I'd submitted my REFRAD paperwork to the Squadron Adjutant. The events of the deployment thus far had led me to the decision to leave the Army at the end of my contract, which ended shortly after our deployment. The SCO now held that paperwork in his hands.

"Are you pussing out on me, Rueben?"

"It's Rye, Sir," I corrected. "It's there on the folder."

He glared and I wondered if he ever got tired of glaring. He put his cigar back in his mouth.

"I know how to read, asshat," he said. "I was trying out a nickname for you. Like the Reuben sandwich. Made with Rye bread. Your name is Rye."

He smiled proudly. His face quaked, unused to such a movement.

"Yes, Sir," I said. "I get it, Sir. That's very clever."

"Are you mocking me?"

"No Sir," I said. "I've never heard that one before."

I'd heard it a million times. In fact, it was my least favorite bread-related nickname.

"So why are you getting out?" He pressed.

About a million reasons I couldn't say gushed through my head.

"It's just time, Sir," I lied again. "After my knee injury, I don't seem to be much use to the Army."

"Don't be an idiot," said The SCO. "Of course you're of use to the Army. You're a good officer, Rye. We can't all be door-kickers though."

Shock.

Good officer. The words pinballed inside my skull. He'd just called me a good officer and got my name right all in the same breath. It was my turn to be suspicious.

"Thank you, Sir, but I think this is the right step for me. I never intended to make the Army a career anyway."

"Don't want to end up like me, huh?" He picked at the back of his hand. "Old, broken and crazy."

"It's not that, Sir—" I started, but he waved me off.

"It's okay," he said. "The plywood walls are thin. I hear people talk. But I don't have to justify my actions to them. I've spent twenty five years in the military. I've done some great things and I've made some deals with the devil."

This was a whole side of The SCO I'd never seen.

"Are you sure there's nothing I can do to keep you in?" He asked. "No guaranteed duty assignments? I could get you an ROTC gig at a Big Ten university. We could dump this folder in the trash right now and pretend this never happened."

I paused to give the appearance of consideration. In reality, I was more concerned about the floor giving way, sending both of us falling into the piss soaked rubble below, which only seemed slightly less enjoyable than my current situation.

"No, Sir. I think I'm making the right decision for me."

"Fine," he growled. "One less 'shit-officer' clogging up the ranks."

There he was.

"And you're wrong about Squadron morale," he went on. "Morale is tanking right now. And quitting is contagious, so I'd appreciate it—the Army would appreciate it—if you'd keep your trap shut about getting out. Don't go around bragging about being 'free' in a couple months."

"I won't, Sir."

But I was going to.

There was a knock on the door. The SCO jumped a mile high before crouching low behind his desk. I hoped it was Nasir, coming to put us both out of our misery.

"Who's there?" Shouted The SCO.

"Is Ivan, Sir," came a thick Russian accent. The SCO sat back up and smiled.

"C'mon in." He shouted.

I got grilled at the door, but the Russian ex-pat gets invited in like an old pal. I was going to wallpaper Alternator with copies of my REFRAD paperwork.

The smell of vodka entered the room well before Ivan did. He too nearly went sprawling before realizing sandbags covered the floor. He scanned The SCO's bunker-office in foggy befuddlement.

"I love the decorations," he sloshed.

"Thank you, Ivan. One can't be too cautious," the SCO said before turning to me. "Get out."

I turned to the door.

"Stop," the SCO shouted. "Is that how you leave a superior officer's presence?"

Customs and courtesies.

I turned sharply, snapped to attention and rendered a salute. Ivan giggled, but I think it was because he'd spotted the urinal on the wall.

"Tomorrow, you go up to FOB Shank and meet with Colonel Gunn," The SCO instructed. "He's conducting exit interviews with all the quitters. I'd suggest you give him some better reasons for turning tail."

He tongued his cigar to the other side of his mouth.

"Now, get out."

****

The door to the Command Post swung shut behind me and I took the stairs slowly, processing what had just happened. I wasn't particularly fond of the idea of speaking with Colonel Gunn and I began running through possible conversation scenarios. This quickly snowballed into a fantasy in which I saved Colonel Gunn's life after a mortar attack interrupts my exit interview. He'd present me Silver Star for "gallantry in action", but he'd do so begrudgingly, knowing full well I was still getting the hell out of the Army.

My radio crackled to life, bringing me back to reality.

"Titan 3 Air, this is Titan Big Sexy," came the voice of Sergeant Hunter.

"This is Titan 3 Air," I responded. "And that's not your callsign, Titan Airfield."

"That callsign is so lame," complained Hunter.

"This is an open channel. Cut the crap. What do you need? Over."

"Just got a call from Honcho 45, they're inbound with Task Force Retirement Home. Over."

"You do know Captain Russell's probably tuned in and heard that, right? Over." I asked.

There was silence from the other end.

"Task Force Raven is inbound, Sir," Hunter corrected. "Ten minutes out. Over."

I cut around the back of the staff building, where the ankle-ravaging gravel wasn't as deep. As I rounded the building, I halted, backpedaled quickly, and peeked around the corner again. In the shadows, at the far end of the building, Chappy stood toe to toe with Specialist Thedon. I couldn't hear them, but Chappy was visibly upset. As he spoke, he waved his arms high over his head and pointed knife-hands in Thedon's pudgy face. Thedon only smiled smugly under his greasy mustache.

I stepped around the corner, deciding to interject for Chappy's sake and Thedon's safety. Suddenly, Chappy shoved Thedon, pinning him to the wall with a python sized arm. I backpedaled again. Chappy cocked his fist back as if intending to bash Thedon's head. Then he did. I heard the meat-packing slap of the solid blow to Thedon's eye. There was a yelp and a gasp. I wasn't sure which sound I'd made and which came from the stunned Specialist. Thedon wriggled free and stumbled off through the loose gravel, clutching his eye with both hands. Chappy strutted back and forth in quick cuts, his hulking frame puffed like a champion rooster.

I folded back around the other side of the building, feeling no need to acknowledge what I'd just witnessed. When I came around the building, Chappy was still there pacing angrily.

"Hey there, Chappy," I croaked. Chappy woke from his daze.

"Jared," he nodded. "Where're you headed?"

"Airfield," I said, trying to sound nonchalant. "Captain Russell's team is inbound with today's catch. Sounds like they have a detainee that might have intel on Coucher."

"Step into my office a minute," he beckoned toward the stairs leading into the staff building.

"I really need to—"

"Step into my office a minute," he repeated sternly.

"I'll step into your office for just a minute."

We walked in silence up the stairs and down the hall to Chappy's office.

"How much of that did you see and hear?" he asked before opening his door.

"How'd you know I was there?" I asked.

"You yelped like a little bitch."

"Chappy, you know I fear for your soul, right?"

I followed him into his office and stood in awe for the second time that day. The room was a spider web. Trails of red yarn criss-crossed the room from all four walls. At the end of each thread, photographs of soldiers, official documents, old newspaper articles and cut-outs of maps now served as wallpaper covering every visible square inch. Chappy weaved through the tangled mess before taking a seat at his desk.

"How much?" he repeated.

"Heard nothing, saw the important parts," I said. "What is all this?"

"Nothing you need concern yourself with," he sounded like a pastor again. "Trust me that my actions were justified. And necessary."

"I'm not judging," I said, "but *you are* a Chaplain and an Army officer and you just struck a low ranking enlisted soldier. In the face. Hard. That's not gonna to report well," I said.

Chappy didn't bat an eye.

"It won't get reported."

"Are you serious?" I scoffed. "It's probably *already* been reported."

"It won't get reported," Chappy said calmly. "For two reasons. Number one, as you stated, I'm a Chaplain and an Army officer. In the battle of 'he said, she said', I think I have him trumped."

"Well that's a bit conceited," I said. "And a gross abuse of power. What's number two?"

"Number two, and I haven't proved this definitively yet," he motioned to the chaotic cat's cradle around us, "but if what I've uncovered is true, ol'Thedon's not even part of our unit. He may not even be in the Army at all anymore."

"What in God's name are you talking about?" I asked.

Chappy leaned in.

“This is only the tip of the iceberg,” he said. “This Thedon guy is the head of some sort of Specialist syndicate. An E4 mafia, if you will.”

“If he’s not in the Army anymore, how’d he get all the way to Afghanistan with us?” I asked, playing along.

“That’s the beauty of it,” Chappy’s eyes brightened. “There are already Specialists in every aspect—every department—of the Army. All they’d have to do is alter some records, move some names around and bingo-bango.”

“So, this is some sort of Army wide conspiracy now?” I asked.

“Goddamn right it is,” Chappy said, smacking his palm down on the table. The vibration popped a tack from the wall. A length of red yard fluttered down and rested across his legs.

“Think about it,” he said. “If Thedon’s only in charge here on FOB Alternator, imagine if every FOB out there has their own ‘Thedon’. They could have their own rank structure within their little mafia. Who knows how high up the ladder this goes. There could be some ‘head Specialist Thedon’ out there that’s getting coffee for the Chief Of Staff of the Army.”

He was working himself into a frenzy.

“Okay,” I said calmly. “I’ll play along. Let’s say, for argument's sake, there is some secret Specialist mafia that has their hands in every aspect of the Army. Let’s say they do hear and see everything. You’re not at all worried you just punched one of their leaders in the face?”

Chappy considered this.

“No. That guy's a little bitch too,” he said. And if I hear of him pullin’ any of his shit again, I’ll knock that dirt stache right off his oily little face.”

“I love it when you quote scripture,” I said.

“‘A time to love and a time to hate. A time for war and a time for peace.’ Ecclesiastes 3:8,” Chappy quoted.

“There’s one thing I still don’t understand,” I said. “What is it all for? If there is this grand secret society you claim, what is their goal? Their purpose? What are they working toward?”

“Nothing,” Chappy said matter-of-factly.

“Nothing?” I asked.

“Nothing,” he repeated. “Their sole purpose is the shirking of their soldierly duties. I dare you to walk the Alternator grounds and find a Specialist who is gainfully employed, doing his assigned job. You won't. They've either delegated their job to a Private or they've vanished entirely. If my sources are correct, they've even developed an 'underground railroad' of sorts to escape their day to day work."

"It doesn't seem like a grievous offense," I sighed. "Sounds like their preparing for careers in middle management if you ask me. And who are these 'sources' you're talking about?"

Chappy leaned back.

"I have Specialists coming in for confessional all the time," he said. "Well, they usually come in for other reasons, but I'm pretty good at turning it into a confessional."

He popped a couple knuckles on his right hand.

"Chappy," I said, "You can't just beat up—"

"It's sloth," Chappy hissed, slamming his fist down on his desk again. Somewhere another tack popped and tinkled across the floor. "It's one of the seven deadly sins, Jared. 'One who slacks in his work is brother to one who destroys.' Proverbs 18: 9."

"What does that mean?" I asked.

Chappy leaned forward in his seat. The former sergeant in him shown through in one menacing look.

"It means, if they are slacking off, I have to destroy them."

Chapter 22: Shank

September 8, 2009

It was too early and too hot to be sandwiched between Kevlar plates. Sweat already trickled from my body armor down the small of my back. I stood on the edge of the airfield, rifle slung across my chest and assault-pack slung across my back. I was hitching a ride to FOB Shank, for what promised to be an uncomfortable exit interview with Colonel Gunn.

Ivan's white whale was parked on the far end of the airfield, but he was nowhere to be seen. He'd become a regular fixture on Alternator, since the search for Coucher had ramped up again. The rumor was, The SCO was using him as a freelance search party, sending him into regions deemed too dangerous for unescorted Army aircraft. Lord knows how The SCO was paying him. Probably in black market booze. But The SCO needed to find Coucher to get a feather back in his cap and Ivan didn't seem to mind the danger. Ivan didn't seem to mind Alternator either. He could often be found loitering around the cafeteria in between missions, heckling anyone foolish enough to pull a nonalcoholic beer from the drink cooler.

"Real men drink vodka," he'd shout. He said "vodka" the way all Russians say "vodka". I was growing quite fond of him.

I radioed the Command Post, but no one there had seen him. It was 0830 and my appointment with the Colonel wasn't until 1030 hours. I had time to kill anyway. I leaned back against a concrete barrier and slowly slid down until I was sitting in the pea gravel. I wriggled my hips until I'd formed a sufficient ass-divot and leaned back to relax. Resting my helmet on the top of my pack, I began running through possible scenarios for my upcoming meeting.

I'd made myself too comfortable and before long I was asleep. I found myself in Colonel Gunn's office, sitting in a low chair in front of his towering desk. His giant, square frame sat opposite me, backlit by the sun. A bikini clad Lieutenant Barrett sat across his lap, stroking the chest hair protruding from his unfastened uniform. I remember thinking how incredibly unprofessional it seemed. Most shocking of all, on his desk sat the severed head of Nasir, black beret and all. The head was pale and waxy, but a wicked laugh still contorted its thin mustache. A single purple thumbprint adorned its forehead, directly between the eyes.

From a side door, Sergeant Loredo entered the room. She was dressed in an American flag bikini and her wavy brown locks danced lightly across her cleavage as she walked my way. Stopping in front of me, she placed both hands on her nearly bare hips. With her foot, she playfully nudged mine.

"Are you ready to go?" She asked, fluttering long lashes.

I looked to the Colonel in confusion. His eyes were hidden behind his aviator sunglasses and he was gnawing one of The SCO's cigars. From behind his desk he pulled a pistol and pointed it directly at my head.

"Are you ready to go?" He shouted.

"Shit!" I spat, waking to find Ivan tapping my boot with his foot.

"Are you ready to go?" Asked Ivan again.

Cold beads of sweat dotted my forehead. They felt better than the hot beads that dotted everywhere else. Ivan reached a coffee free hand and helped me to my feet. He didn't smell like vodka yet, which concerned me.

"Where were you? I asked as we started toward his helicopter. I checked my watch. I'd only been asleep ten minutes.

"Intelligent briev-ing," he said before changing the subject. "You shouldn't sleep in open. Makes easy for Taliban to cut throat."

He ran a thumb across his neck. I rubbed my throat, thinking of the ANA soldier's election day neck smile.

"Bad dream?" He asked.

"Parts of it," I said. I was pretty fond of the Sergeant Loredo part. "I'm just a bit on edge. I'm meeting with Colonel Gunn today. I have to tell him why I'm leaving the Army."

We walked in silence for a moment.

"Blow hard," said Ivan.

"I don't think my situation is *that* desperate," I gasped.

"No. 'Blow-hard'," he repeated. "This ess way of saying 'arrogant', yes?"

I nodded.

"Colonel Gunn ess blow-hard," he said. "You are strong American Captain."

He flexed both arms over his head, then lightly punched my shoulder.

“He’s going to guilt me into staying in,” I said. “And I’m going to cave, cause I don’t like disappointing people.”

Ivan crunched to a halt and grabbed my shoulder.

“You stand ground,” he said, shaking a finger in front of my nose. “Life ess too short for caring of others’ opinions. Can be much shorter here.”

“Easy for you to say,” I said. “You’re not about to tender your resignation to your boss’s, boss’s, boss.”

Ivan smiled.

“I was like you,” he said. “Long time ago. I wanted make name for self here. And I did. But not for good things.”

“What happened?” I asked.

“Made name for self, but not for good things,” he repeated flatly. “But I move on. I try to be best person. Maybe redeem self.”

Ivan pulled down the step ladder and I climbed aboard. He climbed into the pilot seat and began flipping switches and turning knobs, one leg still hanging out the driver door. The rotors began turning slowly. Once he was satisfied he’d turned every knob and flipped every switch, he leaned back out the door and heaved the rest of his coffee into the rocks below. Then, pulling a brown paper bag from under his seat, he produced a bottle of vodka and filled the empty Styrofoam cup to the rim. Returning the bottle back to its hiding place, he took a man-sized pull, emptying half the cup. He smiled at me as he wiped his mouth with his sleeve.

“Now ready to fly,” he announced.

“Good God,” I said. “You drink that stuff plain?”

“Is better on rocks,” he grinned. “But ice ess hard to find in Afghanistan.”

I checked my watch. It was 0915. There wouldn’t be time to find another ride to Shank, so I devoted some extra time to securing my seatbelt as tightly as possible.

I watched Ivan empty the rest of his cup as we took to the air. Then, mid flight, he produced the bottle again and gave himself a refill. He kept pointing to different features of the landscape and yelling gibberish over his shoulder. The rotors washed out everything. I’d just nod, he’d thumbs-up, and we’d fly on. To be honest, the flight was the smoothest I’d ever been on and we landed on FOB Shank with barely a bump.

I gave Ivan's shoulder a pat of thanks as I climbed out. He swung the door open and leaned sloppily out. His eyes had a nice sheen to them.

"Cap'n Rye," he called.

"What?" I shouted over the rotorwash.

"If Gunn gives you dir'-mo, you punch him in iz hooy," he slurred matter of factly.

I nodded though I didn't understand, but he'd already slammed his door. Before I reached the edge of the airfield, his helicopter had disappeared over the FOB walls.

****

Lieutenant Barrett escorted me into the Colonel's office. She wasn't dressed in a bikini, so the meeting was starting off worse than my subconscious had planned. It was too late in the day to be in a Physical Training uniform, but that didn't seem to bother her. The PT uniform, on most soldiers, is baggy and unflattering, but Barrett's was form fitting. As though it was tailored specifically to her hourglass figure.

I took a seat in front of the Colonel's desk and Barrett took a seat on the desk's edge, facing me. Her shorts slid high up on her thigh exposing a mile of soft pink skin. I thought about how long deployment had been and about all the things we'd been deprived. That's a lie. I was only thinking about one thing we'd been deprived. Barrett cleared her throat. I'd been caught staring.

My face flushed, but she went back to paying me little mind.

"So, will the Colonel be here soon?" I asked.

"Sure," she yawned.

She checked her watch and looked around the room, as if the Colonel could materialize anywhere.

"You don't have to babysit me you know," I said. "I can handle sitting by myself if you want to go put your uniform on."

Barrett leaned back and smiled.

"Its Saturday," she stated. "This *is* the uniform today."

Saturday. Days of the week had lost all meaning. Every day blended into the last and the next.

"You get to wear that *all* day?"

"And tomorrow." She bragged. "All weekend."

"There are no weekends on Alternator," I grumbled. "Must be nice living up here in la-la-land."

She looked annoyed, but I didn't care. I had no chance with her, nor did I want one anymore. That's also a lie.

Before she could respond, the door burst open and Colonel Gunn barreled into the room. He was also in his weekend uniform. Lieutenant Barrett remained seated on the edge of the desk and I stood to attention, seemingly for no reason. The Colonel never picked his head up from the newspaper he was reading. He crashed into his chair and spread the paper out across his desk.

"The goddamn election is going to have to be redone," he complained. "They're saying the whole thing was rife with corruption. Can you believe that, Sarah?"

"No, Sir." She cleared her throat again and he looked up.

"Who are you?" He asked me. "I mean, how can I help you?"

Barrett interjected on my behalf.

"This is your 1030 appointment, Sir."

"I had a 1030 appointment?" The Colonel checked his watch. "What's this about?"

I was about to answer when Barrett ran interference again.

"He's quitting or something, Sir," Barrett yawned and did a little cat stretch. "His file is there on the desk."

The Colonel watched her stretch and I wondered if he'd heard anything she said.

"That so?" he said, shaking loose his daze. "What's your name, son?"

"Captain Ray, Sir," Barrett interjected again.

"Rye, Sir," I corrected.

"His file's on the desk, Sir," she sighed in annoyance.

"We've met before?" Colonel Gunn asked, pulling my file from beneath his newspaper and flipping it open.

"Yes, Sir," I said. "A few times, actually. Most recently in Kherwar, on election morning."

He looked up and squinted at me. I'd never seen him without his aviator sunglasses. His eyes added ten years to his appearance.

"Ah, yes. Sorry about that, Ray. It's been a crazy few weeks. It's hard to keep names, faces and places straight sometimes," he smiled.

"It's Rye, Sir. And I completely understand."

He went back to my file and his smile faded.

"Well can you believe this, with the election? They're going to have to do the whole damn thing over again in the Spring when they can come up with a better system. How do you like that?"

"Yes, Sir, it's quite a shame. Lot of wasted effort and resources," I said. "But on the other hand at least they're staying committed to making sure that it gets done right. They could have just—"

"You sure you don't want to stay in?" The Colonel interrupted. His head was down as he scribbled something on my REFRAD paperwork. Barrett looked off into oblivion and had started slowly drumming her sneakers against the Colonel's desk like an impatient child.

"Sir?"

"Could I tempt you to stay in with a cushy assignment? Maybe a recruiting station near home or an ROTC unit somewhere?"

He kept writing.

"No, Sir," I said. "I'm pretty set on getting out."

"Do you have a plan for when you're out?" He asked.

"Um. Not a specific one, Sir," I said. "I have my degree in-—"

He cut me off again.

"Would you say, 'Pursuing other interests'?" He asked.

"I guess so, Sir."

He made a check on the paper in my file.

"And you don't have any 'grievances that are the catalyst for your separation from the Army'?"

He was just reading off from a form now.

"Sir?"

"No one discriminated against you because of race, religion or gender?"

"No, Sir."

"No one touched you inappropriately, did they?" He looked up. Barrett's interest peaked briefly.

"No." I spat. "Good God, no."

Barrett went back to looking bored.

"A simple 'no' is fine," said the Colonel. He checked some more boxes and then made a large sweeping signature at the bottom.

"That should do it," he said. He gave the paper another "once-over", closed the folder and handed it to Lieutenant Barrett.

"That's it, Sir?" I asked, shocked and a bit insulted.

"That's it," he said. "The Army is fat right now, so the process for trimming the waste has become pretty efficient."

The waste?

That one hurt.

"Listen, son," he went on. "War is a busy place and I'm sure you're a great American. I just don't have extra time to spend with folks who don't want to be here. Sarah, I mean, Lieutenant Barrett will show you out."

I was speechless and I slipped into autopilot. I rose from the chair to the position of attention and rendered a salute.

"Thank you for your time, Sir," I heard myself say. In a way, it was sincere. The meeting had cemented my resolve to leave the Army. The Colonel remained seated and flicked a half salute my way, as he went back to reading his paper. I followed Barrett to the door trying not to stare at her butt. The office could've been on fire and I'd have still been distracted.

"Captain, one more thing," the Colonel called after me. I stopped and turned back around.

"Sir?"

"When a Colonel tells you your name is 'Ray'," he said. "Your name is 'Ray'."

I waited for a joking laugh, but he just went back to reading his paper.

I turned back to find Barrett's butt was gone. It was shaping up to be a real craptacular day.

****

In the short time I'd been in the Colonel's office, a sandstorm had blown in and the whole base was buttoned down for the remainder of the morning. In an effort to put distance between Gunn and myself, I darted from building to building until I reached the main cafeteria. There, I sat in the back corner, shame eating Aunt Mary's Muffins and practicing all the ways I'd never tell him off, if I ever saw him again.

The sandstorm blew over after lunch, but a nasty thunderstorm was hot on its heels, sinking the whole base into a fine, sloppy mess. The cafeteria workers were starting to give me dirty looks and I didn't want to stay one more minute on FOB Shank than I had too, so I took my chances with the rain and headed for the airfield.

The Control Center at the airfield was closed up and I pounded hard on the aluminum door. An old soldier pulled the door open and waited for me to say something. He was in his workout uniform, so I couldn't tell his rank. Behind him, his laptop screen was paused on an explosion in some mind numbing action movie. There were subtitles across the bottom in some foreign language. Probably one of the newest bootlegs at the local bazaar.

"When's the next flight to Alternator?" I asked.

He poked his head out the door and looked at the black clouds over head. Then he looked at me like I was crazy.

"Tomorra," he grunted and swung the door shut.

It wasn't worth the fight, so I sloped back through the rain and mud toward the transient tents. The foreign subtitles made me think of Ivan and how he'd planned to be out flying today. I hoped he'd made it back to Alternator before the sandstorm hit.

I pulled back the flap of the transient tent and stepped out of the rain. The tent was humid and obviously not high on FOB Shank's list of maintenance concerns. Of the eight cots inside, only one was fully functional. It was positioned directly under a leak in the canvas ceiling and now cradled a swimming pool. I decided the staff at the cafeteria would be delighted to see me again and I headed right back out.

"Hey good lookin, need a lift?" Called a familiar voice from a few tents down.

Major Connick smiled under the hood of his camo rain jacket.

"Sir! I most definitely need a lift," I said, hurrying over to him. As I reached him, I stopped and saluted. He returned my salute with a crisp salute of his own, a stream of rainwater pouring from the brim of his patrol cap which jutted out from under his hood.

"You're a hard person to track down, Jared," he grinned. "Come with me."

"How did you get here, Sir? And what do you mean? Have you been looking for me?"

"Diablo Troop," he said. "I was summoned by Colonel Gunn this morning, but you and Ivan had already left. The matter was urgent, so I arranged for Diablo Troop to make a mail run. Once the weather went south, I thought you might need a lift. I figured you'd still be around Brigade Headquarters, but you had already split."

"Sorry, Sir," I said. I truly was too. "Thank you for thinking of me. My meeting with Colonel Gunn was—unpleasant, so I wasn't fond of hanging around." I told him about the meeting and the comments the Colonel had made. He walked quietly, but I never doubted for a second that he was listening. When I finished, he slapped me hard on the shoulder.

"That's really messed up," he chuckled. "Want my advice or were you just venting?"

"Venting, Sir," I said. "But I'll take some advice, as long as you're not reciting a recruitment video."

"Don't let the Colonel, or the SCO for that matter, be the deciding factor in your Army career."

"Or The GIF? Or Captain Jaxon?" I grumbled.

"I understand your point. I'm just saying, don't let a handful of bad—," he paused. "Bad *experiences*, sour you on the whole deal. In a couple months we'll be home and you'll be off to bigger and better things. You may never see any of these folks again. I've worked with some pretty great officers over my years and I've worked with my fair share of schmucks too. It's no different in the civilian world. Gotta take the good with the bad."

"I'll consider it, Sir," I said and I meant it.

We approached the line of Diablo Troop trucks idling outside of an open shipping conex. Major Connick stopped and put a hand on my shoulder.

"You're a good officer, Jared," he said. He stomped his foot hard into the mud. A wave of water rushed out and then quickly returned, submerging the sole of his boot. "Sometimes it's hard to see our footprint through the muck."

He looked at me for understanding and I nodded.

"You splashed mud on my pants, Sir," I said.

"Shut up and get in the truck," he said.

The rain had let up and Diablo Troop soldiers scurried from vehicle to vehicle packing boxes into any available nook and cranny.

"That's a ton of mail," I said.

One Private piped up.

"They found another conex full'a our mail that'd been overlooked for months. It's gonna be Christmas on Alternator tonight," he sang. "Hold on, Sir, I think I saw something for you."

The Soldier disappeared back into the connex and then reemerged with a large box on his shoulder. He lugged the box into my hands. It was light for its size and appeared to have been trampled by several angry elephants. It was post dated, April 21, 2009 and it was from my mom. I already knew what it was.

Chapter 23: Vodka On The Rocks

September 9, 2009

Thump, thump.

I sat up too quick and creased my dome on the cracked concrete overhead. Letting loose a string of obscenities, I groped for my alarm clock. 0700 hours. Experience told me I was hearing a Chinook, but I held out hope I was wrong. Ivan hadn't returned to Alternator yesterday, nor had he checked in anywhere else. With any luck, he'd just been too drunk to keep flying and landed somewhere safe for the night.

Rolling off my bunk, I nearly landed on the ragged box I'd brought back from Shank. It was still unopened. After five months, another day wouldn't hurt it. I smelled a couple pairs of uniforms and dressed in the least offensive option.

Captain Clark was coming out of his room at the same time I stepped through my door.

"When'd *you* get back?" He asked. His lower lip was already packed tight with a horseshoe of dip. He fumbled with an open can of Sergeant Drill's as he locked his door.

"Late last night," I lied. Truth is, Major Connick had taken pity on me and told me to take the evening off; just so long as I stayed out of sight. I'd complied with an evening of bootleg movies and more than few daydreams of Lieutenant Barrett in her tight workout uniform. And a few without it.

"*How'd* you get back?" He asked.

I hesitated.

"I rode back with Major Connick," I said.

"Major Connick was at FOB Shank? For what?"

"I don't know, Nancy Drew, why don't you go ask him," I said. "He said he was meeting with Colonel Gunn about an 'urgent matter'. He hitched a ride with the mail run."

"The mail run was back before dinner, dick," Clark grumbled. "You decided to give yourself a night off?"

"Major Connick did and he told me to keep it on the 'down-low'," I smiled. "He knew bitches like you be crazy."

Clark shoved me into my door while I tried to lock it.

"How'd your thing with the Colonel go?" he asked.

"Well, he referred to me as 'waste' at one point," I sighed, struggling to unstick my key from the knob.

"Cold blooded. But I guess if the shoe fits," he grinned and spit brown sludge into his can. "So you haven't heard about everything that went down last night."

The knob finally gave up my key.

"What happened?" I asked, as we started down the hall. "Did they find him?"

"Oh, they found him alright," said Clark. "But not before he lost a good amount of blood."

I stopped.

"But he's alive?"

"Yeah, he's alive. He actually wasn't that bad off after Doc got him stitched up."

"Where the hell did they find him?" I asked.

"Behind the shower tent on the other side of the cafeteria. Must have got disoriented and crawled back there," Clark explained. He took a long swig from the Sergeant Drill's can and grimaced.

"Wait. What?" I stopped again. "What about his helicopter? Where'd he land? Or crash?"

Clark cocked his head.

"Who're you talkin' about?" He asked.

"Ivan," I said. "Who are *you* talking about?"

"Chappy," said Clarke. "You really didn't hear?"

"No. Hear what?" I spat. "What the hell happened to Chappy?"

He started walking toward the exit, leaving me standing there with an idiot look.

"He got stabbed a bunch'a frick'n times by some porky-ass Specialist that nobody can seem to find."

****

A lit, neon "TATTOO" sign buzzed angrily above the entrance of the aid station. Doc had played off the sign as a joke and been granted permission to keep it lit during daylight hours. The last "O" was dark and I tapped it on my way in. It flickered back to life as I pushed through the canvas door. The smell of latex filled my nose.

The medic's desk was empty, but the curtain was drawn forward on the first of the long row of patient beds. I peeked around it and found my favorite medic lying flat on his back with his feet tucked up to his butt. The same ragged issue of *The Flash* was draped across his face and his arms dangled limp out from each side of the bed.

"The Chaplain back there?" I asked. The humming of the tattoo gun was coming from the back room again.

The comic shook from side to side and the medic, who'd recently been promoted to Specialist, jerked his thumb toward a curtained bed on the far end of the ward. I'd have badgered the medic on proper courtesies, but it's never a good to cross somebody who could potentially be stitching you up later.

The plywood floor creaked as I approached and a deep voice boomed through the tent.

"Pay no attention to the man behind the curtain."

I pulled back the vail to find Chappy lying inclined and undressed from the waist up. Two lengths of white gauze lined each side of his torso and spots of blood were seeping through. He grinned from ear to ear.

"How long have you been waiting to say that?" I asked.

"Since the last visitor left," Chappy confessed. "How are you?"

"Not that great—," I stopped. "*How am I*? How are *you*? What the hell happened?"

"Well, I got stabbed," Chappy said, displaying is bandages. "Turns out I got our mafia buddy all riled up after our last altercation."

"And he did it himself?" I asked. "Doesn't he have minions to do his dirty work?"

Chappy pointed to the medic up front.

"'The Flash' up there says all Thedon's boys are used up looking for Coucher. He's got no muscle. He caught up with me outside the shower tent. Never said a word. Walked up and started jab'n away."

"God bless," I said in disbelief.

"I'm getting to that part," Chappy said impatiently. "He got me two or three good ones before I got my first punch in. His eye was still all puffed up and swollen, you know, from where I whacked him before. I figured it was probably still pretty tender, so I worked that area pretty hard. He was crying toward the end. I don't think he could even see where he was stickin' that knife."

I imagined the whole horrible incident.

"You know what, Chappy?" I said. "I'm proud of you. This whole conversation, in spite of everything, you didn't cuss or use the Lord's name in vain. I'm impressed."

"Oh, I'm a new man," Chappy proclaimed, scooching up in his bed. He winced and clutched his side as he leaned over. From the bloodied uniform crumpled on the chair next to him, he pulled a small Gideon Bible. The cover was ripped nearly in two.

"Thedon's last thrust would've put a hole in my heart," Chappy said, waving the book.

"So you've finally found God?" I asked.

"Turns out he was in my breast pocket the whole time."

"Amazing," I said. "And all it took was attempted murder."

"Hey. Call it 'finding God'. Call it 'being born again'. Hell, just call it, 'being grateful'. Whatever you wanna call it, for the next three months, I'm gonna be the best goddamn Chaplain this Squadron's ever seen."

"Baby steps," I said. "So what happened with Thedon?"

"Gone. Long gone," Chappy said matter-of-factly. "Fat little bastard scaled the FOB wall like a damn spider monkey, blind eye and all. It was a good hour at least before anybody found me, so Lord knows how far he got."

I was blown away.

"He just bolted into the Afghan countryside?" I asked. "You're joking. None of the tower guards saw him?"

Chappy smiled.

"I asked about that too," he said. "And that's the kicker. All the guards on duty were Specialists. Said they didn't see a thing."

I shook my head. None of this was making sense.

"'The Flash' up there said there's a rumor that ol'Thedon was about to be promoted out to Sergeant," Chappy continued. "Sounds like that's the 'kiss of death' in their little organization."

"And 'The Flash' just volunteered this information to you?"

"I may have promised him eternal salvation," Chappy said, lowering his eyes.

"Shame on you," I said. "And they haven't sent anybody out looking for Thedon yet?"

Chappy rubbed his thigh and winced.

"Nope," he said. "Far as I can tell, they won't be either. There's no record of him. So there's technically no one to search for. He either wasn't on the Squadron roster to begin with or the E4 Mafia already ghosted him from the records. Either way, he doesn't exist from an Army standpoint. The GIF was in here earlier for one of his migraines and he said it'd be embarrassing for the Army if the story got out, so the official statement is that an 'enemy combatant' snuck on base posing as an Afghani soldier."

"Sucks for Thedon," I said. "He'll probably find Coucher long before anyone else does."

Chappy laid back and closed his eyes. He grimaced and rubbed his thigh again.

"You want me to grab the medic?" I asked.

He shook his head.

"Did you get stabbed in the thigh too?"

He shook his head.

"Where's Doc? He should be on duty."

"He is," Chappy said, grinding his teeth. "He's hiding in the back cause I told him I'd murder him if I see him again."

"Serious?"

Chappy pulled back the cover of his sheet exposing his bare thigh. The flesh was pink under a bloody cellophane seal. In the center were two stone "Ten Commandment" tablets and a caricature of Moses between them, giving the thumbs up.

"He *is* getting better," I said. "But you shouldn't encourage it."

"I didn't ask for it," he growled. "He put me under to stitch me up and I woke up with this monstrosity on my leg."

"Oh," I said. "Well, that's no good then."

"I'll kill him!" Chappy shouted as loud as he could. The buzzing from the backroom stopped momentarily and then started back up again.

****

That afternoon, Captain Russell and his team returned from yet another manhunt mission. They'd found no trace of Coucher or Thedon, though they weren't officially looking for Thedon at all. What they did find was the smoldering wreckage of a white Sikorski helicopter, which had dashed itself beneath a mountain peak on the far side of the Kherwar bowl, above a small pass known as the Tangi

Valley. The tail number was still intact and confirmed what I'd feared all along.

The base fell into a funk. Ivan had become a Squadron mascot of sorts and everyone missed their loud, egocentric, abrasive drunk. The only hope we held was that his blood alcohol level helped him burn faster, making a quicker death.

In an effort to cheer myself up, I'd opened the package from my mom. Another box of Peeps. I'd thrown it on my desk in disgust, but CSM Storms picked it up with a sly smile.

"I've got a proposition for you, Sir," he grinned.

That evening, every officer and senior sergeant on base converged on the operation office. Word of the gathering had spread like wildfire. But there was no operations brief tonight. No large announcement affecting the Squadron. No, this was something else entirely. This was the night, I'd finally vindicate myself. Redemption from the tragic cookie contest back on Bagram, so many months ago.

"Gentlemen. May I have your attention, please," CSM Storms shouted, standing on a chair in the center of the room.

The idle chatter continued from the surrounding crowd.

"Shut your got-damn pie-holes," he yelled and the room fell silent. "I'd like to thank you all for taking time out of your busy war to attend tonight's event. After the events of the last twenty four hours, we could all use a little good-natured fun. And after eight months of living in complete and utter shame, Captain Rye is returning from retirement to stare death in the face once more."

A cheer rose up from the room. CSM Storms waved his arms for silence.

"I'd like to warn you, what you are about to see may be graphic. Traumatizing even. This could result in PTSD. Anyone feeling faint or ill, should note that Doc Jonston is in attendance, though he's here primarily to resuscitate Captain Rye if—when needed."

SSG Jonston stood up and gave a wave to the crowd. His arms were now sleeved in tattoos.

"Without further adieu," CSM Storms went on, "we'll get to the main event. As you may recall, it was the Dragon Cafetria's monstrous chocolate chip cookies that thwarted, nay, nearly destroyed our beloved, Captain Rye. But he won't be shoving cookies in his face this time. No, he'll face a greater challenge."

He held up a single, yellow Peep. There were giggles from the crowd.

"The rules are simple. The marshmallows must remain intact at all times. No tearing or chewing. Compressing is permitted and Captain Rye is allowed to manually manipulate the marshmallow placement at any time. Finally, Captain Rye must be able to completely seal his lips for the final Peep to be counted. I trust you all have placed your bets."

The whiteboards in the back we're wiped clear of tactical graphics and operational brainstorms, replaced by an elaborate betting chart created by Captain Garcia, who was now busy collecting money from the crowd.

I was in the corner bouncing like a boxer ready to enter the ring. Major Connick gave me a pep talk, mostly because he'd placed a high wager on an even higher number of Peeps. He was saying something about "God and Country" which I'm sure was quite inspiring, but I was watching the room. A group of Specialists had entered uncontested. They were outranked by years upon years of military experience, but seemed to have no qualms about joining the party. At their center was a short chubby Specialist with a dirty blonde mustache. The new mafia Don. I watched them curiously as The New Don whispered something to one of his mongoloid henchmen. The brute turned and placed a bet on the board, shoving a handful of crumpled bills at Captain Garcia.

"So what's your strategy?" Major Connick asked.

"Stuff marshmallows in my face until I can't anymore," I said.

"You've had all day to strategize and that's the best you've got?" The GIF said, butting into the conversation. He'd been off glad-handing officers like he was running for public office. Since I was on his staff, he was taking the publicity very serious. "Pull your head out of your ass and don't you dare make this office look bad."

"Listen, Sir, with all due respect," I said, meaning no due respect, "I'm the professional glutton here, so let me do my job."

I started to do some hamstring stretches. It felt like the right thing to do.

CSM Storms drug a trash barrel to the center of the room, where the Peeps were stacked on a small card table.

"And now for the main event," he bellowed.

There had been no other events. I stepped forward and stood before the great pyramid of Peeps. Everyone's eyes were on me. I imagined if they were gathered to watch a medal for valor being pinned to my chest. I guess pinning Peeps to my face would have to do.

I lifted both hands to silence the crowd and was surprised when it a worked.

"No flash photography, please," I said.

"Shut up and get on with it," someone yelled from the back.

I pulled the first Peep from its conjoined twins. It stretched like hot mozzarella and the granulated sugar coated my fingers. One by one I stuffed the pliable sugar-balls into my mouth. To my surprise, a strategy *did* develop. First I packed the space between my cheeks and gums, all around my lower jaw. With the horseshoe, complete, I did my best Texas-drawl impression of Captain Clark famous mouth full of dip.

"Ya'll know where I can find some lip cancer," I drooled and dodged an empty Sergeant Drill's can thrown by Clark.

The GIF handed me a paper towel.

"Stop talking, you're making me nauseous," he complained.

I was already doing better than most had expected. Fifteen peeps and feeling good. The highest bet was Major Connick's at twenty-two Peeps. The agreement was, anything more and I took the winnings. The quiet chatter around the room had built to a low roar. People laughed and joked and pointed. Half of them weren't even paying attention to my Herculean endeavor, but I didn't care. It was good to see people smiling again.

Twenty Peeps in. Discomfort was setting in. My cheeks were at capacity, but I couldn't stop. I envisioned both cheeks splitting simultaneously. I stuffed another in. Then another. Twenty-two. I'd reached the highest expectation. One more and the prize was mine. I wedged number twenty-three behind my front teeth. A cheer went up from the crowd and Major Connick flipped me the bird. My paper towel was a sloppy mass. I hunched over the trash can, as multicolored drool poured from the corners of my mouth. I pinched my lips shut and sealed the win for good measure, raising a hand victoriously.

Major Connick leaned in, next to my ear.

"Don't you quit now," he winked. "This is *your* moment. Not all heroes wear capes."

I looked around the room. The focus was all back on me. It wasn't on Ivan's deadly crash. It wasn't on Chappy's assault. It wasn't on missing, traitorous Specialists or hyper-paranoid commanders. It wasn't on anything else in this sad corner of the world. It was on me and my silliness. And that was good enough.

Peep twenty-four went in hard and the amalgamation of congealed sugar-mush was pushing its way down the back of my throat. I was reaching "choke point". There was a momentary flashback to the cookie incident on Bagram.

Peep twenty-five. I gagged. There was a gasp from the crowd. I gagged again and Doc Jonston stood. The crowd began chanting and laughing.

"Puke! Puke! Puke!"

My eyes were watering and my cheeks burned. I raised my hand to hold off Doc and reached for another Peep.

Twenty-six, I gagged one last time. Mind over matter. The stream of yellow, blue and pink drool tethered me to the trash can and I placed a hand on both sides. I strained with all my mouth's might and slowly touched my lips together over the sticky mass. CSM Storms leaned in to confirm the seal.

"Twenty-six," he shouted, throwing his hands in the air. A thunderous cheer went up from the crowd. Even The New Don silently nodded his approval.

Suddenly the door slammed open, crashing against the wood wall behind it. Everyone jumped to their feet as the SCO charged into the room. He was thin and frail, but his wild eyes still commanded attention. Cracked lips contorted around his cigar nub and it looked like he may have lost a tooth. He stood silently heaving, studying the room, like a rabid dog about to lunge. He was mortified his staff was having a good time. Not on his watch. He locked eyes with me, still doubled over the trash can.

"There's a goddamn war going on out there," he barked, pointing arbitrarily at a wall. "All of you better cut this fucking shit out."

With that, he turned on his heels and walked out, slamming the door behind him. For a moment everyone looked ashamed, but then they looked back at me.

I hurled Peeps.

A mass resembling an alien slug from some bad Sci-Fi movie slid from my mouth and landed with a solid thud in the trash can. The sound of the The SCO stomping down the hall could still be heard, but I threw my hands up and whispered.

"Twenty-six!"

A hushed cheer went up from the crowd and Major Connick slapped me on the back.

The SCO's door slammed, followed by an agonizing groan of stressed lumber, and then a thundering crash surged through the Command Post.

Chapter 24: Battlefield Circulation

October 19, 2009

Nobody had seen hide nor hair of The SCO since his office floor collapsed under all the sandbag weight. The SCO, though frail and sickly, had miraculously emerged from the rubble unscathed. Like the world's worst phoenix, he rose from the dust, only to take flight to his secondary bunker under the incorrect assumption Nasir had made an attempt on his life. Major Connick and CSM Storms were now the only people permitted to see him and only for urgent Squadron matters. Through them, he'd issue orders from the safe confines of his reinforced living quarters. This is how it had been up until I'd left for two weeks of stateside R&R.

Every soldier is granted two weeks of leave during a year deployment. During this time, soldiers are allowed to travel anywhere in the world under the loose agreement they'll actually return to the war. My R&R was spent back home in a whirlwind of obligatory visits with family and friends. All conversations resulted in a litany of questions about if I'd been shot at, how many terrorists I'd killed and how hot the desert is, occasionally peppered with passive aggressive comments from people who claimed to "support the troops but not the war".

One evening, at the only bar in my single stoplight town, a high school friend, who'd enlisted in the Army after graduation, approached my table and poured himself into the neighboring seat. He boasted of his tours in Iraq, making sure I knew *he'd* been in the *real* war, going into great detail about all the "hajiis" he'd killed. He made crass jokes about shooting women and children on the run and how difficult it was because you don't have to lead them as much. I don't believe he actually did those things, nor did he expect me to believe he did, but it bothered me he'd think I'd find such things funny, that this brutality would be our common ground. I considered telling him about the Peeps. Instead, I told him I couldn't relate, I wasn't a monster. He then made several astute comparisons between me and female genitalia before stumbling back to the bar to continue drinking his guilt into submission.

The change from military to civilian life had been too quick and I was relieved to be boarding the plane back. This relief was short lived, lasting until I set foot back in the bizarre, isolated world of Bagram, the final stepping stone in my journey back to Alternator.

A week earlier, an absent-minded mortar had whistled over the Bagram fences in the wee morning hours. This, in itself, was nothing new. In fact, it happened every two to three months. Having been fired in haste, the mortars would typically impact in some innocuous corner of the base, causing no more consequence than a few nights of restless sleep for the base's residents. Unfortunately, in the most recent incident, a Private walking back from his night shift guard duty was on the receiving end of a direct hit. Upon inspection by an Army coroner, it was determined the Private had indeed been wearing his kevlar helmet, safety glasses, reflector belt, mouthguard, and his pistol belt with two full canteens of water, which was the new Bagram uniform mandate. For days, the populace of Bagram collectively grappled with disillusionment over how this soldier, having taken every precautionary measure fathomable, could've died so unexpectedly.

It was night before I arrived back on FOB Alternator, having caught the first helicopter I could find leaving Bagram. The airfield was black except for the sparks made by the pea gravel kicking off the blades of the Chinook, which was airborne and enroute back to Bagram before I'd even reached the control humvee at the airfield entrance. If anyone had been there when the bird landed, they were long gone now and I was all alone. Home sweet home.

I ditched my bag in my room and headed for the Operations Office. I could've easily played hooky, but I felt the urge to get caught up on the last two weeks.

The last two weeks.

Before long I found myself standing at the base of the stairs to the Command Post. I switched my flashlight off and stood there in the dark, in limbo between two lives.

Red flashlight beams bounced toward me from between a row of tents. Not yet ready to soldier, I ducked into the Port-A-John that stood a few feet from the stairs. The doors hinge announced my entrance and then slapped shut behind me. I stood in silence, trying to recreate the suspended existence I'd felt outside. I took a deep breath and my nostrils burned with ammoniated urine. The moment was gone. A new moment entered. One where I realized I hadn't pissed since Bagram. I switched my flashlight on and held its end between my teeth, so I could unbutton my pants. The warm liquid splashed off the back of the cold urinal, sending a noxious cloud of piss-steam rolling up through the flashlight beam, into my face. I wrenched my head from side to side, my flashlight illuminating the graffiti covered plastic walls. I took a moment to read some clever, albeit vulgar, poetry before buttoning up. Before leaving, I pulled a black marker from my uniform's breast pocket. Above the toilet paper dispenser I wrote "Kilroy Was Here" in big black letters and sketched the familiar face peeking over a wall. My contribution to the war in Afghanistan.

****

I stepped through the Operations Office door and landed millions of miles from my moment of calm. I'd expected the office to be vacant, but it was all-hands-on-deck. Everyone scurried around pointing at maps and looking at their watches.

"It's about damn time," The GIF yelled from his desk "Where the hell have you been?"

"America, Sir."

"I really missed your goddamn sense of humor," The GIF said. His orange hair was an explosion of gnarled tufts. Like an Irish Medusa. "Now get in here and get to work."

"What's the situation?" I asked.

Packages of Peeps were still stacked on my desk. I gagged a little.

"The situation is we had a giant turd of a mission dropped in our laps," The GIF complained. He swiveled his chair back around and began adjusting the font style on an operations slide presentation Captain Clark had probably created for him.

"Colonel Gunn called down and wants a Battlefield Circulation down to Kherwar with The SCO," Clark elaborated. He had a horseshoe of dip in his bottom lip and I think he may have even had some up top.

"What's the big deal about that?" I asked. "Commanders visit troops out on the frontlines all the time."

"He wants to go tomorrow," Captain Garcia chimed in.

"Oh."

"And he wants to go in by ground."

"Oh. Well that's not ideal," I said. "So why the sudden interest in driving?"

Clark and Garcia exchanged looks. The GIF swung his chair back around.

"Officially," The GIF said with an air of annoyance, "aircraft are scarce because they're still looking for that douche bag, Coucher."

"And unofficially?"

The GIF lowered his voice.

"Unofficially, The SCO's brain is a bag of cats and Colonel Gunn is testing him. Wants to see if he's gone full blown crazy-pants."

"Well what better way to test one of your leaders than to put a whole bunch of soldiers' lives at risk," I said.

Nobody disagreed.

"So The SCO's still nosediving?" I asked.

"Actually, he's been better," said Clark. "He even came to the chow hall the other day. I think he's easing up because there hasn't been any Nasir sightings in the last few weeks."

"Is Nasir dead?" I asked.

"Unlikely," said Garcia. "Our sources haven't heard anything concrete, but lots of speculation he packed up and left for Pakistan. Probably after he sold off Coucher. At least until the heat blows over."

"Anyway, news of The SCO's floor collapsing made it up to Brigade," continued Clark. "So, we think the damage is already done on that front."

"And The SCO is onboard with driving to Kherwar?"

"He doesn't have a choice. He can't turn down the Colonel," said The GIF.

"So instead he's turning the convoy into a goddamn armada," Clark elaborated. "Kherwar needed a resupply anyway, so Diablo Troop is going along with as many supplies as they can load. The SCO's even ordered us to arrange jingle trucks of fuel to come down from FOB Shank."

"This is going to be a debacle," I said.

Clark nodded.

"The route clearance team will leave first thing tomorrow at 0900 hours to clear any IED risk. Captain Russell jumped at the opportunity to get his ANA some convoy training, so they'll be in the mix too. They'll roll out thirty minutes behind Route Clearance and then Diablo Troop, with The SCO and the Colonel, will roll out at

1000 hours. That should give Colonel Gunn and the jingle trucks plenty of time to get down here from Shank."

"So what do you need me to do?" I asked. "Sounds like you guys have it all buttoned up."

"You can go pack your bags, my friend," said Major Connick as he walked into the office.

"I don't follow, Sir."

"Go get your gear ready. You're going along."

"Me, Sir? I just got back an hour ago."

"Good, then you're already packed," Major Connick grinned. "The SCO asked for you by name. He said Colonel Gunn will want to find Handboy while you're down there. I guess he considers you the subject-matter expert on all things 'Handboy'."

I wished I were back in the Port-a-john.

"Did he really ask for me by name, Sir?" I asked.

Major Connick grimaced a smile.

"Well—we all knew who he was talking about."

Chapter 25: Murphy's Law

October 20, 2009

On the morning of the convoy, the Route Clearance Team and Special Forces Team, along with the ANA platoon, left exactly as scheduled. That was the end of the things that went right. Shortly after Captain Russell's team departed, word came down from FOB Shank that the jingle truck carrying the fuel for the Kherwar Outpost had blown a tire. Any other truck would've been left behind, but the outpost was almost out of the gas for their generators, so it was deemed too important to be left behind. Initial estimates for fixing the truck were about an hour.

Four hours later, the truck was fixed and Colonel Gunn's convoy had finally departed, enroute to Alternator.

With four extra hours to think about it, the mission was still bugging me. I couldn't see the benefits of Colonel Gunn putting soldiers at risk to drum out one bad commander. Especially with only two months left in the deployment and The SCO having taken himself out of the fight already. Not wanting the responsibility himself, The SCO named The GIF as the convoy commander for the trip to Kherwar much to my dismay. And much to The GIF's dismay. He'd already "earned" his Combat Infantryman Badge and a Bronze Star for his role in the election day firefight he failed to participate in. He had no desire to risk adding a Purple Heart to his list of self-awarded accolades. He never said it, but I think he was also worried Colonel Gunn might recognize him from the whore's bath incident at the hand-wash-station. I knew he wouldn't.

Terp 2 had been tasked as The GIF's terp for the convoy mission and I was glad he was coming along. Not just because he was the only one who could get Handboy to talk, but because he'd been avoiding me since the election. My careless comments to Colonel Gunn about my distrust of Afghanis had not been forgotten. He'd stopped visiting the airfield during our night resupply missions and he rarely loitered in front of the Command Post these days. My embarrassment and my R&R had kept me from seeking him out. Today, we'd be forced into close proximity and I was hoping for a chance to apologize.

For the first hour of our delay, The GIF had been diligent in ensuring the Diablo truck crews were double and triple checking all of their vehicles and equipment for maintenance concerns. His zeal was short-lived and he was soon complaining of a sudden-onset dust migraine. I knew he was going to vanish, but I was hoping he'd at least make a grand production of it and throw some wild excuses our way. He did disappear, slinking off in his regular way, which was yet another disappointment. I'd been slated to ride in his truck, but that didn't mean I was in charge in his absence. The Diablo Troop platoon leader, Lieutenant Narrows, reluctantly took that duty. He'd been a Platoon Leader for the better part of three weeks now. Three mail-runs to FOB Shank dominated his combat resume.

"Sir, how long does it take the Taliban to place a roadside bomb?" Narrows asked. There was shudder in his voice and he looked tired from being hassled by The GIF all morning.

I had no idea.

"Longer than we'll be delayed," I said, feigning confidence. "We'll be out of here in no time. And even if they plant any bombs, the dirt will be to freshly disturbed. We won't miss it."

Lieutenant Narrows eked a smile. Even I felt better. A lie conceived in logic can be a comforting thing.

The truck crews were getting squirrely. Tight rings of soldiers began forming beside the long column of trucks. They smoked cigarettes, chewed nicotine gum and swore loudly while checking their watches. I had to do something before a mutiny began.

Terp 2 was resting against the huge rear tire of one of the Diablo wrecker trucks. Above the the truck's back bumper, a bucket with a hole in the bottom was secured with a bungee cord. This bucket served as a portable toilet for the truck crew during long missions. Someone had cleverly labeled it "Shit Bucket" with a black marker. Unstrapping the shit-bucket, I walked it straight out from the trucks about thirty meters and nestled it down into the pea gravel. Returning to the truck, I kicked Terp 2's feet until his eyes opened.

"What are you doing?" Terp 2 asked, as I helped him up.

"Just follow my lead," I said, as I bent down and picked up a handful of gravel. I poured half of the rocks into his hand and then began throwing mine, one at a time, at the bucket.

Terp 2 got the idea. His second stone landed in the shit-bucket with a solid *thud.*

"Nice shot," I yelled, over enthusiastically.

Within minutes, the groups of frustrated soldiers had dissolved into a single firing line on either side of Terp 2 and I. We heaved rock after rock at the pathetic old bucket. Give a man a target and unlimited ammunition and he'll occupy himself for hours.

I'd just separated two Privates, who'd been fighting over whose stone made it in the bucket, when Colonel Gunn's convoy pulled into the staging area. Their string of vehicles drove between us and the shit-bucket. A few ballsy Privates continued to throw stones over the moving trucks, until the caravan ground to a halt and a passenger door swung open.

The Colonel hopped from his truck and studied our half of the convoy with his hands firm on his hips. The wires from multiple radios tethered his head to his shoulders. With his stark, clean helmet and black sunglasses he looked like a cyborg. He approached our firing line and we stood at attention, with a nearly simultaneous salute. *Nearly* simultaneous, only because some soldiers had become distracted by Lieutenant Barrett and SSG Loredo, who sauntered up behind the Colonel. They were dressed in full-battle-rattle and to the undeployed eye, could have been any gender.

"Sorry for the wait, gentlemen. Turns out it's not easy finding replacement parts for these jingle truck monstrosities," the Colonel said, as if he'd fixed the truck himself.

He checked our chests for rank and settled on me.

"Everything set to go here, Captain—," he checked my name tape, "—Rye."

"Yes, Sir," I said. "We're ready to mount up and hit the road as quick as we can."

"Good, good," he said. "Say, I'm not sure we've met yet. Are you new to the Brigade."

"Yes, Sir," I lied.

Barrett scowled at me.

"Well, make note to set up a meeting with me. I like to get to know all my new junior officers."

He looked up and down the convoy line again.

"Where's Lieutenant Colonel Fink?" He asked. "Isn't he ready to go, for God's sake?"

"I'm here," growled The SCO as he and a small entourage emerged from between two of the Colonel's vehicles. Chappy trailed behind him, clutching his front armor plate with both hands and wincing with every painful step. He rolled his eyes when he saw me staring.

The SCO offered up a sloppy salute without breaking stride. Colonel Gunn didn't bother reciprocating. The SCO's body armor hung loosely over his skeleton. It was a cool day, but he was already sweating profusely. His eyes sunk into dark circles and rarely ventured from the top of Mount Krumpit.

"We'd better get on the road," The SCO muttered as he headed for his truck. "We need to be to the COP before sundown."

"Daniel," called Colonel Gunn.

The dreaded first name.

The SCO stopped cold, his back to the Colonel.

"Are you sure it hasn't been too long since the Route Clearance departed?" Colonel Gunn asked. "If you don't feel good about it, we can call it off."

And there it was. Our one chance. The SCO could chicken out and the Colonel could call off the whole mess.

The SCO pivoted stiffly, his heels grinding in the gravel. He stared coldly at the Colonel and then at all of us on the shit-bucket-firing-line. He slopped his cigar from one corner of his lips to the other. Then suddenly, the storm blew away from his eyes. He licked the free corner of his mouth and smiled.

"I think we'll be just fine, Sir," he said. "Any fresh IEDs should be pretty obvious in the daylight."

I nudged Lieutenant Narrows.

"Perfect," Colonel Gunn said. "Let's get this show on the road."

Turning their backs to each other, they headed to their vehicles. The Diablo soldiers looked at each other nervously. They too had felt their last chance of escape slip away.

I nudged Lieutenant Narrows again.

"You heard 'em," he squeaked. "Mount up."

Not very motivating.

I caught up with Chappy as I headed toward my truck, near the back of the convoy.

"Why's he making you come along?" I asked. "You should still be in the sick bay."

"God shield," was all he replied as he stopped beside The SCO's truck.

"Messed up."

He shook his head as he hobbled up the ramp, disappearing into the back of The SCO's truck.

The engine of my truck was already rumbling when I approached. Terp 2 was strapping his seatbelt on one of the long bench seats that lined both rear walls. The front passenger seat was empty. The GIF was still missing.

Over the radio came the crackled jargon of the lead trucks, who were starting to roll toward the gates. I grabbed the radio hand mic.

"Diablo 1, this is Titan 3 Air, over," I radioed to Lieutenant Narrows.

"This is Diablo 1, send it," he crackled back.

"Diablo 1, I'm without a truck commander back here,' I said. "Titan 3 still hasn't returned. I'll send a runner to find him."

"Roger, Titan 3 Air," came the reply. "We'll hold tight."

At the head of the column, the lead trucks ground to a halt. The line of gunners, whose torsos protruded from the turrets atop each vehicle, threw up their arms in frustration.

"Negative, negative, negative," came The SCO's gruff voice over the radio. "If he isn't here, he isn't coming. I'm not waiting another goddamn minute. Diablo 1, you're now in charge of the convoy. Titan-3-whoever-the-hell-you-are, you're now the truck commander for your vehicle. Call down to the TOC and have'm remove Titan 3 from the convoy manifest. Let's get the hell out of here. Titan 6, over."

Before I could respond, another voiced raised on the radio.

"This is Spartan 6," came Colonel Gunn's voice. "I agree with Titan 6. Let's get this thing moving, gentlemen. We've been held up long enough. If Titan 3 can't be on time, he doesn't get to go."

Doesn't get to go.

Like we were going on a damn field trip. I radioed down to the Command Post to have them remove The GIF from the manifest. The Radio Operator informed me The GIF had been in the Command Post five minutes earlier, dressed in his workout clothes and raiding their snack table. The Radio Operator asked if he should send anyone to inform The GIF. I told him that wouldn't be necessary.

The trucks began creeping forward again, slithering like a giant snake toward the front gates. The Colonel's four MRAPs and two jingle trucks inserted themselves behind The SCO's platoon, who were themselves following two of the Diablo Troop maintenance trucks, a wrecker, and a truck full of potable water. At the very front and very rear of the convoy were two MRAPs each. I was in the second to last vehicle.

I maneuvered from the bench seat, opposite Terp 2, up to the truck commander seat. My driver, an eighteen-year-old named Private Dunn, looked at me skeptically.

"You ever done this before, Sir?" Dunn asked.

"Of course I have," I said. "In training."

He rolled his eyes.

"Okay. Well, it ain't hard," he said. "I've done this a million times. The only thing you need-a remember, is that you've never done this before and I've done it lots, okay, Sir?"

He shifted the truck into drive and a terrible grinding noise came from under the hood. He swore under his breath and jerked the shifter knob into a different position.

"That ain't nothin to worry about," he said.

"Of course it's not," I said. "Cause you've done this lots."

I twisted around in my seat as much as my body armor would allow. Terp 2 was buckled in and looking extra nervous about Dunn's abilities.

"You good?" I shouted over the engine and gave him a thumbs up. I'm not sure he heard what I asked, but he smiled and returned the thumbs up. The gunner must have heard me and thought I was talking to him. He crouched until I could see his face in the turret ring. I was surprised to see he was a Staff Sergeant. If you're a Staff Sergeant serving as a gunner, you've probably made a few mistakes in your career.

"All good," Staff Sergeant Parker said. "Ready to smoke me some hajjis."

"Easy, cowboy," I yelled. "Let's hope we won't have to smoke anyone today."

Parker frowned. I must not have sounded like much of a combat officer to him. He shook his head and stood back up through his hole in the roof.

The MRAP ground across Alternator's gravel road. We moved quickly for a bit, but then slowed to a stand-still as the vehicles ahead navigated the barbwire serpentine at the front gate. Twice our vehicle hit the concertina wire and had to be untangled by the gate guards. I watched Private Dunn, who was mumbling under his breath, knuckles white on the top of the wheel. I doubled checked my seatbelt as we finally rolled out of Alternator's gates.

Chapter 26: Little Blue Truck

October 20, 2009

Sergeant Parker quickly confirmed my suspicions on why a man of his rank would be serving as a truck's gunner when he should've been commanding a truck of his own. As we passed through several small towns, Sergeant Parker threw handfuls of candy to the village children who'd come out to watch our giant iron beasts pass through.

"That's awfully nice of you," I yelled up through the turret.

Parker crouched and his face appeared in the turret hole. He was laughing uncontrollably.

"Halfa them—," he gasped with laughter. "—Halfa them are laxatives, Sir. The whole goddamn village is gonna shit its pants."

A glob of tobacco slipped from his lip and splattered on the floor between his feet. He heckled like a hyena as he slipped his sleeve across his chin to clear away the chew juice.

"What the hell is wrong with you?" I yelled. "Are out of your damn mind? No wonder these people try to blow us up."

Parker looked betrayed.

"Never figured you for a hajii-lover, Sir," he said, shaking his head.

"Well, I am," I yelled. "And quit using that word, 'hajii'. I'd bet my life you don't even have a clue what it means, so keep it outta your mouth. And make an effort to act like a decent human being."

I could hear Parker grumbling about where he'd like to shove his bag of candy as he stood back up in the turret.

Terp 2 never looked up from the book he was reading in the back. He'd asked Captain Clark a month earlier to send away for a book about America for him. When Clark asked which book specifically, Terp 2 had just replied, "whichever best represents America". Being a career soldier, Clark bought him a brick of a book called, *The Complete Military History Of The United States*. He'd been buried in it ever since.

The third village we entered was just north of the narrow pass into the Kherwar Valley. Our reception there was stone cold. I couldn't help but wonder if news of Sergeant Parker's poops-candy had traveled faster than our trucks. The whole village had gathered to watch by the time my end of the convoy passed through. I yelled at Sergeant Parker to keep his bag of treats in the truck.

I turned back to watch out the front window, as we squeezed through tight, qalat-lined roadways. The MRAPs were much larger than any vehicle normally traversing these roads and our side-view mirrors nearly scraped the clay walls that lined each side. The walls stood a few feet taller than our trucks and I feared the ease at which some rifle wielding Taliban-wannabe could pop up and deliver Sergeant Parker a new face hole. Our driver, Private Dunn, was swearing under his breath.

"You okay, Dunn?" I asked.

Dunn stared ahead and rung both hands over the top of the steering wheel.

"Dunn," I called again.

"Huh?" He said, coming out of a trance. "What, Sir?"

"Are you doing alright? You seem—tense."

"Me," he chuckled nervously. "Nah, not me."

He scooted forward in his seat and squinted.

"I've done this lots," he mumbled, settling back in his catatonic concentration.

"Sir!"

Terp 2 yelped so suddenly, both Dunn and I jumped. Scooting quickly across the bench seat, he thrust the open book toward me.

"Sir, I found your face," he said smiling.

"What are you talking about?" I asked, grabbing the book. I was shocked to see the familiar crude doodle of "Kilroy" peeking back at me from the open page.

"See," Terp 2 said proudly. "That's the face you've been seeing all over."

There were old photographs of American soldiers standing next to the graffitied face in World War II, the Korean War and the Vietnam War. Fascinated, I read the caption below the picture:

> *"Kilroy Was Here" became the calling card and geographical tag of the American G.I.'s as they made their way across theaters of war in the twentieth century. Although its origins are disputed, many credit an American Shipyard Inspector, James J. Kilroy, for the signature. During war-ship*

construction, workers were paid daily by the number of rivets placed and James Kilroy would end his day's count by circling the last rivet and scribing "KILROY WAS HERE". World War II soldiers, being transported to both the European and Pacific in the hulls of these great ships, picked up on the message and carried it with them around the world.

"Well, I'll be damned," I said, handing the book back to Terp 2.

"We might all be damned, Sir," said Private Dunn.

I turned back to the road ahead. We had exited the village, but the convoy had slowed even more.

"What is it?" I asked.

"The road gets real narrow up there, Sir," Dunn sighed. "If we roll, it's a long way down. This mission was a bad frick'n idea."

"We'll be fine," I said, tightening my seat belt. I slapped the roof, which had no effect on the thick metal plating. "Parker, be ready to tuck in if we roll."

"Roger."

I turned to Terp 2 again, who was already back to his seat buckling back up. He gave me the thumbs.

"Sir! Sir! Sir!" Private Dunn began slapping wildly at my arm. "Look at this shit!"

I whipped around in time to watch a jingle truck up ahead begin to slide off a particularly narrow stretch of road. Loose bungee cords, hanging from the trucks side, became pendulums indicating the exact degree to which the truck was screwed. At first it slid into the ravine, still on all four wheels, but as gravity took over and the terrain degraded, the heavy cargo truck slammed hard on its driver's side panels. It scraped along the rocks the remaining fifteen feet, leaving a cloud of dust in its wake, and then rested at the bottom of the hill.

****

It took the better part of two hours to position the wrecker where its wench could reach the overturned jingle truck. The Diablo Troop soldiers went to work and they were good at their jobs. What they weren't good at was get a petrified Afghani truck driver out from behind the wheel of his overturned truck. The driver was uninjured, but unresponsive all the same. Terp 2 volunteered to go down and coax him out, but all he got was a glassy-eyed stare-down.

The surrounding terrain was rugged and evoked thoughts of Captain Applegate's wartorn cheeks. The not-so-distant ridges and the town, still in our rearview mirrors, had me feeling uneasy. Especially being at the tail end of the convoy. Anybody could be lurking beyond those rocky mounds, so I decided somebody should put a better set of eyes on them. After all, we weren't going anywhere for a while.

"Titan Six, this is Titan Three Air," I radio.

Silence.

"Titan Six, this is Titan Three Air," I tried again. "Do you copy?"

"I ain't a goddamn Kinko's," The SCO growled. "So no, I don't copy. What the hell do you want?"

"Permission to round up a few soldiers and take them up to an overwatch position?"

Silence.

"We're still observable from the village," I continued. "And there's no visibility beyond the ridgeline."

"Permission denied."

The static crackled for a second then died. Sergeant Parker drummed obnoxiously on the turret's inner ring to a song only he knew. The radio crackled again.

"Titan Three Air, this is Spartan Six," Colonel Gunn's voice broke through.

"This is Titan Three Air," I said, excited someone had used my callsign.

"I just had a good idea," the Colonel said. "Why don't you round up a few soldiers and go set up an overwatch position on the ridgeline. We should keep our eyes on the village."

I shook my head. My only consolation was the thought of The SCO swearing up a storm in his truck.

"Roger, Spartan Six," I said. "Will set up overwatch, over."

"Spartan Six, out."

"Colonel Gunn's fulla good ideas," Dunn said smiling.

"Shut up, Dunn."

****

"Do you think God's real?" Chappy asked.

He was lying with his fingers locked on top of his helmet, watching billowing cumulus clouds roll by. He pointed up at a particularly long one.

"That one looks like an AK-47," he said, changing his own subject.

"I'm glad you're having a relaxing afternoon," I grumbled.

Chappy had convinced The SCO that the wrecker crew needed God's help to right the jingle truck and The SCO, desperate to get the convoy moving, had let him escape. Chappy found me just after I'd found two Diablo Troop soldiers whose sole contribution to the recovery was taking bets on whether or not the winch cable would snap. Together, the four of us had climbed to the ridgeline south of the village. From there we could easily observe the crowd forming outside the village walls, the progress of the jingle truck recovery, and the miles of oscillating landscape that bounced off into the horizon.

I seemed to be the only one concerned about the crowd outside the village and I watched them through my rifle scope, as they watched the progress of the wrecker. The two Diablo Troopers took turns throwing rocks into the ravine on the other side of the ridge.

"I'm serious," Chappy said. "Do you think God's real?"

"Of course, I do," I said. I'd focused my attention on a particularly suspicious looking military aged man in the village crowd.

"Why?" Chappy asked. His voice was distant; on the verge of sleep.

"Christ, I don't know. Because I always have?" I hadn't meant it to be a question. "Because if I didn't believe we were part of something bigger, I'd be too depressed to go on, I guess. You're not having doubts after your near death experience, are you?"

Chappy was silent. I figured he'd drifted off, so I kept studying the crowd. After a few minutes he picked his head up.

"You think they'll get Coucher back?" He asked. "Alive?"

I'd almost forgotten about Coucher's plight.

"No," I said flatly. The young man I'd been watching had pulled a cell phone from the pocket of his blue vest and pressed it to his ear. He moved away from the group of villagers as he spoke, but continued to watch the wrecker's progress, occasionally glancing at my group on the hill. But he wasn't the only one watching me. Chappy had craned his neck, looking for an explanation.

"I said I believe in God," I sighed. "But Darwin wasn't all wrong either. God gave us free will. Some people, like Coucher, use it to make dumbass decisions. And then they get their heads removed by religious extremists. So it goes."

"I feel like it's partially my fault," Chappy said. He settled back into watching clouds. "If I hadn't grilled him so hard for info, he might not have bugged out."

"If you hadn't badgered him, you wouldn't have found out about the Specialist Mafia, and you'd never have confronted Thedon. And then you'd have missed getting yourself stabbed nearly to death, which was the catalyst for your life-altering, religious awakening. So, in a way, Coucher saved *your* soul."

"That's a pretty 'bass-akwards' rational," Chappy accused.

The wrecker was making progress with the jingle truck, which was now back on four wheels. It appeared the plan was now to have the wrecker's winch crank the truck straight back up the hill. Terp 2 was still talking to the driver, who still hadn't moved from behind the wheel. When I looked back to the crowd outside the village, the young man in the vest had vanished.

"Well, that's no good," I gumbled. I explained to Chappy about the man I'd seen and how he'd been watching us, while talking on his cell phone.

"People have phones," Chappy stated, trying not to sound concerned. He tried to roll over, but struggled on the curvature of his back armor plate, like a turtle trapped upside-down. He finally gained enough momentum in his rocking to roll to his stomach.

"What the hell was that?" He asked, pointing toward the village.

"What was what?" I looked back through my scope. There was dust billowing from behind a qalat.

"I just saw something moving between those two qalats on the west side," Chappy said. "It was heading east."

I moved my scope and trained it on the next gap in the qalat walls to the east. The plume of dust continued to move slowly that direction. Before long I caught a glimpse of its creator as it moved slowly across the opening. A little blue truck.

By the time we made it back to the wrecker, the jingle truck was back on the road. Diablo Troop soldiers hustled about unhooking it from the wrecker and doing basic maintenance checks. They moved quicker than I'd ever seen. None of them wanted to be in the valley after dark.

Aside from some major cosmetic issues to the driver's side, the damage was minimal. The truck huffed with exhaustion for a few strokes before coughing back to life. The driver looked pleased with himself, having never even left his seat.

Colonel Gunn was now pacing around the recovery site, occasionally stopping to reprimand soldier's who'd become distracted by the two androgynous beauties following close behind him.

"Sir," I shouted as I jogged up. "Sir, I think something's up."

"I'll say," the Colonel said. "This is the most undisciplined group of wrench-monkeys I've ever seen. Not a damn one can focus on his job. They're not your soldiers are they?"

"No, Sir."

"Good. Or I'd have your ass," he said. "If they're not yours, then who are you?"

"Captain Rye," I groaned.

"Don't sound so disappointed in yourself, son," he said slapping me on the back. He walloped me so hard it knocked the wind from my chest.

"Have we ever met before, Captain Rye?" he asked, surveying the ridgeline of the hill that rose from the road.

"Yes, Sir. Many times, Sir," I said.

"Ah, well don't take it personally, son. I have a lot of Captains under my command. More than a few with bread related names too. Why, over in the 1-89 Infantry, there's Captain Wheaton, Captain White, and Captain Pumpernickel. And that's just in one battalion mind you."

"That's nice, Sir, but I think we have a real problem," I said, pointing back up toward the village. The Colonel was still staring off in the opposite direction.

"I believe there's a Captain Naan in the Field Artillery battalion. Indian fellow, I think. I could be wrong," he said and turned to Lieutenant Barrett. "Sarah, is there a Naan in Field Artillery?"

She shrugged with her typical bored indifference.

"Jesus, Sir," I said. "I need to tell you this. I spotted a blue truck moving through the village right before we came down. And there was a guy in the crowd watching us and talking on his cell phone.

The Colonel turned to me with a calm smile under his aviators.

"Easy, son," he said. "No need to take the Lord's name in vain. The Chaplain is standing right behind you for Christ's sake."

Chappy shook his head in disapproval, as the Colonel continued.

"People drive trucks, Captain Bread," he said. "Even blue ones. People also have phones. Which they make calls on. He was probably wishing his grandmother a happy birthday. If we waterboarded every Tom, Dick, and Akmed who made a phone call, we'd never get anywhere."

He began walking back in the direction of his own truck.

"Sir," I pleaded. "People don't make casual calls out here. And I've seen this truck before. Its Nasir's truck. I know it. There's an alert out for his sky blue truck."

Colonel Gunn stopped and turned around. He looked annoyed now.

"Captain, you don't get where I am by not paying attention to the intelligence reports," he lectured. "I've seen the alert and if I recall correctly, which I usually do, Nasir's truck is described as a 'periwinkle blue', not 'sky blue'. You clearly did not see the same truck."

The Colonel started walking again and I followed after.

"Sir, I've seen the truck before," I said. "In person. I know this was the same truck, whatever kinda blue you want to call it."

We were striding along fast now and I felt like the Colonel was trying to lose me. Chappy and the Colonel's harem followed close behind.

"Sir," I finally said again, "I believe this is a credible threat."

The Colonel stopped abruptly.

"Speaking of credible threats," the Colonel said. "Let's see what your Squadron Commander thinks."

We'd stopped right next to The SCO's vehicle. I could see his silhouette sitting like a stone inside, his gaze lost out the front windshield. The Colonel reached up and pounded on the truck door's window. The thick metal almost muted The SCO's yelp as he jumped in his seat.

"Open up, Daniel," the Colonel shouted. "It's your boss."

The SCO hung his head and then the door creaked open. A sandbag fell from the floor of the truck to the ground below.

"What is it, Sir?" The SCO made only the slightest effort to not sound annoyed. He bit down hard on his cigar nub and brown juice pooled under it against his lip.

"Your junior officer here has some intel to report, Daniel," the Colonel said looking back to me. "Go on. Tell him what you saw, son."

I took a deep breath.

"I saw a truck in the village, Sir. A blue truck," I said.

The SCO's gray complexion turned to green. He looked at Colonel Gunn cautiously.

"Well, Jesus, Reuben," The SCO said, laughing nervously. "There's gotta be a hundred blue trucks in this province."

"It's Rye, Sir," I corrected.

"Can we all stop using the Lord's name in vain in front of the goddamn Chaplain," the Colonel grumbled.

Chappy shook his head again.

"What shade of blue was it?" Asked The SCO.

"Periwinkle blue," I said.

The SCO's face went a shade greener. He looked at the Colonel again and reigned in his composure.

"Well there, you have it," The SCO said. "The truck alert says it should be a 'sky blue' truck. Not periwinkle."

"That's exactly what I told him, Daniel," gloated the Colonel. "What kind of combat officer knows what shade 'periwinkle' is anyway? Honestly, it makes me think you might be a little light in the loafers."

My face was hot.

"Listen, Reuben," The SCO said. "Diablo is loading up and we're about ready to roll again. I don't know about you, but I'd like to get the hell out of this valley before sundown. If it'll makes you feel better, you can call up your truck sighting to the Command Post when you get back to your truck."

His eyes plead with me to do just that, while the Colonel rolled his.

"Alright, ladies," the Colonel said. "Let's get moving."

The SCO snarled before realizing Colonel Gunn was talking to his assistants. The three of them continued down the line toward their truck. The SCO leaned out his doors and locked onto Chappy.

"Get in," he demanded and then slammed the door without another glance in my direction. The back hatch of the truck dropped slowly and Chappy climbed sadly aboard.

"Godspeed," he said on his way up the ramp. The hatch began to close before he'd even made it inside.

I rushed back to my truck and climbed aboard. Dunn and Parker hadn't left their positions and Terp 2 was climbing back in at the same time. I jumped on the radio immediately. Communication in the valley was spotty at best, but the Alternator Command Post seemed to pick up the important parts of my message. Captain Applegate refused to put Captain Garcia on the line and assured me I had nothing to worry about. According to him the alert was for a 'cadet blue' truck. Not sky or periwinkle. I slammed the hand mic down.

"Everybody seems tense," Parker called down from his turret hole. "Why don't you all enjoy a couple pieces of candy."

The trucks in front of us started creeping forward and Private Dunn followed suit.

"You think we're going to get hit before we leave this valley, Sir," Dunn asked.

"I hope not," I said. "Maybe I'm just being paranoid."

"Bring'em on," called Parker.

There was a brilliant flash of red in front of the windshield and the truck lifted violently into the air. The cabin filled with smoke as we slammed back down.

Chapter 27: Fire Fight

October 20, 2009

There's a series of subconscious steps taken in the seconds following an explosion. Most people don't know this because most people have never been blown up before. First, you check yourself. It's natural instinct. Self preservation. Call it whatever you want, except selfish. Following a blast, a soldier must confirm he's physically whole and still in possession of all critical appendages and eyeballs. The Army calls this, "Life, Limb, and Eyesight". This is a critical step before rendering aid to comrades. It does no good fixing your buddy's broken fingers while your own leg is dangling from a bloody stump.

I gave myself a quick once over. No bloody stumps. My eyes burned from the smoke that still billowed around the truck's cab, but that meant my eyes were still there, so that was good. My ears were what worried me. The ringing was deafening, but at least I could hear it. I guess that was something too.

The second step is assessing the surrounding area. Like my "wayward appendage scenario", patching up a buddy in a burning vehicle is counterproductive. I scanned the truck's cabin. No fires. The biggest hazard was the black smoke choking the air. It rolled across the roof like an inverted ocean. I glanced at the ceiling above my seat, thinking maybe my helmet had left a mark.

Third, and most important, render aid to fellow soldiers. Now that you've confirmed the absence of imminent danger and that you're not personally bleeding out in a vehicle that's about to erupt, it's time to attend to those in need. There is no order in which to proceed. Formal rank is irrelevant. Priority of aid is determined by the ferocity of the blood spurting from gaping flesh wounds.

"Dunn," I called through the haze. "Dunn, talk to me. You alright?"

Dunn's head appeared through a curtain of smoke.

"I luuk awlwight?" He sputtered. Blood poured from his nose, which was now bent sideways on his face. One pupil was dilated and his bottom lip puffed out to twice its normal size, catching the blood that streamed from his nose.

"Good God," I recoiled. "Is the rest of you okay?"

"I fink so," Dunn said, looking down. He swiped his sleeve across his mouth, leaving a streak of gory war paint across one cheek. "Ya, I fink I'n okay."

"Good," I said. "I think the radio's out. See what you can do." I twisted around in my seat too fast. My vision blurred and waved like a funhouse mirror. I blinked hard and the world focused. I reached back and gave Sergeant Parker's pant leg a tug. He was still standing in the turret, so I could only see him from the waist down. As far as I knew, that could've been where he ended.

"You all good up there, Parker?" I called.

There was an uneasy silence and then his gloved hand dropped downward through the turret opening. Thumbs-up.

The smoke beyond Parker's legs dissipated and Terp 2 became visible. He was on his knees between the seats, his face was blue and eyes wild with panic. One hand clasped tightly around his throat. Empty MRE wrappers littered the floor around him.

"Are you okay, Ahmad?" I shouted, knowing full well he wasn't. I thrashed wildly to get out of my seat, sliding on my armor chest plate across ammo boxes stacked between the seats for Parker's fifty-caliber machine gun. I kicked my feet for momentum and would've accidently kicked the radio had Dunn's fingers not been in the way.

He yelped, spitting blood across the dashboard.

"Sorry," I called back as I rushed toward Terp 2. He was on his back now, gulping like a fish in a boat. I yanked him to the sitting position and swung my legs in behind him.

I'd never been trained in the Heimlich Maneuver, but I'd seen it done on television. It turns out, it's a whole lot harder when the victim is wearing a flak jacket. I wrapped my hands around the padded vest, giving a solid pull with no effect. Terp 2 reached back, grabbing my shoulder over his own. Terror coursed through the white tips of his fingers. I gave three more hard thrusts below his chest, but the thick flak jacket made it futile. I felt his grip begin to loosen.

"It's not working," I yelled, mostly to myself.

I scrambled to my feet, searching frantically for any tool to help. Desperate, I jerked Terp 2 to his knees and with all my strength, thrust his torso into the bench seat in front of him. He hit the seat with a dull thud and a golf ball sized hunk of lemon-poppyseed, MRE pound cake launched from his throat and adhered itself to the seat back, just inches from his face.

Terp 2 gasped, coughed and cried simultaneously.

For a second my vision tunneled and I slumped against the opposite bench.

"You used my real name," Terp 2 squeaked out between coughing fits.

"Take smaller bites," I groaned.

Terp 2 nodded, still hunched over the seat.

"Dunn," I called. "Where are we on the radio."

"I goh nuffin, Sir," he yelled. "And ooh boke my finga."

"That wasn't me, that was the bomb," I said. "You're delirious. You need a doctor."

Dunn went back to nursing his fingers, when suddenly Parker's legs went limp. The canvas gunner's harness twanged, as Parker's ass hit the end of the slack. Now in a sitting position, he dangled from the harness, spinning lightly on the tips of his boots like a combat ballerina.

"Parker," I called again. I leaned in, but couldn't get a look at his face, which was still level with the turret ring. "Parker, are you okay?"

No response.

"Parker! Answer, dammit."

No response.

"Dunn, I need your help," I yelled, scrambling over to Parker's legs. I stepped on Terp 2's fingers on my way by and I heard him yelp.

"Sorry," I called back.

I heaved Parker up, but Dunn was still navigating his seatbelt release with two broken fingers. Terp 2 rushed in and unhooked the harness strap, allowing me to ease Parker to the truck floor.

I gagged.

Parker's right sleeve was torn clean at the shoulder and hung loose around his forearm His shoulder was split open like an over-microwaved hotdog. Whatever debris had hit him was hot as hell. The wound had been cauterized on contact and was barely bleeding. Small mercies, I guess.

"Wat do ee do naw, Sah," Dunn garbled, finally making it over the stack of ammo boxes.

I suddenly became aware of the sound of bullets pinging against the truck's armor outside.

"I'll take care of Parker," I explained as calmly as I could and then pointed into the turret. "*You* get on that gun and return fire."

Dunn looked relieved not to be responsible for the life, limb and eyesight of Sergeant Parker.

"Wha doo I shoo?" he asked as he climbed into position.

"Anything that moves, Dunn. Anything that moves."

I removed the field dressing from Parker's body armor kit. It's best practice to always use the injured man's field dressing first; you never know when you'll need your own. Parker was conscious, but miles away. His eyes followed the wisps of smoke that drifted overhead. He was mumbling something over and over again, but his dictum was too quiet for me to hear. I finished wrapping the dressing over the wound. It wasn't perfect. It wasn't even pretty.

Parker continued his chant and I leaned in close, placing my ear right to his lips.

"They're all gonna shit their pants," he mumbled.

"Amen, brother," I said, giving his other shoulder a pat. "You got 'em good."

There was a knock on the back hatch. Terp 2 stood next to the door, his eyes staring right through Sergeant Parker. I waved my hand to get his attention, pointing to a button along the back hatch. He hit the button and the ramp dropped. Fresh air flooded the vehicle, replacing the dust-smoke cocktail we'd grown accustomed too. The door hit the ground and Sergeant Jonston stepped inside.

"Anybody need a medic?" he smiled.

Sergeant Jonston went to work on Parker, removing the field dressing I'd applied, which he labeled "atrocious". Terp 2 watched the process intently, while munching on what remained of his lemon poppyseed pound cake. We'd need a MEDEVAC helicopter for Parker, so I slid back over the ammo cans to the radio. After ten seconds of mashing buttons and twisting knobs, it was clear the MEDEVAC request wouldn't be coming from our truck. If I was going to talk to anyone, I'd be going for a walk.

****

The sun had already dipped behind the western hills as I darted between vehicles. All the enemy gunfire was coming from the east ridge, so I used the vehicles as cover. Behind me, Private Dunn let loose burst after burst with the truck's fifty caliber machine gun, though I wasn't sure he'd identified any targets.

Two more columns of smoke billowed up from farther down the long convoy of trucks. My truck was not the only one hit.

The next truck I reached was The SCO's. Pressing my back armor plate against the truck, I drew in a deep breath. The sprints between trucks had left me lightheaded. I was about to take a knee when The SCO's door cracked open.

"What the hell are you doing outside your goddamn truck," The SCO growled, poking his head slightly out to see me.

I could barely hear him over the rhythmic thumping of his own truck's machine gun.

"The blast took out my radio, Sir," I yelled over the racket. "I'm trying to find out what the hell's going on."

"We're all going to die," The SCO yelled. "That's what's going on, you twit."

His eyes scanned wildly across the western ridgeline for any signs of movement in the growing dusk. The cigar dropped from his mouth and landed in dirt.

"Sir, the enemy fire seems light. I think we'll be alright if we—," my attempt to rationalize was cut short.

"You don't get it, Rueben," he said. "Its Nasir. He's out there. You saw his damn truck yourself. He's not going to stop until I'm dead."

"I don't think he's targeting you specifically, Sir. Besides, I think we've got him out-gunned" I said, pointing to the fifty-caliber barking away on his roof.

"Of course he's targeting me, you fool," he yelled. "After all the promises I broke—"

"What promises, Sir?"

He was in survival mode and pretended not to hear me.

"Get back to your truck," he growled. "We're turning this convoy around. Hard telling what Nasir has planted farther down."

"Sir, we can't turn around. Half my truck's engine is gone and there's at least two other trucks disabled farther down."

The SCO followed my finger as I pointed down the road. As he looked, a rocket propelled grenade, or RPG, cut between the two trucks ahead of us and slammed into the opposing hillside, showering the vehicles with rocks and dirt.

"Suit yourself," The SCO snapped. "I can't force you to follow orders. *I'm* heading back to Alternator, with or without you. And, I'll be documenting this insubordination immediately."

The SCO leaned back inside his truck and grabbed the radio hand mic.

"Raven One, this is Titan Six."

"This is Raven One," crackled the voice of the SCO's platoon leader, Lieutenant Carrier.

"Get our vehicles turned around," the SCO said. "Raven Platoon is returning to Alternator. The situation here is too hot."

"Sir?" Carrier was confused. "There's a truck ahead of us that's in bad shape. It's Colonel Gunn's truck, Sir."

"I have eyes, Raven One," The SCO yelled. "I repeat, the situation is too hot. If I wanted a status report, I'd ask for it. Get these goddamn trucks turned around. Now. Titan 6, out."

He slammed the hand mic on top of the radio.

"You can't just leave," I yelled. We were beyond formal courtesies.

When The SCO turned back, his face was placid. The panic was gone.

"Listen," he said. "The Colonel's here and who knows what kind of shape he's in. The last thing this brigade needs is two of its senior leaders killed in the same firefight."

There was so much conviction in his rationalization, I almost considered it. Another RPG impacted the rocks behind the truck. The SCO slammed his door, denying me a rebuttal.

I yelled at him again, but he pointed to his ears, shrugging like a petulant child. He shooed me away, as his truck began making its eighteen-point turn in the narrow road. The truck ahead and the truck behind began the same process.

"You coward," I yelled, even though I knew he couldn't hear me. I ran to take cover behind the next set of vehicles. Reaching the next truck, I doubled over. The tunnel-vision set in, but only for a few nauseating moments.

I was two trucks back from the second bomb site. The smoke rolled from Colonel Gunn's truck and crept toward me along the road, caught in a downdraft. Light was fading and I squinted into the smoke. I rubbed my eyes as two phantoms bounded in my direction. A mirage perhaps. Before I knew it, the two figures emerged from the smokescreen, shimmering as they passed through the heat exhaust of the next truck. They ran single file, carrying a stretcher between them. The Colonel's entourage. Their tightly-bunned hair had been knocked loose and flowed behind them from under their helmets. Despite their heavy load, they moved gracefully. Their faces were marred with soot and dirt, but their locks bounced together like models in a shampoo commercial. They seemed to move in slow motion. Like Valkyrie goddesses, removing the worthy dead from the battlefield. Majestic.

"The fuck you looking at?" Spat Barrett as she reached me.

"The Colonel's wounded you dumb son-of-a-bitch," huffed Sergeant Loredo. Her hands and lower sleeves were drenched in blood.

"It's not that bad," yelled Colonel Gunn from the stretcher. "And I'm not going anywhere, so don't even try it."

One lens was missing from his aviator sunglasses. His leg was bad. Real bad. The left pant leg was shredded and soaked in blood at the middle of his shin. A tourniquet was expertly placed below the knee and a field dressing was tied to cover as much of the gaping wound as possible. His lower leg and foot remained attached by nothing more than a two inch strip of meat that quivered and jerked involuntarily. Bile rose in my throat.

"Sir, we gotta get you out of here," I choked.

"No shit, Sherlock," interjected Barrett. "We heard Fink say he's turning around, but our radios were busted. We gotta get the Colonel on one of those trucks."

"I told you, I'm not going anywhere," yelled the Colonel.

"With all due respect, shut the hell up, Sir," yelled Loredo.

"He's probably right about that anyway," I said, pointing toward The SCO's platoon.

Three trucks were in the process snaking around the roadblock that was my truck. Private Dunn watched them with confusion as he continued to fire away at nothing in particular on the ridgeline.

"Where the hell does he think he's going?" Barrett demanded.

"Back to America is my bet," I said.

"Why are there only three trucks leaving?" Loredo asked.

"What?"

"Three trucks, idiot," she snapped, pointing toward The SCO's retreat. "He's got four in his platoon."

In the chaos, it hadn't occurred to me. The SCO was leaving a truck short. I checked the tail number of the truck we were crouched behind. It was from The SCO's platoon.

"Hey!" I called up to the gunner. "Whose truck is this?"

The gunner, who'd stopped firing to reload his MK-19 grenade launcher, leaned over the edge of the truck.

"Sergeant Major Storms, Sir," he said with smile.

A bullet snapped overhead. The gunner slapped the feed tray closed and went back to work, lobbing explosives into the hilltops. I banged on the passenger door until it cracked open. The seat was empty, so I hopped up. The driver, a kid who barely looked eighteen, was settling back into his seat.

"Where'd Sergeant Major go?" I asked.

"Up the line to check on the burning trucks," the driver said pointing out the windshield. "He headed up there a few minutes ago.".

"Well, I've been out there a few minutes and I haven't seen him."

"He went up the other side of the trucks, Sir."

"Why would he take that side? Is he suicidal?"

"He said he was gonna draw fire to give the gunners somethin' to shoot at," the driver shook his head. "He's batshit crazy."

I snatched the radio hand mic and rooted through a pouch on my body armor, finally producing a laminated index card. My MEDEVAC request cheat-sheet. The Army's MEDEVAC request has a very rigid format and requires nine lines of information. These nine points ensure the medical helicopter brings all necessary equipment to perform a successful evacuation and save a soldier's life. Miss a line and someone could die. My nerves were shot, but I stumbled through the request, giving them all the info they needed. The radio operator on the receiving end was cordial, despite my bumbling, and assured me the evac helicopter would be onsite as soon as possible.

When I climbed back down from the truck, CSM Storms had returned. He kneeled beside Colonel Gunn along with Sergeant Jonston, who'd returned after patching up Sergeant Parker. They were attempting to administer an I.V. to Colonel Gunn, who wanted no part of it.

"Get that thing away from me," he shouted. "My leg is fine. It's always been like this. I'll run circles around any one of you."

Storms pinned the Colonel's arms down, so Sergeant Johnston could insert the I.V. As soon as the needle pierced his skin, the Colonel went ballistic. I thought about adding a straight-jacket and an exorcist to my MEDEVAC request. The sudden exertion, coupled with an extreme loss of blood, was enough to make the Colonel lose consciousness. Sergeant Jonston checked his pulse for good measure and set to replacing the I.V. which had been ripped out during the Colonel's tantrum.

"MEDEVAC should be inbound soon," I told CSM Storms.

"How long did they say?" Barrett asked quickly. Her and Loredo were at either end of the truck, rifles raised and scanning the eastern ridgeline for targets.

"They said 'as soon as possible'."

Storms shook his head, as he zip-tied the Colonels wrist to the stretcher poles.

"Then they're not likely to be here anytime soon," he said.

He motioned to Barrett and Loredo to come back. As they left their positions, a barrage of bullets came in, snapping overhead or pinging sweetly off the truck's armor.

"You two," Storms pointed. "Get Colonel Gunn in the truck. When he wakes up, keep him calm and make sure he doesn't buck that I.V. again."

He gave two whacks to the passenger door of his truck and the back hatch dropped like magic. Barrett and Loredo collected the stretcher and hustled up the ramp, disappearing into the truck. Sergeant Jonston followed behind them to monitor the Colonel until needed elsewhere.

"Absolutely no tattoos," I said, pointing a strict finger at him.

He smiled and disappeared into the steel belly of the beast.

"What now?" I asked CSM Storms.

He lifted his hand, signaling for silence. Squatting with his back against the truck's running board, he pulled his night-vision goggles from a side pouch in his body armor and mounted them to his helmet. All the while, paying close attention to the bullets pinging intermittently off the trucks.

When in doubt, do what the sergeants do.

I squatted against the truck and mounted my own night-vision goggles. I too listened to the sounds of the incoming fire.

"What do you hear?" CSM Storms asked.

"The sounds of people trying to kill us?"

"They're down to two men," came a voice a few feet away. CSM Storms nodded and I jumped, as Chappy swooped in to share in the cover of our vehicle.

"Chappy," I exclaimed. "I thought you were with The SCO. How'd you get out?"

"I may have broken a few 'Chaplain Rules'," he stated, squatting down next to me.

"Such as?" I asked.

"Such as stealing The SCO's sidearm and threatening to pistol whip Frank to death with it," Chappy sighed.

He didn't like my disapproving look.

"I *barely* pistol whipped him at all," Chappy defended. "The SCO was pretty eager to get outta dodge."

"You shoulda pistol whipped The SCO," Storms muttered.

"So, what's the plan?" Chappy asked eagerly.

"That's what I was just asking," I said. We both looked to Storms.

"When I was down by the Colonel's truck," he said, "I got a quick look at the bomb crater. There's a detonation wire leaving the hole, heading straight up that hill.

He pointed over the truck to the highest hill top.

"If I were a bet'n man, I'd say if we followed that wire, it'd take us straight up the hill and we'd find a nice little fighting position on top. And we aren't gonna get any break from this rifle fire until somebody goes up there and knocks that position out."

"So you wanna take some guys and assault that hilltop?" I asked.

"Hell no," Storms said. "These guys are all mechanics, medics and line cooks. Most of'em haven't assaulted an objective since Basic Training. *You* want to take them?"

"*Me*?" I asked. "You're not coming?"

"Hey, Sir, I'm all about taking the fight to the enemy," he said. "But my place is here, prepping a landing zone for the MEDEVAC and making sure the gunners stay supplied with ammo."

"I think I got one," shouted the gunner above us. "Saw that sum-bitch bounce ten feet in the air."

We listened again and sure enough, the alternating rifle fire had reduced to the sporadic fire of one lone shooter.

"See," Storms smiled. "The tide is already turning in your favor."

Chappy pulled back the slide of The SCO's pistol, chambering a round, and then letting it slam forward.

"We got this," he said to me.

I wasn't convinced.

"So, it's supposed to be me and Chappy here?" I asked. "Going off, in the dark, to assault a high-ground-objective of questionable resistance?"

"I'm coming too," came another voice from the back of the truck. Lieutenant Barrett was coming back down the ramp of the truck, her hair pinned back up under her helmet.

I rubbed my eyes in frustration.

"And why, may I ask, are you going?"

"Revenge," she stated matter-of-factly.

CSM Storms put a hand on my shoulder and smiled at me with his big white teeth glowing in the last light.

"Have confidence, Sir," he said. "That's your primary job as an officer. 'Audacity, audacity, always audacity.' You do that, you'll be just fine.

He flipped his NVGs down over his eyes and flicked the switch. A crescendoed whine cut the darkness as they powered up.

"Besides, Sir, we own the night."

Chapter 28: No One Owns The Night

October 20, 2009

The second gunman started firing again while Chappy and Lieutenant Barrett were mounting their night-vision goggles to their helmets. Our odds were worse again. The gunner on top of the truck, who'd claimed the kill, cursed and pounded his fists.

"Don't be so hard on yourself," I called. "You prolly winged him at least. I bet he's just slowly bleeding out."

"You're just saying that to be nice," he said glumly.

"No," I defended. "I'd bet on it. In fact, we're gonna go up there to prove it to you."

The gunner allowed himself a smile.

"But just to be safe," I continued. "Why don't you keep hammering him and see if you can get him to bleed out a little quicker."

The gunner nodded and continued the rhythmic *whump whump* of the grenade launcher.

"Stay alert, stay alive," CSM Storms had touted before trotting off down the line of trucks. He was off to round up any more wounded and to check ammunition levels of the gunners, who by now were all laying waste to the eastern ridgeline.

Even with the darkness and the heavy suppressive fire, the enemy was somehow managing accurate shots. Going straight up the hill was out of the question. Besides, no self-respecting cavalry officer would ever lead a frontal assault against an elevated position, unless your name was Teddy Roosevelt and you had a pair of brass balls.

"So where're we heading," Barrett asked, trying to adjust the focus on her NVGs.

"If we head that way, the road curves around the hill," Chappy said, pointing The SCO's pistol in the direction of Colonel Gunn's smoldering truck. "We can use the trucks as cover and then come up the side of the hill on their flank."

I shook my head. The NVGs made my helmet front heavy and I felt like a bobble-head doll.

"That's the way they'll expected us to come," I said, tightening the chin straps of my helmet. All of my gear suddenly felt foreign, after months of minimal use. I was double checking everything and trying not to look like a soup-sandwich. "Chappy, remember that ravine we had to climb through to get to our overwatch position this afternoon?"

"You can't be serious," Chappy complained.

"As a heart attack," I said, trying to sound confident.

"That ravine was rocky as shit. It's gonna take forever to navigate in the dark," Chappy complained.

"Have a little faith," I said. "It's familiar ground and it runs right along the north of this hill. Plus, if these guys retreat to anywhere, it's going to be back to Nasir's truck. If we take the ravine, we have a good chance of cutting them off."

"Yes, but—," Chappy started.

"Good God," Barrett hissed. "Do you hens ever stop clucking? Let's get this shit-show underway."

She slapped the bolt release on the side of her rifle. The bolt slammed forward with a *ka-chunk*, chambering a round. Without a second glance at Chappy or I, she bolted across the opening between trucks, heading back toward my truck.

"Well, I guess that decides it," I shrugged.

"Better hurry, Jared," Chappy sighed. "Or she's going to take the hill all by herself."

"How does the saying go?" I asked. "'Hell hath no fury like a woman you just tried to kill'?"

"Something like that," Chappy said as he darted to the next truck.

We leapfrogged from truck to truck, taking turns going first across the openings. We weren't getting actively shot at and we wanted to keep it that way. By the time we got back to my truck, I was out of breath again. An extra fifty pounds of body armor bouncing on my chest and shoulders didn't exactly make me feel like an elite warrior.

The front of my truck still smoldered and Private Dunn remained vigilant behind his fifty caliber machine gun. He'd slowed down his rate of fire, realizing he'd have to make his bullets last. We approached cautiously, as a dark silhouette leaned against the rear of the truck.

"Who's that?" I asked cautiously. My NVGs were still off, because I didn't like the way they impaired my vision.

"It is Terp 2," came a reply. It was odd hearing him refer to himself as "Terp 2". I regretted not using his real name more. He had a can of Sergeant Drill's in one hand and was eating an Aunt Marge's muffin like it was an apple.

"What're you doing out here?" I asked.

"It was too noisy inside," he informed.

PVT Dunn let loose a burst that bludgeoned my ear drums.

"Jesus, don't you think you should have your helmet on?" Chappy asked, as he and Barrett came up behind me.

Terp 2 shrugged and took another bite of his muffin.

"How's Sergeant Parker?" I asked.

"He seems okay. Sergeant Jonston gave him many drugs."

"He's sleeping through all this racket?"

"Not sleeping," said Terp 2. "He is yelling very bad things about Afghani people. And about Muslims. Really about brown people in general. He is so very racist. This is why I came out here. Too noisy in there."

"Sorry about him," I said, moving past and peering around the back of the truck. I was scouting my route to the ravine.

"Why are you sorry?" Terp 2 asked. "You did not make him say these things."

"I know," I said, still gauging the distance in the dark. "But he's my countryman—I guess."

"Does this mean I should apologize for the trucks blowing up?" Terp 2 asked.

"C'mon, Sir," Barrett interrupted. She rocked back and forth like she was about to start a race. "Quit your gabbing and let's do this thing."

"Where are you all going?" Asked Terp 2 with interest.

"To kill some bad mama-jamas," said Chappy. "We're the swift right hand of God."

Terp 2 looked to me with confusion.

"We're going to assault the hilltop."

"I want to come with you," he declared, spiking the rest of his muffin into the dirt.

"Absolutely not," said Chappy, before I could answer. "You're not armed, you're not trained, and my pistol doesn't need a translator."

Terp 2 puffed his chest.

"Fuck you," he said. "This is my country, not yours. I am coming."

Chappy gave me wide-eyes as Terp 2 swung open the passenger door and crawled in to retrieve his helmet. From inside, I could hear Parker yelling something about "camel-jockeys".

"You're seriously gonna let him come along," Chappy asked.

"He's right," I said. "It's his country. If he wants to fight for it, why shouldn't he be able to?"

Terp 2 climbed down from the truck with Sergeant Parker's rifle in hand.

"You even know how to use that thing?" Chappy asked.

Terp 2 shook his head.

"Here. You use this and stay behind us," Chappy said, handing Terp 2, The SCO's pistol and taking the rifle for himself. "Flip the safety and when you need to shoot, point it at whatever you want to kill."

Terp 2 swallowed hard and nodded. He looked like he was regretting his own audaciousness.

"Dunn," I shouted up between bursts.

He looked like a sci-fi nightmare with dried blood caked around his mouth and chin, below his night vision goggles.

"We're going around the hill and assaulting up the north side," I yelled, pointing in our desired direction. "Watch for our I.R. lights. Shift your fire south once you see us."

Dunn nodded as I tucked an infrared chemlight in the band around my helmet. I tossed a chemlight to Chappy, Barrett and Terp 2, who all followed suit. The glow of infrared chemlights can only be seen through night-vision goggles and it's assumed that ill equipped insurgents have neither.

Lieutenant Barrett was the only one with a radio, so she relayed our assault plans to CSM Storms and any other vehicles that could hear us. She was in a hurry, so she left out a lot of details I probably would have included, but that's just me. Storms chuckled when she told him Terp 2 was coming along.

"Good," he replied. "The kid has guts. I like it,"

Terp 2 beamed. And with that we were off.

****

Traversing the ravine was rough and unpleasant. The carved walls raised a foot above our heads in most places. In the wet season, the ravine would be filled with churning, muddy water, but now the ground was nothing but loose rock. Not unlike the gravel covering of FOB Alternator, but with a few boulders added to the mix. I felt pleasantly well trained for the terrain. Finally, life on the base was paying off.

I'd turned on my NVGs before leaving the truck and the world in front of me became a grainy green glow. A ghastly world where every boulder or bush had the potential to reveal itself as a hiding place for vicious men. I counted my paces to estimate our distance and occasionally climbed the banks to view our surroundings. Each time I expected a bullet between the eyes.

Terp 2 stumbled along behind us. His helmet wasn't equipped for NVGs, so he walked nearly blind in the dim light of the crescent moon. I could hear him muttering to himself and Chappy kept shushing him.

"What is the plan?" whispered Terp 2.

"The plan is for you to shut the hell up," hissed Chappy.

"I mean, where are we turning?" Terp 2 asked. "How much farther?"

I stopped and held my fist over my shoulder. The universal sign for "stop". Chappy and Barrett took a knee, followed closely by Terp 2. The tread of a small sneaker had been stamped in a rare sandy washout. The rocky walls above it were scuffed where someone, or multiple someones, had climbed. The tracks were coming from the opposite direction, where the wadi continued on before disappearing around the curvature of the hill. I poked my head above the wall. We were directly between the hill and the village.

"Looks like a popular place," Chappy said. "Over the wall?"

I nodded to Lieutenant Barrett, who whispered into her radio as loud as she dared.

"Shift fire, shift fire, shift fire, over."

I made a step with my interlocked fingers and hoisted Chappy over the ledge. He lay on his stomach and helped Barrett next, followed by Terp 2, who was significantly lighter without all the armor and gear. I jumped up next, with Chappy and Terp 2 taking the underside of my arms. Grunting and sputtering, I kicked for traction against the wall and slithered out of the cutt.

Pausing on the ledge, I rested on my hands and knees. My vision began to tunnel again and the small green circle of night vision grew even smaller.

Not now.

I shook my head, but the circle kept shrinking.

"What is it?" Chappy whispered, putting a hand on my shoulder. "You hear somethin'?"

It seemed like a valid excuse.

"I think I hear someth—," I vomited on the ground beneath me. The retching brought back my vision and the small circle of green light widened again.

"What the hell is wrong with you?" Barrett whispered. "Puke quieter."

"He hit his head in the explosion," stated Terp 2.

"I'm fine."

"He's spent too much time behind his goddamn desk," Barrett grumbled.

"I'm fine," I said again, unsure which of their assessments was most true. "I'm fine."

We spread out across the hill, with Chappy fifteen feet to my left and Barrett the same to my right. Terp 2 followed behind me at a distance. The footing on the hill was infinitely better than in the ravine. The spring thaw-waters had swept it's surface clean of large rocks. Villainous shrubs dotted the climb, appearing as menacing dark orbs until coming into focus.

The incline was heartbreaking. My legs and thighs burned with each footfall. Were I capable of wielding my rifle one-handed, I could have leaned forward into a bear-crawl. Terp 2 *did* bear crawl with The SCO's pistol tucked in his waistband. Barrett seemed to be the only one not struggling and I had to keep motioning for her to slow down and stay on line with Chappy and me.

The trucks on the road below continued belching rounds at the far end of our hill.

Snap!

An apparition burst from the ground a few feet to my right. I stared at the green cloud as it danced and then settled back to earth.

Zing!

The sound was a hummingbird in my ear. The wake of the bullet stroked my cheek.

"Contact front!" Chappy yelled.

I hugged the hill. Two more rounds snapped into the ground near Chappy. I scanned the hilltop for any sign of a shooter, but could only see black-blob shrubs.

"I can't see shit," I yelled.

"Me either," shouted Barrett.

I looked back at Terp 2, praying I wouldn't find him with a gaping hole in his face. But he'd crawled up beside me and lay with his arms outstretched and pistol drawn.

"Me either," he shouted, between huffs.

"I got nothing," Chappy called. "Let me give you a target."

"Chappy, don't be—," I stopped as Chappy stood and bound forward up the hill. Two more shots ripped the air and he thudded to the ground.

"Chappy!"

Far beyond him, a black-blob shrub rose, taking the form of a man's silhouette. The silhouette pumped its arms furiously, retreating farther up the hill. I raised my rifle and focused down the site. The small lit dot of the scope rested on the center of the running black mass. I steadied my breathing and moved my finger toward to the trigger.

Pop. Pop. Pop.

The silhouette crumpled to the ground. My finger still hovered millimeters above the trigger.

"Hell, yeah," screamed Barrett, pumping her fist in the air. "Got you, you son-of-a-bitch."

"Chappy," I yelled again, getting to my feet.

"What?" he finally yelled back.

"I thought he got you," I huffed, running up to him. "The way you hit the ground—"

"Well it wouldn't have been very smart to stay standing," he said, sitting back on his heels.

"Besides," he said, pointing a thumb at his chest. "God shield."

"Did you see me blast that fool?" Barrett asked, as she and Terp 2 moved cautiously up to us. Her teeth glowed through my night-vision. "Bitch bounced like a bad check."

We were near the hilltop now. Tracer rounds impacted the ridge farther to the south, answering the sporadic bursts that still peppered the trucks with harassing fire. This was a particularly tenacious cell of fighters. A normal firefight in Afghanistan lasts only a few minutes.

"Something's off," I said. "They should've broke contact a long time ago."

We continued on to the top of the hill, fanning out to our original positions with me in the center. Barrett's kill was directly in my path and I kicked the rifle from its lifeless hands. Blood soaked the cloth of his blue vest coat around two large exit wounds. It was the cell phone user I'd seen earlier outside the village. One of Barrett's rounds had exited through his mouth and took his bottom jaw with it. Strips of cheek hung down like tentacles. Bile filled my mouth and I looked away before my vision narrow again.

"It's the guy from the village," I hissed at Chappy. "The guy with the cell phone."

Chappy pressed his fingers to his lips, hushing me like a Sunday-school teacher. He pointed down the backside of the ridge. Twenty meters away, sandbags had been stacked in a semicircle. A board covered the top and more sandbags had been stacked on top. A perfect fighting position. But in a peculiar place. It had no line of fire to the road and only a few feet from where I perceived the entrance would be, the hill dropped off to a nearly vertical decline.

"I'd bet that's where the wires from the bombs lead," I offered in a whisper.

Chappy hushed me again, then pointed to his eyes, then to his boot, and then back to the fighting position.

"You're going to throw your boot to draw someone out?" I asked. I wished we'd had grenades instead.

"No, dumbass," Chappy scolded. "Look at the far side of the hole. Someone's feet are stickin' out. Could be a dead fighter."

"Could be a live fighter," I said.

Blood pulsed through my ears as we approached. I kept the rifle trained on the back side of the bunker, while Chappy swung around to the front and Barrett stayed on line with us, scanning the ridgle-line for more scrub-bush-blob-men.

"Jared," Chappy called as he skirted around the bunk. "We have a situation."

When I reached the bunker, Chappy was squatting in front of the entrance. The legs protruding from the bunker were connected to a person, so that was a bonus. The man lying in the bunker was dressed in a long white tunic. His wrists were bound and his arms were tied to his sides around his abdomen. Over the tops of his hands, thick white gauze had been tapped, each with a large dark splotch of blood staining the top. He had no thumbs. Over his head was a black hood. The hood was enormous.

Chapter 29: Little Black Backpack

October 20, 2009

Chappy crawled into the bunker and yanked the hood off unceremoniously. Specialist Coucher's eyes were wild and he rallied against his restraints. He looked fatter than before.

"*Mmmmph mmph mmmmph*," he screamed from behind a silver strip of tape.

Before Chappy could tear the tape away, a snake of smoke curled inches over my shoulder.

"Shit!"

I dropped to a knee as an RPG slammed into dirt farther down the hill and exploded. I raised my rifle again and panned the horizon frantically. My scope finally settled on a crouching silhouette. Had he not been shaking his arms, I would have never distinguished him from the other shrubs. He was trying to drop something.

I fired two rounds. The figure reeled from impact and spun to the dirt. I felt instant remorse. But there was no time for that. I turned back to Chappy, who nodded approval.

"Aaaaaahh," Terp 2 screamed from down the hill. I felt sick. The RPG would've impacted near where he'd been standing.

"Ahmad," I shouted. Searching the hillside.

"I've got him," came Barrett's voice from down the hill.

They appeared in my night-vision. Terp 2's arm was draped over Barrett's shoulder. She staggered forward, bearing the burden of his weight.

"Is he okay?" I called.

"Ass full of shrapnel," she puffed. "He'll live."

"YEEEOOOWWW," came a scream from inside the bunker. Chappy had torn the tape from Coucher's mouth in one quick stroke.

"Shut your goddamn mouth, you deserter-bastard," Chappy snapped. Then he wrapped Coucher's bigass head in a hug, pulling it close to his chest plate. "I'm glad you're not dead."

"I didn't desert," Coucher insisted. "I was gonna come back after."

"After what?" Chappy demanded.

"After I talked to the Taliban," Coucher said. "Geez, didn't you guys find my note?"

Chappy shook his head and started to lift Coucher to a sitting position.

"No," yelled Coucher. "There's a bomb."

Chappy dropped him.

"What are you talking about?" I demanded. "Where?"

"It's under the tunic. Strapped around my tummy, under my arms," he begged.

I took a step back.

"Why the hell didn't you start by telling us that?" I yelled.

"Who says 'tummy'?" Chappy asked. "What are you, five years old?"

Chappy grabbed the tunic collar with both hands, ripping it aggressively down the middle, similar to the way he broke bread in communion. With his red lens flashlight, he illuminated the black backpack under Coucher's arms. The same black backpack Handboy had carried the night of the election. The straps crossed on Coucher's chest before disappearing under his shoulders.

"What do we do?" Coucher asked.

"*You* sit still and try not to explode," I snapped. "Chappy, what do we do? Leave him here and call up the EOD team from Alternator?"

Chappy shook his head.

"It could take hours for the bomb squad to get here," he said. "And who's to say we won't get attacked again."

He kept shaking in disagreement with his own assessments.

"No, we gotta get him outta here," he said. "The bomb hasn't blown yet, so it probably required a triggerman. And it sounds like all the triggermen are dead or on the run."

He was right. An eerie silence had settled over the hill. The convoy's guns were now silent and all I could hear was the low rumble of their engines far below.

"We gotta get this backpack off him," Chappy declared. "You good with that?"

"You're the God-shield," I relented.

"I'm not good with that at all," Coucher whined. "You don't know what you're doing and neither did the kid who rig—mmmph mmmmmph."

Chappy silenced him with the tape and began a closer inspection of the backpack, looking for protruding wires and boobytraps.

In the distance, another engine coughed to life. But this was no Army truck. The sound came from the village. I flipped my NVGs back down and scanned the village, but all I could see were the grainy, green qalat walls. No signs of life. Then suddenly, but slowly, the outline of a small truck emerged from behind the village walls. I'd have bet anything it was periwinkle blue or sky blue or whatever-the-hell blue color it needed to be. It crept carefully down the hill in our direction. Then, using a wash in the bank, it dropped into the ravine. Using the ravine as a road, the truck disappeared behind another set of hills to our east.

"Son-of-a-bitch is getting away," I grumbled.

"Not necessarily," Barrett said. She had lugged Terp 2 up to the far side of the bunker. The two of them rested against the sandbag walls. Before she could explain, I heard it too.

Thump, thump.

"It's just the MEDEVAC," I said.

"Not just the MEDEVAC," Chappy said looking up.

He was right. Two more sets of rotor blades pummeled the night air.

"Apache escorts," I smiled.

Within moments the angry hornets buzzed over head. Barrett used her radio to relay the last known direction of Nasir's retreating truck. The Apaches, in turn, relayed that the hill appeared clear of any immediate threats and then ventured off to hunt down their prey.

I waited anxiously for them to find the truck or for Coucher to explode, whichever came first. Barrett's radio crackled away, as the pilots chatted between themselves:

"Viper 3, this Viper 2, we've got eyes on the BOLO truck."

"Roger Viper 2, we see it. Truck appears to have stopped."

"This is Viper 3, can you positively identify any threat?"

"Male suspect emerging from vehicle.... Appears to be armed."

"Can you confirm he is—"

"Break, break break, we are being engaged. Returning fire."

From beyond the hill, I could hear the unmistakable belch of the Apache's thirty-millimeter chain-gun, firing rounds so fast they merged into one long vibration.

"This is Viper 3, enemy combatant neutralized. Permission to disable vehicle?"

"This is Viper 2. We're just waiting for permission from higher to use Hellfire Miss--permission granted."

"Fire."

"On the way."

There was a bright flash behind the hills and then a clap of thunder chased it from the valley.

"Target destroyed."

I sighed and lifted my NVGs. The MEDEVAC helicopter had landed near the convoy and was collecting the wounded. I suddenly became very aware of my sweat drenched uniform, which clung to my skin. The exposure on the hilltop sent a chill to my bones.

"How's it coming down there?" I asked Chappy, through chattering teeth.

Chappy wiped sweat from his brow. His head hovered an inch above Coucher's chest, as he slowly eased back the two zippers that converged at the top of the bag.

"We'll see in just a second here," he finally said through his concentration.

He gingerly opened the bag, shining in the red light from his flashlight.

"Well, what is it?" I asked impatiently.

Chappy squinted into the bag.

"Looks like we've got four blocks of C4 wired to a cellphone," he said. The rest is a 'terrorist party mix' of rusty nails, ball bearings, and severed purple thumbs."

"Mmmmmph, mmmph, mmmmmph," Coucher said with raised eyebrows.

"Yes, I'm sure yours are in there too," Chappy reassured him, before his attention was caught by something else in the bag. "Hello, what's this little guy."

He carefully reached into the bag and pulled out a folded piece of notebook paper.

"Death to America," he read, shaking his head. "How unoriginal."

He handed the paper to me. I unfolded the paper and held it up, holding my own flashlight to it. On the inside was a crudely drawn image of a naked woman. The woman had her fist raised defiantly in the air, clutching a flaming American flag. The style in the art was the same I'd seen in the old Kherwar log book, but something had changed. The smooth, graceful lines of the woman's curves, where no longer so. They bumped and jittered erratically. There was a loss of control in the sketch. A sadness.

I should be an art critic.

"What've you got there, you perv?" Barrett asked mockingly.

I jumped.

"It's not mine," I blurted, jamming it into my cargo pocket.

"I've got good news and I've got bad news," Chappy said. I was grateful for the change of subject. "The good news is that the bomb's not wired to anything outside the bag and its meant to detonated when someone calls the cellphone. And since all the bad guys seem to be deceased, there shouldn't be any inconvenient calls."

"And the bad news?"

"The bad news is that I'm still not real comfortable jostling this thing around a lot. We're gonna have to cut the shoulder straps and lift it outta here."

We all nodded in agreement. Except Coucher, who shook his head emphatically.

Chappy pulled his Kabar from its sheath and sliced through the straps like an MRE pound-cake. He worked the straps out from under Coucher, with little participation from Coucher himself. With the straps free, he carefully lifted the bag and pushed it toward me.

"Here," he said.

"Me? What happened to 'God-shield'?"

Chappy didn't say anything. He just kept the bag hovering there, the severed black straps swaying beneath his hands.

"Alright, alright," I said, reaching out and taking the bag. Chappy's hands stayed frozen in place. He was looking beyond me now.

"Jared," he whispered. "Behi—"

CLICK.

The sound of a pistol's hammer cocking back sounds exactly like it does in the movies. I turned slowly, still holding the bomb-bag out in front of me; one foot still in the bunker. Above me, loomed a thin figure. The barrel of a tarnished, old revolver shivered a foot from my face. The figure's other hand, ensnared in a metal cage, held an outdated cell phone pinched in its twisted fingers.

"Handboy," I muttered.

"What?" Handboy demanded. His words were a blend of fear and rage.

"Handboy," I said louder, with a little more shame. "It's, um, kinda what we call you."

"You, Americans," Handboy snarled. "So arrogant. So cold hearted, you would make up names for a boy crippled by your own men. Shame to you."

"Well, you did run away," I said. "So we didn't know what else to call—"

"Shut up. You are worst of all" Handboy shouted, thrusting the pistol toward me. "I was great artist. I was going to leave Kherwar. Leave Afghanistan and be famous cartoonist for the Playboy magazine. But you stole this dream from me."

I kept my eyes locked on the phone in his hand, as his thumb gilded back and forth over the keys.

"I'm very sorry about your hand," I said. "We can get you some proper rehab—"

"Quiet," Handboy said. "Your offers mean nothing to me. It is too late for you. It is too late for all of us."

His thumb mashed the phone.

"Think fast," I yelled, heaving the bag-bomb at him and wishing I'd had something wittier or more heroic to say. Swiping at the bag with his caged arm, Handboy stumbled backward discharging his pistol into Coucher's foot.

"MMMMMMMPHHH"

An awful ringtone of middle-eastern pop music jingled from inside the bag. Handboy tried to shake the bag from his caged forearm, where the loose straps had become tangled. I lunged forward to push him over the hill. The shrieking bag, still swinging wildly, served a vicious blow to the side of my head, knocking me off balance. My vision tunneled. I stumbled sideways, waiting for the blast or at the very least, a bullet from Handboy's revolver.

Pop, pop, pop.

I cringed, but felt nothing. On the other side of the bunker, Terp 2 stood with The SCO's pistol drawn. Handboy was a statue, staring down at the dark circles forming on his chest. The awful music jingled from inside the bag. He stumbled backwards, loosing his balance as the hill picked up pace behind him and disappeared over the edge.

The sound of a rolling body clattered in time with the gyrating ringtone, growing farther and farther away. I peered over the edge, straining to see his progress. There was an intense flash from below. My feet left the earth and I found myself gazing at the night sky. I felt a peculiar optimism, staring up at those stars. Like hundreds of luminous warriors fending off a darkness descending on the crescent moon.

Chapter 30: Flatline

October 21, 2009

My boots were skidding over rocks and dirt. I could smell a woman's shampoo.

Darkness.

A truck's engine idled. There were stars again. I puked bile into a patch of dried grass beside my head.

Darkness.

I was inside a truck. Terp 2 was on his belly next to me. Doc Jonston prayed over his ass and then raised a twisted piece of metal into the air. An offering to the war gods. Terp 2 wailed.

Darkness.

A fluorescent light hummed overhead. I shielded my eyes and found a tube in my arm. I could hear bees.

Darkness.

****

I woke to the sound of canvas lapping behind my head. The fluorescent light hummed gently and was still much too bright. Scratchy linen sheets were pulled up to my armpits and the smell of latex was tainted with wintergreen chewing tobacco. My head throbbed.

"He's back," declared a voice from the foot of my bed.

Major Connick stood in a huddle with Captain Clark and The GIF. I had the feeling my consciousness had inadvertently interrupted a secret meeting, but Major Connick smiled all the same.

"Welcome back, hardcore," said Captain Clark.

"It's about damn time," The GIF yawned. "Thought we were going to have to pull the plug on you."

I surveyed my horizontal body. No tubes, no wires, no missing appendages.

"Was I on life support?" I asked, still hazy.

"It's just an expression," The GIF said.

"I don't think it is," I said. "How did I get here? Where's everyone else?"

"Dead," said The GIF.

My stomach turned.

Major Connick smacked him in the chest.

"Geez, he knows I'm kidding," The GIF complained.

"I did not, you sick—"

"Everyone's fine," Major Connick said, raising his hand. "Aside from the shrapnel in Terp 2's butt and Coucher losing a toe, everyone's fine and resting."

"You've been out a good ten hours," said Clark. "Doc thinks it's a pretty severe concussion."

"What about Colonel Gunn and Sergeant Parker?" I asked.

"In Bagram," Major Connick said. "Both needed extensive surgery. More extensive than we could provide here."

"Well, what happened to me?" I asked. "I don't remember anything after Handboy fell."

"That's why you don't look at explosions, genius," The GIF said.

"Terp 2 said you took three pretty bad blows to the head yesterday," explained Major Connick. "I guess the last one put you out. Chappy said Lieutenant Barrett dragged your butt all the way down the hill, while Chappy helped Terp 2."

"And Coucher?" I asked.

"Chappy made him walk," Clark said smiling.

"Coldblooded," I said, laying my throbbing head back on the pillow. "Well, at least we got Nasir."

Connick and Clark exchanged a look, while The GIF fiddled with a vital-signs monitor behind them.

"About that," Connick said. "We didn't get Nasir."

I sat up to quickly and my skull cracked down the middle.

"How is that possible?" I groaned. "I heard the pilots confirm it. They destroyed his truck."

"The pilots said they destroyed 'a truck'," The GIF sighed. "Lots of people drive trucks."

The madder I got, the more my head felt like exploding, so I tried to stay calm.

"I know what I saw," I argued. "I saw Nasir's truck. I saw the damn sky blue truck. Did somebody go look at it? Didn't they find the bodies?"

"Captain Russell's team came back to interrogate the scene," Clark explained. "They found *some* bodies. All of'em had rifles, but none of'em were Nasir."

I closed my eyes.

"Captain Russell said the truck was more of a 'baby blue' anyway," said Major Connick.

I opened my eyes, ready to scream. Major Connick snorted, holding back laughter.

"Well, I guess The SCO's descent into paranoid madness can continue," I sighed.

The three men exchanged glance again.

"What?" I asked. "He's pissed, isn't he? Because I didn't follow orders? So now I'm going to be on some shit detail for the rest of the deployment."

Major Connick ran his hand through his hair.

"You don't have to worry about The SCO."

"You're gonna have to give me more than that," I said.

"The SCO's not in command anymore," Major Connick said. "Colonel Gunn, despite his leg hanging by a thread, was quite clear on the matter. The SCO was a on helicopter to Bagram this morning. He'll be on a plane to the States tonight."

"You shoulda seen his sleeping quarters," The GIF interjected excitedly. "Talk about a mess. And can you believe he'd been sleeping on one of those nasty old Army cots this whole time? Nobody knew it, so nobody bothered to get him a mattress."

"Sleep deprivation," I mumbled. It had been one of my major concerns my first day in Bagram.

"What?" Major Connick asked.

"Nothing. Who will be acting commander? You, Sir?"

Major Connick smiled.

"That would be the chain of command, yes. I'll be acting Commander until they bring in a replacement of appropriate rank."

The GIF shook his head, as he continued to fidget with the buttons on the monitor.

"Congratulations, Sir," I said to Major Connick, but continued watching The GIF. "I can't think of anyone who deserves it more."

The GIF mashed a button with his thumb and the heart rate monitor began to flatline.

"Dammit," he grumbled.

Doc Jonston raced in from the back of the room wearing nothing but gym shorts and panic. Under his right eye was a large bruise.

"What the hell is going on here?" he yelled.

The front of his chest and legs were covered in tattoos. Each located and positioned where he could easily do them himself. One tattoo on his stomach was upside-down. He was a walking page of doodles.

"Your damn monitor is broke," grumbled The GiF.

"Were you playing with this, Sir?" Doc accused, wheeling the monitor away from The GIF.

"Playing? No, I was not playing," said The GIF, shaking his head. "I was running a diagnostic on it to make sure your equipment is in working order. Which it clearly isn't."

"My machines are fine," Doc grumbled as he wheeled it away. "And I see my patient, who's been unconscious for the last ten hours, is finally awake. I'm sure glad somebody had the common sense to come notify his doctor."

"Your patient is awake," Clark said, gulping down some chew juice.

"You're not a real doctor," The GIF mumbled, embarrassed over being chastised.

Doc ignored them both and sat on the edge of my bed.

"How are you feeling, Sir?"

"My head is pound—"

"He's fine," The GIF interrupted again. "We need him back in the office ASAP."

"Sirs," Doc said, turning back to the group. "Captain Rye has suffered a traumatic brain injury. He could have intracranial pressure and need a craniectomy. He could suffer a decline in fine motor skills, as well as verbal communication skills. He'll likely have post traumatic stress episodes for the rest of his life. At the very *least*, he needs to get some rest. And *I* need to run some doctorly tests. Visiting hours are over."

"You have actual visiting hours?" The GIF asked.

"Yes. And they are not now."

Major Connick and Captain Clark said their farewells and the three men exited the Med Station. Doc returned to my bedside with a packet of paper and a pen.

"Was all that stuff you just said true?" I asked.

"Oh, God no," Doc smiled. "You're gonna be fine, Sir. I just wanted them to leave. I do need to ask you a few questions though.

They're a little like brain teasers. Just to make sure you didn't get any wires crossed in the ol'noggin."

"What happened to your eye?" I asked. Pointing to his bruise.

Doc frowned.

"You happened," he said.

"I did that?"

"You regained consciousness briefly and started yelling about bees," Doc explained. "I caught a fist when you started swatting at them."

"I'm really sorry."

"Don't be," Doc said. "I probably deserved it."

"Did something happen to my arm?" I asked. "It stings awful bad."

I reached up to rub it. Doc's cheeks flushed red.

"Don't be mad," he said, scooting farther down the bed.

I lifted the sleeve of my undershirt. Just above my bicep, was a familiar face. The words "Kilroy Was Here" were inked below it. The flesh around it was pink and tender.

"Don't be mad," Doc repeated. "It was Terp 2's idea."

"I love it," I said.

Chapter 31: Flight Of The Terps

December 5, 2009

The sky was a deceiving blue. The kind that makes a winter day look warm. Through the hot-breath-fog on the Humvee windows, I watched wafts of powdery snow twisted across my frozen airfield. The low rumble of the Humvee's engine was lulling me to sleep. I checked my watch. Helicopters were due in fifteen minutes, but not a single passenger had arrived. The Squadron was two weeks out from re-deploying home and some "non-essential personnel" were already shipping out. I'd been placed in charge of arranging flights for the first leg to Bagram. Watching people leave was bittersweet, but today would be harder than most.

There was a tap on the passenger window and the frosty hinges squawked open.

"Got room for another?" Chappy asked. Not waiting for a response, he shucked off his bags and climbed in. He removed the fleece beanie covering his bald head and wiped a hole into the fog on the windshield. Leaning forward, he squinted down the empty airfield, across the bright snow.

"Am I the only one leaving today?" He asked.

"Nah, you're just the only one willing to stand in the cold," I said. "They'll all come running when they hear the birds."

"The rhythmic bludgeoning of freedom," Chappy smiled.

"I can't believe they're sending you home already," I teased. "Apparently God is non-essential personnel now?"

Chappy scoffed.

"They need me back there to counsel all the broken-hearted Privates, returning home to an empty bank account and 'Jody' in bed with their wives."

"Jody is the worst," I said.

"Should be punishable by death," Chappy grumbled.

We sat in silence for a few minutes, while I weighed a subject I'd been hoping to broach and Chappy fantasized about capital punishment for adulterers.

"You ever worry that maybe you haven't made a difference?" I asked.

"Hell no," Chappy said bluntly. "I always make a difference. Sometimes it's just not the one I intended to make."

I nodded and Chappy did me a favor by changing the subject.

"Who's flying out with me anyway? You got the roster, right?"

I pulled a paper from my coat pocket and unfolded it.

"Looks like mostly Diablo Troop guys. And Captain Applegate."

"Dammit," Chappy said. "That dumbass is gonna try to sit by me. He treats every interaction with me like a frickin' confessional."

I couldn't help laughing.

"I'm serious," Chappy said, chuckling now himself. "I'm not his damn Catholic priest. I don't give two shits how many times he's looked at porn this week."

He gave me a minute to catch my breath.

"I thought I heard the terps were flying out today too," he said.

"Yeah, they're on there too."

"Good," Chappy said. "I'll try to sit next to Terp 2. Course, I probably should still apologize to Frank for the whole 'pistol whipping' incident."

"Nah," I said. "He had it coming."

"How's he doing by the way?" Chappy asked.

"Frank?"

"No, Terp 2," Chappy said. "I haven't seen him since Major Russell stole him."

Major Russell had been impressed with Terp 2's actions on the hill and had recruited him to serve as his personal interpreter on the Kherwar Outpost. In exchange for his services, Major Russell offered to train him in basic soldiering skills. I had trouble imagining him doing combat training in between mouthfuls of Marge's muffins, but I guess the night on the hill had flipped a switch for him.

"I haven't heard anything either," I said. "I was hoping he'd come up early, so I could catch up with him."

Chappy stuck out his lower lip.

"Aw, Captain Rye misses his lil' buddy."

"It's your empathy that makes you such a good chaplain," I said.

I glanced out my window. A lone figure in a Terp uniform and a heavy, black coat walked up the road to the airfield. His face was bundled in a scarf and his kevlar helmet was pulled low over his eyes.

"Speak of the devil," Chappy said.

I hopped out and approached the man, only to find the fat face of Frank smiling his obnoxious smile, when he pulled down his scarf.

"Oh," I said in my most disappointed tone. "It's you."

Frank's parasitic relationship with The SCO had made him a lot of enemies and he'd been in hiding ever since The SCO's departure. Every now and then, he was spotted darting in and out of the cafeteria between meals, his arms full of Marge's Muffins and cans of Sergeant Drill's, but no one ever made an effort to track him down.

"Don't look so happy to see me," he sneered. "Besides, this is the last time you *ever* have to see me again."

"I could've done without it."

"You and me both, my friend. I'm going to go sit in the Humvee while I wait."

"Chappy's in the Humvee," I said.

"I'm going to go stand in the staging area," Frank said, abruptly changing his mind. He huffed over to the cement barriers and dropped his bags, occasionally shooting a wary glance at the Humvee.

One by one, soldiers began filtering into the airfield, forming a line along the cement barrier beside Frank. They spoke excitedly about going home and snapped final pictures of their drab, year long, all-inclusive resort. I chit-chatted with Chappy until Captain Applegate arrived and pulled him into a private conversation. There was still no sign of Terp 2.

It wasn't long before the familiar *thump, thump* filled the air. Soldiers began collecting their bags, front loading them in anticipation of the tiny Chinook seats. I had everyone from my roster except Terp 2. I radioed down to the Command Post, but the sleepy radio operator hadn't seen him and wasn't volunteering to go find him.

The helicopter touched down, its dual rotors kicking up the soft snow into an icy tornado. I felt a hand rest on my shoulder and turned to find the smiling face of my friend.

His appearance had changed dramatically over the last two months. The baby fat of his face had melted away and his once unkempt, curly hair had been sheared into a bold, military high-and-tight. His shoulders were squared, his back straight. He looked like a man on a mission.

"You're late," I said.

He peered around me at the helicopter.

"It appears I'm exactly on time," he smiled.

"You made me talk to Frank by myself again," I said.

"That was not my intention," he laughed. "I'm glad to see you one last time."

"I'm glad you're well," I said. "It's been an honor."

I extended my hand to shake, but was pulled into a hug.

"The honor is mine," Terp 2 said, straightened himself and his uniform. He squared up and rendered a salute, which I quickly returned. Picking up his bags, he headed for the helicopter.

"Have you decided what's next for you?" I called after him.

He never broke stride, but I saw him smile as he shouted over his shoulder.

"Afghanistan!"

Chapter 32: Kilroy Was Here

December 16, 2009

I was alone in the Operations Office. The officers from the new unit had left early for lunch. Their family pictures and knick-knacks had replaced ours around the room and two full boxes of Peeps still sat at the back of my old desk.

The GIF had left for home already. He'd claimed an allergy to the laundry detergent used by his replacement, despite the fact we all used the same laundry service. Major Connick and CSM Storms were staying on a few days longer to ensure the new unit had everything they needed. Captain Clark was waiting for me on the airfield.

I swiveled my chair, taking in the room one last time. I thought about the year and the chaos that shaped it. And about what I was taking away from the experience, besides a recurring headache that could bring a man to his knees. I checked the clock. Ten minutes until the helicopter was due, assuming it was on time. They never were. I picked up my bags and headed for the door, bouncing recklessly through the jam as I squeezed out.

The steps of the Command Post had been salted, but were still covered in ice. Gripping the wood railing, I eased my way down to the snow-gravel mixture below and set my bags down next to the Port-A-John. The door screeched its familiar warning of the smell inside. It was going to be a long time before Bagram and another bathroom. Cocking my head to the side, I dodged the piss steam rising from the urinal. Above the toilet paper dispenser, buried in the noise of lesser graffiti, I spotted my own artwork.

"*Kilroy Was Here*"

Reaching into my breast pocket, I pulled out the same permanent marker. With one quick swipe, I slashed a line through "Kilroy" and wrote "Rye" above it.

You don't have to pull a trigger to make an impact.

Satisfied with my legacy, I put my marker away. Satisfied with my pee, I put my pencil away. The door screeched its goodbye, as I stepped back into the snow. In the distance was the sound of freedom.

Thump, thump.

Epilogue

August 3, 2013

In a small office on the second floor of the old Kherwar school house, the new ANA Company Commander sat precariously on a small strip of his chair. The toes of his glossy, black boots tapped concrete as he studied a stack of intel reports. The reports had been left by the Americans, who'd turned the outpost over to him and his soldiers only a week earlier as part of recent efforts to hand off security operations to the Afghani Army. This was the Commander's third time through the same reports, but today the words bounced off him. His mind was elsewhere.

Gradually, the low rumble of a pickup truck drifted through the window and lifted his ears. He stood with considerable effort, more than one would expect from a man so young. A trait he'd earned over several years of rigorous training and gritty combat. From his window he could see the entire western valley, the Kherwar village and the road to the outpost. On that road, a pickup truck approached with much hast, sending spiraling red dust into the air behind it.

There was a knock on the office door.

"Enter."

The Commander looked over briefly to find a young soldier in the doorway. He recognized him as one of the new recruits. The soldier couldn't have been more than five years his junior, but he felt a lifetime older than the poor boy looked.

"Sir, the patrol is returning from the village," the young soldier said, before realizing the Commander was watching exactly that. "Looks like the intel was right. They have one detainee."

The Commander nodded without looking back. When the soldier had left, he bent down to pick up his green beret, which had slithered from his desk behind the fray of shuffled papers. He winced as he straightened and rubbed a charlie-horse from his right butt cheek as he exited the room.

The truck crunched to a halt in front of the guard shack before the Commander arrived. Two particularly weathered soldiers hopped from the truck's bed and chatted excitedly with the guards about the raid they'd just completed. Another four soldiers burst forth from the trucks cab to corroborate their stories. All six fell silent when their Commander approached.

"Excellent work men," he said. "Where is he?"

The men pointed to the bed of the pickup truck.

"Bring him to me."

The two soldiers, who'd been riding in the truck bed, went back and dropped the tailgate. Lying face down was a man, whose hands were zip-tied behind his back and head was shrouded in a burlap sack. The soldiers grabbed the man under each armpit and pulled him forward. He protested briefly before his feet dropped from the tailgate to the ground with a heavy thud. The tips of the man's boots left twin trenches in the dirt behind him and the soldiers dropped him on his knees before the Commander, then stood tall beside their prize.

The Commander examined the man in burlap.

"Did he have anything on him when you captured him?" The Commander asked.

"Not much, Sir," one of the soldiers replied and began digging into his cargo pocket. "These were the contents of his pockets, Sir."

He bent down and, one by one, began laying items onto the ground in front of the prisoner. A buck knife. A cell phone with a cracked screen. Several hundred dollars in American currency. A black beret. A crumpled sketch of a naked woman.

The Commander squatted down before the prisoner's personal effects and lifted the black beret. He turned it over in his hands to find an American Combat Infantry Badge pinned to its face.

"Do we have the right man?" One of the soldiers interrupted.

With care, the Commander removed the pin and discarded the beret back to the dirt. He turned the pin over in his hands, feeling its weight and deciding its fate. Then, unbuttoning the flap of his breast pocket, he tucked the pin neatly inside.

"Yes. Yes, we have the right man."

ARMY JARGON

ANA Afghan National Army
ANP Afghan National Police
BOLO Be On Look Out
CP Command Post
COP Combat Outpost
DFAC Dining Facility
FOB Forward Operating Base
IED Improvised Explosive Device
IR Infrared
JDAM Joint Direct Attack Munitions (big bomb)
KIA Killed In Action
LZ Landing Zone
MEDEVAC Medical Evacuation
MRAP Mine-Resistant Ambush Protected (tactical truck)
MRE Meal, Ready-to-Eat
MSgt Air Force Master Sergeant
NCO Noncommissioned Officer
NVG Night Vision Goggles
OCS Officer Candidate School
OP Outpost
PT Physical Training
ROTC Reserve Officers' Training Corps
RPG Rocket-Propelled Grenade
RTO Radio Telephone Operator
SCO Squadron Commander (usually Lieutenant Colonel in rank)
TOC Tactical Operations Center

Officer Rank Structure:

2LT	Second Lieutenant
1LT	First Lieutenant
CPT	Captain
MAJ	Major
LTC	Lieutenant Colonel
COL	Colonel ("Full-Bird Colonel")
BG	Brigadier General
MG	Major General
LTG	Lieutenant General
GEN	General

Enlisted Rank Structure:

PVT	Private
PV2	Private
PFC	Private First Class
SPC	Specialist
CPL	Corporal
SGT	Sergeant
SSG	Staff Sergeant
SFC	Sergeant First Class
MSG	Master Sergeant
1SG	First Sergeant
SGM	Sergeant Major
CSM	Command Sergeant Major
SMA	Sergeant Major Of The Army

Cavalry Unit Structure (Small To Large)

Section
Platoon
Troop (Company)
Squadron (Battalion)
Brigade

ACKNOWLEGDEMENT

The writing of *Kilroy Was Here* has been quite the undertaking to say the least. When I began putting words to paper over eight years ago, I knew virtually nothing about the writing process, long-form storytelling, or even how to build a coherent scene. After reading countless books on the subject of writing, novels in similar genres, and endless trial and error, I can still safely say I know virtually nothing about the writing process, long-form storytelling, or even how to build a coherent scene. So I wouldn't have been able to complete this book without the help of a whole lot of people.

Thank you to Travis Russell for allowing me the opportunity to work for you, but most importantly for being the sounding board for my ridiculous ideas.

Thank you to Adam Hillary for reading the rawest form of my garbage words and helping me turn them into less garbage words. I'm sorry for all the ill placed comas.

Thank you to my wife Carlye, my mom Patti, my brother Scott, Paul W, Jason W, Jake M, Marc C, and all of my other friends and family who helped me beyond words by serving as beta readers.

Thank you to Mr. Steve Parolini, The Novel Doctor, whose expertise in editing helped immensely in polishing the initial work.

Thank you to the fine people of A15 Publishing for helping me make this dream a reality.

Thank you to Mr. Patrick Tillery and *www.kilroywashere.org* for granting me the permission to use the Kilroy Was Here phrase and iconic image.

Thank you to my friend Lucas for your incredible cover design. It turned out better than I ever imagined. You are a truly talented individual.

And finally, thank you once more to my wife, Carlye, for your never ending support and love and your willingness to overlook my "writing mornings" as a thinly veiled excuse to go sit at the donut shop.

AUTHOR BIO

Brett Allen is a graduate of Michigan State University and commissioned into the U.S. Army from its ROTC program. After college, he served as an armor officer (cavalry) with the 3rd Squadron, 71st Cavalry Regiment (10th Mountain Division) posted at Fort Drum, New York. His 2009 deployment to Afghanistan in support of Operation Enduring Freedom provided the subject matter for his freshman novel, *Kilroy Was Here*. He left the Army in 2010 at the rank of Captain and currently resides in Ada, Michigan with his beautiful wife, two small children, and their dog Gatsby.

*Special thank you to Cidermill Photography and Tessa Muir for the great photos.

Made in the USA
Las Vegas, NV
26 December 2021